Dethroned

Dethroned

Patel, Menon and the Integration of Princely India

John Zubrzycki

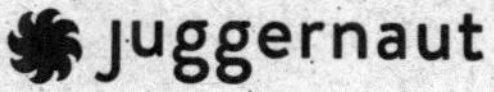

juggernaut

JUGGERNAUT BOOKS
C-I-128, First Floor, Sangam Vihar, Near Holi Chowk,
New Delhi 110080, India

First published in hardback by Juggernaut Books 2023
Published in paperback by Juggernaut Books 2024

10 9 8 7 6 5 4 3 2 1

P-ISBN: 9789353459130
E-ISBN: 9789353451677

The international boundaries on the maps of India are neither purported to be correct nor authentic by Survey of India directives.

Typeset in Adobe Caslon Pro by R. Ajith Kumar, Noida

Printed at Thomson Press India Ltd

To April

Contents

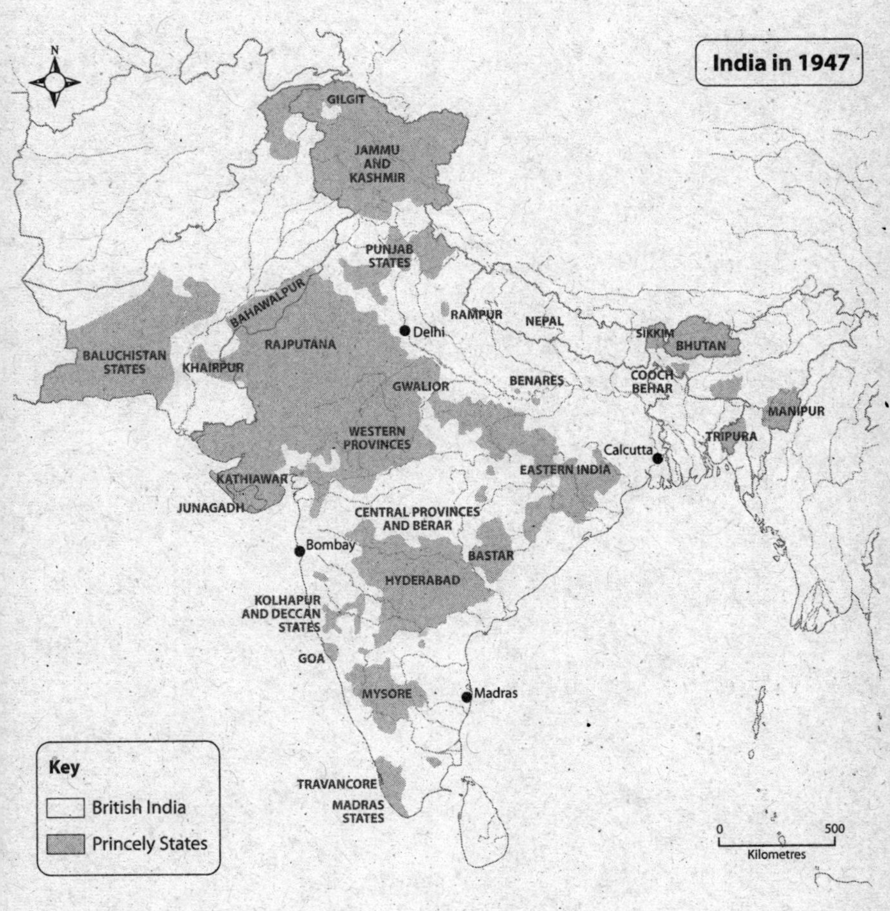
India in 1947
N
GILGIT
JAMMU AND KASHMIR
PUNJAB STATES
BAHAWALPUR
RAMPUR
NEPAL
Delhi
SIKKIM
BHUTAN
BALUCHISTAN STATES
KHAIRPUR
RAJPUTANA
COOCH BEHAR
GWALIOR
BENARES
MANIPUR
WESTERN PROVINCES
TRIPURA
Calcutta
EASTERN INDIA
KATHIAWAR
JUNAGADH
CENTRAL PROVINCES AND BERAR
Bombay
BASTAR
HYDERABAD
KOLHAPUR AND DECCAN STATES
GOA
MYSORE
Madras
TRAVANCORE
MADRAS STATES
Key
British India
Princely States
0
500
Kilometres

Prologue: The Last Durbar

India was beginning to burn. Communal violence was erupting across large swathes of the Punjab and Bengal. In the rubble-strewn laneways of Lahore, the grey light of dawn revealed the bodies of Hindus, Muslims and Sikhs massacred the night before. Those who had not fled the smouldering cities and towns battled each other with bricks, stones and home-made bombs. Blood turned the waters of canals a dull red and congealed in parched and abandoned wheat fields. Yet the potentates who assembled in the Chamber of Princes (COP) in Delhi on 25 July 1947 seemed oblivious to the butchery. Nearly one hundred rajas, maharajas, maharaj ranas, khans, nawabs and dewans were meeting as a body for the last time in the Council House, the huge circular Herbert Baker–designed building that would house the future Parliament of independent India. Never to miss an opportunity to turn on an audacious display of pomp and privilege, they arrived bedecked in richly embroidered achkans buttoned up to their necks, belts studded with sapphires, rubies radiating from their turbans to their shoe buckles. In just three weeks, half a century of nationalist struggle would culminate in Britain's departure. From his quarters in the Viceregal Estate, Sir Cyril Radcliffe was consulting census reports as he finalized the boundaries of the new dominions of India and Pakistan. In offices around the subcontinent, officials were furiously calculating the final division of everything from rolling stock to rice reserves, from typewriters to telephones. The only uncertainty that remained was how the 562 princely states[1] – a motley collection once described as 'the oddest political set-up that the world has ever seen' – would fit into this new paradigm.[2]

It was not just the heat on that day – a stifling 44.5 degrees Celsius – that was piling discomfort on an already prickly and politically charged summer. Just a week earlier, the Indian Independence Act had received royal assent. It provided for the handover of power to two new dominions on 15 August. All treaties with the British Crown would lapse, technically leaving the princes free to join either India or Pakistan, or if they chose, to declare themselves independent. Among the princes, the imminent departure of the Raj evoked a range of emotions. A handful had accepted the inevitability of independence and the necessity of preparing for the new realities it would bring. Many palpably dreaded and resented what they saw as their future once Britain's political and military protection was withdrawn. Despite the provisions of the Independence Act, they would, they feared, be absorbed into the new India against their will. Their autocratic powers and privileges would be washed away, their palaces and treasuries seized, their right to impose customs duties and earn royalties on their mineral wealth wrested from them, and their personal fortunes taxed. They could keep their Rolls-Royces and royal stables, but these would be empty symbols of lost prestige. Hallowed decorations and knighthoods bestowed by the King Emperor in return for their loyalty would be a thing of the past.

The remainder had adopted a posture of insouciant denial. When the former Indian Civil Service (ICS) officer Philip Mason arrived in Hyderabad in 1946 to tutor the two grandsons of Nizam Osman Ali Khan, he found the nobility carrying on as if nothing was about to change. At a garden party, a sixty-piece string orchestra conducted by an Anglo-Indian named Henry Luschwitz played waltzes and foxtrots. 'It was like the spring of 1789 at Versailles . . . The men were elegant in black sherwanis or gorgeous in gold brocade, the ladies wore saris of sapphire or flame-colour or starlit blue . . . Everyone seemed to be happy and witty and amused.'[3]

As the rulers and their representatives waited for the entrance of Lord Louis Mountbatten, conflicting rumours swept through the assemblage. Some heard that India's last viceroy was about to declare the princes independent, others that he would make a dramatic announcement that would effectively sever the century-old sacred compact between the Crown and its feudatories. Entering the chamber, Mountbatten seemed to draw strength from the heat like a salamander. Dressed in his full viceregal ivory-white uniform, 'his chest flashing with a breastplate of orders, decorations, and medals', he looked every inch the cousin of the British monarch King George VI.[4]

Walking on the red carpet alongside him was the imposing figure of Vallabhbhai Patel, the head of the recently formed States Department. His broad and heavy features and glassy, hooded eyes gave the impression of a man worn down by years of struggle. Yet the seventy-two-year-old politician, described by one nationalist leader as 'a rough diamond in an iron casket',[5] was the most powerful figure inside the Congress party after the interim prime minister, Jawaharlal Nehru. Patel kept the cogs of Congress turning by wooing industrialists to fill the party's coffers, while acting as a brake against its more radical elements. Had he achieved his ambition of becoming India's first prime minister, his centrist pro-market ideology would have seen the country take a radically different course from the socialist model espoused by Nehru. Today, Patel is often called the 'Bismarck of India' for repeating the German chancellor's feat of cajoling a group of scattered and disparate princedoms into giving up their sovereignty and creating a cohesive nation state. In reality, as his biographer D.V. Tahmankar notes: 'the task in India was infinitely more difficult and complex' than Bismarck's, with not dozens but hundreds of potentates 'reluctant to give up ancestral estates, great privileges and ruling powers'.[6] Writing a few months after Independence, a Western journalist described Patel as 'a Hindu Cromwell courteously decapitating hundreds of little King Charleses', in the process turning the princes into pensioners and giving their subjects political unity and a voice they had never known before.[7] This feat drew admiration from some unlikely quarters, including the Soviet premier, Nikita Khrushchev, who exclaimed: 'You Indians are a remarkable people. How did you manage to liquidate the princely states without liquidating the princes?'[8]

The feat was not Patel's alone. In fact, the real architect of the accession and integration of the states was a diminutive Malayali with a penchant for Savile Row suits, Cuban cigars and slate-blue Cadillacs. Over a remarkable three-decade-long career, Vappala Pangunni (V.P.) Menon had gone from being a coolie in the mines of the Kolar Gold Fields to holding the highest position in the government ever held by an Indian, serving as reforms commissioner and constitutional adviser to three viceroys, Lord Linlithgow, Lord Wavell and now Mountbatten. It was the slightly rotund, balding and bespeckled Menon, the secretary of the States Department, who had come up with the deceptively simple plan of accession limited to three subjects – defence, foreign affairs and communications – which would be used, to great effect, to disarm the princes. In the weeks and months to come, Patel's powerful personality, which mixed fury with charm and persuasion with coercion, would complement Menon's skills as a tactician. When Patel, in a rare moment of hesitation, expressed unease that the departure of the British would mean that treaties would be torn up and undertakings abandoned, Menon responded: 'We start with a clean slate. It is now our turn to say how the princes will behave.'[9] This frankness would appeal to Patel, who would increasingly rely on the man who became his deputy in the States Department to formulate and implement the policies that would ultimately redraw the map of India.

Missing from the historic conclave was the only British official who knew each of the rulers personally. Conrad Corfield, the viceroy's adviser on the princely states until his position and powers were taken over by Patel and Menon, had submitted his resignation and boarded a plane for London just a few days earlier. Indian nationalists regarded Corfield as the man who wanted to Balkanize India by encouraging the states to exercise their legal right to choose between the two dominions or to become independent entities. After serving in the states for more than three decades, Corfield believed it was his job to protect the princes' interests and their bargaining power. He was also convinced that Mountbatten was about to make a set of promises to the princes that he could not guarantee. One of Corfield's final acts had been to destroy thousands of secret files maintained by the British on the often-scandalous private lives of India's potentates.

Also striking in their absence were the princes who had ignored Mountbatten's invitation to attend the COP meeting. Chief among them were Indore's ruler Yeshwant Rao Holkar and the nawab of Bhopal, Hamidullah Khan. The pair were viewed by Patel, Menon and others in the States Department as the co-conspirators of a scheme to plunge 'a dagger into the very heart of India' by lobbying a slew of contiguous states to accede to Pakistan. Borrowing a metaphor from Lewis Carroll, Hamidullah said he felt that the princes had been invited 'like the oysters to attend the tea party with the walruses and the carpenters'.[10] (By the end of Carroll's poem, the oysters get gobbled up by their hosts.) Other notable absentees were the dewan of Travancore, C.P. Ramaswami Aiyar, and the mightiest ruler of all, the dangerously eccentric Osman Ali Khan of Hyderabad. Bhopal, Hyderabad and Travancore had declared their states would become independent once the British departed, with Aiyar adamant that his maharaja took orders from God and no one else. Inspired by the example of these three states, other headstrong potentates were re-evaluating their future too.

As Mountbatten took his place on the dais, the gloom seemed to lift, and a frisson of excitement mixed with anticipation filled the room where, for the past quarter century, India's chiefs had tried in vain to overcome their divisions and petty feuds and face their challenges head-on. If there was anything resembling a consensus among them as they waited for Mountbatten to begin his speech, it was the view that as a blue-blooded royal with a passion for polo and pigsticking, Mountbatten would prove an ally when they needed one the most. He knew many of the princes personally, counting among his close friends the maharajas of Bikaner and Jaipur and the Nawab of Bhopal. Only the canniest of those present noticed a slight but significant departure from tradition. Normally, only the viceroy occupied the dais. This time a special seat was prepared for Patel – a placement the Maharawal of Dungarpur interpreted as a not-so-subtle signal that the tide was turning against the princes. After ruling over nearly half of India's land mass and holding the power of life and death over a third of its population, their day of reckoning had come.

Labour Prime Minister Clement Attlee is said to have chosen

Mountbatten to oversee India's independence because he could 'not only talk the hind leg off a donkey but also the throne from under a prince'.[11] For the next hour, the viceroy lived up to this estimation, speaking without notes and giving one of the most impressive performances of his long career – 'the apogee of persuasion', as Menon later put it.[12] Using every weapon in his oratorical armoury, Mountbatten told the princes that he was about to present them with a 'take it or leave it' offer, which would not be repeated. They would be given instruments to sign, which provided for accession on just three subjects – defence, foreign affairs and communications. Their internal affairs would be left untouched. There would be no financial liability on the part of the states, nor would the central government have any power to encroach on their internal autonomy or sovereignty. It was a bargain so advantageous, Mountbatten assured them, that he wasn't even sure the Indian government would accept it. 'My scheme leaves you with all the practical independence you can possibly use and makes you free of all those subjects which you cannot possibly manage on your own.' The core message from the speech, and one that made the headlines in Indian newspapers the following day, was: 'You cannot run away from the Dominion Government which is your neighbour any more than you can run away from subjects for whose welfare you are responsible.' Playing to their love of titles, Mountbatten told the assembled monarchs that if they signed on the dotted line, there was every likelihood that Patel and the Congress would not interfere with their receiving honours and titles from the king.[13] He also issued a blunt reminder – one that would come back to haunt the Indian government as it grappled with the Kashmir crisis:

> The States are theoretically free to link their future with whichever Dominion they may care [to]. But when I say that they are at

> liberty to link up with either of the Dominions, may I point out that there are certain geographical compulsions which cannot be evaded. Out of something like 565 States, the vast majority are irretrievably linked . . . with the Dominion of India.[14]

'His control of the meeting never faltered,' writes Mountbatten's biographer Philip Ziegler. 'He sensed precisely when to curdle the blood with fearful prophesies, when to relieve them with a joke.'[15] Answering questions from the floor, Mountbatten at one point resorted to pantomime, 'reading' an absent prince's mind with the aid of a paperweight that he pretended was a crystal ball. Should this absent prince sign the Instrument of Accession? he asked the paperweight. The answer was, of course, yes. While the gag elicited some laughter from those assembled, by the end of the gathering, 'the expression on the face of even the richest of them was the sad, lost look of men in defeat'.[16] Buried beneath the gravitas was the fact that Mountbatten was making promises on behalf of entities that had yet to come into existence, namely, the dominions of India and Pakistan. Sessions of the COP normally lasted two days. This final one lasted less than two hours. The princes were told that the viceroy was preoccupied with other matters and had to leave.

Having observed the reaction to the speech, Mountbatten's press secretary Alan Campbell-Johnson saw how the princes, 'leaderless, riven with dynastic and political dissensions, tried desperately to hide behind opportunism and indecision, but events were moving much too fast and on too large a scale to allow of any such halting tactics'.[17] Mountbatten's immediate assessment of the gathering was blunter. 'Very few of the Princes or their representatives seemed to have any idea of what was going on around them. Unless they accepted the Instrument they would be finished',[18] swept away by the forces of nationalism that were opposed to autocratic rule. That afternoon, Campbell-Johnson and Menon prepared a sanitized official transcript of the speech Mountbatten had delivered. 'He threatened sanctions – such as withholding arms, ammunitions and other supplies – against States not agreeing to accede,' his joint private secretary, W.H.J. Christie noted in his diary. He also let Travancore's absent dewan 'have it' for daring to make overtures to Britain and the United Nations and pledged to do 'everything in his power' to make life difficult for the state if it continued to resist joining India.[19] Mountbatten was determined to go down in history as the man who brought the princes to heel. He would show no pity to those who dared oppose him.

While the viceroy projected unshakeable confidence, Patel and Menon were watchful. A slew of states from Travancore on the Malabar coast to tiny Bilaspur in the Himalayan foothills were daring to dream of independence. Filled with dread at the prospect of acceding to either India or Pakistan, Kashmir's Maharaja Hari Singh was clinging to the belief that his state could become the 'Switzerland of the East'. The leader of the Muslim League Muhammad Ali Jinnah was busy wooing future border states such as Jodhpur as well as Sikh princes, thrusting blank sheets of paper in front of them and promising to agree to any terms for accession they demanded. In Alwar and Bharatpur, Muslims were attempting to join forces with their co-religionists in the Punjab to form an independent Meostan, while the Jats hankered for a separate Jatistan. Dholpur's ruler believed he had a divine right to do what he wanted. Kathiawar had to be brought to heel when word leaked out that several of this peninsula's princely states might form a union and ally with Pakistan. In Rampur, the nawab briefly flirted with acceding only to be forced to appeal for outside intervention to prevent his state from descending into communal bloodshed when he rejected Jinnah's overtures. Even Gwalior, a state so pro-British that its ruler George Jiwajirao Scindia was named after the king of England, deviated from the path laid out by the viceroy by begging at the last moment to be allowed to determine its own future.

The urgency with which the princes were being dealt with stemmed from the very real fear that while an India deprived of its eastern and western wings because of Partition would survive, an India deprived of its states would lose 'all coherence'. In an influential essay published in 1944, the constitutional expert Reginald Coupland wrote:

> [The states] form a great cruciform barrier separating all four quarters of the country. If no more than the Central Indian States and Hyderabad and Mysore were excluded from the Union, the United Provinces would be almost completely cut off from Bombay, and Bombay completely from Sind. The strategic and economic implications are obvious enough. The practicability of Pakistan must be admitted, but the more the separation of the States from British India is considered, the more impracticable it seems. India could live if its Moslem limbs in the North-West and North-East were amputated, but could it live without its heart?[20]

Mountbatten would later congratulate himself for giving Patel and Menon what they wanted: the accession of all but a handful of the hundreds of disparate states in the space of just a few weeks. The new dominion gained political cohesion, land and money. By the end of 1949, it had added 13 lakh square kilometres of territory and more than 9 crore subjects, easily offsetting what it had lost because of Partition. One estimate put the total value of public holdings transferred from the princes to the new Indian Union to be around Rs 100 crore. But there were costs. The process was nowhere near as painless or as bloodless as its architects would assert – the most obvious exception to this claim being the thousands of lives lost during the misnamed 'Police Action' in Hyderabad. The nizam's doomed attempt to exercise his legal right to independence resulted in at least 25,000 lives lost and the displacement of many thousands more. And accession was not 'in itself a final solution', as Menon put it – an unfortunate choice of phrase, given its Nazi echoes – to the problem of the states. That would require Patel and him to roll back their promises not to interfere in the princes' internal affairs. The map of India would have to be redrawn, ancient boundaries erased and once-proud lineages reduced to scraps of paper.

The motivations of the main players in this endgame of empire differed greatly. For Congress leaders, the princely states were bastions of despotism, debauchery and decay. Nehru derided them as 'sinks of reaction and incompetence and unrestrained autocratic power, sometimes exercised by vicious and degraded individuals'.[21] Corfield and others who had served in them, including many Indian dewans, ministers and administrators, took a more nuanced view. Yes, there were tyrants who should have been deposed had it not been for their usefulness to the British, but there were also many states such as Mysore, Baroda and Aundh where indigenous rule was benevolent, devoid of communal friction, based on a stable social structure and carried out in an atmosphere of security and loyalty. Given time, it would be possible for the princes to put their houses in order. While Nehru was making no secret of his abhorrence of feudal autocracy, the father of Hindutva, Vinayak Damodar Savarkar, saw the states as representing the true India, 'portals to a pure, ancient past', and even as 'the foundation on which the future nation' could be launched.[22] As for the princes, all but the most myopic had some inkling that the tide of history was turning against them, that the prospect of dozens of 'mini Ulsters' made up of larger states exercising their right to independence and of small states creating their own federations would never be tolerated by the leaders of a newly independent dominion of India or Pakistan.

Aside from a voluminous amount of archival material available in India and Great Britain, anyone working on the princely states can draw on a wealth of excellent scholarship, including Ian Copland's *The Princes of India in the Endgame of Empire:1917–1947*, Stephen Ashton's *British Policy Towards the Indian States: 1905–1939* and Barbara Ramusack's *The Indian Princes and Their States*. These have been supplemented in recent years by the publication of several outstanding books on individual states, their rulers and administrators, notably Manu Pillai's *The Ivory Throne* and *False Allies*, and Rahul Sagar's *The Progressive Maharaj*. Scholarship on the princely states that found themselves within the borders of Pakistan remains sparse, with the exception of Yaqoob Khan Bangash's *A Princely Affair* and Anabel Lloyd's *Bahawalpur: The Kingdom that Vanished.* Even when taken together, these surveys leave unanswered questions of what happened to the states after Partition, what motivated men like Menon and Patel to work so hard to integrate them into the new India and what agency the princes retained as they adjusted to a democratic order that increasingly viewed them as anachronisms.

Drawing on confidential government and diplomatic reports as well as the correspondence and writings of the main protagonists, the following pages attempt to fill this gap by charting the story of India's centuries-old princely order, from the arrival of

Mountbatten as viceroy in March 1947 until the abolition of titles, privileges and privy purses in December 1971. This three-part drama was enacted with ruthless determination against the backdrop of the subcontinent's bloody division and its aftermath. Act One opens with the sudden and unscripted sprint to independence as Menon and Patel, aided by Mountbatten, arm-twisted hundreds of absolute autocrats to sign away their kingdoms and become part of the new India. Not all were ready to surrender without a fight. Encouraged by Corfield and Jinnah, states such as Bhopal, Jodhpur and Indore were taking their cue from Britain's promise that they would be free to determine their own future following the transfer of power. Act Two took longer but was no less dramatic: the integration of the states into new units or their merger with existing provinces. The threat to India's territorial integrity thrown up by Junagadh's accession to Pakistan, the tribal invasion of Kashmir and Hyderabad's declaration of independence brought the two dominions perilously close to war, unleashed communal tensions and widened the rift between Patel and Nehru. Once proudly independent princes were coaxed and coerced into giving up their powers with new administrative posts, privy purses that were guaranteed for life and privileges that the ordinary Indian could hardly comprehend. During this second act, the constant redrawing of the map of India would have taxed the patience of the most talented cartographers – the boundaries of just one state, Rajasthan, going through several iterations in the space of a single year. Threatened by the growing power of the princes on the political stage and desperate to shore up her political credentials, Indira Gandhi emerged as the chief protagonist in the final act of this drama. Wielding her parliamentary sword, and with the help of a compliant president, she deftly and definitively consigned the princely order to the history books.

Until the final curtain call, the princes were undermined by division and delusion, their parochial perspective of their importance and their God-given rights curtailing their ability to manoeuvre in the rapidly changing circumstances they found themselves in. Whether or not the rulers were responsible for the debacle of their own downfall, whether their demise was premeditated or inevitable, the story of the unmaking of the princely order and those who orchestrated it is an inseparable part of India's story. It deserves to be told.

1

The 'Iron Man' and the Civil Servant

A brass band and a full bodyguard were waiting for Rear Admiral Viscount Louis Mountbatten of Burma and his wife Edwina when their York transporter landed at Delhi's Palam airport on 22 March 1947. As India's last viceroy stepped onto the tarmac, he felt overjoyed to be 'endowed with an almost heavenly power. I realised that I had been made into the most powerful man on earth. One fifth of humanity I held in my hand. A power of life and death.'[1]

The couple's arrival marked the start of a summer of discontent. As he followed Mountbatten off the plane, Alan Campbell-Johnson was overcome by a sense of despair. Everywhere the viceroy's press attaché looked the situation seemed hopeless. The British government had made a pledge to the Indian people without knowing how to implement it. The worst rioting and communal violence in a century had left thousands dead, mostly Sikhs at the hands of Muslims, in Rawalpindi and Multan. The Congress and the Muslim League were at loggerheads. Partition seemed inevitable. 'In short, we have the people rioting, the Princes falling out among themselves, the entire Indian Civil Service and Police running down, and the British, who are left sceptical and full of foreboding.'[2] When a sullen Lord Wavell met Mountbatten at the Viceregal Lodge later that day to brief him on the handover, he handed him a manilla file titled 'Operation Madhouse'. 'This is called "Madhouse" because it is a problem for a madhouse,' Wavell explained, referring to the crisis engulfing the subcontinent. 'Alas, I can see no other way out.'[3]

Attlee's announcement to the House of Commons on 10 February 1947 of Mountbatten's appointment was followed by a declaration ten days later that Britain would transfer power into 'responsible Indian hands' no later than June 1948.[4] To achieve this would need a new personal approach. During Mountbatten's first two weeks in India, that personal approach translated into a staggering 133 meetings with ministers in the interim government, commanders-in-chief of the armed services, leading princes and other prominent figures. Jinnah scored the lion's share, meeting Mountbatten no fewer than six times.

On 26 March, two days after his brief swearing-in ceremony, it was the turn of the interim home minister in the Constituent Assembly Sardar Vallabhbhai Patel. In late 1946, Wavell wrote to King George VI giving his frank assessment of the leading figures in the nationalist movement. Gandhi was a 'shrewd, malevolent politician' prone to making pronouncements 'so qualified and so vaguely worded' they can 'be interpreted in whatever sense best suits him at a later stage'. Jinnah was a 'lonely unhappy, arbitrary, self-centred man'. Abdul Kalam Azad, the Congress president, 'stood for good sense, but up against Gandhi he was a rabbit faced by a stoat'. Nehru, though 'sincere, intelligent and personally courageous', was 'unbalanced'. The only individual Wavell expressed unconditional support for was Patel, whom he upheld as 'the recognized tough of the Congress Working Committee and by far the most forceful character amongst them'. Patel, he added, was 'the only one . . .

capable of standing up to Gandhi'.[5] Historians would go on to nickname him the 'Iron Man' of India.

When Campbell-Johnson first saw the dhoti-wearing Patel, he was reminded of a Roman emperor in a toga. 'There are in fact Roman qualities about this man – administrative talent, capacity to take and sustain strong decisions, and a certain serenity, which invariably accompanies real strength of character. Despite his preoccupations, Patel had a shrewd grasp of India's strategic position in the world at large.'[6] Given his reputation as a blunt-mannered, hard-boiled, self-declared 'fascist' when it came to dealing with dissenters in his own party, Mountbatten had been somewhat apprehensive ahead of the meeting. Patel, for his part, had low expectations of the new viceroy, who he dismissed as 'a toy for Jawaharlalji to play with while we arrange the revolution'.[7] By the end of their encounter, however, mutual reservations had evaporated with Mountbatten describing the Congress strongman as 'most charming . . . evincing a considerable sense of humour'.[8] Like Mountbatten himself, he was a pragmatist and a realist, a politician refreshingly free of the complexities of Nehru and Gandhi. And as Patel now saw it, Mountbatten's 'royal status and personal friendship with many of the princes was uniquely suited to help India achieve its aim of leaving no state behind'.[9]

Nationalism ran in Patel's blood. The son of a petty landowner who had fought alongside the Rani of Jhansi in the Mutiny of 1857, he was born in 1875 in the village of Nadiad, approximately 60 kilometres southeast of Ahmedabad. The young Patel would inherit his father's fiery spirit. While in sixth class, he organized a three-day strike to protest against the harsh treatment of a fellow student who had been caned for failing to pay a fine. He went on to become a pleader in criminal cases in the district court in Borsad, where he practised as a barrister for eight years. Patel's steely determination and single-mindedness were evident even then. In 1909, while he was giving the final speech for the defence in a court case in Bombay, his wife Jhaverba died after undergoing surgery for cancer. Patel was given a note about his wife's demise, pocketed it, continued his summing up and won the case. He broke the news to others only after the proceedings had ended. The following year, aged thirty-five, he sailed for London, renting a room in the neighbourhood of Bayswater and working with relentless resolve to pass his Bar exams. On his return to Gujarat three years later, he set up a successful legal practice with his elder brother Vithalbhai.

At the time, in the words of biographer Balraj Krishna, Patel was 'an unabashed scoffer; a smart young man dressed in tip-top English style', a bridge-playing, chain-smoking barrister 'sardonically scanning the Indian political scene from the seclusion of his "fritters club" at Ahmedabad'.[10] His first encounter with Gandhi came in 1916 shortly after the latter's return from South Africa. When Gandhi walked into the Gujarat Club Patel's companions all stood up and rushed to greet him. Patel reportedly remained seated and scoffed at his fellow Gujaratis, sarcastically commenting that he was not interested in lessons on how to clean toilets.

Just a year later, Patel had given up smoking and bridge-playing, quit his legal practice, ditched his tailored suits and donned a dhoti to become one of Gandhi's most trusted lieutenants. While he has left nothing on record to explain his change of heart, it's likely that the rebel spirit he had shown at school attracted him to the Mahatma's campaigns among peasants in Bihar and Gujarat. In 1918, the two men worked together to organize the Nadiad satyagraha in Gujarat over the unjust collection of land tax. When Gandhi departed for Indore a few days after the satyagraha started, Patel took over, showing a remarkable capacity for leadership. 'If Gandhi had a bania's suave, courteous veneer hiding his firmness and determination, Patel had the bluntness of a soldier and the astuteness of an organiser,' Krishna notes.[11] With Gandhi's blessings, Patel went on to arrange the annual meeting of the Congress in Ahmedabad in 1921. The meeting was a watershed moment, consolidating the party's evolution from what Nehru would describe as 'an English-knowing, upper-class affair' where morning coats and well-pressed trousers were greatly in evidence, into a mass grassroots movement.[12] Six years later, Patel led the Bardoli satyagraha. For weeks he cajoled peasants to refuse all payments to the government. Despite arrests, confiscation of property and other pressures, he held the peasants firm until Gandhi stepped in with a proposal of mediation. Noted the *Times of India*: 'Iron discipline prevails in Bardoli. Mr Patel had instituted there a Bolshevik regime in which he plays the role of Lenin.'[13] From then he was known as Gandhi's 'deputy commander' and as 'Sardar', a title that means chief. But the closeness between the two men would not always work in Patel's favour. In 1946, Gandhi ignored the preferences of the party's rank and file and chose Nehru over the more experienced Patel for the role of Congress president. The choice meant it was Nehru who would be the prime minister of newly independent India and the country's face to the world.

Patel's first brush with the princes came in March 1928, when he arranged a dinner party at which the invitees included Bhupinder Singh of Patiala, Motilal Nehru, the freedom fighters Sarojini Naidu and Lajpat Rai, as well as Muhammad Ali Jinnah. Patiala's ruler recalled how Patel served up a piquant warning that the states would be eliminated if they attempted to block British India's march to freedom. From then on there was little ambiguity in his attitude. In 1929, he gave an address to the fifth Kathiawar Political Conference, a grassroots organization set up to give a political voice to the people of the region, in which he decried the situation in the states as being 'disorderly and pitiable . . . For the Princes to claim the Empire's friendship is sheer nonsense, like friendship between a lion and a jackal!' he exclaimed.[14] The expansion in the early 1930s of Praja Mandals, public associations encouraged by the Congress but independent of it, which pressured the states to introduce constitutional reforms, saw Patel's attitude harden even further. 'The red and yellow colours on India's map have to be made one,' he declared, referring to the colours used to distinguish princely India (yellow) from British India in the official maps of the time. 'Unless that is done, we cannot have Swaraj.'[15]

Throughout his rise in the Congress, Patel's mantra was that the states must introduce responsible government and guarantee fundamental rights such as freedom of speech and association to their citizens. To him a ruler was just a trustee:

> He is enjoying the right inherited from his parents; so in every country when the king becomes worthless people have a right to dethrone him. But in our country, our forefathers made us ultra-loyal, and that is the reason why we are being suppressed . . . The worst disease that spreads from power is sycophancy. Rulers like to hear sweet things about them but that is in fact sedition. To tell truth and bitter things is real loyalty. But today everything is being overturned.[16]

Patel's writings and speeches also reflect his utter disdain for princely autocracy:

> There are six hundred native states in India. There is no country in the world which has so many states. Some states are so small that even a person who rules over six or seven villages announces himself a ruler. Simply because the kings wear a crown, they do not

> become totally independent. They are also slaves, and we who are their subjects are slaves of slaves.[17]

When dealing with crises in the princely states, Patel was a fast learner. In 1938, he met with the Maharaja of Mysore and his dewan, Mirza Ismail, to defuse clashes between Congress workers and state forces over the hoisting of the tricoloured national flag on 26 January, which was being marked as India's future Independence Day. Patel's negotiations resulted in a settlement which would see the Mysore state flag flying alongside the Congress flag at all ceremonial occasions involving the party. For its part, the Mysore government expressed deep regret over the misunderstanding that had caused the crisis and the resulting deaths and injuries. But Patel also recommended that the Congress mellow its approach to the states:

> I do not think it is unpatriotic to have friendly relations with States' officials. You must remember that they are Indian States and not foreign States. The struggle for freedom under the aegis of the Indian National Congress is freedom for 350 million people including Indian States' people and Indian Princes. Once the Princes are free, we shall settle our accounts with them without third party intervention.[18]

No sooner had the Mysore crisis been defused than another broke out in Rajkot on the Kathiawar peninsula. Following the death of the state's widely respected ruler, Lakhajirajsinhji, his eldest, somewhat wayward, son Dharmendrasinhji was placed on the gaddi. He promptly dismissed his father's elected assembly. Patel launched a highly effective campaign to restore the assembly, which included strikes, withholding of land revenue, boycotts of cotton produced at the state's mills, an embargo on electricity from the state power station and even a run on the state bank. Dharmendrasinhji caved in and agreed to the formation of a committee to reconstitute the assembly. At this point the British blocked Patel's nominees to the assembly. Meanwhile, the state's dewan, Durbar Virawala, responded to the campaign to restore the assembly by clamping down on political activities and jailing activists, including Patel's daughter Maniben and Gandhi's wife Kasturba. In January 1938, Gandhi went to Rajkot, a city he had lived in for thirteen years as a young man, and threatened to fast unto death unless Virawala released all those jailed and accepted Patel's nominees. During Gandhi's visit, a Muslim mob attacked a meeting he was addressing, looking to kill Patel. Finally, the then viceroy, Lord Linlithgow, intervened and left the final decision to his chief justice, who supported Patel's position. The assembly was restored.

Although he did not fully appreciate it at first, Mountbatten had on his staff one of the most capable civil servants India had ever produced. V.P. Menon was the head of the Reforms Commission, the highest office held by an Indian in the bureaucracy of the Raj. Wavell, the former viceroy, had been suspicious of him, regarding him as Patel's 'mouthpiece'.[19] Mountbatten's private secretary, George Abell, feared Menon might leak some of the viceroy's secrets to the Congress because of his closeness to Patel, and because both men were Hindus. 'Though he is an old friend of mine, and one of the people I like best in Delhi, I am convinced that it is not possible to take him into confidence as fully as has been done in the past,' Abell warned his superior.[20] Acting on his advice, Mountbatten had kept Menon in the background during the first several weeks of his viceroyalty. 'He never sent for me,' Menon would later tell his close friend Henry 'Harry' Vincent Hodson. 'That whole first month that he was here, he never sent for me.'[21] It would not be long, however, before Menon would become indispensable.

Menon's life story was extraordinary. The son of a schoolmaster, he was born in 1893 in a small village near the town of Ottapalam in Kerala. As a boy he was a prodigious learner, mastering Malayalam, Sanskrit, English and mathematics while at school. He also devoured news, spending much of his spare time by the newspaper vendor's stall at the local railway station, his head buried in the latest copy of the *Madras Mail*. According to Menon family lore, he left home after setting fire to his school in retaliation for his Tamilian headmaster failing him in his exams because of poor attendance. The fact that he had to walk two hours each way to reach school had mattered little to the headmaster; nor that he was such a bright student. Menon's explanation for his actions hints at the risk-taking, rebellious spirit that would eventually propel him ever higher: 'There was no space for such a school, and such teachers there . . . I didn't know what I would do now, but the confidence of youth is sometimes stupid. I just knew I wanted to leave.'[22]

Terrified of being punished for his act of defiance, he caught the first train to pass through Ottapalam station without knowing its destination. It was headed for the Kolar Gold Fields in present-day Karnataka. Aged just thirteen, he did manual work, carrying heavy loads of soil on his head from the underground mine shafts and then sifting for gold with his bare hands. His weekly salary was 2 annas. His lucky break came a few years later when two vacancies were advertised at the mine – for the posts of clerk and overseer. He applied for both. Impressed by his confidence, his interviewer, an Englishman, offered him a choice of positions. Menon took the overseer's job, managing a group of mine workers and earning a commission based on the amount of gold they mined. He lasted barely a year before he was sacked for negligence. Menon's coolies had taken advantage of their young boss's soft-heartedness and spent their time drinking home brew in the mine shaft instead of digging for the precious metal. Fortunately, the same Englishman who had hired Menon remained impressed enough to give him a letter recommending him for a clerical position with the Imperial Tobacco Company in Bangalore.

For the next few years, lucky breaks were punctuated by periods of absolute despair. From Bangalore Menon went to Bombay, making the four-day train journey in a third-class carriage. Arriving exhausted, he fell asleep on the pavement outside the Gateway of India. When he awoke, he found that his money had been stolen. After wandering the streets, he came across a fellow Malayali hawker outside Victoria Terminus. The two became friends and within days Menon found himself selling towels to passers-by. After a short stint working as a clerk, he was down on his luck again. Having borrowed money, he decided to return to Kerala. On his way to the station, an Englishman he had met while clerking in Bombay crossed the road to greet him. He was head of the Home Department in Delhi. When he heard of Menon's plight, he offered him a job. 'God has been very kind to me,' Menon wrote to his brother at the time. 'I have been given my fair share of second and third chances. I will make this one work.'[23] It nearly didn't.

Aged twenty-one, Menon arrived in Delhi at the beginning of the summer of 1914 just as the Government of India was making its annual pilgrimage to Simla. When he went to the railway station to buy a ticket, he discovered that he had been robbed for a second time. Once again it was a Malayali who helped by giving him enough money to cover the train fare. What started as a job as a temporary typist with the Home Department became a springboard for a steady rise through the bureaucracy. Displaying the acumen that would mark his career, he became the principal typist of the first draft of the Montagu–Chelmsford Report that in 1919 recommended the introduction of self-governing units in India. Sixteen years later, he was appointed as a stenographer in the newly established Reforms Branch (later known as the Reforms Commission), which was tasked with implementing the report's recommendations.

In November 1930, Menon boarded the SS *Multan*, one of the so-called 'conference ships' that transported delegates to and from the three Round Table Conferences (RTCs) held in London between December 1930 and December 1932 to map out India's constitutional future. The ship's passengers represented a cross-section of classes and political complexions – Congress moderates and Hindu nationalists, trade unionists and business leaders, pan-Islamists and bejewelled princes. Aside from scheduled port visits that enabled telegrams to be sent and mail and messages to be received, the three-week voyage was in a hermetically sealed environment, where political intriguing and gossip-mongering alternated with games of bridge and fancy-dress balls – the theatricals closely observed by accompanying journalists and curious holiday-makers. Though his work would be mind-numbingly boring – typing up the minutes of the RTC sessions – the voyages to and from London and the two months Menon spent there would give him an opportunity to engage with luminaries such as Jinnah, the lawyer B.R. Ambedkar, the dewan of Travancore, C.P. Ramaswami Aiyar, and K.M. Panikkar, who held the same post in Bikaner. One of the princes attending the first RTC was Narendra Singh Sarila, who was representing the smaller Indian states. It was Sarila who told Menon that to impress his English 'masters', 'the key lay in direct talk, while maintaining steady eye-contact'. Any kind of ingratiation would be immediately seen for what it was.[24] It was a lesson he would never forget.

By 1940, the rebellious ex-child labourer had become a crucial cog in the machinery of the Raj, serving as under-secretary in the Reforms Commission for Viceroy Lord Linlithgow. Menon's boss at the Reforms Commission was H.V. Hodson. Educated at Balliol College at Oxford, he was ranked among the top five applicants for the ICS in 1928. In his 'Preliminary Report on the Indian Political Situation', written in 1932 for the RTCs in London, he pointed out that the nascent movement for a separate Muslim state was stronger than generally recognized. He would even call it by its eventual name: Pakistan.[25] For Menon, there was no better mentor than Hodson, and the two men became close friends, referring to each other as VP and HV. Hodson's interviews with Menon, taped in 1965 and kept at the School of Oriental and African Studies in London, provide an invaluable insight into Menon's thinking and are far more candid than the anodyne version of events presented in Menon's own widely referenced work, *The Story of the Integration of the Indian States*. Hodson's *The Great Divide: Britain, India, Pakistan* remains one of the most perceptive works on the subject of Partition.

Menon's attitude to the princes was shaped by his experiences during his early days as a civil servant. 'When I came up here years ago, a poor boy from Malabar, I went into a shop one day and watched a Maharani buy a hundred expensive saris,' he recounted to the Delhi correspondent of the *New York Times*, Robert Trumbull:

> Another time I was present when a Maharaja walked into a sporting goods store and casually ordered a hundred thousand rupees' worth of hunting rifles. And one day, on one of my civil

> service assignments, I was stopped at fifteen different state customs posts on a thirty-mile drive through Kathiawar. I thought it was time this nonsense was stopped.[26]

By 1942, Hodson's working relationship with Linlithgow had deteriorated with the reforms commissioner complaining that the viceroy was not only ignoring his advice, he was not even bothering to ask for it. 'Sitting comfortably in a cushy job in a hill station with nothing to do but theorise about a hypothetical future is getting me down,' Hodson wrote in his diary shortly before submitting his resignation in mid-August.[27] Because his offer to resign coincided with the start of the Quit India movement demanding an end to British rule, Linlithgow asked him to delay the official announcement to prevent the appearance of a rift between the two over policy towards Congress. The delay allowed time for Hodson to make a strong case for Menon as his replacement. 'He has great knowledge of and long familiarity with this business and I am sure, will be most useful in collecting material for the next stage,' Linlithgow wrote to the Secretary of State for India, Lord Amery. 'I know that you agree with me as to the importance of maintaining this post as an independent post and of making it a focus of study for later constitutional developments.'[28] Menon got the job.

In September 1946, Menon was appointed Patel's political aide in the home ministry. The Sardar needed hard-working and knowledgeable officers to help with his massive workload. Menon proved more than capable. As their professional and personal relationship developed, they found themselves increasingly drawn into discussions on India's constitutional future. In Menon's view, the proposal for a three-tiered structure of government embracing the provinces and the princely states put forward by the Cabinet Mission in May 1946 was 'an illusion . . . unwieldy and difficult to work; I saw no future for the country under this plan'. Besides, Menon argued, Jinnah had shown no signs of giving up his demand for Pakistan, particularly as he had the support of powerful people in the British establishment and the Indian Army. 'My personal view was that it was better that the country should be divided, rather than it should gravitate towards civil war.'[29] Power would be handed over to two separate central governments – India's and Pakistan's. The two countries would be granted 'Dominion Status', meaning full nationhood within the British Commonwealth. Menon especially objected to the Mission's plan of allowing the successor states to conclude independent treaties with the Crown, which amounted to a direct invitation to the major states to retain their independence as allies or feudatories of Britain.[30] Patel quickly saw the logic of Menon's plan, particularly as it would be a soft landing for the princes, who would find it easier to transition to an India that was part of the Commonwealth with the constitutional monarch as its head.

Such was the animosity between Congress and the princes by the beginning of 1947 that the praise certain states received from some of India's early nationalists for their progress in areas such as responsible government, education and social reform seemed to belong to a distant past. Baroda's ruler Gaekwar Sayajirao had outlawed child marriage and bigamy and made education free and compulsory for all school-age children in the early 1900s. He introduced legislation to ban untouchability in his state, years before Mahatma Gandhi took up the cause. Mysore inaugurated a representative assembly in 1881 and added a legislative council or upper house in 1907. The self-governing nature of the states offered an opportunity for Indians to rise to higher administrative positions than they could in British India. The states had helped develop 'a school for Indian statesmanship' and 'offered fields for men of capacity whose complexion had placed a limit on what they could achieve in foreign-ruled parts of their own motherland', noted K.M. Panikkar.[31] Over the decades, the states nurtured the careers of dozens of enlightened administrators, including Salar Jung I, who held the post of dewan of Hyderabad for more than thirty years, and the reformist Madhava Rao, who ended his career as regent in Baroda in the 1870s. In 1903, Romesh Chandra Dutt, a former ICS officer and minister in Baroda, wrote: 'No part of India is better governed to-day than these States, ruled by their own Princes.'[32] Addressing a rally in Finsbury Park in London, the theosophist and social reformer Annie Besant stated: 'It is a remarkable fact that, where the Indian princes have been left uninterfered with, the famines have not been so serious.'[33]

Born in the princely state of Porbandar in present-day Gujarat, Gandhi had greater affinity with the princes than Patel or Nehru. Both his father and grandfather had held senior positions in the courts of various Kathiawar states. At the urging of the liberal Indian politician G.A. Natesan, the rulers of Bikaner, Mysore and Hyderabad contributed funds to support Gandhi's satyagrahas in Natal, South Africa. In his first recorded thoughts on the princes, Gandhi takes pity on them, attired 'like women' in silk achkans, pearl necklaces and bracelets at Lord Curzon's 1903 durbar. His views on the princes, as on issues such as caste and industrialization, would undergo numerous iterations. 'My ideal of Indian states is Ram Rajya,' he declared in 1925, referring to the ideal kingdom ruled by Lord Rama – a condition he believed the princes could achieve and should make their goal. He was an admirer of Mysore's ruler Krishnaraja Wadiyar, a pious and progressive Hindu whom he referred to as a rajarshi, or 'saintly king'. At the same time, the Mahatma pitied the slavery and emasculation of the princely states at the hands of the British, describing them as being little better than 'puppets, created or tolerated for the upkeep and prestige of the British power'.[34] Allowing the princes to continue their reign was a stain on the Empire's reputation.

> The existence of this gigantic autocracy is the greatest disproof of British democracy and is a credit neither to the Princes nor to the unhappy people who have to live under this undiluted autocracy. It is no credit to the Princes that they allow themselves powers which no human being, conscious of his dignity, should possess. It is no credit to the people who have mutely suffered the loss of elementary human freedom. And it is perhaps the greatest blot on British rule in India.[35]

The official policy of the Indian National Congress towards the states, adopted at Nagpur in 1920, was one of non-intervention. It said the Congress could form committees in the states but not indulge in political activities. It could give moral support to Praja Mandals, but not lend manpower or offer them financial backing. If the states' subjects felt dissatisfied with the performance of their rulers, they were not permitted to organize protests in the name of the Congress but instead could form specific bodies and press their demands through non-violence and non-cooperation. This stand was a rational one. The princely states enjoyed considerable autonomy. Even the British shied away from enforcing administrative reforms except in cases of gross misrule. Involving itself in the affairs of the states would leave the Congress fighting battles on two fronts, with the British and with the princes, for which it was ill prepared. Moreover, it could result in the Government of India lending the rulers even greater support, thereby strengthening British rule. Concluded Gandhi: 'Prudence, therefore, dictates inaction where action would be waste of effort if not folly.'[36] Not everyone agreed with this stand. At the Jabalpur session of the All India Congress Committee in 1935, the prominent left-wing Congressman N.V. Gadgil moved a resolution demanding that the people of the states should get the full cooperation of the Congress in the freedom struggle. Gadgil was opposed by Patel, who told the gathering: 'We were not prepared to go into an Indian State and interfere in its affairs in case it banned the Congress. A necessary consequence of Mr. Gadgil's resolution would be the abolition of Indian States. We were not prepared to subscribe to this policy.'[37] Pragmatism lay behind Patel's statement. For there to be constitutional progress the cooperation of the people of the states would be required. Alienating them would therefore run counter to Congress interests.

Jawaharlal Nehru's views were closer to Gadgil's than to Patel's. According to Sarvepalli Gopal, one of his several biographers, 'the prospect of these puppet princes . . . setting themselves up as independent monarchs drove him to intense exasperation'.[38] Nehru's attitude was coloured by his early exposure to Fabian Socialism and Marxism while he was a student in Cambridge. More directly influential was his experience in Nabha, a thirteen-gun-salute hill state in the Punjab. In 1923, the despotic and sadistic Sikh maharaja, Ripudaman Singh, was forced to abdicate after a one-man British commission of enquiry concluded that he had violated the sovereignty of the neighbouring state of Patiala by covert and overt acts of aggression and had utilized the machinery of the state and his power as a ruler for criminal and illegal purposes. He was also found to have associated with political movements outside his state, which were aimed at subverting the authority of the British government. Nehru had gone to Nabha to observe the Akali Dal-led agitation against Ripudaman's deposition. Representing the interest of the region's Sikhs, the Akali Dal had been organizing marches in support of the ex-ruler. Unaware of a ban on his entry into the state, Nehru found himself arrested with two other Congress workers and confined to a small, damp jail cell. It was the future Congress leader's first taste of prison life. 'At night we slept on the floor, and I would wake up with a start, full of horror, to find that a rat or a mouse had just passed over my face,' he would later recall.[39] After what he termed a mock trial under a magistrate who 'seemed to be wholly uneducated', Nehru was sentenced to thirty months of rigorous imprisonment, but the punishment was suspended and he was told to leave Nabha immediately. It was also his first taste of what the ordinary people in princely states had to endure. 'The semifeudal conditions are retained, autocracy is kept, the old laws and procedure are still supposed to function, all the restrictions on personal liberty and association and expression of opinion (and these are all-embracing) continue.'[40]

~

Strains in the Congress party's policy of non-intervention in the affairs of the princely states began to appear as early as in the mid-1920s as complaints from within them about maladministration and abuse of power became too numerous to ignore. In May 1925, up to 500 unarmed farmers protesting steep hikes in land taxes were massacred by the state forces of Alwar using machine guns. The army then set fire to the village of Neemachna, destroying hundreds of houses and killing dozens of livestock. It was the worst atrocity since the Jallianwala Bagh massacre in Amritsar in 1919. Gandhi responded to news from Alwar by saying: 'If all reports that are published are true, they are proof of Dyerism double distilled.'[41]

A sham official enquiry ordered by Maharaja Jey Singh found that only thirteen people had died and twelve wounded. The willingness of the British government to investigate these reports irked the princes, but their complaints were rebuffed by the secretary of state, who reminded them that he was duty-bound to intervene if administrative or financial mismanagement caused unrest or an uprising.

In 1927, a group of prominent lawyers, including Rajkot barrister Popatlal Chudgar, set up the All India States Peoples' Conference (AISPC). The AISPC's aim was to extend responsible government and basic civil rights to princely India. Although its work was not endorsed by the Congress, it was influential in drawing attention to some of the worst excesses of princely rule. Chudgar's 1927 book *Indian Princes under British Protection* portrayed the typical ruler as a spoilt autocrat fondled, indulged and scrupulously guarded from an early age, 'like a jewel within its velvet case'.[42] Three years later, on the eve of the first RTC in London, the AISPC published a set of allegations against the maharaja of Patiala, Bhupinder Singh. The *Indictment of Patiala* accused Bhupinder of shocking crimes, including the rape and murder of his heavily pregnant wife Bachittar Kaur and the disappearance of her son.[43] It also alleged that public officials were being jailed if they did not supply the maharaja with a constant stream of young peasant girls for his sexual gratification. His army was accused of demanding supplies from villagers without payment. Forced labour was rampant and anyone refusing it was beaten by the police. Despite the atmosphere of fear and intimidation in the state, the authors of *Indictment* were adamant that the allegations had 'the backing of very solid and in many cases startling and shocking facts'.[44] A closed-door official enquiry into the allegations that found no evidence of wrongdoing was dismissed as a whitewash.

Bhupinder was elected for a fifth term as the chancellor of the COP.

In February 1938, the Congress passed a resolution at its session in Haripura declaring that it stood 'for the same political, social and economic freedom in the States as in the rest of India and considers the States as integral parts of India which cannot be separated'. It also reiterated that its objective of complete independence was for the whole of India 'inclusive of the States'.[45] The trigger for the policy U-turn was the jailing of party volunteers who had hoisted the national flag on 26 January 1938 in Mysore. Gandhi also served notice on the states urging them to recognize that the alternative to full self-government was their ultimate extinction. In an editorial in *Harijan* on 3 December 1938, he wrote:

> I am responsible for [the] policy of non-interference hitherto followed by Congress. But with [the] growing influence of Congress it is impossible for me to defend it in the face of injustices perpetrated in the States. If [the] Congress feels that it has [the] power to offer effective interference it will be bound to do so when the time comes.[46]

Two weeks later, the Congress Working Committee authorized party members to directly assist the people of the states in their struggle for responsible government.

The response was swift. In Indore, Kotah and Jodhpur, the Congress party's influence had led to the establishment of organizations pressing for domestic political change. The banning of these organizations by the rulers of the states deprived those pressuring for reform of a platform for venting their grievances. This, together with the pent-up anger against princely misrule and excesses, saw peaceful hartals quickly escalate into violent demonstrations in Travancore, Kashmir, Hyderabad, Jaipur, Rajkot and elsewhere. Violence also erupted in the Eastern States Agency, where the British political agent in Raipur was hacked to death. 'When I toured the State during last winter everything was normal and no grievances were brought to my notice,' the Raja of Sarila wrote to Nehru. Now, 'towns are filled with mobs, parading and taunting officials'.[47] Finally, it was Gandhi's moral authority that kept the more radical elements in the Congress from taking matters into their own hands, earning the princes and the British a reprieve. In April 1939, he called for the agitations to cease. The historian Ian Copland argues that the satyagraha of 1938–39, though short-lived and outwardly unsuccessful, 'radicalized thousands of hitherto docile princely subjects. Never again would these people meekly acquiesce in a system of governance that formally excluded them from power.'[48]

2

The Bonfire of Vices

Night after night the fires burned fiercely. Clouds of grey smoke billowed above the walls surrounding the British Residency, the hot summer breezes spreading feathery white embers across the sprawling city of Indore. Inside the Residency compound, peons sweated profusely as they carried bundles of frayed and yellowing files from steel almirahs, to be cremated without ceremony. Consumed by the insatiable flames during those sultry nights in the summer of 1947 were decades of secret correspondence between the resident and the Political Department, detailing the most intimate details of the personal lives of Indore's rulers – evidence of 'unnatural sexual indulgence', inbred insanity, torture, prostitution, incest, enslavement, conspiracy to murder, and more.

Dozens of such conflagrations were happening at British outposts around India. In Srinagar, the British resident, Colonel Wilfred Webb, was consigning to the funeral pyre the files on the 'Mr A' case, the sexual blackmailing of the maharaja of Kashmir, Hari Singh. In Ajmer, correspondence concerning the ruler of Alwar's practice of tying widows to trees as tiger bait was set ablaze. In Patiala, the names of women that the maharaja had ordered to be abducted and held as sex slaves in his zenana were fed to the flames. In Hyderabad, personal files on the Nizam of Hyderabad, once called 'the most freakish and disreputable person to be at this date placed in a position of authority over some 16 million of his fellow human beings',[1] were similarly being erased. In all, four tonnes of papers concerning the princes and their peccadilloes were destroyed or shipped to the Imperial Archives in London, where they would be safe from prying eyes looking for ways to harm the states.[2]

The order for lighting this bonfire of princely vices came from Conrad Corfield. A missionary's son, Corfield spent his childhood years living in a hunting lodge near Amritsar that once belonged to Ranjit Singh, the 'Lion of the Punjab', and had been converted into a school dormitory and his family's living quarters. After serving with the Cambridgeshire regiment during World War One, he joined the Indian Civil Service and was posted to the Punjab in 1921. Corfield's rationale for this arson-inspired redaction was to prevent files that could be used to blackmail the princes from falling into the hands of the leaders of a future independent India or Pakistan. He had been political adviser on the states to the Crown representative and head of the Political Department since April 1945. It was a critically important position. Paramountcy, or imperial control, was exerted informally through the advice of officers of the Indian Political Service. Known as 'residents' in the larger states and as 'political agents' or just 'politicals' in the smaller ones, the members of this cadre came under the wing of the Political Department and acted both as representatives of the Government of India and as advisers. 'All those who have direct experience of Indian states know that the whisper of the residency is the thunder of the state, and that there is no matter on which the Resident does not feel qualified to give advice,' K.M. Panikkar remarked.[3]

Corfield had replaced Francis Wylie, a former ICS officer. Wylie had been one of three officers recruited by Lord Linlithgow to urge the princes to join an all-Indian federation that had been enshrined in the 1935 Government of India Act. Under the Act, the eleven provinces that made up British India were to be advanced to the status of full-fledged parliamentary democracies with almost complete autonomy, except in the areas of foreign affairs and defence, which remained entirely under viceregal control. The act also contained a provision for a federal structure that was exceedingly generous to the princes, with the latter being able to nominate representatives to a Constituent Assembly, an interim government meant to ensure a smooth transition to independence, without the holding of elections. It also offered the princes the chance to maintain their legal status as separate entities. But there were costs attached. The states would lose a degree of sovereignty as the laws of the central legislature would also apply to them. For some of the larger states, that meant no longer being able to print their own stamps and mint their own coins. The abolition of internal tariffs would mean the end of their own customs regimes, depriving them of important sources of income. The most bitter pill to swallow for the states was the loss of prestige.

Wylie failed to make much headway. None of the princes he visited, he wrote, 'had displayed any practical appreciation of the contents of the Government of India Act', their minds confused by the conflicting advice given by a battery of 'loud-mouthed American experts' they had employed at vast expense. All appeared obsessed by the fear that they would be 'flooded' with federal officials over whom they would have no control or that they would lose their privy purse. Baroda's ruler was too busy attending the horse races in Bombay to see Wylie, while Hari Singh of Kashmir was his usual 'bored and sulky' self.[4] Ganga Singh of Bikaner, whom Wylie described as 'an out-of-date windbag whose capacity for self-advertisement is very nearly exhausted', was openly hostile to the Act, suggesting some 116 limitations and greeting Wylie's every remark with 'scorn and derision'.[5] Wavell considered Wylie 'wise and steady but possibly a little too drastic with the Princes; anyway, they don't like being ridden on his rather tight rein and with his rather sharp spurs'.[6]

Corfield had not been Wavell's preferred choice, but there was no one else with his experience in the Political Department's cadre. A career political officer who had served in multiple states, his sympathies were suspect. As Wylie would later write, he was an 'able person' but excessively conservative. 'He has been all his life in Indian States and has imbibed, perhaps, too successfully, the Princely point of view . . . He does not agree with the present-day political developments in British India which make his task as Adviser . . . very difficult indeed.'[7] Corfield's son later told researcher Madeleine Moëd, that his father's almost clerical upbringing in the Punjab 'may have conditioned the rather high moral stance he took over the abrogation of the Crown's treaties with the Indian Princes'.[8]

For the princely states, the new political challenges that accompanied the preparations for the departure of Britain from India were a painful disruption of their mutually beneficial relationship, in which their excesses were overlooked in return for their loyalty. During the Mutiny of 1857, 'these patches of Native government', in the words of India's first viceroy, Lord Canning, 'served as breakwaters to the storm, which would otherwise have swept us in one great wave'.[9] When control of India had passed from the East India Company to the British Crown in 1858, a royal proclamation was read out in

Queen Victoria's name. It guaranteed the continued existence of the states without the Crown's interference. All treaties and agreements made with them by the company would be 'scrupulously observed'. 'We desire no extension of Our present Territorial Possessions. We shall respect the rights, dignity, and honour of Native Princes as Our Own.'[10]

The proclamation buried forever the notorious Doctrine of Lapse that provided Britain with an excuse to annex states where the ruler was either manifestly incompetent or whose death triggered a succession. The policy had been enthusiastically pursued by Canning's predecessor Lord Dalhousie, who viewed annexation as a way of 'getting rid of those petty intervening principalities which may be a means of annoyance, but which can never, I venture to think, be a source of strength'.[11] Around a dozen states were annexed during his governorship, the most important being Oudh, a rich province that lay between the Ganga and Yamuna rivers. The policy backfired disastrously when Oudh became one of main springboards for the Mutiny a year later.

With Queen Victoria's proclamation, the political map of India was effectively frozen, a jumble of pinks representing British India and yellows representing Indian India or the princely states. In the early 1900s, Sir Bampfylde Fuller, a former governor of Assam, likened the subcontinent 'to an ancient, tessellated pavement, the greater part of which has been destroyed, and has been replaced by slabs of uncoloured stonework. The tesserae represent the Native States: the plain stone-filling the territories that have come under British administration.'[12] The tesserae dissected the plain stonework in almost every direction. Save for a narrow neck of land near Jhansi in central India, it would have been impossible to travel north to south without crossing into the territories of one of the princely states. Travelling east to west would have presented a similar set of obstacles. After passing through Delhi, the yellows of Bahawalpur and Faridkot closed in on the imperial pinks like the pincers of a scorpion. The pincers relaxed their grip as the traveller traversed what is now northern Pakistan before coming up against the tribal areas of the North-West Frontier. In 1930, the Simon Commission noted that the princely states 'constitute an outstanding feature which is without precedent or analogy elsewhere'.[13]

While the origin of kingship in India dates back more than three millennia to the early Vedic period, most of the princely states at the time of Independence owed their existence to the slow collapse of the Mughal empire following the death of Aurangzeb in 1707. Centuries of foreign domination meant that many of the rulers who carved out their own states were outsiders. The nizams of Hyderabad were of Turkoman stock. Bhopal was established by one of Aurangzeb's Afghan generals. Rampur's first ruler, Nawab Faizullah Khan, was a Pashtun. Tonk in present-day Rajasthan was founded by Pindari freebooters. The seaboard state of Janjira was the creation of an Abyssinian pirate. Among the Hindu kingdoms, most of the rulers were Kshatriya, but there were notable exceptions, such as the robber-caste rajas of the south Indian state of Pudukkottai. Only the Rajput states and a scattering of south Indian kingdoms could trace their lineages to the pre-Mughal period. The Muslim potentates of Hyderabad and Junagadh ruled over majority-Hindu populations. The situation was reversed in Kashmir. Most of the subjects of Kapurthala's Sikh maharaja were Muslims.

State creation was haphazard at best. When the East India Company defeated the last of the Maratha chiefs in 1818, it accepted the status quo in the territories it now ruled without any regard for checking titles or status. The subjugation of the Sikh chieftains in Punjab spawned the formation of important states such as Patiala and Kapurthala. Mysore and Jammu and Kashmir were the creation of the Raj – Mysore being restored to its Hindu rulers after the defeat of Tipu Sultan, and Kashmir being sold by the East India Company to a Dogra adventurer in return for assistance rendered during the Sikh war of 1846. Khairpur was allowed to retain its independence after the conquest of Sind, while Kalat was drawn into British India because of its strategic importance on the Afghan border. 'Princely India is a perfect example of the well-known fact that Britain acquired her empire in a fit of absentmindedness,' quipped the *New York Times* correspondent Herbert Matthews in June 1947.

> She did not plan this picture-puzzle India. It just happened. At one moment, the British conquerors said, 'Enough!' They deposed no more rulers, seized no more territory, made treaties with those rulers who were left, and India so to speak was frozen into her present patchwork pattern.[14]

States such as Udaipur and Rewa were considered bastions of conservatism. Shortly after coming to the throne in 1884, Udaipur's Maharana Fateh Singh refused to have a railway built to connect his capital with the rest of Rajputana. When Lord Minto attended a state banquet in his honour at the Lake Palace, Maharana Fateh Singh's mania for ritual purity meant he dined separately. 'He is held in the deepest reverence, and when any of his subjects speak to him a towel is held over the mouth in order that the Maharana should not be desecrated by their breath,' Lady Minto noted.[15] Rewa's Gulab Singh refused to allow a railway line to pass through his state after his Brahmin advisers warned that beef might be on the menu in the restaurant cars. Mysore's long-serving ruler Krishnaraja Wadiyar was another devout Hindu, who for many years refused to leave India because to cross the ocean would mean loss of caste. But he was also a visionary whose achievements included the setting up of a hydroelectric power project, a steel mill, an eye hospital, the Indian Institute of Science and the State Bank of Mysore. His successor Jayachamarajendra Wadiyar was a trained classical musician who was equally at ease with a Carnatic kriti and a Chopin sonata. Following Independence, he provided funds to London's Philharmonic Orchestra and helped pay the salary of its conductor Herbert von Karajan.

The largest state was Kashmir, with an area of 218,799 square kilometres, followed closely by Hyderabad. Located in the Deccan, Hyderabad's income and expenditure rivalled that of Belgium, and in 1947 was larger than that of twenty members of the UN. At the other end of the scale were more than 300 microstates. The bulk were in the peninsula of Kathiawar, where numerous individual fiefdoms yielded 'a revenue not greater than that of the annual income of an ordinary artisan'.[16] Maharaja Ganga Singh of Bikaner once remarked that he knew of a Kathiawar state with a income of 'forty-three rupees and whose kingdom is a well'.[17] The other concentration of microstates was in the Punjab hills, where Herbert Thompson, who served as the political agent, recalled visiting one raja who 'would share his palace with his cattle which walked through the front door and occupied the ground floor'.[18] As to the prize for the smallest of the states, opinion was divided as to whether size or population was the marker. Was it Bilbari, with an area of 4.3 square kilometres and a population of twenty-seven? Or was it Veja-no-ness, with an area of 2 square kilometres and a population of 184?

Regardless of the size of their states, India's princes were the final source of all authority, their actions never questioned by judiciaries or elected legislative bodies. As *Life* magazine photographer and reporter Margaret Bourke-White noted:

> If you were a citizen of a state, you might be taxed with an elephant levy if the prince were buying a new elephant; and maharajas buy a lot of elephants. You might be taxed with a dowry levy if a princess were getting married; with a motor levy if the prince were buying a Rolls-Royce, and they buy a lot of Rolls-Royces.[19]

Whatever laws existed tended to be a jumble of personal decrees, British Indian laws and local customs. Their citizens of the princely states were not British subjects but, in legal parlance, 'British Protected Persons'. Common to all, even for those who would have been village squires had their fiefdoms been in Britain, was their subordinate relationship to the Paramount Power. The relationship absolved the need for Britain to take over more territory and set up complex administrative systems. At the same time, Britain could count on the cooperation and support of the princes when it needed it.

In exchange for guaranteed protection against internal unrest or attacks by his enemies, a ruler would have to accept a British resident or political agent at his court and, in the case of the larger states, pay for a subsidiary military force commanded by British officers. Through its network of residents and political agents, the India Office in London was the final authority on recognizing successions and determining when to hand over full ruling powers in the case of minors. About forty states had actual treaties with Great Britain. Hyderabad's committed Britain to maintain 5,000 troops for the protection of the state, while Bhopal's spoke of 'perpetual friendship'. Another hundred or so had signed *sanads* or agreements that acknowledged the authority of the Paramount Power, while the remainder enjoyed some form of recognition of their status by the Crown. Such guarantees came at a price. As K.M. Panikkar, the dewan of Bikaner, complained:

> The rulers were not to call their sons princes, they were not supposed to reign but only to rule: they did not ascend 'thrones' but only acceded to 'gaddis', their troops were not armies but only 'forces', their governments were not to be styled as such but only as 'durbars'. Lord Curzon even objected to the colour of the liveries.[20]

Walter Lawrence, who served as settlement commissioner for Jammu and Kashmir and then as Curzon's private secretary, recalls meeting one Rajput ruler who compared the interference of the political agent stationed at his court to the 'sensation of a rat in his pyjamas'. Lawrence hinted that the irritability of the relationship might have had something to do with the officer's objection to the ruler's habit of harnessing the state's bankers like horses to tow his carriage or of forcing them to row his pleasure barge.[21]

To constitute the princes into a feudal hierarchy, the British devised a system of gun salutes, ranging from twenty-one for the five largest states down to nine. Out of 562 states at the time of Independence, 149 had gun salutes. In determining a state's ranking, size and population often mattered less than loyalty and lineage. Only five states enjoyed twenty-one-gun status – Hyderabad, Kashmir, Mysore, Gwalior and Baroda. But even they were a long way down in the imperial pecking order. The King Emperor was entitled to a 101-gun salute, while a viceroy was granted thirty-one.

The obsession with hierarchy deepened the existing insecurities and sensitivities among the Indian feudatories. The ruler of one small state in Rajputana was 'so suspicious of everyone except his private secretary that he invented a secret language known to only the two of them and even issued coinage inscribed in it'.[22] Speaking from first-hand experience, Henry Cotton, who served as chief commissioner of Assam, declared:

> They are consumed by petty jealousies among themselves, by questions of precedence, of salutes, of the strength of their armies. The example of one chief is infectious, the others cannot be outdone, and thus they vie with one another in their enthusiastic receptions of the Viceroy on his occasional visits, and in the display of those barbaric attributes of loyalty which are the surest passport for recognition and favour from the Government.[23]

Pandering to their love of ceremony, the British bestowed on the princes imperial orders as a reward for loyalty and gave them prominence in rituals such as the Imperial Assemblage of 1877 and visits of British officials to the states. The Maharaja of Patiala collected decorations from foreign courts as if they were stamps and had to reproduce them in three-quarter size to fit them on his chest. Nripendra Narayan, the maharaja of Cooch Behar and a frequent guest of Queen Victoria's at Windsor and Sandringham, was such a firm believer in the benefits that British rule conferred that he told Gordon Casserly, a soldier serving at the nearby garrison at Buxar: 'If ever, during [his] lifetime, the British quitted India, my departure would precede theirs.' India would not be worth living in. 'Chaos, bloodshed and confusion would be its lot.'[24] When the Prince of Wales, later Edward VII, visited India, one ruler ordered that the water for His Royal Highness's tea must be boiled on a fire made of banknotes.

Residents and political agents were expected to adhere to a code of practice outlined in the *Manual of Instructions to Officers of the Political Department of the Government of India*. Commissioned by Curzon's successor Lord Minto, it was published in 1909 and ran into almost 350 pages. The manual began by reminding officers that their first duty was 'to cultivate direct, friendly personal relations with the Ruling Chiefs'. A departmental officer 'should be careful to uphold the dignity of the Durbar; he should not interfere between the Durbar and its subjects, encourage petitions and letters against the former; nor should he on his tours inspect the district offices and institutions except at the wish or invitation of the Durbar'. Only when misrule reached 'a pitch which violates the elementary laws of civilisation' should the government take measures for enforcing reform – 'But this would be as a last resort.'[25] The manual's laissez-faire approach was meant to encourage good governance in the states by treating the princes as allies rather than as the 'unruly schoolboys' that Curzon so despised.

The premise, however, was fundamentally flawed. It offered power without responsibility and effectively ruled out British intervention except in cases of gross misrule – and even in that matter the goalposts were constantly shifting. The leeway given to a prince was considerable. He could spend most of his state's income on himself – if he did it discreetly; torture and murder his subjects – as long it was only done occasionally; and take as many mistresses as he pleased – preferably Indian, not European. In all these areas Bhupinder Singh of Patiala was among the most excessive, spending around 60 per cent of his state's income on himself. To the embarrassment of the British, he was not averse to flaunting this wealth in public, rarely appearing without the great Sans Souci diamond as a pendant and a 3.8 centimetres flat emerald across on his arm. There were 500 horses for his personal use, kennels containing dozens of champion gun dogs and dozens of wardrobes bursting with Savile Row suits. The royal garage contained twenty-seven Rolls-Royces, their upkeep managed by an Englishman trained by the firm. Only his prominence as a princely power broker protected him from being toppled. Despite the decades of mostly gentle arm-twisting by residents and political agents, the rulers of the states were at best mildly limited by constitutional checks and at worst were total autocrats. They could be encouraged but not coerced into making reforms.

~

Persistent lobbying by the leading princes for a greater say in policy matters led to the formation of the Chamber of Princes in 1921. Inaugurated by the Duke of Connaught at the Diwan-i-Am, the former audience hall of the Mughal emperor inside the Red Fort in Delhi, it brought the rulers of the leading states together under one umbrella for the first time. Membership was open to the 108 princes who were entitled to salutes of eleven guns or more. Another twelve rulers represented 127 smaller states. Its first chancellor was Maharaja Ganga Singh of Bikaner.

The Chamber's many critics dismissed it as being little more than a glorified debating society. Three of the five twenty-one-gun-salute states – Hyderabad, Mysore and Baroda – refused to join. Prominent states such as Jaipur, Indore, Udaipur, Travancore and Cochin also stayed away, collectively bristling at the prospect of a bunch of lesser states taking decisions that would impinge on their sovereignty. 'I should not like any questions affecting my State being determined on the advice of other Ruling Princes, or of their representatives, Hindus or Muhammadens,' scoffed Hyderabad's nizam.[26]

As a body for collective action, the COP would never live up to its own expectations. Attendance at its annual meetings rarely exceeded forty. Among those who attended, few took an active part in the deliberations, while the others, in the words of one nationalist critic, sat 'like dummies nodding their heads at everything that passes'.[27] The apathy was in large part due to the COP's toothless nature and its unwieldy decision-making process. It was essentially an advisory body; its resolutions were binding neither on the British nor on the princes who had voted for them, nor on any other princes. Any discussion of the private affairs of individual states and rulers was strictly off limits, as was any intervention by the Chamber on behalf of rulers who had to endure the interference of the Raj. All this mattered little to the British. The COP represented a bulwark of autocracy and conservatism, which the British hoped would counter nationalist forces and prolong the lifespan of their Indian empire.

It is also clear that many residents and political agents saw the states through rose-tinted glasses – or, more accurately, through the sights of a .450 Martini carbine while hunting tigers in their private reserves. Corfield blames the overindulgence of the princes on the attractions of 'old world' India to viceroys and governors who wanted an escape from the drudgery of day-to-day administration.

> What viceroy could bear to refuse an invitation to shoot tigers in Alwar, within such easy reach of Delhi? Especially when the invitation came from a ruler who was known to be a personal friend of the Secretary of State, a brilliant speaker and a leader amongst the princes. What political officer in these circumstances would be inclined to point out the villages which had been expropriated, the roads which had been closed and the fields which remained uncultivated in order to provide the playground of this sport?[28]

There was also the mania among some princes for all things European that played its part in this relationship. Yeshwant Rao Holkar of Indore commissioned Le Corbusier to design a tubular chaise-longue cover in leopard skin. The Maharawal of Dungarpur travelled specially to Brighton to take lessons on how to do the foxtrot. Sport was another passion. Aside from polo, cricket and hockey, lawn tennis was a highly favoured pastime in princely circles, and it was not uncommon for the princes to employ Europeans skilled in the game on their personal staff. The Maharaja of Orchha and the Nawab of Jaora maintained golf courses whose greens were meticulously tended by convicts from the local jails.

By the early 1940s it was becoming clear that this strange symbiotic relationship could not last. With the momentum towards independence now unstoppable, it was clear that no state would be left untouched. 'We shall have to come out into the open with the Princes sooner or later,' Wavell declared shortly before departing from India. 'We are at present being dishonest in pretending we can maintain all these small states, knowing full well that in practice we shall be unable to do so.'[29]

3

Allies and Agitators

He was the king's cousin, had proven himself as an astute wartime commander, was extremely hard-working, popular with his contemporaries and 'blessed with a very unusual wife'.[1] His liberal views would appeal to Indian nationalists and his royal pedigree would earn him the trust of the princes. When British prime minister Clement Attlee began canvassing his peers for Lord Wavell's replacement as viceroy, Mountbatten had no rivals. Outside Attlee's immediate circle, however, opinion was divided. Mountbatten had a reputation for being a playboy and was widely perceived to have used his political and social connections rather than his knowledge of India to secure the prized post. He was also known for acting impulsively. He 'did not only leap before he looked', wrote Philip Ziegler, 'he leaped before he even knew whence he was leaping'.[2] That was particularly dangerous, given that he would be granted unprecedented plenipotentiary powers by Attlee, allowing him to take decisions at his own discretion without seeking approval from London. At a time when the Congress party's demands for a unified India were being violently opposed by the Muslim League, Mountbatten's limited understanding of the subcontinent did not bode well for the future.

Before taking up his viceroyalty, Mountbatten was summoned by King George VI to Buckingham Palace. The British monarch was worried about the position of the states in the coming negotiations over India's independence. Do what you can 'to see fair play for the Princes', he urged Mountbatten. It was an instruction Mountbatten would interpret very loosely.[3] Though he had been charged with ensuring that the princes would not be neglected, he admitted later: 'I had been given no inkling that this [state's problem] was going to be as hard if not harder to solve, as that of British India.'[4]

Mountbatten's mission had been complicated by the last botched attempt at meeting the demands of the princes. When the three-man Cabinet Mission put together by Clement Attlee arrived in Delhi in March 1946 to consult with political leaders on India's constitutional future, Conrad Corfield made sure that a large map showing the extent of the princely states was hung in the viceroy's private conference room. 'Lord Pethick-Lawrence and Mr [A.V.] Alexander were astonished, and even Sir Stafford Cripps was surprised, by the sheer magnitude of the territorial possessions of the Indian Princes,' wrote Edmund Wakefield, a senior member of the Political Department who had been tasked with briefing the delegation. Only Cripps displayed 'anything but the most elementary knowledge'.[5] Asked at a press conference the day after the Mission's arrival whether the cooperation of the princes would be mandatory, Pethick-Lawrence replied: 'If I invite you to dinner, it is not obligatory for you to come.'[6]

As it turned out, there was not enough seating at the Cabinet Mission's table for those princes clamouring to make their opinions heard. Dungarpur and Bilaspur were delegated to represent the smaller states, and the dewans of Jaipur, Hyderabad and Travancore were also included in the consultation process. When the question came up as to whether to involve representatives of the 9 crore or so subjects of the states in the consultations, the response from the chancellor of the COP, Hamidullah Khan, was a firm no. None of the Cabinet Mission members raised an eyebrow at his objection.

It was an inauspicious start to the Mission's two-month consultative process that culminated in its memorandum of 16 May 1946 recommending that there should be a union of British India encompassing both Hindu- and Muslim-majority provinces as well as the Indian states, with foreign relations, defence and communications held in common. A Constituent Assembly would be formed that would act as an interim government until independence, with the princes free to nominate their representatives rather than have them elected democratically. Paramountcy would lapse on Britain's withdrawal from India and the states would be free to chart their own future. In a separate memorandum on states' treaties and paramountcy, the Cabinet Mission affirmed that the states would get back all the powers they had turned over to the British. The resulting void was 'to be filled either by the States entering into a federal relationship with the successor Government or Governments in British India, or failing this, entering into particular political arrangements with it or them'.[7] The ambiguity surrounding the phrase 'particular political arrangements' was not helped by Cripps subsequently telling a press conference that the logical outcome of the Mission's proposals was that the states would 'become wholly independent'. This was music to the ears of the princes who, on 11 June at a meeting of the Standing Committee of the COP, unanimously endorsed the broad parameters of the Cabinet Mission's plan. What they neglected to realize was that once power had been transferred, they would have to rely on themselves for protection. As Corfield warned, 'a powerful Indian government under democratic rule would hardly be interested in preserving their personal rule, however limited'.[8]

The unanimity of the princes would prove to be short-lived. By the time Mountbatten took up his post, they had split into two camps: those who took Cripps at his word and those who realized that the only way forward was to make some sort of accommodation with Congress. The pro-independence group was led by the nawab of Bhopal and the chancellor of the COP, Hamidullah Khan, while Bikaner's maharaja Sadul Singh became the figurehead for those taking a more inclusive approach. Both rulers had absented themselves from Mountbatten's inauguration, despite being among the viceroy's closest friends in India – a sure sign, noted Campbell-Johnson, 'of the disunity and crisis within their ranks'. The press attaché was right. After making some half-baked excuse for not attending the morning's inauguration, Hamidullah would spend much of his meeting with Mountbatten portraying Singh and the dissident princes as 'tools of Congress'. For his part, Singh poured blame on the COP's chancellor for dividing India along communal lines.

Described by one viceroy as an able administrator but prone to behaving like 'a mischievous boy with a catapult',[9] Hamidullah was the youngest son of Sultana Jahan Begum, the last of four women who had ruled the nineteen-gun state for more than a century. He was a brilliant polo player and had a reputation for being a fearless hunter who stalked and killed tigers on foot. His redoubtable daughters indulged in the equally dangerous sport of hockey on roller skates on the marble floor of one of the family's palaces. His experience as his mother's private secretary, including his holding of the post of chief secretary during her rule, had honed his administrative skills and familiarized him with the workings of the COP. Hamidullah would make no secret of his ties with the Muslim League. For him it was a matter of survival. A Muslim ruling over a Hindu-majority state, he had grown increasingly aware of the communal orientation of the other princes. Since the early 1930s, several leading Hindu rulers had developed close ties with Vinayak Damodar Savarkar's Hindu Mahasabha and were providing funds to the organization for running schools and for office space and propaganda work. This drew Hamidullah closer to the League, and at the urging of his adviser Liaqat Hayat Khan he announced his candidacy for the position of chancellor of the COP in early 1946.

Once elected, Bhopal's nawab breathed new life into the organization. It began demanding assurances that princely states would not be at the mercy of a hostile Congress once the British left India and started tackling the all-important issue of internal reform in the states. But Hamidullah was also a divisive force. His plan to set up a 'Rajastan' made up of all the princely states that would be on par with a future India and Pakistan would split the Chamber and see him branded as being anti-national. Under his plan, the leadership of 'Rajastan' would fall on Hyderabad as the pre-eminent state, thus increasing Muslim influence in the centre and curtailing the power of Hindus in an independent India. Driving the plan was the expectation that there was no future for Muslim dynasties in a Hindu-dominated India.[10] When Hamidullah proposed the plan at a meeting of the COP in May 1946; he was initially supported by the majority of the rulers present. It was only when K.M. Panikkar, the dewan of Bikaner, pointed out that the Hindu princes would not only forfeit their status but also be exposed to the wrath of their subjects under such a scheme that the proposal was rejected. Hamidullah's pro-Muslim stance alarmed Vallabhbhai Patel: 'The Princes' Chamber is in alliance with the Muslim League,' he wrote to B.L. Mitter, the dewan of Baroda, in December 1946. 'It is a matter of surprise to us that the League should hold so much influence on the Princes' Chamber when the chamber is composed of a vast majority of Hindu princes.'[11] For his part, V.P. Menon believed Hamidullah's strategy was to turn the rulers into a 'Third Force' in Indian politics. 'He was an advocate of a loose centre with residuary powers in the States. With such a centre and with the Congress and the Muslim League pitted against each other, the States would occupy a key position and hold the balance.'[12]

Sadul Singh, who had been waiting patiently for his turn to meet the viceroy, had been placed on the gaddi in 1943 after the death of his father Ganga Singh. Considered the elder statesman of princely India, Ganga was the first ruler to propose an assembly of princes, which eventually became the COP. During World War One, he was the only Indian on the Imperial War Cabinet and attended the signing of the Treaty of Versailles in 1919, where he was one of the two signatories representing British India along with Secretary of State Edwin Montagu. Now his son was the acknowledged leader of a progressive bloc of rulers who saw themselves as partners with the Congress in building a new India. When Mountbatten first met Sadul Singh in April 1945, he found his 'views on India as reasonable as any ruling prince could be expected to express'.[13] In contrast to Bhopal's nawab, who believed the June 1948 timetable for Britain's withdrawal was impossible and if enforced would result in bloodshed and chaos, Sadul was upbeat. A dissident block of prominent princely states, including Bikaner, Jaipur, Jodhpur, Baroda and Patiala, was intending to join the Constituent Assembly with the active backing of the Congress. The split in the princely ranks was not along communal lines, he assured the viceroy, but a recognition that the Congress 'was the one central party which possessed the potential to extend itself beyond communities'.[14]

~

In the first few weeks of his viceroyalty, Mountbatten had little time to foster a closer relationship with the princes, let alone engage himself at a policy level on the question of their future. Both Menon and Patel had yet to take on what would be their decisive roles in determining the fate of the states. It was the Political Department headed by Corfield that still called the shots, and as far as its detractors were concerned was doing its best to keep the princes out of the Union. The dynamics between Mountbatten and his political adviser would prove critical in determining the deal eventually struck between Britain, India's nationalist leaders and the princes. Corfield's invaluable knowledge of the states and his personal relationship with many of their most prominent rulers could have been an asset, but ended up as an obstacle. His reputation as 'friend, guide and philosopher' to the rulers made him suspect in the eyes of the Congress leaders. Patel had clashed with him in 1946 over the Nizam of Hyderabad's bid to take advantage of the death of the ruler of Bastar to absorb the mineral-rich state into his own. Corfield insisted that 'his Department was the guardian of the minor ruler [of Bastar] and at liberty to enter into the contract [with Hyderabad] in his interests'. Patel retorted that he would not 'allow the interests of the people [of Bastar] to be bartered away'.[15] The Sardar won the day. Menon's dislike of the Political

Department dated back to the early 1940s, when it had vetoed his appointment as dewan of a large princely state because he was 'not sufficiently above his nationality'.[16] As for Mountbatten, by the time he came up with an agenda for dealing with the states problem, he was at best ignoring Corfield's advice and at worst sabotaging his efforts to make the British government stick to the promises the Cabinet Mission had made to the princes – promises that even the viceroy was quickly beginning to realize could never be honoured.

On 11 April 1947, Mountbatten attended the opening proceedings of the Residents' Conference, but left immediately afterwards, citing other priorities. By doing so, a crucial opportunity to understand the logistics of winding down the Political Department that had been at the coalface of dealing with the princes since the days of the East India Company had been missed. After two days of deliberations, the conference set out a timetable that would see the withdrawal of all political agents by autumn of 1947 and all residents by the end of the year. The main functions of the Political Department would terminate in March 1948. In the meantime, it would undertake to destroy files that were deemed unimportant or contained sensitive information on the private lives of the princes. As the department's head, Corfield's overriding priority was to relieve it 'of its duties as swiftly as possible', encourage the states to make alternative arrangements and put them in contact with the central and provincial governments. 'Any other course would be interpreted as a breach of faith and would not lead to satisfactory conclusions.'[17] When Corfield travelled to London to seek endorsement for the plan from the secretary of state for India, he neglected to tell Mountbatten about it or to brief him on his return. On hearing of Corfield's trip, the viceroy reportedly said to Menon: 'Do you know what that son-of-a-bitch

Corfield has done? Sneaked back to India without telling me. I wonder what he's up to?'[18]

~

The summer heat came on early in 1947, and with the cooling monsoon rains still months away tempers were beginning to fray. As March merged into April, five cities, including Delhi, Calcutta and Amritsar, were placed under curfew to prevent communal clashes. To the south of Delhi, mobs of Jats were attacking Muslim Meo villages – in one incident burning to death twenty-six people, including women and children. In retaliation, Meos attacked six Hindu villages. Jinnah was also turning up the temperature. The previous July he had rejected the Cabinet Mission's plan following the Congress party's refusal to share power with the Muslim League. His call a month later for 'direct action' by all Muslims as a show of force in support of a separate nation resulted in unprecedented levels of communal violence. In May 1947, he reiterated his stance on partition, declaring that any division that excluded the Muslim-majority provinces of Sind, the Punjab, Baluchistan, the North-West Frontier Province, Bengal and Assam was unacceptable and would result in a 'truncated or mutilated moth-eaten Pakistan'.[19]

The patience of Congress leaders with the princes was also running out. On 18 April 1947, Nehru made his broadest and most cutting swipe at the princely order yet, telling delegates attending a meeting of the All India States Peoples' Conference in Gwalior: 'I do not like this shopkeeper's mentality. This bargaining spirit will not do good to the princes. It is a very short-sighted policy which will result in creating enmity between them and the rest of India.' The march towards freedom cannot brook any more obstruction, he insisted. 'All those who do not join the Constituent Assembly now will be regarded as hostile States and they will have to bear the consequences of being so regarded.'[20] To the princes it sounded like a declaration of war.

It was a much-chastened Nehru who met with Mountbatten four days later. The viceroy expressed his 'great disappointment that a man whom I had regarded as a statesman and as a friend should have descended once more to the level of a demagogue in making inflammatory speeches'. Nehru defended himself, saying he had been misquoted. Those rulers who failed to send representatives forthwith to the Constituent Assembly were the ones acting in a hostile manner. Far from being a demagogue and a hothead, he was keeping extreme elements in order. He had nothing against monarchy as long as the decisions of rulers were based on consultation with the wishes of their people.[21] But the Congress leader left Mountbatten in no doubt about how incensed he was that officials of the Political Department were actively lobbying the princes to believe that once the British had left they could legitimately stake their claims to independence. The department's deliberate intent, Nehru warned the viceroy as he left the meeting, was to break up India and introduce 'anarchy by the back door'.[22]

Nehru's apocalyptic vision was partly dispelled on 28 April when the representatives of eight princely states – Bikaner, Patiala, Baroda, Cochin, Udaipur, Jaipur, Jodhpur and Rewa – took their places in the Constituent Assembly. Their defection was largely thanks to Sadul Singh, who had fended off a bid by Hamidullah at a meeting of the Standing Committee of the COP to insist that only those states that had begun the process of drafting constitutions – a process that would take at least six months – should be allowed to enter the Constituent Assembly. Realizing the importance of getting the princes on board, Nehru, Patel and others in the Congress high command confirmed their commitment to the monarchical system of government – a promise that would soon be ditched. In a rousing speech, Panikkar declared that the participation of the states had made the Assembly the most representative gathering in India's history. Neatly buried in the congratulatory messages was the fact that aside from Baroda, none of the representatives had been elected by their state legislatures. The very public defection by the Bikaner bloc tore to shreds whatever façade of princely unity remained, with the Maharaj Rana of Dholpur remarking to Mountbatten that 'two different views conspicuously mark the division of thought and action of the Order'.[23] For Hamidullah Khan, the defection left his leadership fatally compromised. At Corfield's urging he resigned from his position as chancellor of the COP on 3 June 1947.

In early May, Louis and Edwina decamped to the cooler climate of Simla. They were soon joined by Nehru, his daughter Indira and India's future foreign minister, Krishna Menon. 'We have made real friends with him', the viceroy later wrote, referring to 'Jawa', his nickname for Nehru, 'and whatever happens I feel this friendship is sincere and will last'.[24] The intention of the Simla sojourn, however, was not to relax but to finalize the details of what became known as Plan Balkan to replace the Cabinet Mission's failed scheme for the devolution of power. Under the viceroy's revised plan, power was to be transferred to each of the eleven provinces, with Punjab and Bengal, both fiercely contested by Congress and the League, given the option to vote for the partition of their units. Rendered independent upon the transfer of power, the princely states would be able to negotiate freely with any confederation of provinces that might emerge. So confident was Mountbatten that Nehru would accept the plan, he scheduled an announcement to be made at 7.30 p.m. on 20 May. It would never see the light of day.

Also present in Simla was V.P. Menon. After weeks of being snubbed by the viceroy, Menon finally had his ear. Plan Balkan, he told him, was never going to work. The only way forward was to accept the inevitability of the partition of the country that Jinnah was demanding, which he believed the Congress would finally accept. Mountbatten put what happened next down to a 'hunch', but it was clear that Menon's warning had rattled him. Instead of waiting a week for a scheduled meeting with the princes and the Indian political leaders, he decided to show the latest draft of the plan to Nehru on 10 May. Nehru's response was so incendiary Mountbatten termed it 'Nehru's bombshell'. Plan Balkan, he thundered, was a 'picture of fragmentation and conflict and disorder, and, unhappily also, of a worsening of relations between India and Britain'. It would fragment India by spawning 'little Ulsters' made up of provinces and princely states all over the subcontinent. 'If my reactions were so powerful,' Nehru continued, 'you can well imagine what my colleagues and others will feel.'[25]

Desperate to retrieve the situation, Mountbatten turned to Menon who told him: 'Sir, you have never listened to me before, but I beg you to listen to me now.'[26] Locked away in his guest house with a bottle of whiskey, smoking his way through packets of cigarettes, Menon had just three hours to turn what was a 'few notes and some essential points scribbled on some sheets of paper' into a blueprint for the transfer of power to two central governments, one in India and one in Pakistan.[27] The handover would be based on dominion status, which would give both countries independence as members of the Commonwealth. The Congress would be left in charge of the lion's share of the capital as well as the military and bureaucratic machinery of the Raj. Satisfied with the new plan, the viceroy took it to Nehru, promising that he would exert his influence to ensure the states would integrate into India or Pakistan. Nehru signalled he was on board, describing the plan as 'very desirable' and expressing his preference that 'there should be a transfer of power as soon as possible on a Dominion status basis'.[28] He then rang Patel in Delhi, shouting to make himself heard on the crackling line. Nehru said he was worried that the plan would not get Congress's approval. 'Leave that to me, that is my business,' Patel replied.[29] The fate of the Indian empire had just been sealed on a barely audible phone call.

On 18 May, Mountbatten departed for London to get endorsement for the plan to partition India. He was accompanied by Menon. The man who just a few weeks earlier was considered too untrustworthy to be allowed into the upper echelons of the Raj had just saved Mountbatten's reputation – and most probably his job. During his meetings with the India Committee of Cabinet, Mountbatten argued that the prospect of direct relationships between the Crown and the independent princely states would encourage the 'disintegration of India'. It was also likely to see the Congress withdraw from accepting dominion status. On 24 May, the committee accepted that the government's 'prime object should be to facilitate the exclusive association of the States with one of the new Dominions'. However, it also acknowledged that if a state chose to become independent the government would have to consider separate relations with it.[30]

Having obtained the Cabinet's endorsement of the broad parameters of the plan, Mountbatten returned to India on 30 May. Two days later he disclosed its contents to the Indian political leaders assembled at the Viceroy's House, later commenting that he 'could remember no meeting at which decisions had been taken which would have such a profound influence on world history'.[31] He then showed the plan separately to Sadul Singh and Hamidullah

Khan. The ruler of Bikaner welcomed it, saying that the prospect of dominion status for the successor nation states and their continued association with the Crown would make a great difference to the states entering the Constituent Assembly. But Bhopal's nawab was bitterly disappointed, saying: 'Once more, His Majesty's Government have left the Princes in the lurch . . . Whichever Dominion we join . . . will utterly destroy us.'[32] Disillusioned by the outcome of the meeting, Hamidullah declared that his state would become independent once paramountcy ceased. 'The State of Bhopal does not wish to remain associated in any manner whatsoever with the Chamber of Princes or any of its subordinate organisations,' he wrote to Mountbatten. 'It cannot therefore be represented by the Standing Committee of that body and will negotiate directly with the successor Governments of British India in regard to its interests, and its future political relationship with Pakistan and Hindustan.'[33] The fragmentation of India that Menon and Mountbatten had been hoping to avoid was suddenly becoming a very real prospect.

Armed with acceptance of the new plan by Congress and the Muslim League, Mountbatten faced the press on 4 June with Menon by his side. Campbell-Johnson referred to it as 'the most brilliant performance I have ever witnessed at a major press conference'.[34] Most of the more than one hundred questions fielded by the viceroy concerned the willingness of the Congress, the Muslim League and the Sikhs to accept Partition, but several touched on the states. Asked whether the states would be allowed to become independent on the transfer of power, Mountbatten was adamant: 'British Paramountcy over the Indian States would end as soon as power is transferred in British India. The States would then be free agents though they would not be invited to join the British Commonwealth.' When probed again, an angry

Mountbatten responded by throwing the question back at the reporter: 'Are you suggesting that we, in our last act, should tear up those treaties and say we are going to compel them to join this or that . . . Constituent Assembly? . . . I cannot go back on a pledge based on treaties entered into many years ago.'[35]

The following day's headlines were dominated by Mountbatten's off-the-cuff comment that the date of India's independence would be brought forward by almost a year to 15 August. The proclamation, which Mountbatten later said came to him as an inspiration, created shock and consternation. Upended by the announcement were Corfield's plans for readying the princes for the day when their great protector and patron, the British Raj, would depart forever. 'When the date [for the transfer of power] was fixed for August 15, it became more important than ever that he [Mountbatten] should appreciate the difficult position of the Indian States. It proved impossible, however, to distract his attention from the British Indian problem,' Corfield wrote despairingly.[36] The government now had just ten weeks to come up with policies for the retraction of paramountcy, defining the status of the states in relation to the new dominions, and finally and most difficult of all, determining Britain's relations with states that opted out. To solve these problems would require all parties, including Mountbatten and his staff, Corfield and the Political Department as well as Congress and the League, to work together towards the same ends – and for now that seemed like a distant dream.

It was a demoralized Standing Committee of the COP that met on 4 June to consider Hamidullah's resignation and the Menon–Mountbatten plan, but had to adjourn for lack of quorum. When the meeting resumed the next day under the chancellorship of Yadavindra Singh, the maharaja of Patiala, it recommended that the Chamber be wound up once the transfer of power had been completed. Few would shed tears for its passing. It would meet for only one last time.

By laying the groundwork for Partition, the Menon–Mountbatten plan was indeed historic, but like every other plan the British had come up with so far, it made little or no mention of what would happen to the princely states. Having delayed addressing the states problem directly for the best part of three months, Mountbatten finally announced that a meeting of all the relevant parties would take place on 13 June to consider the issue. Present at the conclave were Corfield, Nehru, Patel, Jinnah and a clutch of senior officials, including Pakistan's future prime minister Liaqat Ali Khan, the viceroy's chief of staff, Hastings 'Pug' Ismay, and his private secretary, Eric Miéville. It almost seemed too late. Just two days earlier, Osman Ali Khan had issued a *farman* declaring that Hyderabad would not accede to either of the newly announced dominions. 'The result in law of the departure of the Paramount Power in the near future will be that I shall become entitled to resume the status of an independent sovereign,' the nizam asserted.[37] On the same day, C.P. Ramaswami Aiyar made a similar declaration to Travancore's legislature. Two of India's most important and strategic states had now joined Bhopal in declaring their intention to go it alone. 'The situation was indeed fraught with immeasurable potentialities of disruption,' Patel later recalled.[38]

Corfield's hope that an agreement on fundamental issues, such as the freedom of the states to choose their own fate, might finally be achieved at the 13 June meeting proved to be wishful thinking. Nehru had been waiting for months to confront the man he believed was conspiring with the princes to sabotage the freedom struggle. Mountbatten had just begun making his opening remarks when Nehru interrupted him and accused Corfield of trying to Balkanize India by insisting that no successor government was entitled to assume paramountcy after the transfer of power. 'I charge the Political Department and Sir Conrad Corfield particularly with misfeasance,' he shouted. 'I consider that a judicial enquiry on the highest level into their actions is necessary.' Topping the list of misdemeanours he accused the department of was the destruction of records concerning the princely states. Corfield's defence was that the process was being carried out in consultation with the Imperial Records Department, and anything of value would be retained and turned over to the British high commissioner. Anticipating the fallout from the destruction of the documents, he had hurriedly prepared an annexure to the order of business for the meeting. In it he argued that if the destruction of certain files was not carried out 'there will remain a mass of useless records'.[39] 'I have nothing to hide. Everywhere I have acted under the instructions of the Crown representative and with the approval of the Secretary of State,' he insisted.[40]

All the while Corfield kept looking at Mountbatten. But instead of coming to his defence, the viceroy maintained a stony silence. It was Jinnah who finally intervened, threatening to put an end to the meeting if Nehru continued to make bombastic speeches and unverified accusations. Taking Corfield's side in the full knowledge that a Balkanized India would be a weak entity, he declared that 'every Indian State was a sovereign State' and the princes were 'free to do as they liked'. But the reprieve was short-lived. Next on the order of business was the establishment of a States Department as soon as possible. Corfield was stunned. There had been no warning that such a move was being contemplated. The fate of the princes would no longer be in the hands of the Political Department. His attempts to protect their independence were to no avail. He left the meeting a broken man.

The task ahead for the new States Department was enormous. From Bahawalpur in the west to Orissa in the east, rulers were discussing the formation of federations to strengthen their positions ahead of the transfer of power. Bhopal, Hyderabad and Travancore, powerhouses in their own right, were preparing to split from the Union. The future of Kashmir was anyone's guess. By leaving the states problem to simmer for so long, Mountbatten had created a political vacuum that threatened to derail the very viability of the new dominions of India and Pakistan. As the *Economist* noted in an editorial on 26 June:

> Lord Mountbatten's tactics for covering the evacuation of the British Raj from India appear to consist in keeping everybody so busy that the new India will take shape before anyone has time to think about it and British official responsibility can finally be unloaded while the going is still good.[41]

Rescuing the situation would require nothing short of a miracle. The two men who would help Mountbatten deliver it would be Menon and Patel.

4

A Basket-full of States

On 27 June 1947, the States Department was set up, comprising an Indian section headed by Sardar Patel and a Pakistan section headed by Muslim League stalwart Abdur Rab Nishtar. Patel's appointment came as a relief to Mountbatten because of his less abrasive approach to the princes. 'I am glad to say that Nehru has not been put in charge of the new States Department, which would have wrecked everything,' he wrote in a memo to London.[1] He even went so far as to advise Patel to drop his other portfolios so he could devote more time to his new ministry. 'The one portfolio you must not give up is the states,' he insisted. 'For the princes have come to trust you in a quite remarkable way and so long as you have got V.P. Menon to carry out your policy so loyally, the Ministry of States will continue to be the mainstay of the Dominion.'[2] Three days after his appointment, Patel called in Menon and asked him to accept the job of secretary of the States Department. Menon told him his intention had been to retire from government service after 15 August. He was about to be persuaded to do otherwise.

> Sardar told me that because of the abnormal situation in the country, people like myself should not think in terms of rest or retirement. He added that I had taken a prominent part in the transfer of power and that I should consider it my bounden duty to work for the consolidation of freedom. I naturally agreed that the country's interests, and not my personal predilections, should be the guiding factor.[3]

Nehru would have preferred his principal private secretary H.V.R. Iyengar for the post, but Patel held firm. He had been working closely with Menon for almost a year and considered him trustworthy and knowledgeable as well as an invaluable conduit to the Imperial Secretariat.

For Corfield and the princes, Patel and Menon were a chilling combination, and one that they were ill-equipped to counter. Patel's biographer, Balraj Krishna, opines that when dealing with the states he would demonstrate 'the strength of a Hercules and the political acumen of a Chanakya to meet the formidable challenge and avert the catastrophe'.[4] As for Menon, there was arguably no other civil servant in India who better understood the gravity of the situation with regard to the princes. He was determined to out-manoeuvre the 'prophets of gloom' who were predicting that 'the ship of Indian freedom would founder on the rock of the States'. If he failed, two-fifths of India's land mass would revert to a state of complete political isolation. Nothing less than 'the integrity of the country' was at stake.[5]

Menon's first act was to write to Sir Paul Patrick, the permanent political secretary in the India Office, asking him to refrain from encouraging any 'reckless' bids for independence. 'Even an inkling that His Majesty's Government would accord independent recognition would make infinitely difficult all attempts to bring the States and the new Dominions together on all vital matters of common concern.'[6] His next priority was to draft an Instrument of Accession based on three subjects: defence, external affairs and communications. Menon's reasoning was that defence was not a matter that could be conducted by the states themselves, external affairs was linked to defence, and communications were by nature a federal concern because roads, railways and lines of telecommunications criss-crossed India. A Standstill Agreement to maintain the existing arrangements for customs, currency, postal services and similar matters until the transfer of power was also drafted. It was a transparent two-step process that might just be enough to bring the princes to the party. They would be reminded that two out of the three functions they were 'surrendering' had not been theirs earlier (responsibility for defence and foreign affairs rested with the Crown), and they would be reassured that there would be no interference in their internal political structures.

The plan was brilliant, both in its simplicity and in solving the problem of paramountcy lapsing or being transferred to India. As Menon later told the writer Leonard Mosley, the lapse of paramountcy was 'a blessing in disguise'. Had paramountcy been transferred to the Indian dominion, Delhi would have had to honour the treaties and agreements signed between the princes and the British Crown and the privileges that came with them, such as non-interference in their internal affairs. 'We would have had to go on treating the Princes as demi-gods in their own States. But not now. Paramountcy lapses. So do the privileges.'[7] Patel immediately saw its logic.

The second plank of Menon's strategy was to get Mountbatten to take ownership of the princely states problem. 'Apart from his position, his grace and his gifts, his relationship to the Royal Family was bound to influence the rulers,' Menon observed. 'Sardar [Patel] whole-heartedly agreed and asked me to approach him without delay . . . I should add that the Prime Minister, with the approval of the Cabinet, readily entrusted Lord Mountbatten with the task of negotiating with the rulers on the question of accession and also with the task of dealing with Hyderabad.'[8]

Armed with Patel's endorsement, Menon approached Mountbatten, pointing out that the plan's success would require a great deal of statesmanship that only he possessed. The flattery worked. 'I felt that he was deeply touched by my remark that the wounds of partition might to some extent be healed by the States entering into a relationship with the Government of India and that he would be earning the gratitude of generations of Indians if he could assist in achieving the basic unity of the country,' Menon later wrote.[9] After some initial hesitation, the viceroy signalled he was on board.

Mountbatten's agreement reflected a major shift in his attitude towards the states. Any form of independence, either individually or as a grouping, he now believed, would lead to both the fragmentation of India and creation of what H.V. Hodson described as an 'indefensible, irrational frontier of the Commonwealth within the sub-continent'.[10] The Indian Independence Act that had been introduced in the House of Commons on 4 July would not only see India partitioned but would also mean that the paramountcy of the British parliament over the princely states would lapse and all treaties and agreements between the British government and the Indian rulers would be void. This, as Menon warned him, would 'produce administrative chaos of [the] gravest kind'. Agreements covering railways, customs, harbours and irrigation canals would all disappear.[11] Mountbatten was also swayed after meeting the distinguished jurist and constitutional adviser to the Constituent Assembly, Benegal Narsing Rau, who pointed out that after

15 August, the rulers of 327 petty states, with an average area of about 50 square kilometres, an average population of about 3,000 and average revenue of £1,000 per annum, would gain the same powers of life and death over their subjects as a state such as Hyderabad. Rau urged Mountbatten to have a clause inserted in the Indian Independence Act, which would restrict their powers and guarantee that the authority of the Crown representative in respect of the small states would be exercised by the new dominions. This was deemed unfeasible by the secretary of state for India, Lord Listowel, who told Mountbatten that such a clause 'would fundamentally alter the intention of the Bill towards the Princely States; that the lapse of paramountcy must stand, and that no alteration could be made'.[12] Mountbatten found himself in a quandary. Publicly he had to stand by London, but by doing so he would be giving the more recalcitrant rulers enough rope to undermine the viability of an independent India.

Alarmed by the possible breakout of princely anarchy, Mountbatten took Menon's draft instrument to Patel. There is a conflict of opinion as to what occurred at this meeting. According to the viceroy's rendering, the Sardar told him not to bother about the states. After independence, their people would rise, depose their rulers and throw in their lot with the Congress. Mountbatten maintained that he corrected him by pointing out that many states had armies equipped by the British and were probably preparing for such an eventuality on the advice of the Political Department. The result would be civil war. Several historians, however, have contested this version of events, pointing out that Patel had been actively engaging with the rulers from late 1946. As his biographer Rajmohan Gandhi writes: 'In supplying this account, which is not backed by any other evidence, Mountbatten sought credit for this successful formula under which almost all the states acceded to India by 15.8.47.'[13]

According to H.V. Hodson, Patel told Mountbatten at their next meeting that he would accept the plan for the states to accede only on the subjects of foreign affairs, defence and communications, provided he gave him 'a full basket of apples'. Asked what he meant, Patel replied: 'I'll buy a basket of 565 apples' – his reading of the number of states – 'but if there are even two or three apples missing, the deal is off.' Mountbatten told him he could not completely accept these conditions, 'but I will do my best. If I give you a basket with, say, 560 apples will you buy it?' 'Well, I might,' Patel replied.[14] Although Hodson is the sole source for the exchange between Patel and Mountbatten, this conversation has come to represent the 'moment' at which the Sardar and the Crown representative sealed the princes' fate. Whether they haggled like a couple of fruit vendors or held a statesman-like exchange is irrelevant. The task of convincing more than 560 disparate, divided and mostly frightened rulers to accede to India was placed in Mountbatten's hands, with the ever-watchful Menon and Patel on call to use their influence when necessary.

Realizing the very real possibility of failure, Mountbatten decided against keeping the India Office in the loop, in case Attlee or Listowel should get wind of the terms Patel and he had agreed on before he won over most of the states. When Mountbatten did finally inform London a few weeks later, he argued that the arrangement would be a strong bargaining point. 'I am positive that if I can bring in a basket-full of states before the 15th August, Congress will pay whatever price I insist on for the basket,' he wrote, knowing how desperate its leaders were for a solution to the states problem. 'I need hardly say that unless we can pull this off, India will be in a bit of a mess after the 15th August.'[15]

In his first pronouncement as states minister on 5 July (the text was drafted by Menon), Patel appealed to the princes' proud, glorious past, when their ancestors 'had played highly patriotic roles in the defence of their family honour and the freedom of their land'. Join hands with the Congress in the creation of a new India, he pleaded: 'We are knit together by bonds of blood and feeling, no less than of self-interest. None can segregate into segments; no impassable barriers can be set up between us.' The price to pay was insignificant. 'We ask no more of them than accession on three subjects in which the common interests of the country are involved. In other matters we would scrupulously respect their autonomous existence.' The Congress had no desire 'to interfere in any manner whatever in the domestic affairs of the States' or become an enemy of the princely order. On the contrary, the party's leadership 'wish them and their people under their aegis all prosperity, contentment and happiness'. The alternative to cooperation, he warned, was 'anarchy and chaos'.[16]

Underpinning the statement's largely conciliatory tone was the realization that in less than six weeks, paramountcy would cease and the states would be technically free to do what they liked. Patel had long been aware of the Attlee government's concern that the Churchill-led Tories, some of whom who had close ties with the states, might slow down passage of the Indian Independence Act if there was any sign the princes were being coerced to act against their will. In fact, London was treading so carefully that as late as early August it had yet to reach a conclusion as to how to deal with the frightening potential of states with seaports declaring their independence and then placing orders for British arms.

The formation of the States Department did not mean an end to Corfield's lobbying of the princes. In a bid to outmanoeuvre the viceroy's political adviser, Menon met with the COP chancellor,

Yadavindra Singh. 'I asked for his co-operation in implementing the policy of accession and I told him frankly that "independent of us, you cannot exist".'[17] Shortly afterwards, Patel invited the rulers and ministers of ten states that had joined the Constituent Assembly in April to his residence and urged them to accede to India immediately. This, he argued, would put them in a stronger position to influence government policy. All those present agreed and pledged to hold informal discussions with other rulers and their advisers. Menon avows that it was this meeting 'which at last broke the ice, clearing away a mass of vague suspicions which the rulers had entertained about the new States Department'.[18] Patel then leaked the news of the meeting to the press, knowing that favourable coverage would bring more rulers on board. Meanwhile, Nehru, as prime minister in the interim government, wrote personally to many of the princes. The maharaja of the distant state of Manipur on the Burmese border was reminded that his kingdom 'can hardly be expected to defend itself unaided in case of troubles on the frontier. This business of defence must be shouldered by the Union.' Nehru was similarly blunt in his letter to the Gaekwar of Baroda, warning him that 'there is no future for any State in India, however big it may be, if it stays outside the Union. Within the Union it will have a large measure of autonomy and will participate in the progress of India as a whole.'[19]

For the first time since the transfer of power had been announced, it seemed that all parties, aside from Corfield at his Political Department, were on the same page as far as the states were concerned. Gandhi was urging Mountbatten to do everything in his power to ensure that the British did not leave a legacy of Balkanization. Defence Minister Baldev Singh was trying to close a loophole that allowed states to acquire arms from abroad. Patel and Nehru held meetings with the viceroy, sounding him out on what he was planning to do about India's 'most pressing difficulty – relations with the states'. To everyone's relief, Mountbatten reassured them that he had made the cause of getting the princes on board his own. To that end he would address the Chamber of Princes later that month. Officially, he would be using the address to acquaint the princes with the Instruments of Accession and Standstill Agreements Menon was drawing up. In reality, it would be his moment to settle the states problem once and for all by leaving the princes with no choice but to sign away their future.

Having a mandate and having the time to implement it were two different things. As the viceroy admitted in mid-July, just four weeks away from the transfer of power: 'I have not been able to grip the States problem before.'[20] When asked about the admission, Corfield later told Hodson that it was

> ...naive of a Viceroy who knew that the states comprised one third of India; who had been charged personally by the King to consider the States' future, and who was alone responsible for shortening the time required to tackle the problem, to plead ignorance of its complexity and anxiety about being rushed![21]

W.H. Morris-Jones, Mountbatten's constitutional adviser, later called it 'a case of culpable negligence'.[22] Nor was the viceroy consistent in his messaging. When meeting with representatives from Hyderabad on 11 July, he told them there was 'no shadow of doubt that the legal position was that the States would be absolutely free after 15 August' – a scenario that was technically true but one he was attempting to avoid at all costs. This statement was music to the ears of the Hyderabad delegation but struck a discordant note in the states ministry where officials were watching in alarm as a slew of rulers, including Jodhpur's and Indore's, looked like they would follow Bhopal, Hyderabad and Travancore and take Mountbatten at his word.

On 11 July, Menon and Patel drew up the agenda for the Conference of Rulers and Representatives of Indian States in the COP to be held on 25 July. The main items were the accession of the states on defence, external affairs and communications as well as the drawing up of a Standstill Agreement. The conference would mark the first and last time Mountbatten addressed the COP. Neither Menon nor Patel had any idea of the tactics and promises the viceroy would use to get the rest of the princes across the line. On the eve of the conference, they met another delegation, which included the rulers of Patiala, Gwalior, Bikaner, Nawanagar and Jodhpur. Menon interpreted the attendance of the last two states as a sign that they 'had broken away from the leadership of the Nawab of Bhopal and were prepared to come in with us'.[23] His optimism was misplaced. Hamidullah might have resigned as the COP chancellor, but he still wielded considerable influence and had not given up his dream of a 'Rajastan' made up of princely states. According to K.M Panikkar, the real threat to India's unity at this time was not from Hyderabad or Travancore, but from the miscellany of states that littered the vast hinterland between Delhi and the future state of Pakistan. These included Dungarpur, Pratapgarh and Narsingarh, who were receptive to Hamidullah's idea of forming a single unit to play Pakistan against India, thereby weakening India and increasing the influence of the princes.[24]

Although he had been effectively sidelined following the establishment of the States Department, Corfield was expected to participate in the 25 July conference. He had other ideas. 'It would have been against my conscience to attend,' he later wrote. 'He [Mountbatten] had agreed to use his influence as the representative of the paramount power to recommend a bargain that could not be guaranteed after independence,' he ruefully noted.[25] On 22 July, he offered his resignation – which was accepted by Mountbatten without comment – and left India for good. 'I boarded the plane at Karachi with a feeling of nausea, as though my own honour had been smirched and I had deserted my friends.'[26]

Menon was clearly relieved at Corfield's departure. Just a few weeks earlier, he had heard rumours of the political adviser's attempts to persuade Bhopal and several other princes to form a 'Third Front'. Convinced of what he termed as the Political Department's intolerable interference, he told Mountbatten: 'The position is such, that I am afraid that a choice must be made. Either Sir Conrad Corfield goes, or I go.'[27] As Menon later recalled: 'I felt that if both Sir Conrad Corfield and myself operated in the same field, it was like trying to walk simultaneously in two opposite directions.'[28]

Corfield had also been working at cross purposes with the viceroy. Where he saw treaties that gave the states the right to be independent, his superior saw a looming vacuum that had to be filled by the states joining one or other of the new dominions. Where he believed he had the backing of Attlee and Listowel, Mountbatten felt the urgency of the situation gave him the authority to use his plenipotentiary powers to forge his own course to ensure the smoothest possible end to British rule in India. For Patel and Menon, the very real fear of Balkanization, and of the obfuscatory behaviour of certain princes such as Hamidullah Khan and Osman Ali Khan, had convinced them that they had no choice but to enlist what Menon termed 'stopgap' measures to preserve India's unity. As Campbell-Johnson wrote in his journal on 20 July 1947, fitting the 9 crore people governed by the princes into the new India was in many ways a greater challenge than getting an agreement between Congress and the Muslim League. 'After 15th August there will be no Viceroy, Paramountcy will be retroceded, and each Indian Prince will become an autocratic independent sovereign. Unless Mountbatten can get a workable solution accepted by all before 15th August, I tremble to think of the chaos that will supervene throughout the subcontinent.'[29] The immensity of the princely states problem had finally dawned on everyone.

~

Mountbatten's 25 July address was a reality check for India's hereditary rulers. Their cosy relationship with their protector was about to be severed. If nothing was put in its place, the only alternative would be chaos, and it would be the states that would rulers first, he warned. While Pakistan was prepared to negotiate with each state individually, India, because of the large number of rulers involved, would do so only collectively, based on the draft Instrument of Accession. All they were being asked to surrender were three subjects – defence, external affairs and communications. In no other matters would the central government have any authority to encroach on their internal autonomy or sovereignty. There was no room for compromise on the timetable for accession. Stressed the viceroy: 'If you are prepared to come [in], you must come before 15 August.'[30]

When the text of Mountbatten's speech reached London, it set off alarm bells. It was clear from even the diluted version before them that the Crown representative had given the princes an ultimatum that was out of step with Listowel's assurances in a recent House of Lords debate on the Indian Independence Act that there would not be 'the slightest pressure to influence their [the princes'] momentous and voluntary decision'.[31] The deputy secretary of the India Office, H.A.F. Rumbold, called for

Mountbatten to be censured. In the end, Mountbatten was not even issued a warning. Everyone knew that once Mountbatten had made up his mind, nothing could make him change it. Moreover, Attlee had agreed to grant him plenipotentiary powers, something no previous viceroy had enjoyed. He had a free rein to formulate and execute his own policies, untrammelled by the need to seek London's approval. Whether the pressure he brought to bear on the princes was morally correct or not was up for debate.

On the evening of 25 July, Mountbatten dined with Jinnah and his sister Fatima. He had a low opinion of the Quaid-i-Azam, whom he would later describe as 'this clot' who was the 'evil genius of this whole thing [India's partition]'.[32] The tenor of the conversation was awkward, with Jinnah spending much of the time cracking a series of lengthy and generally bad jokes. When the discussion turned to the princely states, he urged Mountbatten 'not to be in such a mortal hurry' to pin down their rulers. 'After all, one could not make the world as one wanted it to be in a week.' With an eye on the disruption he knew it would cause, Jinnah suggested 'a period of suspense and delay' while the new dominions got established and the states adjusted themselves to a post-British reality.[33]

Rejecting Jinnah's 'suspense and delay' advice, Mountbatten sprang into action. His task seemed impossible: He had just twenty days to get some 550 states located within the boundaries of a future India to sign Instruments of Accession. On 28 July, dozens of princes and their advisers gathered for a reception at the Viceregal Palace. Menon, who was present, likened the event to 'a last-minute canvassing of voters near the polling booth'.[34] As waiters glided through the throng carrying trays of chhota gins and whiskeys and the band played tunes such as 'The Roast Beef of Old England', those princes who had not signalled their intention to sign the Instrument of Accession were brought before the viceroy for a friendly chat before being passed on to Menon, who in turn conducted them across the room to see Patel. Standing three deep in a semicircle, a clutch of potentates watched the process in a state of bewilderment. Others, as one dewan remarked, wandered about 'like letters without a stamp'. 'Who's HE getting to work on now?' one of the old rulers joked, referring to Mountbatten.[35] Narendra Singh Sarila, one of Mountbatten's ADCs and son of the Raja of Sarila, commented:

> What I saw that day in the Viceroy's Palace was how Patel handled the princes. He first flattered them as scions of a race that had fought for centuries to protect India's integrity and honour and then asked abruptly whether they would let India down now when it was approaching freedom after centuries of subjugation.[36]

Whatever the tactics, the cajoling worked. By 31 July 1947, twenty-five states had sat down with Menon and signed away their rights to independence.

On 1 August, there was another meeting of princes hosted by Sadul Singh at Bikaner House. Four months earlier, Sadul had split the princes by leading a breakaway group to join the Constituent Assembly. Now he was trying to convince those still wavering of the benefits of accession. Narendra Singh Sarila recalls him sitting calmly as the rulers expressed their misgivings about Mountbatten's promise that there would be no interference in their administrations. Some thought that by holding out they might get better terms from the Congress party. Others wanted firmer guarantees that the party would not instigate revolutions in their territories. At this point, Digvijaysinhji Ranjitsinhji, the pro-accession Jam Saheb of Nawanagar, intervened saying: 'Without your highnesses entering into some kind of organic relationship with the future central government you will be even more vulnerable to the Congress Party-inspired agitations.' After this reminder, Sarila saw 'the euphoria among the rulers that they would become independent on British withdrawal to do as they wished' visibly evaporate.[37]

Despite these signs of success, the danger of Balkanization was still very real in the stormy weeks before the Crown's final goodbye. As July melted into August, Mountbatten's priority was to keep a lid on the communal tensions between Sikhs, Muslims and Hindus, which were rapidly heading for civil war. It was like 'sitting on top of a volcano', he wrote to the secretary of state for India. 'It was touch and go whether I could hold the place together.'[38] Where the states were concerned the situation remained fluid, despite the persuasive powers and the tactical brilliance of Team Mountbatten–Patel–Menon. A clutch of rulers had already thrown up challenges that even Menon's accession plan would find almost impossible to countermand.

5

Dangerous Liaisons

Situated on India's southwest coast, Travancore had access to the main trade routes crossing the Indian Ocean, putting it, as the India Office conceded, in a position 'to assert effective independence'.[1] Its population of 60 lakh in 1947 had a literacy rate of 47 per cent – three times higher than the rest of British India. It was also progressive. In 1936, it became the first state to open its temples to Untouchables, though the reasons for its doing so were largely pragmatic. Thousands of Untouchables were converting to Christianity and becoming politically active.

Travancore was verdant and resource rich, with forests of teak, ebony and sandalwood. It produced tea and spices, rubber, coconut and coir products, and also had mineral deposits, including graphite, mica and kaolin. Most importantly, Travancore had the second largest known deposits of monazite in the world. The strategic value of the rare earth had soared after the US dropped two atomic bombs on Hiroshima and Nagasaki in August 1945. A by-product of monazite was thorium, a crucial ingredient in the operation of nuclear reactors and in the manufacture of nuclear weapons.

C.P. Ramaswami Aiyar's 11 June declaration that his state

would become independent once power was transferred had rattled Mountbatten, Nehru and the Congress leadership. In a press conference a few days later, the dewan cited the defeat of a Dutch naval fleet in 1741 as proof of Travancore's former glory. As an independent nation, his state would be in 'no worse position than Denmark, Switzerland and Siam'.[2] An additional reason to not accede was India's decision to open diplomatic relations with the Soviet Union. This, in Aiyar's view, would lead to the establishment of Russian embassies and consulates all over India, affording 'immense facilities for infiltration of Communist propaganda, money and violent activities which have already been notorious in Cochin and British Malabar'.[3] He insisted his position was final and there could be no negotiations as the state was ruled 'in the name and on behalf of the tutelary deity, Sri Padmanabha'.[4]

Born the son of a Brahmin lawyer in 1879, Aiyar followed the same path as his father, graduating with distinction from the Law School in Madras and joining the Madras High Court Bar in 1903. He went on to become the advocate general in Madras, law member of the viceroy's Executive Council and a representative of the British India delegation at the first two Round Table Conferences in London. In 1931, he agreed to serve as legal and constitutional adviser to the Maharaja of Travancore and then as legal adviser to the maharaja's mother, Sethu Parvathi, also known as Junior Maharani. Despite persistent rumours that he was in a relationship with her, he was elevated to the post of dewan in 1937. According to Clarmont Skrine, who served as the resident in Travancore in 1938, 'The most striking feature of the situation is the intense, almost hysterical, hatred shown by the educated and semi-educated classes for the Dewan. With a few exceptions, everyone in the State seems to long for his removal, and many yearn also for his ruin and disgrace.' Though his aims were the peace and prosperity of Travancore, 'his methods are Machiavellian; he rules by dividing, he bribes with office and other favours, he sets traps for his critics and plays on the weaknesses of his enemies. It is no wonder that the man in the street does not love him.'[5] Skrine's successor as resident, H.J. Todd dismissed Aiyar as a vain man, 'very susceptible to flattery . . . Likes to be treated as a cosmopolitan, man of the world rather than as an Indian; and although he pays lip service to nationalism and his religion he voices, privately, much contempt for his politically minded compatriots and the superstitions of the ultra-devout.'[6] It was a view that Wavell concurred with, noting in his journal in 1946: 'There is no doubt that Travancore is a one-man show, and the one man is Sir C.P. There is no doubt about his efficiency, his charm when he chooses to exert it, or his determination to get his own way.'[7]

Support for Travancore came from an unexpected quarter. In June 1947, Vinayak Damodar Savarkar wrote to Aiyar backing the maharaja and his 'courageous and far-sighted determination' to seek independence. 'The Nizam, Muslim Ruler of Hyderabad, has already proclaimed his independence and other Muslim states are likely to do so. Hindu states are bold enough to assert they have the same rights.'[8] Savarkar's views were not shared among the nationalist leaders. Gandhi blasted Travancore's bid as 'tantamount to a declaration of war on free millions of India'.[9] Nehru warned that the state 'would be starved out' and that an economic blockade 'would lead to the elimination of independence within three months'.[10] Responding to what he called a 'pistol at my head', Aiyar raised the stakes by banning the Travancore state unit of the Congress party and starting negotiations for the purchase of rice from Sind to break a possible embargo on foodgrains. Similar deals were being negotiated with Burma and Siam. To compensate for the closure of the Indian markets to Travancore's exports, arrangements were made for the sale of copra and coconut oil products to Pakistan and Australia. When Indian textile mills refused to supply Travancore with cotton, Aiyar planned discussions with British and American mills.

Closely watching the developments, Jinnah wired Aiyar on 20 June promising that Pakistan was 'ready to establish a relationship with Travancore which will be of mutual advantage'.[11] Maharaja Rama Varma Tiruvithamkoor had already named Khan Bahadur Abdul Karim Sahib, former inspector general of police, as the state's trade representative to Pakistan. Aiyar responded by proposing that a treaty be signed between the 'independent Sovereign State' of Travancore and the government of Pakistan. Jinnah followed up with promises of food aid if India imposed an embargo. Writing to Mountbatten, Aiyar lauded the Muslim League's leader as 'a realist'. 'I was concerned with the unity of India. It had been lost now and therefore I had come to certain arrangements with Mr. Jinnah.'[12]

Fortunately, the most valuable of Travancore's commodities, monazite, remained off the table thanks to Nehru's quick-wittedness. In 1946 and 1947, the leftist weekly *Blitz* had published a series of articles by journalist K.N. Bamzai exposing the secret negotiations being conducted by the maharaja with monazite-extracting companies. Under one of the deals, 9,000 tonnes of monazite were to be sent to Britain over three years. In return, the British government had promised to get the company Thorium Ltd to construct a processing plant in the state. When Nehru read about the deal, he moved quickly. At the Indian Science Congress in January 1947 he pushed through a resolution that the Indian state should own and control all minerals required to produce nuclear energy. Speaking at a cabinet meeting in April 1947, he warned of using air power against Travancore to bring its recalcitrant Aiyar and the maharaja to heel. Two months later, he sent Sir Shanti Swarup Bhatnagar, head of the Council of Scientific and Industrial Research, to Travancore to block any deals for export of monazite to England. Surprisingly, Tiruvithamkoor and Aiyar capitulated without a fight, leading to the establishment of the Travancore-India Joint Commission on Atomic Energy.

Although Aiyar knew of the strategic value of thorium early on, he failed to use it as a card to play in his state's bid for independence. Writing to the maharaja a few days after the bombing of Nagasaki in 1945, he declared: 'If thorium can be utilized for the manufacture of atomic bombs (there is no reason why it should not be), Travancore will enjoy a very high position in the world.' The historian Itty Abraham speculates that Aiyar realized that withholding thorium to India would be a step too far. 'Denial of a strategic resource would open the door to a military response against which he could not defend, and which he was desperately trying to avoid.'[13]

With Aiyar showing no signs of backing away from his bid for independence and going so far as to sign a treaty with Pakistan, Menon and Patel swung into action. Tactfully taking him aside, Menon reminded the dewan that his state was the main breeding ground for communism in India. If there was a communist uprising after 15 August, an independent Travancore could expect no aid from Delhi. Then it was Patel's turn to point out that the wealthy industrialist Seth Dalmia had given the local Congress party Rs 5 lakh to stir up trouble. If Aiyar returned to Travancore without giving up his idea of independence, his 'life could be in danger'. The dewan responded by saying: 'I am aware that you can have me assassinated but then there will be only one left to fight Communism.'[14]

Of all the fortnightly reports that Mountbatten sent to London during his viceroyalty, the most unusual was the one that recorded his 22 July encounter with Aiyar. The dewan had declined to attend the final meeting of the Chamber of Princes on the basis that his state had already decided not to accede to India. What was scheduled as an opportunity to change his mind turned into a comic opera as the dewan pulled out of his briefcase a set of files that contained a 'number of rather amusing cartoons, to which he took the greatest exception, and in particular one published that very morning showing him being spanked by me at this very meeting!' Another contained several 'rude cuttings about himself'. The final file

> . . . contained cuttings to prove that Gandhi was a dangerous sex maniac who could not keep his hands off young girls. He considered him to be the most dangerous influence in India and said that if he insisted on backing the unstable Nehru against the realistic Patel, he would break up the Congress Party within two years. Sir C.P. said that he was not prepared to ally himself with such an unreliable Dominion.[15]

Despite the viceroy's attempt to appeal to Aiyar's patriotism by suggesting it would be an 'act of statesmanship on his part if his state acceded to India', he was unmoved. Instead, he threatened to incite the Moplah Muslims from the Malabar to invade Cochin to prove his point. At the end of their two-hour meeting, Aiyar had softened his stand slightly, saying he might consider a treaty with India.[16] But, very shortly, there would be a dramatic turnaround.

On 25 July, as Aiyar was leaving a music concert in Trivandrum, he was attacked by a knife-wielding activist from the Kerala Socialist Party. Bleeding heavily from wounds to his head, he was rushed to hospital. The attacker escaped, leaving behind for some unexplained reason a pair of khaki shorts and the knife. A waiting lorry took him to Madurai. From there he caught a train to Bombay, where he was sheltered by an old classmate at the city's Communist Party headquarters. Fearing that the forces behind the attack were capable of ever greater violence, Aiyar wrote to the maharaja from his hospital bed, advising him to follow the path of compromise. Ten days after Aiyar's meeting with the viceroy, the maharaja telegraphed his acceptance of the Instrument of Accession to the viceroy personally. 'The adherence of Travancore after all C.P.'s declarations of independence has had a profound effect on all the other States and is sure to shake the Nizam,' Mountbatten wrote, somewhat optimistically.[17] Aiyar would retire on 19 August 1947, only to be remembered as the most hated dewan in the history of Travancore.

While Travancore's intention to become independent after 15 August had posed a dangerous precedent, the crisis unfolding in Hyderabad was potentially a greater threat to India's unity than Partition, and therefore of far more significance to Jinnah. If Hyderabad had been an independent nation when the UN was established in 1945, it would have featured among the top thirty member states for its size and among the top forty in terms of income. Although it lacked a seaport, it was rich in resources such as coal, iron ore and cotton. Located in the heart of the Deccan, it was India's most strategically important state. As Patel would later remark: Hyderabad was 'situated in India's belly. How can the belly breathe if it is cut off from the main body?'[18] This was precisely the predicament that Jinnah wanted.

Osman Ali Khan, the state's seventh nizam and India's premier Muslim prince, cut a lean and somewhat haggard figure. But his ragged moustache, dandruff-encrusted fez and generally shabby clothes belied his reputation as a shrewd if somewhat eccentric operator. After being installed on the gaddi in 1911 at the age of twenty-four, he had embarked on a series of reforms that included the issue of a farman or decree restraining Hyderabad's eunuchs from luring fresh recruits into their ranks to stem an alarming rise in their numbers. The institution of devadasis was outlawed, as were some of the more indulgent pastimes enjoyed by Hyderabad's nawabs, such as cockfighting and bullfights. His other achievements were more far-reaching, including the foundation of Osmania University, the first institution of higher education in India to offer courses in a vernacular medium – in this case Urdu, the official language of the state. He ordered the building of dams, and Hyderabad became one of the first cities in India to have a reliable supply of drinking water. Schools were expanded and primary education was made compulsory. Railways were extended, collieries and power stations were set up.

The concept of a separate Muslim zone in the Deccan had long been canvassed by Islamic propagandists. It even had a name, 'Usmanistan', coined in 1940 by Choudhary Rahmat Ali, who wrote that Hyderabad 'is a part of our patrimony', and its de jure sovereignty must be given international recognition.[19] On the transfer of power, the nizam assumed that Hyderabad would automatically become a kingdom and he would proclaim himself 'His Majesty the King of Hyderabad'.

Khan's political adviser was Sir Walter Monckton, who had been engaged at a reputed cost of £1,000 a day. One of the leading barristers in England, he had represented the interests of King Edward VIII and his future American wife during the Abdication Crisis of 1936. He had earlier served as Hyderabad's legal counsel when the state was considering its response to the Government of

India Act of 1935. A solicitor general in Churchill's government, he was close to those Conservatives opposed to the Congress, was sceptical of Mountbatten and sympathetic to the princes.

Since taking up his post in 1946, Monckton had been busy. In April 1947, he contacted the former secretary of state for India, Samuel Hoare, to discuss the acquisition by Hyderabad of port facilities at Marmagao in Portuguese Goa and a rail link to the landlocked state. More reports suggesting that Hyderabad was not going to fall in line with the rest of India soon followed. On 19 May, Panikkar wrote to Patel that the nizam's government had negotiated a mining lease in Bastar, together with the right to extend its railway and acquire 39,000 square kilometres of rich mineral deposits in the state. News then surfaced of an arms supply agreement with the Birmingham Small Arms Company and of a Rs 4 crore order for ammunition with a Czech arms dealer. Since Mountbatten's 3 June announcement on Partition and the bringing forward of the transfer of power, Hyderabad had appointed a trade commissioner in London, had begun discussions with France about establishing a Hyderabad diplomatic mission for Europe and had asked Britain's retired air chief marshal, Sir Christopher Courtnay, for advice on creating a modern air force.[20]

The tipping point for Hyderabad in deciding not to join the Indian Union came when Monckton and the nizam realized that the plan for the partition of India into two dominions excluded the possibility of separate dominion-hood for Hyderabad. Despite remaining a faithful ally of the British through the two world wars, 'Hyderabad was to be denied association with the Commonwealth except through India or Pakistan. I think this is rather a shameful performance. How ready we are to appease our enemies at the expense of our friends,' Monckton complained. There was little sympathy for Hyderabad's position in London. When pressed, Listowel reaffirmed that on the lapse of paramountcy the states would be 'masters of their own fate', entirely free to choose whether to associate with one or the other of the dominion governments or to stand alone. But he refused to make any commitments on international recognition, other than that it would be 'left open to be considered on its own merits when such a position arises'.[21]

On 11 July, Monckton travelled to Delhi as part of a delegation comprising the prime minister, the Nawab of Chhatari, the home minister, Ali Yavar Jung, and one representative each from Hyderabad's Hindu and Muslim communities. Monckton's proposal, to which the nizam agreed, was for Hyderabad to sign a treaty with India under which the latter would be responsible for Hyderabad's foreign relations, defence and communications. The delegates then met with Mountbatten, Corfield and Menon representing the States Department, but the talks got bogged down over the question of accession, which India insisted on. With negotiations at an impasse, Menon suggested the drafting of a Standstill Agreement to allow time for further negotiations. Khan, however, remained unmoved, and as the date for transfer of power approached it was clear that no settlement would be reached. When Menon insisted that Standstill Agreements could only be made with acceding states and that the nizam had no hope of survival unless he did so, Monckton retorted: '[The nizam] would go down (if at all) fighting and the Mussalmans would help him all over India. It would not take a few months but probably three years of bloodshed and I was not betting that Congress would last that long.'[22] On 12 August, Mountbatten wrote to the nizam that in view of Hyderabad's special position and peculiar problems, the offer of accession would remain open for another two months. The Hyderabad crisis would continue to fester well after Independence.

Kashmir, with its disaffected Muslim majority ruled over by a Hindu maharaja, was the mirror image of Hyderabad – and just as problematic. Sitting astride the future border of India and Pakistan, it would become the most contested corner of the subcontinent following Partition. Since coming to the gaddi in 1926, Hari Singh had spent much of his time abroad, becoming a familiar figure at Irish race meetings, where his horses Sir Lancelot and Magical Mike were the bookies' favourites. In 1919, he was caught in bed in a Paris hotel room with a shapely blonde named Mrs Robinson by an enraged Englishman who claimed to be her husband. The two men argued, with the alleged husband threatening to divorce his wife and then demanding that Singh pay £125,000 in hush money. The prince's ADC, Captain C.W. Arthur, warned Singh that being implicated in such a case would disqualify him from succeeding to the gaddi. The whole episode turned out to be an elaborate blackmail plot conceived by Arthur. When the case went to court, the government issued a suppression order on Singh's name, and he was only identified as 'Mr A'. The English press respected the order, but there were enough references to 'houseboats' – synonymous with Srinagar's Dal Lake – in the court hearings for the American and European newspapers to identify the mystery witness as the prince. When he returned to Kashmir, his welcome by the Hindu priests and his subjects was hardly effusive. Their main objection was not on moral grounds but to the fact that the woman he had sex with was European. There was also disgruntlement over the millions of rupees he had squandered on living the high life abroad instead of spending it on his people at home. The penances instructed by the Hindu priests included the shaving of his head and moustache and a ten-day purification period in the forest.

The situation in Kashmir went on to deteriorate sharply after demonstrations against the maharaja turned violent in July 1931. Behind the picture-postcard scenes of saffron fields, cherry orchards and exquisitely decorated houseboats moored on Dal Lake lay one of the most impoverished and backward parts of India. In 1901, only 2 per cent of Srinagar's 60,000 inhabitants were literate. Until 1920, Muslim peasants, most living in abject misery, faced the death penalty for killing cows. Sir Albion Banerjee, who served as the state's prime minister from 1927 to 1929, likened the Muslim population to 'dumb driven cattle. There is no touch between the Government and the people, no suitable opportunity for representing grievances.'[23] A decade later, little had changed. 'The poverty of the Muslim masses is appalling,' wrote the Kashmiri author and politician Prem Nath Bazaz. 'Dressed in rags and barefoot, a Muslim peasant presents the appearance of a starving beggar. Most are landless labourers, working as serfs for absentee landlords – almost the whole brunt of official corruption has been borne by the Muslim masses . . . rural indebtedness is staggering.'[24] Kashmiri Brahmins, or Pandits, as they were known, and Sikhs, dominated the government, holding 78 per cent of all appointments.

The July 1931 violence was sparked after a mosque in Jammu district was allegedly demolished by Hindus with the maharaja's permission. Similar outrages were reported elsewhere, as well as a rumour that pages of the Koran had been found in a latrine. A month earlier, Abdul Qadeer, a firebrand preacher from the North-West Frontier Province, was arrested after urging demonstrators to demolish the maharaja's palace 'brick by brick'. Anger over the preacher's show trial erupted on 13 July with police firing on crowds of protesters. Twenty-one people were killed and many more wounded. Muslims retaliated by attacking Hindu shopkeepers. Hari Singh followed up by ordering mass arrests, imprisonment and floggings. When the unrest looked set to get out of hand, the British sent three companies to restore order. Despite the patently anti-monarchical character of the protests, they were officially referred to as 'communal' disturbances, a description that jarred with the fact that not a single Hindu had been killed. Singh was made to accept an official investigation led by Bertrand Glancy, a senior colonial administrator, which confirmed that the protests were the result of popular dissatisfaction with his rule. A humiliated maharaja was forced to appoint an English ICS officer as his prime minister.

Since the early 1940s, Singh had grown increasingly reliant on a Hindu mystic, Swami Sant Dev, a Rasputin-like figure who had enjoyed considerable influence during his uncle's reign. Under the swami's influence, he began to fantasize about building an independent kingdom and extending his territory and rule over a much larger dominion, which would encompass the neighbouring districts of Kangra and the adjacent hill states to the south of Kashmir. Some in his court were already referring to a future Dogristan and restoration of the glory of the Dogra dynasty, to which Singh belonged. The other key figure urging Singh to declare independence was his prime minister, Pandit Ram Chandra Kak.

None of this was palatable to the Congress president and future prime minister. Nehru was a Kashmiri Pandit himself, and although his family had left the state in the middle of the nineteenth century, he still felt a strong affinity for his ancestral homeland, comparing it to a 'supremely beautiful woman whose beauty is impersonal and above desire'.[25] Beyond this gushing sentimentality was an ideological imperative. If Kashmir went to India, it would be living proof that the Congress had created a secular India in which a Muslim-majority province could take its place among Hindu-majority provinces. Accession to India would be the 'normal and obvious course' after Partition, Nehru briefed Mountbatten ahead of the visit. It would be 'absurd to think that Pakistan would create trouble if this happens'.[26]

On 18 June 1947, the Mountbattens flew to Srinagar to gauge the maharaja's mood. The Kashmir Valley was one of the couple's favourite destinations and they had holidayed there in 1946. After weathering the ignominy of the 'Mr A' affair, Singh had made a promising start to his rule, declaring in 1926 that as ruler he had 'no religion; all religions are mine and my religion is Justice'.[27] However, the longer he reigned the less engaged he became in the affairs of the state, preferring to gamble in the casinos of Cannes and Monte Carlo, playing polo in England, and horse racing and hunting to politics. By the 1940s, the high life was having an effect on his health and he was so obese that polo was out of the question. Meanwhile, the British resident in Srinagar was sending a steady stream of telegrams to London describing Singh's treatment of officials as arrogant and often vindictive, as well as complaining of his delusions of grandeur, his growing 'tendency towards extravagance' and, alarmingly, his taste for independence.[28]

Nehru was also personal friends with Sheikh Mohammad Abdullah, the National Conference leader. A committed nationalist, Abdullah had emerged as the voice of Muslim opinion in Kashmir during the unrest of 1931. Born in 1905, the son of a shawl merchant, he studied science at Aligarh University before moving to Srinagar in 1930 to work as a teacher. In 1932, he became president of the Kashmir Muslim Conference (later the National Conference), the state's first political party. In June 1946, he launched a 'Quit Kashmir' campaign targeting the maharaja, his dewan and the British. Convinced that Abdullah was a dangerous revolutionary, Kak ordered his arrest along with senior leaders of the National Conference. In June 1947, Abdullah was still in jail. As Nehru reminded the viceroy: 'The National Conference has stood for and still stands for Kashmir joining the Constituent Assembly of India.'[29]

With independence approaching, the choices before Singh were unenviable. Joining Pakistan was not an option. There was no future for a Hindu ruler in a predominantly Muslim state. A similar fate awaited him if he joined a Congress-ruled India, despite assurances from Mountbatten that the states would in no way be adversely affected and that the rulers would continue to function as constitutional monarchs. Joining India also risked sparking an uprising among the Muslim-majority population. Mountbatten was aware of the conundrum and of the need to engage Singh personally. Instead, all the maharaja wanted was for the viceroy to enjoy some trout fishing. When Mountbatten was finally able to grab his ear while being driven around the Valley, he reassured Singh that the final decision on Kashmir's future was up to him, adding, however, that he 'should consider it very carefully since after all 90 per cent of your people are Muslim'. Patel, he added, had assured him that 'if Kashmir joined Pakistan this would not be regarded as unfriendly by the Government of India'.[30] For a landlocked, underpopulated country, independence, he emphasized, was not an option:

> What I mind is that your attitude is bound to lead to strife between India and Pakistan . . . You are going to have two rival countries at daggers drawn for your neighbours. You will be the tug-of-war between them. You will end up being a battlefield. That is what

> will happen. You will lose your throne and your life too, if you are not careful.[31]

It was the last time the two would meet. As Campbell-Johnson noted: 'Mountbatten had seen for himself the paralysis of Princely uncertainty.'[32]

Historians have cited Mountbatten's remark that no consequences would arise if the maharaja opted for Pakistan as proof that the British would have preferred such an option. The viceroy's preference was confirmed in an interview with the authors Larry Collins and Dominique Lapierre, when he stated: 'I MUST tell you honestly. I wanted Kashmir to join Pakistan.'[33] It was also backed up by a letter Hari Singh wrote to India's first president, Rajendra Prasad, from Pune in August 1952, in which he said: 'The impression which I gathered from my talks with Lord Mountbatten who explained the situation with plans and maps was that, in his opinion, it was advisable for me to accede to Pakistan.'[34]

But Mountbatten was also being swayed by the importance of Kashmir for Nehru. Writing to Singh on 3 July, Patel assured him that the Congress was not his enemy. 'As an organisation, the Congress is not opposed to any Prince in India. It has no quarrel with the States . . . Jawaharlal Nehru belongs to Kashmir. He is proud of it, and rest assured he can never be your enemy.' Patel was quick to add that it was in Kashmir's interest to join the Indian Union and its Constituent Assembly without delay. 'Its past history and traditions demand it, and all India looks up to you and expects you to take that decision. Eighty per cent of India is on this side.'[35] Singh did not respond. When Mountbatten's chief of staff, Hastings 'Pug' Ismay, visited Kashmir shortly after Mountbatten's visit, he found the maharaja evasive:

> Each time that I tried to broach the question [of the state's future], the Maharaja changed the subject. Did I remember our polo match at Cheltenham in 1935? He had a colt which he thought might win the Indian Derby! Whenever I tried to talk serious business, he abruptly left me for one of the other guests.[36]

On 17 July, nine days after Cyril Radcliffe arrived to draw up the future border between India and Pakistan, Mountbatten reminded Menon that for India to have road access to Kashmir, a passage was needed through the district of Gurdaspur in Punjab, the only overland route from Delhi to Srinagar. Although the district had a Muslim majority, Radcliffe duly awarded it to India. According to Christopher Beaumont, Radcliffe's secretary, this highly controversial decision was ordered by Mountbatten under pressure from Nehru, based on the argument that failure to alter the boundary would lead to war between the two nations.[37] However, the viceroy was also under pressure from Sadul Singh, who warned him that if Ferozepur tehsil in Gurdaspur went to Pakistan, 'it may gravely prejudice [the] interest of Bikaner state'. The only source of water for his state was the Harike headworks on the confluence of the Sutlej and Beas rivers, located in Ferozepur. On hearing that Harike might go to Pakistan, the state's dewan, K.M. Panikkar, flew to Delhi to meet with Mountbatten. He was granted just five minutes and had barely begun to speak before Mountbatten interrupted him and said that Radcliffe reported to the British government and not to him. In response, Panikkar allegedly issued a threat – that if Ferozepur went to Pakistan so would his state.[38] Highly critical of the viceroy's stand was Conrad Corfield, who saw the possibility of bargaining Hyderabad against Kashmir after Partition. 'But Mountbatten did not listen to me.

And when he visited Kashmir, he did not even invite his political adviser to accompany him, as was the custom. Anything that I said to Mountbatten about Kashmir carried no weight against the long-standing determination of Nehru to keep it in India.'[39]

For his part, Nehru was disappointed that Mountbatten had failed to secure Abdullah's release, let alone visit him in jail. The problem of Kashmir, he insisted, would not be solved until the sheikh was free and the people's rights restored. He felt it was his 'particular duty' to go there, maintaining that 'Kashmir has become a first priority for me'. But the visit was vetoed by Mountbatten, on the grounds that it would only add to the difficulties of the maharaja and his prime minister in coming to a decision. He was also afraid that Kak might create an incident that would see Nehru arrested just as he was about to become the new prime minister of India. As Mountbatten pointed out, there were 40 crore people in India, but only 40 lakh in Kashmir, and chances were they would be joining Pakistan. When he was told that Gandhi would go in his place, Nehru broke down and wept.

6

'A Dagger into the Very Heart of India'

As Kashmir and Hyderabad continued their cat-and-mouse games, and the states, large and small, individually or in groupings, weighed up their future, Menon and Patel could see potential 'mini-Ulsters' breaking out around the subcontinent. To make things harder for them, Jinnah, after sitting on the sidelines, was finally turning his patrician gaze at the princes. The Mountbatten–Menon plan for the devolution of power had represented a setback for the Muslim League leader's ambitions by depriving him of a 'big Pakistan' that would have included large parts of the Punjab, northeast India as well as Calcutta. Faced with a 'moth-eaten' polity, there was only one course of action left. If he could persuade enough princely states to join Pakistan or remain independent, Nehru and Patel would have their own 'moth-eaten' India.

Jinnah had some catching up to do. The All-India States Muslim League, formed by the League in 1940 with the aim of seeking 'an honourable political future' for Muslims in princely India, was tiny and perennially short of money. Compared to the inroads the Congress had made in princely India, its influence was limited. It was also stymied by the fears of its parent body, the Muslim League, that meddling in the affairs of the states might turn the Hindu subjects in other Muslim-ruled states against their khans, mirs and nawabs. Nowhere was this more apparent than in Kashmir. Jinnah's restraint was partly influenced by a secret report he commissioned in 1943 to investigate Kashmir's potential as a field for League activity. It found that the state had never been a centre for Islam and that its people were at the mercy of 'counterfeit mullahs'. 'They lack a love of Islam, they are the most greedy people going', prone to 'treachery, lies and cheating' and therefore not fit to become Muslim Leaguers. It would require 'considerable effort, spread over a long period of time, to reform them and convert them into true Muslims, willing to suffer and sacrifice for high Islamic purposes', the report concluded.[1]

Visiting Kashmir a year later, Jinnah exhorted its Muslims to organize themselves under one banner and one platform. Instead of flocking to his cause, he had to bear the ignominy of being shouted down by National Conference members at his only rally in Srinagar. The National Conference leader Sheikh Abdullah despised Jinnah, declaring that 'he was not a true Muslim' and 'had little knowledge of the Koran'. Having conceded that the League was no match for the secularist National Conference, Jinnah switched tack and urged Kashmiri Muslims to remain loyal to the durbar. 'So far as the League is concerned,' its mouthpiece *Dawn* editorialized in 1946, 'it has no wish or desire to stir up trouble in the States or to engage in a campaign of . . . vilification against the princely order.'[2] As late as July 1947, Jinnah told a delegation of Kashmiri Muslim leaders to stop campaigning for the state's accession to Pakistan and to support Hari Singh's bid for autonomy. His reasoning was that once Pakistan was created, the sheer weight of geographical and demographic factors would bring Kashmir into its camp.

With the announcement of the transfer of power on 15 August

1947, it was clear that most of the ten Muslim-majority states lying inside Pakistan – including Bahawalpur, Swat, Dir and Chitral – would be absorbed into the new dominion. But that left more than a dozen states with Muslim rulers, notably Hyderabad and Bhopal, as well as a clutch of smaller entities such as Junagadh, Tonk, Rampur, Palanpur and Radhanpur, inside Indian territory. Mountbatten would later scoff at the suggestion that any of these states could have joined Pakistan, telling Dominique Lapierre and Larry Collins: 'I mean, the idea that Junagadh could join with Pakistan across all the other Kathiawar states was just stupid. The idea that Hyderabad could join . . . Pakistan was equally stupid.'[3] But, as the historian Ian Copland points out:

> The idea of having an island of Pakistani territory stuck in the middle of the Deccan was inherently no more absurd than having one stuck in East Bengal; in fact, from one point of view, somewhat less so, as Hyderabad is a good deal closer to Karachi than is Dhaka.[4]

Jinnah disapproved of Patel and Menon's approach of dealing with the states collectively and paid little heed to Mountbatten's statement that separate negotiations with individual princes were out of the question. He sent overtures to some states that the League had its eye on, such as Jodhpur and Nawanagar, making vague promises of at least semi-independence or, in the case of the larger states, eventual provincial status. On 15 June, two days after the conclave at the Viceroy's Palace, Jinnah issued a statement reaffirming that 'constitutionally and legally the Indian States will be independent sovereign States on the termination of paramountcy, and they will be free to decide for themselves to adopt any course they like'. Any state wishing to negotiate its accession to Pakistan, he added, 'shall find us ready and willing to do so'.[5] Ironically, the most vocal critic of Jinnah's approach was the Punjabi nationalist Choudhary Rahmat Ali, who is credited with first coining the word Pakistan in an essay he wrote in 1933. Rahmat Ali argued that Jinnah was committing a grave mistake by 'accepting . . . the principle of the sovereignty of the Princes', as that would undermine his claim to Kashmir and other states that 'are integral and inseparable parts of Pakistan'. He ended with a dire warning: Jinnah's approach would create '200 caste Hindoostans and 6 sovereign Sikhistans within Pakistan and . . . dismember Pakistan itself before its rise and recognition'.[6]

Jinnah, however, was too busy surveying the low-hanging fruit he could pick for his basket to heed such advice, and some of his overtures seemed to be working. In May 1947, Bhavnagar announced that it would dissociate itself from the newly formed Kathiawar Confederation, which was planning a union with India, and would 'give consideration to the desirability of combining with other states in the area headed by Muslim princes and of joining a Pakistan Government'.[7] Nothing more was heard of the state's declaration. A few months later, the Muslim rulers of five small states in Kathiawar – Dasuda, Vanod, Jainabad, Bajuna and Radhanpur – declared their desire to join Pakistan and asked to begin discussions regarding the terms and conditions of accession. 'Send Sind Muslim League deputation or Pakistan deputation at once. It will be a boon for Kathiawar Muslims as Pakistan will extend up to Viramgum,' pleaded the nawab of Dasuda, Sadula Khan.[8]

Another set of targets for Jinnah consisted of those states located astride the partition boundary or close enough to consider some form of union with Pakistan. They included the Rajput states of Jodhpur and Jaisalmer, as well as the Sikh states of Faridkot and Kapurthala. Alwar might also have fallen to Jinnah's lot had he got the whole of Punjab, the state's dewan, Narayan Bhaskar Khare, wrote later.[9] In Rajputana, Bikaner was an outlier, having no qualms about joining the Constituent Assembly or signing the Instrument of Accession. Neighbouring Jaipur could also imagine a future in India, especially since its size and importance would see it continue as an entity in its own right – at least in the short term. But most of the other Rajput states feared that accession would see their power and privileges severely eroded or disappear altogether. In January 1943, Sir Arthur Lothian, the British resident in Rajputana, noted that the Rajput princes had such a lack of trust in 'the willingness of a Congress-controlled . . . Union [Government] to give them a fair deal' that they would be willing to enter into a union with Muslim-dominated provinces such as the Punjab, even though they might be part of a future Pakistan.[10]

Many Sikhs felt similarly alienated because of the Congress party's lack of support for an independent Sikh homeland, prompting the India Office to speculate that it was not 'inconceivable that . . . some of those [states] bordering on Pakistan might prefer to throw their lot in with Pakistan rather than a Congress-dominated Hindustan'.[11] Despite the greater affinity of Sikhs for Hindus than for Muslims, it was a gamble that Jinnah was prepared to take, in the belief that the chaos of Partition would create a power vacuum in the Punjab that Pakistan and the Sikh states could occupy. When Jinnah met Baldev Singh, the Sikh defence minister, in London in December 1946, he showed him a matchbox and said, 'Even if Pakistan of this size is offered to me, I will gladly accept it. If you persuade the Sikhs to join hands with the Muslim League we will have a glorious Pakistan, the gates of which will be near about Delhi if not in Delhi itself.'[12]

In May 1947, Mountbatten invited the maharaja of Patiala, Yadavindra Singh, to a private dinner with Jinnah and Liaqat Ali

Khan, at which the Pakistani side offered 'practically everything under the sun', Yadavindra later recalled. Two plans were put on the table: one based on the idea of a 'Rajastan' or a confederation of states for Sikhs, and the other for a separate Sikh state. 'I was to be the Head of this new Sikh State, the same as in Patiala. The Sikhs would have their own army and so on.' But Yadavindra turned down the offer.[13] Not to be deterred, two days later Jinnah invited Patiala's ruler to his Aurangzeb Road residence, where his sister Fatima made 'excellent tea' while the Quaid repeated his offer. Once more the maharaja remained unmoved, his patriotism impressing Menon, who would later praise him for his efforts in convincing other Sikh states such as Faridkot and Kapurthala to accede to India.

Jinnah, however, was not prepared to give up, and a few days later attended a meeting with the maharaja and his prime minister, H.S. Malik, as well as prominent Sikhs, including the sixty-one-year-old Akali Dal political and religious figure Master Tara Singh. Jinnah told the gathering he was very anxious to have the Sikhs agree to Pakistan and was prepared to give them a blank sheet of paper for them to list their demands on, which he would sign without giving it a glance. When pressed on what guarantees he could give to honour his promises, Jinnah's reply was so astounding that Malik was convinced the Quaid 'was going mad. He said, "My friend, my word in Pakistan will be like the word of God. No one will go back on it." There was nothing to be said after this and the meeting ended.'[14] Malik was not far off the mark in dismissing Jinnah's assurances. There was little sympathy for the Quaid in the Sikh areas after attacks by Muslims on Sikhs in March that year had left thousands dead in western Punjab. Sikh leaders were circulating photographs from the village of Thoa Kalsa showing the bloated corpses of dozens of women who hurled themselves into a well rather than face rape. Yadavindra would later tell the wife of a British official at a party at his palace that if the British gave Jinnah his own country: 'We won't leave a Moslem [in Patiala]. Nor in the districts around. Every Sikh will draw his kirpan and it will be, "Death to all Moslems."'[15] (Bizarrely, the party ended with the maharaja leading a conga line through the palace, 'over and under the chairs and tables – great fun!', a participant reported.)[16]

While there was no prospect of the Sikh states joining Pakistan, calls for the formation of an independent Sikhistan grew in the months leading up to Partition, fuelled in part by the lack of sympathy being shown by the Congress towards the plight of the Sikhs. In March 1947, Tara Singh sent secret letters to Yadavindra Singh and the raja of Faridkot, Harinder Singh, appealing for arms and soldiers. In a plot that one British general compared to a seventeenth-century intrigue – 'all very reminiscent of de Boigne, Dupleix, and the rest' – the Sikhs would seize the Punjab for themselves. The plan envisaged Patiala's and Faridkot's battalions occupying the British-run districts and surrounding their territories. Tara Singh would raise an irregular force of blue-turbaned Akalis to seize Lahore, Amritsar and the Sikh holy places. Jinnah could have the far western reaches of the province. The rest would unite in an independent Sikhistan.[17]

There was nothing fanciful about the idea. Even though Yadavindra would have no truck with Jinnah, a Sikh plan for revival of their past glory excited his imagination. His court astrologer had recently discovered a passage in an old Sikh text prophesying the emergence of a ruler who would rebuild the Kingdom of Lahore. The ruler's physical description matched Yadavindra's. Many Sikh rulers and Akali leaders were promising him 'kingship' of the new Sikh kingdom that would emerge from the ashes of a Punjab civil war in return for his assistance in driving Pakistan out of the state.

His answer was to publicly announce that his army was always ready to protect the community. Other Sikh-ruled states such as Jind, Faridkot and Kapurthala offered arms and soldiers. However, in the end the uprising did not take place. Instead, Mountbatten's announcement that independence would be brought forward diverted attention towards retribution and revenge. By the end of 1947, less than 50,000 Muslims remained in the Punjab states, compared to almost 10 lakh a year earlier.

If Jinnah was looking for a jewel to adorn his karakul cap with, it would be Jodhpur. The state had joined the Constituent Assembly in April 1947 and Maharaja Umed Singh had been adamant that its future lay with the Indian Union. But his sudden death two months later saw power shift to his son Hanwant Singh. Young, inexperienced, corpulent and headstrong, the new ruler's passions included flying, British brides, dancing girls and conjuring, the latter a hobby that he took seriously enough to see him eventually elected as a member of the prestigious Magic Circle in London. On coming to the gaddi, Hanwant first announced that his state would remain in the Constituent Assembly. The presence at the investiture of Hamidullah Khan, who had been likening the Instrument of Accession to a 'death warrant', led to speculation that he was aiming to lure the new ruler into the hands of Jinnah. In early August, Jodhpur's dewan, Cadambi Venkatachar, wrote to Mountbatten that Hanwant had decided to seek independence. This occurred after a meeting with Jinnah, which was also attended by Hamidullah and the League's legal adviser, Muhammad Zafarullah Khan. Jinnah had got straight to the point, offering Hanwant the use of Karachi as a free port; free import of arms; jurisdiction over the Jodhpur–Hyderabad (Sind) railway; and a supply of grain to the kingdom's famine-threatened districts, on the condition that Jodhpur would declare its independence on 15 August and then join Pakistan.

Although only 22 per cent of Jodhpur's population was Muslim, there was a degree of logic to the offer. Historically, the state had ruled the district of Amarkot in the eastern part of Sind and its territory had stretched all the way to the Sindhi city of Hyderabad on the Indus river. These lands were lost after Sind was occupied by General Sir Charles James Napier in 1843. As compensation, the state received a miserly Rs 10,000 rent a year, an amount that had not been increased for nearly a century. 'The Maharaja was dazzled with the prospect of becoming a sort of emperor of all Rajasthan with the help of Pakistan,' K.M. Panikkar wrote at the time, noting that it was an ancestor of the Jodhpur maharaja who had invited the eleventh-century invader Muhammad Ghori to India. The dynasty had also won favour with the Mughals by offering their women in marriage to them. 'The secret pact with Jinnah was thus quite in character.'[18]

Mountbatten had once counted Hamidullah as his second-best friend in India, and as late as July 1947 was courting him to convince Jinnah that the two dominions should share the same governor general, that is, himself. Now the two men were on opposite sides of the fence. When Mountbatten was told of the meeting between Hanwant and Jinnah, he castigated Bhopal's ruler for 'behaving as a friend to my face whilst engineering a break-up of my scheme behind my back'.[19] Officials in the states ministry would come to a similar conclusion, charging Bhopal with

> . . . acting as an agent of Pakistan . . . [and] circulating to other rulers false statements to the effect that, as a result of the efforts of

> his group of rulers, the Instrument of Accession was being revised, and that, if all of them stood firm, they would be able to obtain or extract more favourable terms.[20]

Hamidullah saw his position as an ethical one. He had long been arguing with Mountbatten that the partition plan carried in it the seeds of the destruction of princely India and the doctrine of paramountcy. 'Nobody appears to have paid any attention to what the reaction of the States might be,' he wrote to Mountbatten on 15 June. 'In fact, the States have . . . been completely ignored as if they form no part of India at all.'[21] Brushing his arguments aside, Mountbatten advised him to accede to India. His rejoinder came in the form of a long, meandering letter in which he accused the Congress of pressuring the princes by means of 'coercion, bribery and intimidation reminiscent more of the tactics of Pindaris early in the 19th century rather than responsible politicians and statesmen'. And the British were aiding this, he charged. 'Are we,' he asked angrily, 'to write out a blank cheque and leave it to the leaders of the Congress party to fill in the amount?'[22]

Hamidullah's next target was Bhupal Singhji, the maharana of Udaipur. At his urging, Hanwant sought to persuade the ruler to accede to Pakistan. Logic was at work here: Udaipur was the link between Jodhpur in the west and Indore and Bhopal in central India. If the maharana acquiesced, Bhopal would attain contiguity with Pakistan with the help of an already compliant Indore, enabling its nawab to realize his desire to accede to Pakistan. Rajput disunity, distrust and friction had helped the Mughals expand their empire in India, and now Jinnah was angling for a similar role and opportunity for Pakistan, with Jodhpur as the weakest link. But once again, an alert pro-India dewan played whistle-blower. When Venkatachar found out about Bhopal's plan, he sent H.V.R.

Iyengar, home secretary to the Government of India, a handwritten note through a special messenger, 'to avoid being spied upon', giving news of the 'utmost gravity for the very stability of India'. The note stated that 'the ruler had been approached by Jinnah and had been persuaded to stay out of the Indian Dominion'.[23] Iyengar took the note to Patel and apprised him of the severity of the situation. Patel instantly grasped the implications of the plan – a Jodhpur–Udaipur–Indore–Bhopal axis would create what he termed 'a dagger into the very heart of India'.[24]

It all seemed to be falling into place. At their final meeting, Jinnah dramatically handed Hanwant a blank sheet of paper with his signature on it and asked him to 'fill in all your conditions'. For a moment it appeared as if Hanwant would do just that. It was only his ADC Colonel Thakur Kesari Singh's last-minute intervention that prevented him from putting pen to paper and signing away his state. Singh implored the maharaja to first consult his mother. Hanwant duly returned to Jodhpur, where he found not just his mother but also his guru warning him of the consequences of a Hindu state agreeing to accede to Muslim-dominated Pakistan. He then met with Mountbatten in New Delhi. Realizing the gravity of the situation, the viceroy wasted no time in outlining the legal implications of acceding to Pakistan, noting it would go against the principles underlying Partition, namely, the division of the subcontinent into Muslim- and non-Muslim-majority areas. When that failed to sway Hanwant, he reminded the young ruler that he had been a friend of his father's for twenty-six years and knew that he would have wanted to be with India. 'To me it was tragic that his successor should not follow the wisdom of his father and should have been misled by Jinnah,' Mountbatten wrote later. He also cautioned him about the danger of igniting communal violence in the state.[25] Then it was Menon's turn. When a yet-to-be persuaded Hanwant was ushered into his office, the States Department secretary urged him not to be swayed by false promises and promptly proceeded to offer the state several concessions to match Jinnah's, including free import of arms, food for the famine-struck districts and the building of a railway from Jodhpur to a port in Kutch. 'In any case you won't be able to go to Pakistan,' Menon added matter-of-factly. 'Your jagirdars won't agree, your people won't agree; your own mother won't countenance it. How can you go?'[26]

Finally, it was Patel who delivered the coup de grace. 'Your Highness is free to stay out, if you like,' he told Hanwant. 'But if there is trouble in your State as a result of your decision, you will not get the slightest support from the Government of India.' Patel ended the conversation by reminding him that the maharaja's father had left him to his care as a ward. If he did not behave properly, he was obliged to discipline him. By now Hanwant had broken out in a cold sweat. Sobered by the warning, he got up from his seat and told Patel: 'Well Sir, I have decided to go back to Lord Mountbatten and sign the Instrument of Accession right now.'[27]

Mountbatten's authoritativeness and Patel's knack for appearing reasonable and persuasive were still no guarantee, Menon realized, that Hanwant would do as directed. When he personally drove Hanwant straight to the viceroy's office, he was doing so not as a courtesy but as a foil against further prevarication. After signing the Instrument of Accession, Hanwant was directed to Menon's suite while Mountbatten dealt with a Hyderabad delegation in Edwina's study next door. As Menon would later narrate, Hanwant suddenly 'whipped out a revolver', levelled it at him and said, 'I refuse to accept your dictation.' Menon told Hanwant he was seriously mistaken if he thought threatening him could get the accession abrogated, adding: 'Don't indulge in juvenile theatricals.'[28] There is a different account of the event in Onkar Singh Babra's book *Ek Maharaja ki Antarkatha*, which describes Hanwant's stunt as a joke that 'backfired', and says that Menon's account in *The Story of the Integration of the Indian States* was an exercise in self-aggrandizement.[29] The 'revolver' Menon refers to was a 7 centimetre-long gold-plated pen with a 22-calibre bore made in Hanwant's magic props workshop. When Mountbatten heard of the incident, he made light of it. It became a standing joke between the three men. In 1952, while campaigning in the Lok Sabha elections, Hanwant asked Menon to stand as a candidate from the Jodhpur constituency. Menon immediately turned down the offer. As a gesture of reconciliation, the maharaja gifted the pen gun to the viceroy. Years later, Mountbatten, by then a member of the Magic Circle, donated it to the society's museum. In 2013, it was sold for £13,000 to the Royal Armouries Museum in Leeds, West Yorkshire.

Even if Jodhpur had not been brought to heel, the 'dagger in the heart of India' that Patel feared was blunted by the Udaipur ruler's refusal to have anything to do with Hanwant's plan. 'The choice was made by my ancestors,' Bhupal Singhji told him. 'If they had faltered, they would have left us a kingdom as large as Hyderabad. They did not. Neither shall I. I am with India.'[30]

Nationalist historians have written off Hamidullah as 'sly and aggressive', 'a peerless Machiavellian' and even as a 'Muslim partisan and enemy of the Hindus'.[31] His popularity in his own state – up to 50,000 Bhopalis turned out to give him their support in July 1947, following rumours that he was about to step down from the gaddi – has not changed that narrative. Bhopal had two objectives, Balraj Krishna writes:

> to establish the Princes as a potential 'Third Force' on behalf of Corfield; and, on behalf of Jinnah, to secure their accession to Pakistan, if not immediately but ultimately. Along with the Residents and Agents, he endeavoured to persuade the Hamlets among the Princes to form independent confederations outside the Indian Union.[32]

The accusation that he supported a 'Third Force' is one that Corfield categorically denied. 'I know nothing of the Nawab of Bhopal's attempt, shortly before the transfer of power, to form a union consisting of a number of states in central India,' he said in 1970.

> It was, I imagine, a last-minute attempt to fortify the bargaining power of these states. It had no substance to the best of my knowledge. I had already discouraged a similar scheme in the Deccan states which the resident advisedly supported. These and similar schemes were not real mergers and offered no solution to the problem of viable units.[33]

The picture that emerges of Hamidullah in the final weeks and days before Independence is more of a pathetic Polonius clutching at straws and looking for support from a mostly indifferent Jinnah, who had more pressing nation-building concerns to deal with – not to mention his rapidly deteriorating health. In a grovelling letter sent on 2 August, Hamidullah reminded the Quaid-i-Azam that for the past eight or ten years he had been 'in my humble way a staunch supporter of Pakistan'. He complained that Bhopal stood 'alone with an 80 per cent Hindu majority in the midst of Hindu India, surrounded by my personal enemies'. He was prepared for a confrontation but wanted to know how much Pakistan would help. If Bhopal was eventually forced to join India, then the signature would be that of his successor. 'My own personal wish is to abdicate and to serve Islam. I am a poor man not having amassed a fortune at the expense of my people, but that does not matter as long as I can serve Islam and Pakistan . . . I am prepared to serve Pakistan in any capacity.'[34] Jinnah never bothered to reply.

On 10 August, Hamidullah asked Mountbatten for a postponement of his accession, adding that he was considering abdicating in favour of his daughter, Princess Abida Sultan. With large dollops of pathos, he told the Viceroy:

> I am delaying my final act with the intention of doing everything possible in finding a solution which would enable me to sign our death warrant with a clear conscience. If I fail to find such a solution, I must abdicate rather than take any action which, in my judgment, is not in the true interests of my dynasty and my people.[35]

He also sought an assurance that Patel and Menon would not renege on the terms they were offering. Mountbatten replied tartly that he would be in an extremely strong position to expose them if they did, considering that he was going to remain in India until June the following year.

Patel refused point blank to consider Bhopal's request for a postponement. He had personally blamed the nawab for interfering in the process of accession. 'It is so taxing,' he confided in a letter to Gandhi on 11 August. 'There seems to be no end to the Nawab of Bhopal's intrigues. He is working day and night to cause a split among the Princes and to keep them out of the Indian Union. The Princes are weak beyond measure. They are full of selfishness, falsehood and hypocrisy.'[36] Despite Patel's opposition, Mountbatten found a face-saving compromise. Hamidullah would sign the Instrument of Accession before midnight of 14 August. The document would then be kept in safe custody by Mountbatten until 25 August. The motive for seeking the postponement emerged just three days before the grace period expired. In talks with Patel and then Mountbatten, Hamidullah admitted to having 'ambitions to play a big role in the Muslim world in the future', and he feared that if he acceded to India 'Jinnah would denounce him as a traitor to the Muslim cause'.[37] His hopes evaporated after he flew to Karachi to meet the Pakistani leader. Instead of receiving a warm welcome, he sensed distrust from the country's new leadership. The day after the sealed Instrument of Accession was opened and Bhopal officially became a part of India, he wrote to Patel stating: 'I do not disguise the fact that while the struggle was on, I used every means in my power to preserve the independence and neutrality of my State. Now that I have conceded defeat, I hope that you will find that I can be as staunch a friend as I have been an inveterate opponent.'[38]

Ever since his address to the Chamber of Princes, Mountbatten had been working hard to sign up as many states as possible. With Corfield's departure they were largely on their own and most offered little resistance. 'I have been making unbelievable progress,' he wrote to his daughter on 3 August. 'I gave a lunch [yesterday] to . . . 22 [rulers] in Delhi and all agreed to announce their accession to India that afternoon.'[39] By the end of the week another fifty or so had signed. But with less than ten days to go before the transfer of power, that still left dozens of states whose future theoretically hung in the balance.

Of the undecideds, Indore's Yeshwant Rao Holkar took the art of taxing the patience of all sides to new heights. The Holkars, who ruled the nineteen-gun state, were descendants of the Maratha chiefs who had kept the British at bay until the early 1800s. Yeshwant was installed on the gaddi in 1926 after his father Tukoji Rao was implicated in a sensational murder case and abdicated rather than face an investigation. On the evening of 12 January 1925, a Bombay businessman, Abdul Kadir Bawla, was ambushed and shot dead while driving his six-cylinder red Studebaker past the Hanging Gardens in Malabar Hill. The assailants dragged his mistress Mumtaz Begum out of the car and slashed her face with a knife. The ambush was witnessed by four British officers, who captured the assailants as they tried to escape with Mumtaz. When news of the attack reached Bertrand Glancy, the agent to the governor-general for central India, he sent a telegram to his superiors in London that he had 'little doubt' the attack was instigated by Tukoji.

The great-granddaughter of a courtesan in the Sikh emperor Ranjit Singh's establishment, Mumtaz Begum had come to the Indore durbar as a young 'singing girl'. Captivated by her beauty and her voice, Tukoji made her his mistress and took her with him on his trips to Europe. After a run-in with a senior official at the durbar, who accused her of stealing jewellery, she fled Indore, eventually arriving in Bombay, where she began a relationship with Bawla. The attack having been linked directly to Tukoji, the maharaja was given an ultimatum – either abdicate or face an enquiry. He chose the first option, and on 26 February 1926, Glancy received a formal letter of abdication. Tukoji left for Europe, moved to a villa he owned in Switzerland and married an American woman, who converted to Hinduism. Mumtaz Begum's story was immortalized in a silent film called *Kulin Kanta*.

Yeshwant's tumultuous and often torturous personal life, coupled with his preference for living abroad, would constantly undermine his capacity as a ruler. The premature death of his wife Sanyogita

Bai left him devastated. By 1937, he was admitted to a California hospital suffering from the effects of drug addiction, alcoholism and insomnia. One of the nurses caring for him in the California hospital was Marguerite Lawler. Yeshwant begged her to look after his four-year-old daughter Usha and to be his full-time carer. One year later, the two married amid newspaper stories of a working-class girl's Arabian Nights romance with an Indian ruler who lived off his $70 million fortune. Three months later, she announced she was returning to America, blaming her poor health and the machinations of the court. Between one of his visits to his wife in America, Yeshwant met Euphemia 'Fay' Crane of Los Angeles, whose husband was a senior executive at the Hindustan Aircraft Factory in Bangalore. Yeshwant travelled to America in 1942 with Crane posing as his secretary, ostensibly to check on Lawler's health. The real reason was to end the marriage. A year later, Holkar and Crane were granted their divorces on the same morning, both claiming extreme cruelty at the hands of their partners, and later that day were married in Reno, Nevada.

Following his marriage to Fay, Yeshwant applied himself vigorously though erratically to the affairs of his state, becoming an active though controversial member of the COP. It was his impulsiveness that taxed the patience of the British government to its limit. After not even bothering to reply to Mountbatten's invitation to attend his 25 July address to the princes, Hamidullah and he began sending out telegrams and emissaries to rulers who were wavering about accession, urging them to seek better terms. Yeshwant admitted to Mountbatten that his relationship with Bhopal's nawab was 'very close' and that they had pledged themselves 'to unity of action in regard to all matters relating to . . . future constitutional developments'.[40] Writing to Nehru, he said he took pride in the fact that the two states were following a common policy, describing it as 'a practical demonstration of Hindu–Muslim cooperation, which has so far eluded British India'.[41]

On 30 July, Mountbatten dispatched a team of six Maratha princes to cajole Yeshwant into signing the Instrument of Accession. He viewed the maharaja as 'a most unsatisfactory Ruler' and vowed to leave 'no stone unturned'.[42] The six – the Gaekwar of Baroda, the maharajas of Kolhapur, Gwalior, Dhar and Dewas Junior and the raja of Sandor, Yeshwant's oldest friend – flew to Indore on 30 July, only to find that Yeshwant had decamped to Bhopal. Kolhapur's dewan was sent to fetch him, but Hamidullah insisted that no meeting could take place without his permission. After negotiating for six hours, Yeshwant finally returned to Indore and went straight to his palace. Instead of acknowledging the presence of the visiting rulers, he hurried straight past them pretending they did not exist. After a whole night of trying to contact Bhopal's ruler by telephone to get his consent to speak to Indore, the princes gave up and returned to Delhi. 'I saw four of the Committee who are all horrified at their treatment. The Gaekwar wished me to depose [Yeshwant] at once, but I pointed out that I had no grounds for doing this before the 15th August,' Mountbatten wrote. 'It may not be a bad thing to have a thoroughly unsatisfactory State like Indore remaining outside the Dominion, as an example of what happens to States that try and stand on their own. If he does not change his mind and come in, I prophesy that the people of Indore will kick their Ruler off the Gaddi before the end of September.'[43]

On 4 August, Yeshwant and Hamidullah held a stormy meeting with Mountbatten, who denied he was using threats to make them sign the Instrument of Accession and reiterated that each state was at complete liberty to do exactly what it liked. The meeting ended with Mountbatten pointing out that while

> . . . he could guarantee the terms of the present Instrument up to 15th August, he could do nothing to help after that date. There was no other reason for speed. If the Maharaja of Indore thought that he would get better terms after 15th August, it was open to him to wait until then.[44]

As he later reported privately to the India Office: 'Indore looks as though he has almost missed the bus.'[45]

After his grilling by the viceroy, Yeshwant met with Jinnah, who listened patiently to his requests but strangely offered nothing concrete. He then met with Henry Grady, the American ambassador to India. 'Jinnah has taken [a] much more conciliatory attitude toward States than has Congress,' Grady wrote to his State Department bosses in Washington:

> Jinnah would like to build up a bloc of States with pro-Pakistan leanings in central India using Indore and Bhopal as a nucleus. I doubt that he will be successful in his effort, but Jinnah is undoubtedly treating the States with great caution and courtesy. By contrast Patel was telling [Yeshwant] Rao that if he didn't join the Indian Union, 'we shall starve you out'.[46]

Yeshwant also met with Howard Donovan, the counsellor at the embassy, telling him he had offered the now-disgraced C.P. Ramaswami Aiyar of Travancore the position of dewan. Still thrashing around, Yeshwant then asked Jinnah to spell out his terms for accession.[47] Around the same time, Nehru received an angry letter from Indore, protesting at being 'rushed' into accession and asking for time to study 'Pakistan's terms'.[48] Several days later, however, a manila envelope arrived for Menon at the States Department. In it were the Standstill

Agreement and the Instrument of Accession with Yeshwant's signature. 'There was no note, nor was there an accompanying emissary. For a few hours, an astonished V.P. was left wondering if this was a joke.'[49]

7

Endgames of Empire

A self-confessed advocate of 'fatherly despotism', Udai Bhan Singh, the maharaj rana of the fifteen-gun state of Dholpur in eastern Rajputana, believed his position was bestowed on him by God and objected to having any intermediate authority between himself and his subjects. As a result, he took on the administration of his state himself, supported by just a few secretaries, and was deaf to appeals for any form of democratization. One of India's longest-serving rulers, he had taken part in the Round Table Conferences on India's constitutional future held in London from 1930 to 1933. Once considered 'the finest game shot in India', he became a conservationist in his later years and turned his country estate into a game reserve where the wildlife was so timid that sambar would come up to his car to be hand-fed. Conrad Corfield recalls taking a launch around a lake and seeing 'tigers yawning in your face from the bank ten yards away'.[1]

Udai Bhan's belief in his divine rights was one he shared with the conservative rulers of Panna, Alwar and Bharatpur. Like many rulers, he had been unnerved by Nehru's 18 April address in Gwalior, in which he warned that states refusing to accede would be treated as hostile. After the speech, Udai Bhan told Mountbatten that the princes now had 'no option but to take up the challenge, since it appeared to be grossly unfair to try and blackmail them in this way'. Rather that accede, he demanded a treaty relationship in respect of common matters with India.[2]

The viceroy had little time for Udai Bhan, whom he considered to be a man of minor intelligence. His response was that India would do nothing, leaving Dholpur completely isolated in the middle of an indifferent India. 'Although Your Highness, being a man of such great wealth, may be able to abdicate and leave your State, I know that your loyalty to your subjects and your belief in the position and obligations of a Ruler will not let you desert your subjects,' Mountbatten wrote. 'I shall grieve indeed as I read reports of the plight of Dholpur month-by-month during 1948.'[3]

Another state flirting with independence despite being well within the proposed borders of the new India was Bilaspur, a Hindu-majority eleven-gun-salute princedom that covered just 1,300 square kilometres in the Himalayan foothills. Shortly after Partition was announced, Anand Chand, its young, lawyerish-looking raja, asked for an assurance from the viceroy that the decision on which Constituent Assembly to join was 'a matter of free choice for [the states]'.[4] Chand was a popular ruler who had modernized and democratized his state, setting up a 110-member legislative assembly. A British official returning to Bilaspur in the early 1940s after a gap of several years noted: 'On all sides were new buildings – a girls' school, a hospital for women, a men's club, a public library, a cinema. The progress made in a few years was astonishing.'[5]

It was not the first time Chand had toyed with the idea of

independence. At a meeting with Wavell in April 1946, he had spoken out against amalgamation of the smaller states, arguing that the survival value of a state lay 'not in its size or power, but in its geography and history'. His kingdom, he pointed out, had been in existence since 700 AD and had resisted the Mughals and the Sikhs. Three thousand of its soldiers had fought bravely in World War Two. If the treaty relationships with the Crown could not be honoured for any reason, he told Wavell, 'each State must be allowed to regain its former independence and left to itself to do what it wanted'. While this view might not have wide support, he insisted it was 'just as much a right of the States to have independence as it was for British India. Bilaspur would in the last resort fight to protect itself.'[6]

A third state nursing dreams of freedom was Gwalior, in the heart of central India. After being one of the first princes to join the Constituent Assembly in April, the state's ruler George Jiwajirao Scindia was now begging Menon for Gwalior to be allowed to remain a separate entity on account of the size of its territory, the soundness of its finances, and because its people had been subjects of the Scindias for nearly two centuries. 'Why not at least ask the people if they want Gwalior to be joined to some other territory?' he asked. 'Surely, in a democracy, they should have the right to decide that?'[7] To change Scindia's mind, Menon chartered a plane to fly him and his wife Vijayaraje to Delhi. At first she was just as obstinate, but finally, what Menon called her 'progressive outlook' worked in his favour. 'We lapsed into good manners and smiled bravely . . . trying to make out that the abandoning of four million subjects to the mercies of the Congress nominees was not breaking our hearts,' Vijayaraje, who was to become a prominent politician in independent India, later wrote.[8]

To the north of Gwalior, surrounded by the United Provinces

and not far from Delhi, was Rampur. Its ruler, Nawab Raza Ali Khan, was a Rohilla whose Afghan-Pashtun ancestors had established the state in 1775. Even though the majority of the population was Hindu, Raza Ali was briefly tempted by Jinnah's overtures but turned down his offer when told that Pakistan would only be able to give 'moral support' in case of a showdown with India. Rampur's decision to accede to India prompted widespread rioting instigated by local Muslim League activists. Numerous government buildings were set alight and an inspector of police burnt alive. On 5 August, the nawab, together with his chief minister, Bashir Hussain Zaidi, drove through the rioting mobs, eventually making it to Delhi where they appealed to Mountbatten for troops to quell the unrest. Raza Ali told Mountbatten that 'Jinnah had been bringing every possible pressure to bear on him personally to stop him from acceding to the Dominion of India', the viceroy reported back to London. Zaidi described a meeting with Liaqat and other Muslim Leaguers at which threats were made about what would happen to Rampur if it deserted Pakistan and joined India. Zaidi had replied that if the League could arrange to magically move Rampur to the border with Pakistan they would gladly accede, but as that was impossible the state had no choice but to become part of India.[9] 'You can imagine what would have been the position in Rampur, if this had occurred after 15th August and they had declared their independence, particularly if the riots had been organized by the Hindus who form nearly 90 per cent of the population,' Mountbatten wrote to Listowel.[10] At Menon's urging, troops were sent to Rampur to quell the unrest – and to serve as a warning to other states 'to fall in line with Congress policy' on accession.[11]

Two other princely states with significant Muslim populations would be consumed by violence in the lead-up to Independence. Incensed by reports of communal killings in the Punjab and alarmed by rumours of pro-Pakistan activities closer to home, Hindus in Alwar and neighbouring Bharatpur unleashed a pogrom against their Muslim neighbours. In the first several months of 1947, as many as 30,000 Muslims were killed, up to 20,000 forcefully converted, and an estimated 1 lakh forced to flee the two states for the relative safety of the neighbouring district of Gurgaon. Whole villages were razed and scores of mosques desecrated by activists belonging to local branches of the Rashtriya Swayamsevak Sangh (RSS) and the Hindu Mahasabha. Many of the Muslims who fled these states never returned, preferring to migrate to Pakistan.[12]

The Muslims targeted in the attacks mainly belonged to the Meo caste who had a tradition of defying authority and serving with the Indian Army. For decades they had suffered discriminatory policies introduced by the British that included bans on wearing beards in police and military departments and the use of Hindi not Urdu in government service. Bharatpur's ruler Brijendra Singh was just eleven years old when his father was deposed, which normally would have provided ample time for imperial indoctrination before he became eligible to sit on the gaddi. Despite the best efforts of his British overlords, including three years at exclusive schools in England and Switzerland, he turned out to be a sickly, indolent and intensely conceited ruler. He had once remarked to a courtier: 'I must have committed some very slight sin in my previous incarnation for instead of remaining God I have been sent back a Maharaja.' Spurning the guidance given to him while growing up, Singh behaved 'like an oversized prep-school bully and had indiscreet homosexual affairs with members of the household infantry'.[13]

Tej Singhji of Alwar did not turn out much better. Asked for his opinion in 1941, Francis Wylie, agent to the governor general for Rajputana, wrote of him: 'His Highness . . . has acquired a very good opinion of himself . . . [but] he is petty-minded, greedy both for money and power and a prig.'[14] Nehru dubbed him 'a paranoiac'.[15] Ominously for their states' Muslims, the rulers of both Bharatpur and Alwar grew up to be pious Hindus with a strong commitment to Hindu nationalism.

Threatened by the activities of the Praja Mandals, the rulers turned to communities such as the Rajputs and the Jats who were solidly anti-Congress for support. Brijendra Singh was convinced that Jats from Bharatpur to Delhi and beyond would support him in creating a separate state of Jatistan by teaming up with his cousin, the Sikh ruler of the Punjab state of Faridkot. He went so far as to order maps of his putative state replete with borders and briefly flirted with the idea of setting up an underground movement to oppose accession. In August 1947, he wrote to Yeshwant Rao reminding him that if the states played 'their hands carefully' he knew many Congressmen who would 'come to us for help and recognize our leadership. In the end my only request to you, Bhai, is to agree for the present to whatever they suggest and carry on an underground movement.' Brijendra added that he had the support of the Hindu Mahasabha and other Hindu bodies.[16] In April 1947, Tej Singhji told an All India Kshatriya Conference: 'India's salvation lies in a Kshatriya Kingdom alone and the time has now come to establish such a kingdom.'[17] Alwar's maharaja also briefly toyed with the idea of joining Pakistan, seduced by promises of greater autonomy than might be offered by the Congress. Meanwhile, the Muslims of both states began agitating for the creation of a Meostan that would comprise Meo-majority areas of the

United Provinces, Punjab, Alwar and Bharatpur. Spurred by the anticipation that independence would be accompanied by turmoil and that most of Punjab would go to Pakistan, supporters of Meostan believed there would be nothing, in theory, to stop them from following Punjab's lead.

Complicating the Meo issue was Patel's support for Narayan Bhaskar Khare, the fiercely anti-Muslim prime minister of Alwar. After dissuading Tej Singhji from his pro-Pakistan tilt, Khare, who was also the deputy president of the Hindu Mahasabha, aimed his ire against India's Muslim minority. 'No Musalman [*sic*] can be trusted to be faithful to Hindustan. In case of any big emergency, the Musalmans will surely act as saboteurs,' he wrote in July 1947. 'We need a United Hindu National Front, which will gather all the strength of the Hindus of India . . . All Hindus, princes and people, must . . . join it.'[18]

Khare persuaded Patel to believe that if the Meo revolt was not put down the Meo-majority areas of Alwar and Bharatpur would attempt to join Pakistan. Patel, in his capacity as home minister, ordered the armed forces of both states to evict all Muslims from their areas. According to a former Alwar army captain, he told Singhji: 'The killings of Hindus at Noakhali [in Bengal] and Punjab had to be avenged. We called it the "Clearing Up campaign". All the Meos from Firozepur Jhirka down were to be cleared and sent to Pakistan [and] their lands taken over.'[19] Meos retaliated by defiling Hindu temples, prompting further reprisals. Most of those who survived fled across the border into the district of Gurgaon.

On 7 August 1947, Patel wrote to Khare saying that the Meos who had fled Alwar and Bharatpur were 'now in a penitent mood'. The longer they remained as refugees in Gurgaon district, the more desperate they might become.[20] Patel's warning was not intended as a call for restraint but rather to give Khare the green light for dealing with the Meos as he saw fit. The turning point came on 12 August 1947, when a force of 10,000 Meos from Alwar, Bharatpur and Gurgaon was routed by the Alwar army. After being pushed back into the hills, they were systematically hunted down. Travelling through the area at the time, Edward Wakefield, joint secretary of the Political Department, was 'shocked and sickened' by what he saw: 'Charred corpses by the roadside, children with arms and legs chopped off, mutilated women with gaping wounds. I saw houses being set alight, with armed men waiting outside to cut down any who sought escape from the flames.'[21] Lieutenant General Francis Tuker, who commanded the 6th Jat Regiment that restored order in Rampur, would later contrast Patel's 'complete lack of response to our repeated appeal for troops to be sent to the help of the unlucky Muslims being obliterated in the Hindu States of Alwar and Bharatpur'.[22] Tuker also found evidence of state troops and Hindu mobs surrounding Muslim villages and only sparing those who agreed to convert to Hinduism. One of the worst massacres occurred in Silgaon on 7 August, when villagers were tricked into handing over their weapons before being mercilessly machine-gunned down. A group of survivors who fled into Nabha state were looted of their jewellery and possessions before being 'hacked to pieces with swords and axes. None of this party survived the onslaught.'[23]

Kashmir was also unravelling. Just a few days before the transfer of power, Mountbatten had convinced Hari Singh to 'sack' his pro-independence prime minister, Pandit Ram Chandra Kak. A day later, the maharaja signed a Standstill Agreement with Pakistan to ensure that services such as trade, travel and communications would continue as they had with British India. No such agreement was signed with India, Menon's excuse being that his hands were already full and that he had not had any time to think about it. Writing with smug satisfaction to the India Office, Mountbatten noted that the maharaja 'now talks of holding a referendum to decide whether to join Pakistan or India, provided that the Boundary Commission give him land communication between Kashmir and India', an obvious reference to including Gurdaspur on the Indian side of the partition line. Therefore, it appears 'as if this great problem of the States has been satisfactorily solved within the last three weeks of British rule'.[24]

Once again, Mountbatten was getting ahead of himself. Apart from Kashmir, those states that had still not lodged their Instruments of Accession by the deadline of midnight on 14 August included Bhopal, Junagadh and Manavadar, as also several smaller states such as Piploda in central India, which held out until March 1948. Other states, including Dholpur, Bharatpur, Bilaspur and Nabha, had signed at the very last moment after it was made clear there would be no compromise available to them. Still others had forwarded their Instruments and Standstill Agreements with covering letters that sought to lay out conditions subject to which the agreements had been signed. Another state causing headaches was Radhanpur, an eleven-gun-salute state in Kathiawar with a Muslim nawab ruling over a majority-Hindu population. Its signed Instrument of Accession did not reach Delhi until the final week of September 1947. Among the excuses given by the state's dewan were the nawab's incapacitation by an attack of bronchitis and that flooded roads had disrupted the mail service. Radhanpur had been one of five Muslim-ruled states in Kathiawar that had expressed their desire to join Pakistan in July. Lacking the prestige or strategic importance of Junagadh, Pakistan's states ministry had ignored its request. That had not stopped its ruler from intimidating his subjects. According to a report in the Gujarati daily *Janmabhoomi* on 22 August 1947, Hindu peasants who refused to sign a declaration supporting the state's accession to Pakistan were being beaten or threatened with death.[25]

Mountbatten's final report as viceroy captures the mood among the princes as they watched the Union Jack being lowered for the last time on Indian soil. The Maharaj Rana of Dholpur had tears in his eyes as he said: 'This breaks an alliance between my ancestors and your King's ancestors which has existed since 1765.' The viceroy pointed out that the reigning British monarch was still the king of the dominion of India. Rather than being broken, the link had merely changed. Still inconsolable, the maharaj rana said he wanted to leave Delhi while the top office was still held by a viceroy and Crown representative, namely, Mountbatten.[26] Narendra Singh was another ruler who had held on to the hope that Sarila and its brother-state in Bundelkhand, Charkhari, would be independent after the transfer of power. Eventually he signed two Instruments – one for each state. He then told his son, Narendra, who was twenty-one at the time, that he would immediately start preparing for his coronation. By now, however, Narendra was in no doubt 'that sooner or later my father would lose his powers. In any case, I knew I would never rule Sarila.' When he asked Charkhari's regent Shaffat Ali what he thought of Bundelkhand's future, the response was prophetic, 'What does it matter who rules what, once you have lost your princedom and powers?'[27]

The attitude among British officials who had served in the states was just as sullen. 'It was distasteful in the extreme that the British should behave to these people with such contempt for past obligations and such callous disregard for the decencies of diplomacy,' said Philip Mason, tutor to the sons of Osman Ali

Khan. '"In Hyderabad, it is permissible to stab a man in the back, but you must never be rude to him," – a Muslim in Delhi had said to me. We did both.'[28] Kenneth Fitze, who had served in several states and as adviser to the secretary of state for India, recalled one of his Indian friends describing a

> . . . transformation so dramatic and drastic that I often wonder whether I am still living in the same world that I knew only a few years ago – the Princely Order has been completely wiped out once and for all. For two decades they disregarded advice . . . The day of reckoning has come.[29]

In 1947, the size of the serving cadre in the Indian Political Service that Fitze had been part of was just 124-officers strong, of whom 90 were British. The residents and political agents making up the service had been managing the relationship between the Raj and the 562 princely states for more than a century. Now, they and their subordinates were preparing to leave. At the eleven residences spread out across the subcontinent, staff had been busy packing every item of moveable property to ship home. 'I have never talked about it – but every Resident who left, they only left us the Residency building,' Menon would reveal to H.V. Hodson. He termed it an act of revenge.

> They took everything – photographs, silver, carpets, books. Some of them were very stupid in those last days. One of them had the cheek to tell me that as long as he was Resident, he would fly the Union Jack, whether or not the transfer of power occurred. I told him that on the morning of 15th August, if I saw that the Union Jack was still flying and our flag had not been raised, I would have him arrested.[30]

As far as Menon was concerned, the threatened fragmentation of India had been averted, and the whole country had come under one political umbrella. 'My feeling was one of profound thankfulness to God . . . Thus, the gap which had threatened to Balkanize the country was effectively stopped,' he asserted. 'The prophets of gloom who predicted disruption had been belied. We had obtained a breathing space during which we could evolve a permanent relationship between the Government of India and the States.'[31] Welcoming the states to their new reality as units in an independent India, Patel reinforced the message that their accession had been in their best interests and those of their people. The solution to the states problem had been offered in the 'friendliest disposition' with 'nothing but the ultimate good of the Princes and their people at heart'. The surrender of power had been 'voluntary' and done with the knowledge that it 'would increase and not reduce the prestige that they [the rulers] have enjoyed and would create in the hearts of their people a place of lasting affection and regard which would redound to their glory'.[32] Patel's statement dodges the fact that the states were being constantly warned that if they did not sign Instruments of Accession they would be much worse off, treated as 'hostile' and would be at the mercy of popular uprisings directly or indirectly led by the Congress.

For his part, Mountbatten neglected to outline the disadvantages of signing the Instrument of Accession. Leaving defence in the hands of a future Indian government gave it the right to intervene militarily in any state that posed a threat to the integrity of the new dominion – as would be the case in Hyderabad. Had he told the rulers unequivocally that once paramountcy ended, His Majesty's government's obligations were to the new dominions and not to them, the cries of betrayal that were about to echo around the durbar halls of kingdoms great and small would have been muted, if not averted altogether. But it was equally true that the freedom of the states to choose their destiny was fictitious. As the scholar John R. Wood points out: 'They were too dispersed geographically and too interconnected economically with British India ever to be autonomous; moreover, their political backwardness and vulnerability to agitation had virtually sealed their fate before negotiations on their future began.'[33] It is unarguably to their credit that Mountbatten, Menon and Patel, through their shared vision of securing the interests and territories of a new nation, achieved what they did in an astonishingly short time. But, as the coming months would prove, they had merely set the stage for the next act of this three-part drama: the redrawing of the map of newly independent India and the dismantling of the centuries-old princely order.

8

A Pawn in a Chess Game

On official maps of Pakistan, the country's eastern border beyond the Line of Control in Kashmir fades into a ghostly fog marked by the legend 'Frontier Undefined'. But that is not the only cartographic sleight of hand that differentiates it from the official map of India. A breakout at the bottom of Pakistan's includes Junagadh and Manavadar, deep within India, as part of its territory. Both states had exercised their legal right to accede to Pakistan in August 1947. Both had eccentric rulers – Junagadh's nawab was known for his massive menagerie of dogs, and Manavadar's Khan for being a hockey fanatic. Both would be coerced back into India's fold; Pakistan still refuses to recognize, seventy-five years later, that they are part of India. Dismissed at the time as a 'serio-comic' drama by the foreign press, the Junagadh spectacle, co-starring the minuscule states of Manavadar, Babariawad and Mangrol, would have serious implications for the future of Kashmir and Hyderabad.

Manavadar was tiny, just 260 square kilometres, with a population of around 35,000. Babariawad and Mangrol were even smaller. All three were surrounded by Junagadh, the premier state on the Kathiawar peninsula, with an area of 9,000 square kilometres and a population of 7 lakh, 82 per cent of whom were Hindu. Junagadh was also the home of the Somnath temple, one of the holiest places of Hindu worship in India. Rising above its walled capital were two spire-topped mountains, one sacred to the Hindus and the other to the Jains. Its jungles were the last refuge of the Asiatic lion. The state's only link to Pakistan was by sea from the port of Veraval, which was inoperable during the monsoon.

The state's ruler at the time of Independence was Mahabat Khan, a forty-seven-year-old recluse. His father had been 'an opium-sodden old man' who dealt with anyone who earned his displeasure by making them perform a 'walk the plank' ceremony from a high palace balcony on to some particularly sharp rocks below.[1] Mahabat's mother was a cocaine addict, the drug supplied by one of the palace courtiers. She arranged four marriages for her son, tracking down brides from noble families in Bhopal, Junagadh and Khokhar. Exceedingly shy, Mahabat had never attended a meeting of the Chamber of Princes. He eschewed alcohol and smoking and despised debauchery.

Set in Junagadh during the heady days following Independence, Keki N. Daruwalla's historical novel *Ancestral Affairs* describes the nawab and his begums as living in a dreamland 'floating on a magic rug', unaware that the carpet would soon be pulled out from under their feet.[2]

> Within a year you wouldn't be dealing with Political Agents in their tweed coats and neckties and haw-haw accents and talk of cricket, Hutton and Washbrook, and blighty before explaining why instead of the ten per cent of the state's revenue you were allowed to spend on family, harem and kennels, you splurged eighteen per cent. You'd now be dealing with Gujarati-speaking, paan-chewing politicians in dhotis and chappals who would be curt and demanding. While

> you gazed at their hairy shins, they would take your pants off; and the tick-off would be in some native tongue, not in understated, soft-toned Anglo-Saxon! Unbearable thought.[3]

Mahabat's all-consuming passions were breeding dogs and hunting. Estimates of the size of his menagerie ranged from 150 to 3,000. Around his palace was a series of elaborate kennels, each with its own bath, serving table, bed, attendant and telephone. An English vet was employed to look after them. The canines were carried into the palace in palanquins. Hounds from Hunza guarded his palace and were used to hunt prey. Vaghri tribals were employed to provide a constant supply of pigs, hares, foxes and jackals to the nawab's camp. Deliberately starved, the hounds would tear their prey to pieces, much to the nawab's delight.[4] His favourite pooches had diamond-studded collars, and a public holiday was declared when they mated. Mahabat was reputed to have spent Rs 3 lakh on the marriage of his favourite bitch Roshana with a handsome golden retriever named Bobby in a state ceremony attended by 50,000 guests. Roshana wore pearls around her neck while the groom's paws were bedecked with gold. The then viceroy, Lord Irwin, wisely turned down an invitation to attend.

When Mahabat was holidaying in Europe in the summer of 1947, his dewan, Bahadur Abdul Qadir, was overthrown in a palace coup and replaced by a Muslim League politician from Sind, Shah Nawaz Bhutto, the father of Pakistan's future prime minister, Zulfikar Ali Bhutto. The new dewan was soon in communication with Jinnah, who advised him to stay out of the Indian Union. Junagadh need not fear Indian threats, the Quaid reassured Bhutto. 'Veraval is not far from Karachi,' he declared, adding, 'Pakistan [would] not allow Junagadh to be stormed and tyrannised.'[5] Keeping this information under his belt, Bhutto attended Mountbatten's conclave for princes on 25 July and declared that Junagadh would make common cause with the other Kathiawar states – all of which eventually acceded to India. As days turned to weeks with no sign of the nawab signing the Instrument of Accession, Menon and Patel grew anxious. It was not until 14 August that the States Department learned of his decision – not through official channels but through a press communique:

> After anxious consideration and the careful balancing of all factors the Government of the State has decided to accede to Pakistan and hereby announces its decision to that effect. The State is confident that its decision will be welcomed by all loyal subjects of the State who have its real welfare and prosperity at heart.[6]

For Junagadh to join Pakistan flipped on its head the basic principle on which partition had been agreed, namely, that only states contiguous to the new dominions should consider joining India or Pakistan. Geography, religion and economic interests went counter to Junagadh's decision. Rather than accept its accession immediately, Pakistan stalled. When the Indian government telegraphed Pakistan's new prime minister, Liaqat Ali Khan, to ask about his country's intentions with regard to Junagadh, it got no reply. A follow-up enquiry was similarly ignored. The waiting game was partly practical and partly strategic. To embrace Junagadh would have been an administrative nightmare for Pakistan. Except for its coastline, it was surrounded on three sides by Hindu states. Its main port, Veraval, was 325 nautical miles from Karachi. The state itself was a topographical jigsaw puzzle. Fragments of other states were embedded in Junagadh, and fragments of Junagadh were implanted in other states. An arm of Junagadh sliced through Baroda, cutting it off from the sea.

As a pawn in the chess game being played out over Hyderabad and Kashmir, however, Junagadh was invaluable. If India acquiesced to its accession of choice, based on the legal right of the ruler to decide which dominion to join, it would set a precedent for another Muslim prince ruling a Hindu-majority state, namely, Hyderabad, to do so. Not recognizing the accession would mean playing into Pakistan's hands, as it would give it every right to say no to the Hindu ruler of Muslim-dominated Kashmir opting for India. If India agreed to a plebiscite on Junagadh's future, which it was sure to win, the pressure to allow the Kashmiris to vote on their future would be hard to resist. There were other considerations at play. If Junagadh and Manavadar acceded to Pakistan, it would be a blow to the prestige of the new Indian government. It would also erode the confidence of the other princely states, especially neighbouring ones, in India's ability to honour its commitments.

As New Delhi waited for Pakistan's response, Defence Minister Baldev Singh requested Rear Admiral J.T.S. Hall, India's naval chief, to begin patrolling the port of Veraval and searching boats to prevent ammunition from being smuggled in from Pakistan. Hall was reluctant to do so because it was 'perfectly legitimate' for Junagadh, in accordance with Commonwealth conventions, international maritime laws and Joint Defence Council agreements, to import arms from Pakistan, and 'the only circumstances in which such importation could be checked [was] if the arms were exported from India or carried in a ship on the Indian register'.[7] An angry Menon brushed aside Hall's reservations, declaring: 'Junagadh is a state which proposes to accede to Pakistan . . . Import into Junagadh of large quantities of arms without the knowledge of [New Delhi] will be a direct threat to the . . . whole of Kathiawar.'[8] Patel also wanted a more hard-line approach. On 6 September, Bhutto telegraphed Karachi to say that Pakistani intelligence sources in Rajkot had received information that the Sardar had ordered 5,000 Gurkha troops backed by tanks and artillery to invade the tiny state of Babariawad and take up position on Junagadh's border.[9] There was no truth to the report, but it rattled Bhutto. 'If Pakistan is unable to come to our rescue at this critical moment,' he cabled Liaqat, 'we shall be finished.'[10]

Finally, on 13 September 1947, after two reminders from India and a personal appeal from Bhutto asking it to declare its stand, Pakistan officially recognized the accession of Junagadh and Manavadar. In an official statement, it dismissed as nonsense the suggestion that the accessions were a threat to the other Kathiawar states. It also stated it was willing to discuss 'conditions and circumstances wherein a plebiscite should be taken by any state or states' as long as India withdrew its troops from the borders of Junagadh.[11] The statement was clearly designed to get India to agree to a plebiscite in Kashmir while Hari Singh was still dithering about his state's future. Five days later, Jinnah warned Mountbatten in a telegram: 'Any encroachment on Junagadh sovereignty or its territory would amount to hostile act. Kindly ensure that Indian Dominion troops or troops of States acceding to India do not violate Junagadh territory under any pretext whatsoever.'[12] Mountbatten responded to Jinnah's missive on 22 September by pointing out that 'Each acceptance of accession by Pakistan cannot but be regarded by Government of India as an encroachment on India's sovereignty, and territory, and inconsistent with friendly relations that should exist between two Dominions.'[13] Such verbal protests did little to placate the rulers of the neighbouring states in Kathiawar, notably Nawanagar, whose Jam Saheb warned that 'unless the Government of India had the will and capacity to prevent Junagadh from going over to Pakistan, the confidence of the Princes as a whole in the value of their own Accession Instruments would be shattered; and the position of Kathiawar states would be particularly seriously jeopardised'.[14]

Like Patel, Menon wanted India to intervene militarily, but Mountbatten cautioned that any intervention would be seen as an act of war against what was now Pakistani territory. 'My own position was singularly difficult . . . For the Governor-General of a Dominion to have acquiesced in action which might lead to a war with another Dominion would have been completely unprecedented,' he informed London.[15] There were also practical considerations. The bulk of the Indian Army was involved in mopping up the mess of Partition and had few resources to spare. Moreover, as Alan Campbell-Johnson pointed out, all three armed forces' commanders were British officers, making it 'impossible for any of them to take part in a war . . . or to be the instrument of planning or conveying orders to others should the operations now contemplated result in such a war'.[16]

On 17 September, Mountbatten attended a cabinet meeting to consider the Junagadh crisis. Patel and Nehru were adamant that military action was the only answer. Coming from Gujarat, Patel was keen to avoid making India look weak over the Junagadh issue. In Menon's opinion, nothing less that the honour of those who had negotiated the Instruments of Accession with Indian states was at stake. Rather than sanction military action, the meeting decided to 'suitably dispose' around Junagadh troops from India and the neighbouring princely states. Ismay was against even such a limited response. 'Great wars often grow out of very small incidents. It is therefore essential to proceed in the most careful language, along certain recognized channels,' he told Mountbatten.[17]

The governor general, meanwhile, still suspected that the Junagadh crisis was a well-laid trap by Pakistan. His suspicions were vindicated a few days later at a meeting with Liaqat Ali Khan.

'He used one phrase . . . I considered of considerable significance. This was: "All right. Go ahead and commit an act of war and see what happens."'[18] Meanwhile, nerves were beginning to fray in Delhi, with Patel telling Nehru that he intended to resign unless the cabinet 'backed his aggressive policy against Junagadh'. For Patel, Junagadh was a matter of patriotism and prestige. He was a proud Gujarati. To lose a part of his home region to a Muslim-dominated Pakistan would never be allowed under his watch.

As the war of bluster continued, Junagadh's nawab sent his ragtag army to midget-sized Babariawad, which it considered a vassal state. Three days earlier, on 18 September, while on an otherwise fruitless visit to Junagadh, Menon had met with the rulers of Babariawad and Mangrol, another pocket-sized principality that Mahabat claimed as being part of his state. Initially, both rulers declared their accession to India, but Mangrol's sheikh suddenly wilted and reneged, claiming he had not even 'one hour to ponder over [the] matter'. Not rescinding the Instrument of Accession, he decided, 'might lead to some serious and grave consequences'.[19] Menon's response was to ignore the sheikh's withdrawal. Junagadh's rights over both the territories, he insisted, had lapsed with the transfer of power.

Despite comprising less than fifty villages each and, in the words of Hastings 'Pug' Ismay, 'a total annual revenue about large enough to keep a sparrow', Mangrol and Babariawad would consume a disproportionate amount of time and energy over the coming weeks, with Mountbatten at one point wanting to refer Junagadh's occupation of these 'two ridiculous little principalities' to the UN Security Council.[20] More ominously, Patel issued the very real threat of bringing down the government if the Indian Army did not retake Babariawad. The dominion of India, he thundered, must show it 'was not afraid of Pakistan or their machinations and did not intend to be bluffed by Mr Jinnah'.[21] India's service chiefs – and Mountbatten – had other ideas. An invasion of Babariawad, which was so small they had difficultly locating it on a map, could spark a very big war. British officers commanded the armies of both dominions, and if they did not agree with their respective government's orders, they could refuse to carry them out. An aggravated Patel threatened to resign in twenty-four hours if Nehru did not stand up to these foreign commanders. After all-night negotiations chaired by Mountbatten, a compromise was reached. Indian troops would be deployed – not to Junagadh itself but to its borders. The state forces of Nawanagar, Bhavnagar and Porbandar were put under Indian command, ready for action but under strict orders not to violate Junagadh territory.

In response to the escalating crisis, people from Junagadh and other parts of Kathiawar who were currently living outside the states gathered in Bombay and formed, with Patel's encouragement, a government-in-exile known as Arzi Hukumat, with Samaldas Gandhi, a nephew of the Mahatma and a native of Junagadh, as its president. Samaldas immediately started raising money in Bombay and elsewhere for arms and ammunition and recruiting Sikh irregulars in Lucknow, Kanpur and Allahabad. His resolve to use force to end the Junagadh crisis received his uncle's support: 'You must do what your conscience tells you is right. I quite agree that you should liberate Junagadh,' the Mahatma told him.[22] Samaldas's requests for recognition and assistance from the Indian government, however, were turned down, on the grounds that such support would be tantamount to an act of war by India. Undeterred, Samaldas's Sikhs marched to Rajkot, capturing Junagadh House in late September and then proceeded to the state's border. Reports from Rajkot stated that a 700-strong Muslim Home Guard was being formed in the villages of Junagadh. Indian military intelligence, meanwhile, thwarted the importation of boxes of ammunition and petrol from Pakistan at Veraval port.

On 30 September, Nehru and Mountbatten met with Liaqat Ali Khan. Nehru told his Pakistani counterpart that although India objected to the nawab's accession, it was willing to accept the verdict of a general election, plebiscite or referendum in Junagadh. Mountbatten added an assurance that if the need arose, Nehru would apply the principle to other states too, whereupon, in the governor-general's words, 'Pandit Nehru nodded his head sadly. Mr Liaqat Ali Khan's eyes sparkled. There is no doubt that both of them were thinking of Kashmir. Vallabhbhai [Patel] made it plain that a plebiscite in Kashmir would be conditional on one in Hyderabad.'[23] Three days later, the Defence Committee met and demanded that Junagadh's troops be withdrawn from both states. Following the meeting, Nehru sent Liaqat a sharply worded telegram: 'The only basis on which negotiations can start and be fruitful is reversion, in Junagadh, Babariawad and Mangrol to the status quo preceding the accession of Junagadh to Pakistan. The alternative to negotiation is a referendum or plebiscite by the people of Junagadh.'[24]

India was about to be checkmated. In what was seen as a classic case of 'using a small fish as a bait to catch a large one', Pakistan quickly agreed to a plebiscite.[25] With its overwhelming Hindu majority, a plebiscite would see Junagadh go to India, but it would set a precedent for such a vote in the more important state of Kashmir, which would likely go in favour of accession to Pakistan. Meanwhile, on 22 October, a small contingent of Indian police took over the administration of Manavadar on the pretext that its sheikh was importing arms from Pakistan and carrying out reprisals against Hindus in the state.

The justification for the takeover of Junagadh was made as early as on 19 October in a memo prepared by Menon and C.C. Desai of the States Department. It pointed out the weakness of the state's forces and the willingness of neighbouring rulers such as the Jam Saheb of Nawanagar to support Indian military action. The memo ended by warning that a reign of terrorism akin to martial law prevailed in the state.

> Hindus were panicky and fleeing . . . Communal conversions were being resorted to . . . Dacoits were being released and supplied with arms. Temples were desecrated, Islamic slogans raised . . . If Junagadh was not checked in time, we shall have a repetition of Punjab situation in Kathiawar, Gujarat and Bombay.[26]

By now Menon was growing increasingly impatient. A few days earlier he had told J.H.S. Shattock of the British High Commission that India was wasting time, and if it 'had acted determinedly from the outset, the whole trouble could have been cleared up within three or four days'.[27] Patel was also pushing hard for military action. 'They [Pakistan] will either have to go to war which I think they are in a position to do, or they will be exposed for the weak and blustering state that they are.'[28]

Amid reports of uprisings in several parts of Junagadh state by Hindus and with military intervention looking increasingly likely, Mahabat Khan realized his time was up. On 24 October, a convoy of Rolls-Royces carrying the nawab, his four wives, twenty-four children and eight of his prize Pekinese left the city palace for Junagadh's airfield, where a chartered plane was waiting. As the aircraft was preparing to depart for Karachi, one of his four wives suddenly remembered she had left a daughter behind in the palace and asked her husband to wait while she fetched her. The moment she left the airfield, Mahabat loaded two more canines into the plane and took off without her. Before departing, he cleaned out the treasury of every last ruby and rupee.[29] A few days later, a despondent Bhutto wrote to Jinnah: 'Our revenue [has] gone to the bottom. Food situation is terribly embarrassing . . . His Highness and the royal family have had to leave . . . Today our brethren are indifferent and cold. Muslims of Kathiawad seem to have lost all enthusiasm for Pakistan.'[30]

On 1 November, Indian troops entered Mangrol and Babariawad without a shot being fired. Four days later, a meeting of the Junagadh state council agreed to 'a complete reorientation of the State policy and a readjustment of relations with the two Dominions even if it involves a reversal of the earlier decision to accede to Pakistan'.[31] Bhutto was given the authority to begin negotiations with Samaldas to take over the government. This was opposed by the Muslim Jamiat of Junagadh, which demanded that Bhutto hand over the administration directly to the Government of India. The proposal went to N.M. Buch, New Delhi's commissioner for the states of western India and Gujarat. Neither he nor Samaldas voiced any objections. Later that evening Buch phoned Menon, who was attending a dinner with Nehru and Mountbatten to give him the news. At Mountbatten's request, Nehru and Menon drafted a conciliatory telegram to Liaqat, stating that the Government of India was acceding to Bhutto's request but would ascertain the wishes of the people of Junagadh before accepting the state de jure. Shortly after midnight, Menon went to 1 Aurangzeb Road in Delhi, woke Patel up and showed him the draft. Patel objected to the offer of a plebiscite, saying it was 'unnecessary and uncalled for'. Nehru and Menon 'were sissies to want to send any telegram at all'.[32] The telegram was sent anyway.

At 1 a.m. on 8 November, Bhutto formally invited the Indian government 'to assist Junagadh in preservation of law and order without prejudice to honourable understanding that may be arrived at by all concerned'.[33] Bhutto told Liaqat that he was acting with the support of public opinion, the authority of the state council and of the nawab himself, who had earlier given him the authority to use his 'judicious discrimination as the situation demanded'.[34] A battalion of Indian troops entered the state the following day, meeting no resistance along the way. When Junagadh's state forces were disarmed, they comprised a few hundred thoroughly demoralized third-rate infantry armed with little more than rusted lances and swords. There were only two machine guns, neither of which could fire a shot, and sixty country-made cannons, half of which were not serviceable. Six Pakistani army officers were helping the state troops in organizing the defence of the capital, as well as four navy officers. This was hardly the formidable force that Mountbatten, Patel and Menon a few days earlier insisted was making 'large-scale military preparations threatening the neighbouring states'.[35] Having handed over the administration, Bhutto flew to Karachi, later insisting he had merely asked for assistance from India to remove threats to the administration and had not authorized a full-scale occupation, comparing such a request to 'inviting a thief to tea'.[36]

On 13 November, a triumphant Patel visited Junagadh, where he addressed a crowd of 50,000 on the grounds of Bahauddin College. When he asked his audience to indicate whether they wished for the state to accede to India or Pakistan, all those present raised their hands in favour of India. 'The action of the Nawab of Junagadh would be a lesson to those who are persisting in their chimera of attachment to an authority with which they have no natural ties,' Patel told the rapturous crowd. 'The State is no property of a single individual. Paramountcy has lapsed – certainly not by the efforts of the Princes, but by those of the people.'[37] The takeover was a vindication of Menon and Patel's twin strategy of carrying a big stick, while ignoring Mountbatten's preference for a diplomatic solution. With India needing to set an example of its determination to preserve its territorial integrity, the use of force was seen by Menon and Patel as inevitable – something that Mountbatten would have privately concurred with. Noted Campbell-Johnson: 'It is the first time since the transfer of power that the Government have carried out a major act of policy without fully consulting or notifying him in advance of the event. He feels this may be due to Patel's and V.P.'s desire to spare him embarrassment.'[38]

The Muslims of Junagadh, however, found themselves in a precarious position. In a memo to Mountbatten, Nehru, Patel and others, Bhutto claimed the takeover had been accompanied by

> . . . looting, plundering to the extent of crors [*sic*] of rupees, arson, murders, rape, abductions and unimaginable wrong [*sic*] were committed . . . Notwithstanding guarantees and assurances given by Sardar Patel in unequivocal terms that, if Muslims will remain loyal, even a child's hair of Muslims will not be touched . . . mosques [and] saints' tombs have been ransacked and Holy *Quran* torn. Muslims are robbed in daytime by military under the instigation of communal elements all over the State.[39]

Bhutto also claimed that in one village seven hundred people were locked up for days in a room where seventy persons could hardly be accommodated.[40] His allegations were partly backed by the accounts of an English couple, the Tatlocks, who were asked by Indian authorities to leave Junagadh in late 1947. In a letter to her brother, Mrs Tatlock described the scenes of '[Hindus] going to Mahomedan shops, buying things and saying: "Send the bill to your Jinnah in Pakistan" . . . Crowds of wretched Mahomedans are being pushed out of their jobs.'[41] Acknowledgement of the violence also came from the Indian side. In early January, Buch wrote to S.W. Shiveshwarkar, the chief administrator of Junagadh, saying,

> . . . people seem to be taking the law into their hands . . . Our officers are not sure whether they are expected to check this and even if they are, they probably feel that it is not in their interest to do so. Incendiarism is still going on in Veraval . . . There is also a feeling that indirectly troops and police encourage certain harassments.[42]

Despite moves by Pakistan in the UN for its postponement, a plebiscite was held in Junagadh on 20 February 1948. Two days before the vote, Pakistan's foreign minister, Zafrulla Khan, made an impassioned eighty-minute speech to the UN Security Council describing India's invasion of Junagadh and the proposed plebiscite as a 'fait accompli'. He called upon Security Council members to demand that India withdraw its forces from Junagadh, restore the nawab to his position and then conduct a ballot under UN auspices.[43] When the result of the plebiscite came in, just 130 out of a total population of 7,20,000 in Junagadh and its feudatories voted to join Pakistan, against 2,22,184 votes for India.

The infinitesimally low numbers voting for accession raised questions. Douglas Brown, who covered the plebiscite for the *Daily Telegraph*, told Major A.S.B. Shah, joint secretary of the Pakistan Ministry of Foreign Affairs, that 'the Muslim population voted for India for fear of their lives. There were instances galore of electoral rigging and malpractices.' According to Shah, Brown and Jossleyn Hennessy of the *Times* interviewed Muslim members of the Praja Mandal, who told them in confidence that they were 'going to cast their votes for India because they were afraid of their lives, but they added that actually their hearts were in Pakistan'. The correspondents were given the addresses of about a hundred mosques allegedly destroyed or desecrated. They visited several of the mosques and verified the claims. Brown also reported that each voting slip had a number and the name of the voter recorded on it, thereby enabling officials to identify those who cast their ballot for Pakistan. This was explained as a printer's error.[44] Six days after the vote, Zafrulla protested to the Security Council that the plebiscite had been neither free nor fair.

Little was heard of Mahabat Khan after he went into exile in Karachi. One of the nawab's English officers, Captain Eric Markes, who accompanied him, said he felt that the 'royal family want[ed] to return to Junagadh even at the cost of being a prisoner [and] if His Highness is given a chance, this time he will be one of the best constitutional rulers'.[45] In May 1948, the *Dundee Courier* reported that the nawab had chartered a plane in England to bring two whippet puppies, one called Inkspot, to Pakistan. A breeder told the newspaper that the nawab had 600 dogs in underground air-conditioned kennels and employed vets, surgeons, canine nurses and kennel men to look after them, as well as a small army of guards to keep other dogs away. The whippets were to be used for racing on his private course.[46]

Shortly after India's takeover of Junagadh, Liaqat wrote Nehru to say that since the state had lawfully acceded to Pakistan, neither the dewan nor the nawab had the authority to negotiate a settlement with India. He accused India of acting in violation of international law, demanded the withdrawal of its troops and the handing over of the administration back to the nawab. Only if these conditions were met could Pakistan negotiate its status. When the case was taken to the UN, it was decided that the Junagadh dispute should stand over until Kashmir was resolved. Juridically, Junagadh's case is still pending.

9

The Vale of Tears

The telephone call from Kashmir's prime minister, Mehr Chand Mahajan, came at 4 a.m. on 26 October1947. Menon had hardly slept. Just a couple of hours earlier he had watched as a convoy of 300 vehicles carrying Maharaja Hari Singh and his entourage departed from Srinagar for the safety of Jammu. Mahajan sounded distressed. There were reports that tribal raiders from Pakistan had breached the city's outskirts. 'I could hardly believe it, but I had to accept his word,' Menon would tell his friend H.V. Hodson years later. Mahajan, Menon and half a dozen others crammed into a decrepit jeep, and in the predawn darkness made their way to the airport. Crowds of people thronged the terminal, desperate to get on any plane that was leaving. As they were about to board their chartered flight, Menon was stopped by a woman and her two young daughters. 'She recognised me, she said: "Mr. Menon, please, we cannot leave, but please, you take our girls with you."' The woman was in tears and her daughters crying loudly. Menon was too tired to think clearly. On an impulse he took the girls on board.[1]

As soon as their plane landed in Delhi, Menon handed over the girls to the care of one of his officials before rushing to a Defence Committee meeting chaired by Mountbatten and attended by Nehru, Patel, Baldev Singh and other senior officials. After apprising those present of what he had seen in Srinagar, he made an impassioned plea. History was about to repeat itself. Every invasion of India had been from the north. Stopping Pakistan from repeating those tactics required acting now. 'Just imagine, thousands of raiders coming right through Pakistan into Kashmir without a check. What was there to stop them in the future? Today it was Kashmir chalo, tomorrow it could be Delhi chalo. I told Mountbatten that I was quite clear that this was my position.'[2]

Mountbatten remained unmoved, clinging to his stand that there could be no military intervention until the maharaja had signed the Instrument of Accession. Nehru maintained that it was impossible to deploy so many troops at short notice. When an exasperated Mahajan threatened to fly to Lahore to seek Jinnah's terms, Nehru dismissed it as pure bluster. This was the last straw for Patel. Recalled the then Colonel Sam Manekshaw, who was present at the meeting:

> As usual Nehru talked about the United Nations, Russia, Africa, God almighty, everybody, until Sardar Patel lost his temper, He [Patel] said, 'Jawaharlal, do you want Kashmir, or do you want to give it away?' He [Nehru] said, 'Of course, I want Kashmir.' Then he [Patel] said, 'Please give your orders.' And before he could say anything Sardar Patel turned to me and said, 'You have got your orders.'[3]

For Nehru, Kashmir was 'intoxicating', 'overpowering', 'unreal', a place that 'whispers its fairy magic to the ears and whose memory disturbs the mind. How can they who have fallen under its spell release themselves from this enchantment?'[4] What India's prime minister was ignoring was that Kashmir was also, in the words of former army officer and author Lord Birdwood, a 'geographical monstrosity', based on 'political considerations [that] enclosed a completely artificial area'.[5]

Jammu and Kashmir was a state that should never have been created. Sold by the East India Company to the Dogra prince Gulab Singh in 1846 for Rs 75 lakh – the transaction commemorated annually by the giving of one horse, six cashmere shawls and 'twelve shawl goats of approved breed (six male and six female)' to the British government – it was a patchwork of unrelated tracts of different ethnicities and religions lying astride one of Asia's most sensitive fault lines. In 1947, it comprised the districts of Gilgit, Baltistan and Skardu, each with its own brand of Shia Islam; the Kashmir Valley with its Sunni Muslim majority, where Hindu Dogras and Brahmin Pandits dominated and controlled the bureaucracy and administration; the southern district of Jammu, where Muslims constituted around 60 per cent of the population (a census-proven fact that is often neglected in official Indian accounts); and, in the east, Ladakh, which was largely Buddhist and had traditionally owed its religious and political allegiance to Lhasa. Along its western and northern reaches, Afghanistan, the Soviet Union, Tibet and Chinese Sinkiang peered over icy mountain passes and borders that were at best loosely defined and often contested.

And then there was Pakistan, a newly formed state grappling with the violent aftermath of Partition, with a fledgling army and few friends to count on. The view from Delhi, one that would colour its approach to Kashmir, was that if not already a failed state, Pakistan would shortly become one. When agreeing to Partition, Mountbatten believed the division was in the best interests of India because it would 'give Pakistan a greater chance to fail on its demerits'. A 'truncated Pakistan, if conceded now, was bound to come back [to the Indian fold] later'.[6] Nehru saw an 'already a tottering state' that had no chance of surviving. Patel dismissed the idea of Pakistan as Jinnah's 'mad dream' that 'should be forgotten altogether'.[7] Control over Kashmir would give India a strategic advantage, put pressure on Pakistan's northern borders and leave India in command of the headwaters of rivers that irrigated the Punjab. Pakistan would be encircled militarily, and through Gilgit India would gain a common border with Afghanistan. Crucially, Kashmir was an ideological prize. If it went to India, it would deal a blow to Jinnah and the two-nation theory. It would also prove that the Congress could build a secular state in which a Muslim-majority province could take its place among Hindu-dominated provinces.

Behind such misguided assumptions was a false sense of security based largely on Nehruvian nostalgia. Aside from Menon's negligence in not obtaining a Standstill Agreement from Hari Singh, there was also the States Department's decision to omit Kashmir from a committee of state representatives to discuss terms of accession. When a Kashmir government representative sought Menon's guidance on choosing between India and Pakistan, he was, according to H.V. Hodson, given 'no advice in the matter, and [told] that if a formal proposal for accession was received it would be considered in the light of all the relevant matters'.[8] This complacency, which contrasts with the efforts Menon and Patel made to keep Jodhpur in the Union, would also play into the hands of Karachi, ensuring the disputed state would remain a debilitating, festering sore between the countries, with thousands of innocent civilians paying the price. As Nicholas Mansergh warned in 1958:

> There was no State in the sub-Continent the future of which, if left unsettled when the independent imperial authority withdrew, was more likely to occasion dissent between the two Dominions. The failure to concentrate more closely upon the problem it presented was destined to prove an oversight fraught with grave consequences.[9]

However, it is also true that the Kashmir imbroglio, combining geopolitical factors with geopersonal ones, was virtually unsolvable from the outset. Nehru mistakenly assumed that his close personal relationship with Sheikh Abdullah would convince the National Conference leader to accede to India. Patel, who as states minister should have been handling Kashmir, distrusted Abdullah, and to his frustration was kept mostly at arm's length from the crisis, his demands for swift military intervention ignored by those around him. Mountbatten, though notionally in favour of the state acceding to Pakistan, was ultimately swayed by Nehru's insistence that it belonged to India. As for the other main actors, Menon would prove to be an unreliable witness to the crucial question of when Hari Singh signed the Instrument of Accession. Jinnah misread the situation and failed to use his authority to control the Pakistani military and his administration. Finally, there was Hari Singh, who combined indecisiveness with total ignorance of what was at stake. Even his son Karan Singh would be forced to admit:

> It has always seemed to me tragic that a man as intelligent as my father, and in many ways as constitutional and progressive, should

have in those last years so grievously misjudged the political situation in the country. Being a progressive ruler was one thing; coping with a once-in-a-millennium historical phenomenon was another.[10]

The lapse of paramountcy on 15 August meant that Jammu and Kashmir had technically become independent for the first time since the Mughal emperor Akbar invaded the state in 1586. In many districts, Muslim League supporters celebrated by hoisting the Pakistani flag above public buildings – until they were ripped down on the maharaja's orders. 'It was a spectacle to watch streams of people from all directions in the town and its suburbs swarming towards the Post Office in order to have a glimpse of the flag of their hopes and dreams,' a resident of Baramulla reminisced.[11] The state would remain independent for just seventy-three days.

The differing narratives on the events that unfolded between August and October of 1947 pivot around the question of whether Pakistan was behind the tribal invasion of 22 October that forced Hari Singh to accede to India or whether it was the culmination of a spontaneous outpouring of support by Muslims, mostly from Pakistan's North-West Frontier Province, to help their co-religionists who were being persecuted by Hindus. There is plenty of evidence to corroborate India's assertion that sections of Pakistan's military and administration were involved in the tribal incursion – though the extent to which they controlled the raiders is debatable. Had the raiders been properly drilled and commanded, the fate of Kashmir would have been very different, and Srinagar would most probably have fallen within a week. Jinnah's misplaced optimism about the 'ripe fruit' of Kashmir falling into his lap translated into ineptitude. Not a single senior Muslim League leader visited the state in the months before Partition. Overwhelmed by the challenges arising from the creation of the new state of Pakistan, 'the Muslim League leadership, did not apply itself seriously to the Kashmir situation in the period preceding Independence Day', writes the historian Hasan Zaheer.[12]

Early warnings of the impending crisis came from the district of Poonch, where tensions had been running high since the middle of 1947. The district had been ruled by a subsidiary clan of the Dogra dynasty until 1936, when it came under the control of the Srinagar durbar. The takeover was not popular. Poonch's traditional ties were with western Punjab, which was absorbed into the new state of Pakistan. It had supplied the bulk of soldiers from Jammu and Kashmir who had served in the British Indian army in World War Two. After their decommissioning, Hari Singh refused to allow them to serve in the state forces, and instead they found themselves back on their unproductive farms, having to bear the burden of new taxes. As Richard Symonds, a Quaker who worked in the district, wrote: 'There was a tax on every hearth and every window. Every cow, buffalo and sheep was taxed and even every wife.'[13] Poonch was a tinderbox waiting to explode.

When the inhabitants of Pooch mounted a 'no tax' campaign in July 1947, the maharaja clamped down on them, ordering all Muslims to hand over their weapons. Angered by seeing those same weapons being used against them by Sikhs and Hindus from the local military garrison, the Muslims appealed to the tribes on the North-West Frontier for help. By early September, armed rebels had established a base in the Pakistani town of Murree, from where weapons from the tribal areas were smuggled across the border into Poonch. On 27 August, a local landlord, Abdul

Qayyum, gathered his supporters and launched a full-scale rebellion. Symonds wrote:

> Substantial men told me that they would never have joined such a rash enterprise but for the folly of the Dogras, who burnt whole villages where only a single family was involved in the revolt. Rapidly most of the Muslim ex-service men joined Qayyum and in six weeks the whole district except for Poonch city itself was in rebel hands.[14]

The southern district of Jammu was another powder keg. It saw some of the worst post-Partition bloodshed, with bands of armed Hindus and Sikhs together with soldiers from the maharaja's state forces attacking Muslim villages. According to Ian Stephens, editor of the *Statesman* newspaper in Calcutta, more than 5 lakh Muslims were displaced from Jammu and around 2 lakh 'just disappeared, remaining untraceable, having been butchered or died from epidemic or exposure'.[15] The violence reached its zenith on 5 and 6 November, when a Muslim convoy was set upon by members of the RSS who slaughtered men, women and children 'to the last living body'.[16] Accounts of violence organized by units of Hari Singh's army and police were carried by survivors who fled to west Punjab, only increasing demands for retribution in Pakistan. George Cunningham, governor of the North-West Frontier Province, reported: 'I have offers from practically every tribe along the Frontier asking to be allowed to go and kill Sikhs in Eastern Punjab and I think I would only have to hold up my little finger to get a lashkar of 40,000 to 50,000.'[17] With Poonch close to the major cities in Pakistan such as Rawalpindi, it was impossible for the insurrection to go unnoticed at the highest echelons in the new administration. As Cunningham noted in his diary on 6 October,

Pakistan officials were 'wink[ing] at very dangerous activities on the Kashmir border, allowing small parties of Muslims to infiltrate into Kashmir from this side'.[18] Regular military options were still limited. The Pakistan army was still commanded by British officers, who would have vetoed any cross-border action.

The geopolitics of what had until now been a two-way tussle over Jammu and Kashmir was about to undergo a fundamental change. On the morning of 13 September 1947, Patel wrote to Defence Minister Baldev Singh saying that if Kashmir decided to join Pakistan, he would accept that. By the afternoon his position had gone full circle. The trigger was the news that Pakistan had accepted Junagadh's accession. 'From that day Junagadh and Kashmir, the pawn and the Queen, became his simultaneous concerns,' writes Patel's biographer Rajmohan Gandhi:

> He would wrest the one and defend the other. He would also defend Hyderabad, to him the King on the chessboard. Had Jinnah allowed the King and the pawn to go to India, Patel, as we have seen, might have let the Queen go to Pakistan, but Jinnah rejected the deal.[19]

On 27 September, Nehru warned Patel of a 'dangerous and deteriorating' situation and that Pakistan was preparing to send infiltrators into Kashmir. With the state ill-prepared to meet these challenges head-on, it was necessary for Hari Singh to 'make friends with the National Conference so that there might be this popular support against Pakistan'.[20] Nehru was convinced that releasing Sheikh Abdullah would help bring about Kashmir's accession to

India. Two days later, Abdullah and other National Conference leaders were set free. Muslim Conference leader Ghulam Abbas and his colleagues, however, remained behind bars, prompting more protests from Pakistan, accusing India of partisanship. Shortly after his release, Abdullah held a massive rally at which he demanded 'complete transfer of power to the people in Kashmir'. The future of the state and whether it acceded to India or Pakistan must lie with its people, he insisted. If their voice was ignored 'I shall raise the banner of revolt and we shall raise a struggle.'[21] This was definitely not the rhetoric that Nehru wanted to hear. It was also a foretaste of what was to come a few years later as the two men's views on Kashmir's status became increasingly irreconcilable.

For India, the time for settling the accession question was quickly running out. By the beginning of November, much of the state would be cut off by the first snows of winter, giving Pakistan a free rein to take control. The departure of H.L. Scott, the state's British military commander, on 22 September allowed India to start asserting control and to prepare for a possible military intervention. Under Patel's instructions, and unbeknown to Nehru, Srinagar airport's wireless capacity was upgraded to extend its operations throughout the winter. Arms, ammunition and petrol were flown in, preparations were made to station Indian troops near the Jammu border, and road and communication links were expanded. Contingency planning for military aid began in early October: 'There is no time to lose if the reports we hear of similar preparation for intervention on the part of the Pakistan Government are correct,' Patel urged Baldev Singh. 'It appears that the [Pakistan] intervention is going to be true to Nazi pattern.'[22] The Kashmir government also received support from the Maharaja of Patiala, who sent over a battalion of infantry and a battery of mountain artillery from his own state forces.

Accusations that Pakistan, already charged with supporting the Poonch rebellion, was organizing an economic blockade of the border and breaching other aspects of the Standstill Agreement raised tensions further. Pakistan's defence was that truck drivers carrying goods were too frightened to make the journey because of attacks against Muslims by Sikhs and Hindus. Mehr Chand Mahajan wasn't buying the excuse and warned that if the deterioration in political and economic relations between Kashmir and Pakistan continued, 'it would be justified in asking for friendly assistance'. Understanding the statement to be referring to India, Liaqat Ali Khan responded: 'We are astonished to hear your threat to ask for assistance. Presumably meaning thereby assistance from an outside power.' Such an intervention would only lead, he warned, to a coup d'état against 'the declared and well-known will, of the State's Muslim majority'.[23]

In a belated attempt to turn the situation to Pakistan's advantage, A.S.B. Shah, joint secretary of the Ministry of Foreign Affairs, travelled to Srinagar for talks. According to Mahajan, he arrived 'with a whip in one hand and a letter of accession in the other'. Convinced that Pakistan was backing the rebellion in Poonch, the maharaja refused to see Shah, leaving Mahajan to conduct what turned out to be fruitless talks. Before he left, Shah delivered a parting shot, warning that Hari Singh's days were numbered. As Mahajan later recounted: 'I retorted bluntly that the result of such an action on the part of Pakistan would be to forcibly throw the State in the lap of India, no matter what the result.'[24]

~

In the hour before dawn on 22 October, Prithvinath Wanchoo, a divisional engineer staying in a dak bungalow at Domel, was awakened by his servant shouting '*Dushman aagaya* (the enemy has come)!' From his veranda, Wanchoo could see the village of Nalochi in flames. Caught unawares by the suddenness of the invasion, the nearby Dogra garrison had been forced to retreat to safety. The raiders were Afridi and Mahsud tribesmen from Tirah and Waziristan. The jihad against Dogra rule had begun.

The raiders moved swiftly. Numbering anywhere between 2,000 and 5,000, the armed irregulars headed towards Muzaffarabad, capturing the city and bolstering their numbers with Muslim defectors from the Jammu and Kashmir state forces. They then moved east towards Uri before seizing the Mahura power station. Karan Singh would later recall that fateful evening:

> I was left virtually alone in the palace while my father and members of the staff were attending the Darbar in the beautiful hall at the city palace on the Jhelum with its richly decorated papier mache ceiling. Suddenly the lights went out – the invaders had captured and destroyed the only powerhouse . . . After a few minutes the eerie silence was broken by the sudden, blood-chilling howl of jackals. Weirdly the cacophony rose and fell, then rose again into a mad crescendo. Death and destruction were fast approaching Srinagar; our smug world had collapsed around us.[25]

The goal of the invaders was to celebrate Eid in Srinagar on 26 October, and there is little doubt this would have been achievable had they not stalled their advance in Baramulla, where they turned on Hindus and Muslims alike, in the process delegitimizing their campaign. Arriving in the city a few days after it was liberated by Indian troops, the *New York Times* correspondent Robert Trumbull wrote a graphic description of the violence:

> This quiet city in the beautiful Kashmir Valley was left smoking, desolate and full of horrible memories by invading frontier tribesmen who held a thirteen-day saturnalia of looting, raping and killing here. The city had been stripped of its wealth and young women before the tribesmen fled in terror at midnight Friday before the advancing Indian Army. Surviving residents estimate that 3,000 of their fellow townsmen, including four European nuns and a retired British Army officer known only as Colonel Dykes and his pregnant wife, were slain.[26]

Another reporter who saw the aftermath of the carnage was *Life* magazine photojournalist Margaret Bourke-White, who was told that nervous and excited tribesmen had taken six nuns who had been sheltering in the town's hospital and lined them up to be shot.

> It was the accident that one of them had a conspicuous gold tooth that saved the sisters. One of the riflemen wanted to get that tooth, before his colleagues had a chance at it. In the scuffle that followed, one of their chiefs arrived; he had enough vision to realise that shooting nuns was not the thing to do, even in an invasion, and the nuns were saved.[27]

Bourke-White also described how 'trucks and buses would at times come back within a day or two bursting with loot, only to return to Kashmir with more tribesmen, to repeat their indiscriminate "liberating" – and terrorising of Hindu, Sikh, and Muslim villagers alike'.[28]

News of the tribal incursion reached New Delhi on the evening of 24 October, when Mountbatten was hosting a dinner in honour of the foreign minister of Siam. The same evening, a messenger dispatched from Srinagar arrived with two letters from Hari Singh. The first appealed for military help to repel the invaders; the second contained a formal offer by Kashmir to accede to India. The maharaja's plea for military intervention was considered the following morning at a meeting of the Defence Committee presided over by Mountbatten. At the meeting, General Lockhart, commander-in-chief of the Indian Army, read out a telegram from his counterpart in Pakistan, stating that 5,000 tribesmen were involved in the attack and that reinforcements could be expected. The telegram added that the invaders were just 50 kilometres from Srinagar. The Defence Committee agreed to send arms and ammunition, but Mountbatten vetoed a proposal to send in troops until Kashmir had acceded to India. To order troops into what was a 'neutral State, where we had no right to send them', he contended, would give Pakistan the green light to do the same, raising the risk of an all-out war. Even if such an instrument was signed it would be a temporary accession and be subject to 'a referendum, plebiscite, election or even, if these methods were impractical, by representative public meetings'.[29]

Menon was dispatched the same day to Srinagar to meet Hari Singh, while Abdullah flew to Delhi, where he stayed with Nehru. On arriving at the airport, Menon 'was oppressed by the stillness of a graveyard all around. Over everything hung an atmosphere of impending calamity.' He then met with Mahajan, who stressed the urgency of the situation and begged him to do something. This was followed by a meeting with Kashmir's ruler. Menon left no record of what was discussed other than to describe the ruler as being 'completely unnerved by the turn of events'. With practically no state forces left and the raiders on the outskirts of Baramulla, they would be in Srinagar in another day or two. 'It was no use harping on the past or blaming the maharajah for his inaction.'[30] His first priority, Menon states, was to get the ruler and his family to Jammu for their safety.

Hari Singh took Menon's advice, and shortly after midnight on 26 October, a convoy of 300 vehicles finally left Srinagar. It had taken that long to load them with priceless carpets, jade and marble mantelpieces ripped from fireplaces, antique furniture as well as jewels and precious ornaments that had adorned the necks of the goddesses in the state temple. The only government vehicles left behind were a broken-down bus, one aged ambulance and the barely serviceable jeep Menon would ride to the airport in the next morning.[31] Accompanied by his jeweller Victor Rosenthal and a pair of bodyguards, the maharaja did not utter a word during the entire sixteen-hour journey south across the Pir Panjal. It was only when the convoy reached the summer palace in Jammu that he said: 'We have lost Kashmir.'[32]

On the evening of 26 October, Ian Stephens found himself dining with the Mountbattens at Government House, 'startled by their one-sided verdict on affairs'. They had 'become wholly pro-Hindu'. The atmosphere was almost one of war. 'Pakistan, the Muslim League and Mr Jinnah were the enemy. This tribal movement into Kashmir was criminal folly. And it must have been well organised. Mr Jinnah, Lord Mountbatten assured me, was waiting in Abbottabad, ready to drive in triumph to Srinagar if it succeeded.' By contrast to Pakistan, India's policy towards Kashmir and the princely states had been 'impeccable'.[33]

Mountbatten's intelligence on Jinnah's whereabouts was wrong. The Quaid-i-Azam was in Karachi, unnerved by what was unfolding. When the tribal militias crossed into Kashmir, the mood in Pakistan had been far from euphoric. It was clear to many observers that the incursion would push Kashmir into the arms of India. Now that the genie had been let out of the bottle, it would

Alamy Stock Photo

Sardar Vallabhbhai Patel would be remembered as India's great unifier for spearheading the accession and integration of the princely states.

Alamy Stock Photo

V.P. Menon signing the Patiala and East Punjab States Union merging together eight princely states in May 1948. Menon as secretary of the States Department drew up the Instruments of Accession and merger agreements that brought the princely states into the Indian Union.

Alamy Stock Photo

Lord Louis Mountbatten and Jawaharlal Nehru differed in their attitude towards the princely states but shared the view that allowing them to exercise their right to independence would lead to the Balkanization of India.

Wikimedia Commons

Formed in 1921, the Chamber of Princes brought the rulers of the leading states together for the first time, but as a body for collective action it would never live up to its own expectations.

Wikimedia Commons

Muhammad Ali Jinnah offered princes such as Jodhpur's maharaja blank sheets of paper to write their own terms for acceding to Pakistan.

Alamy Stock Photo

At his address to the final meeting of the Chamber of Princes on 25 July 1947, Mountbatten delivered the rulers an ultimatum – accede or face the consequences.

Bhupinder Singh, the maharaja of Patiala and five-time chancellor of the Chamber of Princes, was accused of shocking crimes including the rape and murder of his wife.

Nawab Hamidullah Khan, the Muslim ruler of the Hindu-majority state of Bhopal was accused of creating a 'Third Front' of princes wanting independence or accession to Pakistan.

Nizam Osman Ali Khan's bid for Hyderabad to become independent after the transfer of power was brutally put down by the Indian army in September 1948.

The Hindu ruler of Kashmir, Hari Singh had the unenviable option of being overthrown by his Muslim subjects if he joined India or forfeiting the gaddi if he acceded to Muslim-majority Pakistan.

Alamy Stock Photo

The charismatic leader of the National Conference, Sheikh Abdullah became the first elected prime minister of Kashmir but would be ousted from power in 1953 for his pro-independence views.

Hanwant Singh, the young, headstrong maharaja of Jodhpur, threatened V.P. Menon with a pistol disguised as a pen when finally forced to sign his state's Instrument of Accession.

Alamy Stock Photo

Nawab Mahabat Khan's declaration that Junagadh would accede to Pakistan threatened India's unity just weeks after Independence. Khan was forced to flee his state in October 1947 fearing a popular uprising and Indian military intervention.

Wikimedia Commons

Yeshwant Rao Holkar, the maharaja of Indore, proved to be a thorn in the side of the British and then the Indian government by his refusal to toe the line on accession and the integration of his state.

Alamy Stock Photo

Maharani Gayatri Devi of Jaipur was one of dozens of royals who successfully ran for political office after Independence, often in opposition to the Congress party.

Wikimedia Commons

In December 1971, Indira Gandhi used her two-thirds majority in the Lok Sabha to amend the Constitution and abolish the privy purses, stripping the princely order of its legal status.

be difficult for Pakistan to push it back in. Confronting angry tribals bent on supporting their kin in Kashmir could have sparked a civil war, something that Jinnah was not prepared to risk. When Cunningham asked the commander of the Peshawar division to stop the tribal advance, he was told there were no formed units in the Pakistan army, and even if directed to fight, Pakistani troops would have disregarded the orders and joined the insurgents. On hearing the news of the invasion in Lahore, Faiz Ahmed Faiz, editor of the *Pakistan Times,* remarked: 'There ended the opportunity of Kashmir's accession to Pakistan. The rest is history.'[34] Phillips Talbot of the *Chicago Daily News* quotes an official describing Liaqat Ali Khan's anger on hearing that a deputy commander of the Muslim National Guards, a private army maintained by the Muslim League, had a personal hand in organizing the raiders. 'If any man should be shot, it was he. He got us involved by leading the tribesmen into Kashmir. But once the thing started . . . there was nothing to do but connive at it. I'll go further . . . there was nothing to do but give it passive support,' the official told Talbot.[35]

As for the extent of Jinnah's complicity, the most plausible account comes from Cunningham, based on information given to him by Pakistan's Defence Secretary Iskander Mirza. 'When he first heard about the tribesmen's move, [Jinnah] said: "Don't tell me anything about it. My conscience must be clear."'[36] The view from Henry Grady, the US ambassador in India, was that Jinnah could not have prevented the tribesmen from entering Kashmir even if he had wanted to. If Jinnah planned to take Kashmir by force, he would rather have waited until the weather worsened enough to deter India from flying in troops. Grady also thought that if Jinnah had planned the invasion he would have ensured that the raiders refrained from killing Kashmiri Muslims and looting their property. 'As it is, according to American correspondents returning from

Kashmir, the depredations of the raiders are so bitterly resented by Kashmir Muslims that for the time being Sheikh Abdullah's following is perhaps stronger than ever.'[37]

~

Early on the morning of 27 October, the airlift of Indian troops to Srinagar began. There were only four serviceable Air Force Dakotas available, so civilian aircraft with their seats ripped out to make room for ammunition and equipment were requisitioned. After securing the airport, the troops proceeded to push the tribals back down the Jhelum Valley. While the date for the start of the Indian counterattack is beyond dispute, controversy still rages three-quarters of a century later as to whether Hari Singh had signed the Instrument of Accession before or after the first planes touched down in Srinagar. If it could be proven that Indian forces had landed before Kashmir had acceded to India, Pakistan could argue that India had no business to intervene in a territory it had no right to be in. Menon insists that Mahajan and he went to Jammu on the afternoon of 26 October and obtained the signed Instrument from Singh that evening. Another version of the signing comes from Manekshaw, who claims that Menon told the maharaja that if he did not sign the Instrument of Accession immediately Delhi would be unable to send Indian troops to help him. Faced with this ultimatum, Singh signed the document on the evening of 25 October and Menon took it back to Delhi the next day. Manekshaw did not see the document being signed but recalled Menon coming out of the maharaja's office saying, 'Sam, we have got it!'[38]

Both these versions conflict with Karan Singh's first-hand account – that the family did not reach Jammu until the evening of 26 October and that his father had gone to sleep by the time Menon, together with Mahajan, came on the morning of 27 October. This chronology, which has the Instrument of Accession signed on the day the airlift of troops began, is supported by the official diary of Alexander Symon, Britain's acting high commissioner. Symon describes trying to see Menon before his plane departed for Jammu on the afternoon of the 26th. On reaching Palam airport, he found Menon preparing to return to Delhi because his flight had been cancelled as Jammu's airport had no night-time landing facilities. When he met with Menon later that day, he told him he would 'leave next morning for Jammu and would be returning by lunchtime'.[39] Major William Cranston, a British military attaché, confirms that Menon and Mahajan were on the same morning flight to Jammu that he caught. Cranston flew on to Srinagar and saw Dakota aircraft on the tarmac. In a letter dated 27 October, Nehru confirms Menon's visit to Jammu on that date and notes that he had returned with the signed Instrument of Accession and Standstill Agreement. If these latter accounts are true, then the instrument was signed after the Indian intervention began.[40]

According to the historian Alastair Lamb, the most likely scenario was that the instrument was drawn up at the meeting at Nehru's house and pre-dated to 26 October, ready for the maharaja to sign 'at a moment convenient to him'.[41] Lamb notes that the Instrument of Accession was not published in the 1948 *White Paper* and doubts the authenticity of the document that appeared in Patel's edited correspondence published in 1971. Other historians cite the fact that Hari Singh never suggested during his lifetime that he signed the Instrument after Indian troops landed in Srinagar. However, as the journalist Prem Shankar Jha, who published Manekshaw's account, points out, the multiple versions of events 'could not fail to create the impression that the Indian government had something to hide'.[42]

There are also questions concerning Mountbatten's strategy. If he had agreed to send in troops when Kashmir was still technically an independent state 'there would have been a greater chance of conducting a properly constituted referendum', argues Philip Ziegler, Mountbatten's official biographer, in a rare expression of criticism.

> By exaggerated legalism the Governor-General helped bring about the result he most feared: the protracted occupation of Kashmir by India with no attempt to show that it enjoyed popular support. The embittered hostility of Pakistan and the disapproval of the United Nations followed inexorably from this state of affairs.[43]

Part of the reason for Mountbatten's stand was his genuine belief that Pakistan would not commit the mistake of allowing the raiders to invade. As he explained to Larry Collins and Dominique Lapierre:

> Can you imagine the Pakistanis being so stupid as not to withdraw the tribesmen? I told Liaqat, 'All you've got to do is pull out. Have the plebiscite, and you'll win. You'll get in again. By refusing to pull out the tribesmen, you are playing into Nehru's hands. He's already got himself into trouble with his followers for risking a plebiscite on my account.[44]

On the same day that Indian troops landed in Srinagar, Jinnah ordered Pakistani troops to go into Jammu and Kashmir. But the order was vetoed by Lieutenant General Sir Douglas Gracey, the acting commander-in-chief of the Pakistan army. The Indian Army, like that of Pakistan, still included British officers and the general was not prepared to let them fight each other. The following day, the commander-in-chief of both forces, Field Marshal Claude Auchinleck, flew to Lahore and told Jinnah that sending the Pakistani army to Kashmir would spark a full-blown war. A chastened Quaid retracted his orders. A summit meeting to be attended by Mountbatten, Nehru, Jinnah, Liaqat, Hari Singh and Abdullah was hastily arranged for the following day at Lahore. Jinnah wanted an immediate plebiscite that would allow Kashmir's citizens, who were overwhelmingly Muslim, to decide which country they preferred to join. Mountbatten and Nehru were in favour of holding talks. To Patel, that reeked of a Munich-style appeasement. 'For the prime minister to go crawling to Mr Jinnah when we were the stronger side and in the right would never be forgiven by the people of India,' he declared at a cabinet meeting that evening.[45] Nehru was saved from attending the summit by coming down with fever. It was rescheduled, but on the day before the leaders were due to meet in Lahore on 1 November, Jinnah issued a belligerent statement on Kashmir's accession, terming it a triumph of 'fraud and violence'. Nehru stayed in Delhi, leaving Ismay and Mountbatten to sit through a three-and-a-half-hour haranguing by the Quaid.

By any measure, Pakistan's denial of its involvement in the tribal invasion would remain a slur on its reputation. Just prior to the Kashmir dispute being referred to the UN in early January 1948, Liaqat Ali Khan called the raiders peaceful 'Pawindah shepherds' from Afghanistan. The *Daily Telegraph*'s Douglas Brown, who had previously taken a sympathetic view of Pakistan's position on Junagadh, was aghast at the description. He wrote: 'The lorry loads of armed men whom I have seen day and night driving through that city [Rawalpindi] to Kashmir do not bear any particular resemblance to shepherds.'[46]

Evidence that Pakistan's military and administration supported the tribal invasion would come from multiple sources, the most unusual being a decommissioned US army officer, Russell K. Haight, Jr. During World War Two, Haight had served with the US Army Air Forces and fought in France. After his demobilization, he worked in several jobs, including as a reporter for the *Denver Post*. Wanderlust soon got the better of him, and in July 1947 he took a job with an American road-building company in Afghanistan. Injured in a fall from a cliff and declared unfit for work, he travelled to Rawalpindi, where he had a chance encounter with officials from Azad Kashmir, who offered him a commission with their forces. Despite not knowing a word of Urdu or Pashtu, he was put in charge of an Azad Kashmir unit on the Poonch front. In January 1948, Trumbull interviewed Haight secretly in Lahore for the *New York Times*. Wearing a 'ten-gallon hat with a bullet hole in the brim', he said he was ready to testify that Pakistan had actively supported the tribal invaders, but he also insisted that the Poonch uprising 'was a legitimate local rebellion against the Maharaja, in which a majority of the fighters are still native Kashmiris'. While leading Kashmiri Poonchis in skirmishes with the Indian Army, he learned to handle the unruly tribesmen by exploiting their vanities and tribal rivalries. He told Trumbull that petrol was supplied to the raiders by Pakistan authorities and that army personnel were running the Azad Kashmir radio station and relaying messages to Azad encampments in Pakistan. 'Uniforms, food, arms and ammunition . . . came from Pakistan Army stores through such subterfuges as the "loss" of ammunition shipments.' Tribesmen also carried arms supplied by Afghanistan, as well as Russian rifles and German Lugers and Mausers, which he believed came from Russia. He characterized the Azad Kashmir provisional government headed by Sardar Mohammad Ibrahim Khan as 'Pakistan puppets' and branded the Kashmir Freedom League based in Rawalpindi as communists – 'there wasn't an honest to God Moslem in the bunch'. As for the tribesmen, they 'were mainly interested in loot'. Trumbull agreed to wait until Haight had returned to America before publishing the article. Haight told him there had been three attempts on his life.[47]

~

When Hari Singh signed the Instrument of Accession, he may have abandoned his dream of creating a Switzerland in the East, but he had not given up his rights. The instrument explicitly stated that he would continue to enjoy 'the exercise of any powers, authority and rights now enjoyed by me as Ruler of this state'. But reality proved different. From the moment Abdullah replaced Mahajan as prime minister on 2 March, the maharaja's position became precarious. Explained Karan Singh:

> My father belonged to the feudal order and, with all his intelligence and ability, was not able to accept the new dispensation and swallow the populist policies of Sheikh Abdullah. The Sheikh, on the other hand, while a charismatic mass leader and a superb orator in Kashmiri, was imbued with a bitterly anti-Dogra and anti-monarchical attitude.[48]

For his part, Hari Singh was doing little if anything to endear himself to his people, insisting on marking his birthday with gun salutes while refusing to allow a stud farm outside Jammu to be used as a refugee relief camp. 'Meanwhile children are dying in the Jammu streets. You can imagine the public reaction to this,' Nehru complained to Patel.[49]

Taking a leaf out of the Political Department's pre-Independence playbook on how to deal with troublesome rulers, Patel suggested that a holiday away from the state for the ruler would be beneficial. The maharaja agreed, on the condition that such a step was not a prelude to abdication. Singh departed in May 1949, never to return to Kashmir. He lived out much of the remainder of his days in Bombay, where he died in 1962. His son, Karan Singh, became regent and then enjoyed a successful career as a politician in Indira Gandhi's administration. But the Dogra dynasty was gone forever.

There are three festering legacies of India's intervention in Kashmir. The first was Nehru's promise to allow Kashmiris to decide their own future. 'We have declared that the fate of Kashmir is ultimately to be decided by the people,' Nehru told the nation in a broadcast on All India Radio (AIR) on 2 November 1947. This, he insisted, was a pledge which 'we will not, and cannot back out of'. Once peace and law and order had been established, India was prepared 'to have a referendum held under international auspices like the United Nations'.[50] Among those supporting a referendum was Menon, who told the British high commissioner just prior to Nehru's announcement that the National Conference had the support of 'about 50 per cent' of the Muslim population and most Sikhs and Hindus, guaranteeing India an overall majority.[51]

If a plebiscite had been held in the months after accession it would probably have gone India's way, but this proved to be a very small window of opportunity. After a tour of Indian-held territory in July 1949, Sibbanlal Saxena, a member of the Indian Constituent Assembly, said that it was 'midsummer madness to believe we can win the plebiscite'.[52] A year later, Patel wrote to

Nehru to say that 'it appears that both the National Conference and Sheikh Sahib [Abdullah] are losing their hold on the people of the Valley and are becoming somewhat unpopular . . . In such circumstances I agree with you that a plebiscite is unreal.'[53] Asked later by a journalist why India offered a plebiscite at all when it was technically not necessary, N. Gopalaswami Ayyangar, India's representative to the UN Security Council, smiled and said: 'We hadn't much experience then.'[54]

The second legacy was Patel's clash with Nehru and Ayyangar over taking the Kashmir issue to the UN Security Council in the belief that the international community would recognize Pakistan as the aggressor. Patel mocked what he called the 'insecurity council' for 'disturbing the peace of the world'. He added that if India was released from it, the 'Kashmir problem [could end] very speedily . . .'[55] Given that foreign affairs was Nehru's responsibility, Patel may have overstepped his bounds, but his message was clear. As he told Congress parliamentarian Hari Vishnu Kamath: 'If Jawaharlal and Gopalaswami [Ayyangar] had not made Kashmir their close reserve separating it from my portfolio of Home and states, I would have tackled the problem as purposefully as I had done in Hyderabad.'[56] Ultimately, the only tangible results from the UN involvement were a ceasefire that came into force on 1 January 1949 and the demarcation of the Line of Control, which now marks the de facto border between the two countries. The ceasefire would prove contentious. 'Our forces might have succeeded in evicting the invaders, if the Prime Minister had not held them in check and later ordered the cease-fire,' General S.P.P. Thorat, the officer heading the Indian Army in Kashmir, later said. 'Obviously, great pressure must have been brought to bear on him by the Governor-General.'[57] Thorat's statement ignores the obvious question of whether the Indian Army had the means to take all of Kashmir, still one of the world's most challenging theatres of war. Referring Kashmir to the UN condemned it to smoulder as an issue in the Security Council, enabling Pakistan, as the socialist leader Jayaprakash Narayan would remark:

> . . . to rake it up every now and then . . . [H]ad the matter been handled by the Sardar . . . he would have found a satisfactory solution, and thus prevented it becoming a perennial headache for us and a cause of bitterness and animosity between India and Pakistan.[58]

The third legacy was the souring of relations between Nehru and Abdullah. To Nehru, the 'Lion of Kashmir' was a Congressman in everything but name – a popular leader, a democratic socialist, and above all a secularist. But he was no 'Frontier Nehru', and steadily became more pro-Muslim to preserve his base. The tone set by his pro-independence speech following his release from prison would grow shriller in the months and years to come. Starting with Phillips Talbot, who later became US assistant secretary of state for Near Eastern and South Asian Affairs, and continuing with other officials he met, including Loy Henderson, US ambassador to India, Warren Austin, US permanent representative to the UN, and Patrick Gordon Walker, Britain's Commonwealth secretary, his line to each of them was: 'Kashmir would be "finished" if it had to join one Dominion and thereby incur the enmity of the other.' Far preferable 'was an arrangement by which Kashmir could have normal relations with both countries' – in other words, independence.[59] In 1953, the Bombay journal *Current*, known for its pro-American sympathies, reported that the Democrat presidential nominee Adlai Stevenson had assured Abdullah during a visit to Kashmir that the US was prepared to loan the state

$US15 million if it became sovereign. Moreover, 'the Valley would have a permanent population of at least 5,000 American families, houseboats and hotels would be filled to capacity, Americans would buy Kashmiri crafts and within three years every village in Kashmir would be electrified'.[60]

When rumours started circulating that Abdullah would declare independence on 21 August 1953, the day of the Eid festival, and then seek the protection of the UN against 'Indian aggression', New Delhi moved pre-emptively. On 8 August, Abdullah was deposed as prime minister and jailed 'for conspiring against the state'. His deputy, Bakshi Ghulam Mohammad, who was complicit in his overthrow, assumed the post of prime minister. Abdullah would remain in jail without formal charges being laid until January 1958. So rapturous was the Kashmiri public's reception to him when he was released that he was arrested just three months later, this time for conspiring with Pakistan to break up India. The 'Lion of Kashmir' would not return to political office until 1975, by which time he was seventy years old. Bakshi, who left school when he was in class eight, stayed in power for a decade and is remembered today as the most ruthless and corrupt chief minister Kashmir has ever known – his reign setting the stage for years of repression, dysfunction and increasing alienation of the Kashmiri population from the rest of India.

On 23 July 1948, Menon met with officials from the US Embassy in Delhi. He told them the Government of India was willing to accept a settlement of the Kashmir dispute based on the ceding of the districts of Mirpur, Poonch, Muzaffarabad and Gilgit to Pakistan. As for the Kashmir Valley, its future would be determined by a plebiscite and India would be willing to withdraw all Indian troops from the Valley while it was being held. India's only qualification was that Pakistan withdraw from the areas it now occupied. 'He said that the Government of India would not take advantage of such a withdrawal by sending Indian troops into the areas concerned and that, if the cease-fire order should break down, Indian troops would not take advantage of the withdrawal of the Pakistan troops to enter the area.'[61]

Menon's chance to be the champion of reason came too late. The opportunity for holding a plebiscite had passed and is unlikely to ever present itself again. The near-impossible precondition of a Pakistani withdrawal gives India an excuse to renege on its commitment indefinitely. Similarly, decades of brutal repression means that the chances of the state's population voting for accession to India are almost zero, further diluting the promises made by Nehru more than seventy years ago.

10

The Killing Fields

Osman Ali Khan knew his state was special. If Hyderabad had not sided with the British during the Mutiny, the tide of rebellion might have overwhelmed the East India Company's armies. And without its support in sending men and material, the fate of numerous battles fought in the muddy trenches of the two world wars might have gone against the Allies. When Turkey's rulers sided with the Axis powers during World War One and issued an appeal to Muslims in India and elsewhere to revolt against the imperialist powers, the nizam had to choose between supporting the Ottoman caliph, who was the spiritual head of Islam, and declaring his allegiance to the Crown. To the relief of the British, he issued a manifesto calling on all Indian Muslims to remain loyal to the Allied cause. For this he was rewarded with the title of 'His Exalted Highness' and confirmed with the appellation of 'Faithfull Ally of the British Government'. Such flattery did not take long to wear off. After the war, he decided that being known as His Exalted Highness had little meaning and that he should instead be given the title of 'King'.

The negotiations with Hyderabad, conducted primarily by Mountbatten, Nehru and Menon between August 1947 and June 1948, were long and tortuous. Mountbatten's account of them in his final dispatch to the king as governor-general ran to more than 27,000 words, with Menon's about the same length. Several times during these months, agreements were frustrated by last-minute brinkmanship on the part of the nizam, spurred on by the nationalist Ittihad ul-Musslimeen (IUM) and its fanatical leader Kasim Razvi.

An ex-lawyer from Uttar Pradesh, Razvi had taken over the IUM from Bahadur Yar Jung, who died suddenly in 1944, the apparent victim of a poisoned hookah. Jung had founded the IUM in 1928 as a social service organization. By the beginning of 1948, it had 9 lakh members, of whom at least 1 lakh were trained as paramilitary volunteers known as Razakars. Menon would later describe Razvi as a man 'with gleaming eyes' and 'a beard which he sported beneath a fez worn at a rakish angle. The moment he started talking I could see that his was a fanaticism bordering on frenzy.'[1] Others in the Indian government referred to him as 'the Nizam's Frankenstein monster'. A powerful speaker, he used his public rallies to protest submission to Indian rule in any form. 'Death with the sword in hand is always preferable to extinction by a mere stroke of the pen,' he told his followers. The waters of the Bay of Bengal, he promised, would wash the feet of the nizam. 'We are the grandsons of Mahmood Ghaznavi and the sons of Babur. When determined, we shall fly the Asaf Jahi Flag on the Red fort.' Every Razakar had taken a vow in the name of Allah to 'fight to the last to maintain the supremacy of Muslim power in the Deccan'.[2] In their quest, Razvi and his stormtroopers had drawn sustenance from Jinnah's promise that if Congress 'attempted to exert any pressure on Hyderabad, every Muslim throughout the whole of India, yes, all the hundred million Muslims, would rise as one man to defend the oldest Muslim dynasty in India'.[3]

The first of these showdowns occurred on 12 August after the two-month grace period allowed by Mountbatten to the indecisive nizam had expired. In contrast to his involvement in Junagadh, Patel took a hands-off approach to Hyderabad – at least in the early stages of the crisis. 'You are dealing with a fox. I do not trust that fellow, the Nizam. I think he will let you down,' he told Nehru. 'Nevertheless, as you say that you are going to deal with him, I will keep off and let you handle this problem yourself.'[4] At Menon's suggestion, a Standstill Agreement was drawn up, which Mountbatten hoped would be close enough to an Instrument of Accession to satisfy all parties. On 25 October, Khan gave his oral consent to the agreement, but then, as usual, procrastinated. To break the impasse, Mountbatten rang the nizam's legal adviser, Walter Monckton, who was in Hyderabad. The two men spoke in French, in case the call was tapped. The line was bad and the call was periodically interrupted by Mountbatten's son-in-law John Brabourne informing him he had just become a grandfather. The secrecy was unnecessary. In the early hours of 28 October 1947, thousands of IUM supporters surrounded the houses of Monckton and the two other delegates of the negotiating team, the Nawab of Chhatari and Sir Sultan Ahmed, threatening to burn them down unless Khan promised to jettison the agreement. When the nizam conferred with the delegates later that day, Razvi burst into the meeting and called for the agreement to be torn up and for fresh negotiations with Delhi. The delegates immediately submitted their resignations. 'The problem of Hyderabad can rarely have seemed more intractable,' Ziegler writes.[5]

On 31 October, a delegation led by Moin Nawaz Jung, Hyderabad's minister for police and information, arrived in Delhi to hammer out a new Standstill Agreement that would be more acceptable to the IUM. But the delegation found Mountbatten, Nehru and Menon steadfast in their refusal to change a single word, and the agreement was signed unaltered on 27 November 1947. This represented a defeat for the nizam, who by now had lost the confidence of the Government of India, and of Patel in particular. The fact that India was prepared to settle for a mere Standstill Agreement also represented a considerable concession, as its policy until now had been 'no accession, no standstill'. It was Menon who stressed the need for compromise. The situation in Junagadh and Kashmir had clearly frayed his nerves. Fearful that the army might not be able to control the communal situation, a Standstill Agreement would at least buy some much-needed time. It didn't. Both sides would violate the terms of the agreement – Hyderabad by secretly lending Rs 20 crore to Pakistan, supporting the Razakars and interfering with road and rail traffic at its borders, and India by launching a semi-official economic blockade that Monckton decried as coercive.

As Khan's control over the course of events in Hyderabad slipped further out of control, reports of Razakar atrocities gained nationwide attention. In February 1948, G. Ramchar, a Congress MP serving in Prime Minister Laik Ali's cabinet, resigned after making the alarming declaration that in Hyderabad 'arson, loot and murder formed the normal events of the day . . . Village after village was burnt down.' The goal of the Razakars, he said, was to establish an 'Islamic State'.[6] The violence was also turning communal. On 22 May, newspapers reported that a Muslim mob had attacked Hindus travelling by train at Gangapur station, killing at least two and seriously wounding eleven as armed Razakars and Hyderabad policemen looked on.

Not everyone took these reports at face value. Maurice Cheesewright, the correspondent for the *Daily Express*, travelled to Gangapur station to interview survivors. He found that no Hindus had been killed or injured, though there had been a reprisal attack at the station following the murder of three Muslims the day before. He blamed what he termed 'fabricated reports' on K.M. Munshi, the India-appointed agent to Hyderabad, a close ally of Patel's and 'the most hated Hindu in Hyderabad'. 'The stories of attacks on Hindus, eagerly and naively reported by the Indian Press, nearly all came from the big house in Bolarum, ten miles from Hyderabad city, where Munshi used to curl up on a water-cooled verandah to gather tittle-tattle from his own political agitators,' Cheesewright reported.[7] Exaggerated or not, the press coverage spread enough fear for thousands of Hindus to flee Hyderabad. At the same time, large numbers of Muslims from the Central Provinces arrived in Hyderabad, mistakenly believing they would be safer there.

~

Shortly after returning in mid-March from a visit to Burma, Mountbatten discovered that plans had been drawn up by the Indian government for a military invasion of Hyderabad, codenamed 'Operation POLO'. His first reaction was one of disbelief – that a military plan had been named after his beloved sport. 'It could hardly have been better calculated to add insult to injury to me personally,' he wrote to King George VI.[8] When questioned, Nehru insisted that it was no more than a contingency plan in case of a massacre of Hindus in Hyderabad. Mountbatten was not convinced and told Nehru that if an invasion were to take place he would take 'an extremely poor view of any such action'. Adding fuel to the fire were newspaper reports that appeared after Nehru addressed an AICC meeting in Bombay on 24 April, headlined 'War or Accession'. According to the reports, Nehru told the Committee:

> There are two courses now open to Hyderabad – war or accession. War is a prolonged affair, and if we resort to it, many new problems may arise. We have therefore been trying to solve this problem by negotiation, but that does not mean we are afraid of following the path of war.[9]

When questioned by Mountbatten, Nehru insisted that the reports had misquoted from his speech, given in Hindi. For the prime minister, an invasion was the last resort, especially as a large part of India's army was tied up in Kashmir. But his patience was wearing thin, particularly after the rejection by the nizam one day earlier of the latest compromise offer – a four-point plan to introduce responsible government.

After attending a meeting of the Defence Committee in mid-May, Mountbatten summarized Nehru and Menon's attitude to military intervention as follows:

> It is rather the prestige of the Government backed by potential armed action which keeps the people in order. We believe that at the moment the prestige of the Government is sufficiently high for us to take action against Hyderabad and to maintain internal law and order at the same time. If the Government delays action against Hyderabad much longer, then its prestige will fall to such an extent that no amount of troops will be sufficient for internal security.[10]

In reality, blueprints had already been drawn up for an invasion. In late April, Patel ordered the stationing of an armoured division in Pune district and the construction of airstrips close to Hyderabad's borders to enable movement of troops. According to Nehru's principal private secretary, H.V.R. Iyengar: 'There were only three people who knew, apart from Sardar, that the date had been fixed. One was V.P. Menon, the other was H.M. Patel (Defence Secretary), and the third was myself.' The date set for the invasion was 13 September 1948.[11]

To compound what was an already volatile situation, a simmering communist insurgency in Telangana was intensifying. 'The incidents now occurring [in Telangana] are not sporadic outbursts but betray a carefully laid plan which is usually executed with ease and impunity,' a March 1948 intelligence report read. 'Communist bands numbering anything from 500 to 2000 and armed not only with guns and rifles but with automatic weapons have in several instances emerged victorious from their encounters with the police and are emboldened in consequence.'[12] So desperate was the nizam to broaden his support base that he took the unprecedented step in early May of lifting the ban on the Communist Party.

Laik Ali, the prime minister of Hyderabad, spent long evenings with Menon trying to hammer out a new agreement that would settle the crisis. 'While V.P. had at least the satisfaction of liberally and continuously moistening his throat with large doses of sherry, there was nothing corresponding that I could use for the lubrication of my ear drums,' he lamented.[13] He also met regularly with Nehru, who seemed to be taking a back seat in the negotiations and, rather than focusing on Hyderabad, spoke of the impact of the 'atomic age on civilization' and 'theories on human emotions'. When Laik Ali complained about the unofficial Indian economic blockade of his state, Nehru 'burst out in fury', saying that if Hyderabad refused to accede, he would make it impossible even for a blade of grass to enter the state. 'He then worked himself up to a high pitch of excitement and snapping his fingers in my face added, "I shall reduce Hyderabad to smithereens." I had never before been so abjectly conscious of the physical weakness of Hyderabad against the military might of India,' Laik Ali wrote later.[14]

With a little over a month to go before he was due to depart from India on 21 June, Mountbatten stepped up his efforts to find a solution to the Hyderabad crisis, holding talks with Laik Ali and inviting the nizam to New Delhi. When Laik Ali remonstrated, saying the nizam would rather be shot than accede to India, Mountbatten retorted: 'If Hyderabad was occupied by an Armoured Division there would be very little shooting.'[15] Instead of travelling to the Indian capital, the nizam proposed that Mountbatten visit Hyderabad. The governor-general declined, and instead sent Alan Campbell-Johnson. The press attaché's mission achieved little, but his report provided an extraordinary insight into the state of mind of the two main players in the Hyderabad drama. The nizam was in a mood of 'aggressive fatalism' and was 'ready to perform a "Samson Act"' on the Government of India. 'In other words, if he goes under, full preparations have been made to ensure that the political and social structure of the State should go under with him,' Campbell-Johnson wrote in his report. He also met with Razvi, whom he described as 'a complete fanatic'.

> He looks at you with eyes that bore holes into you, but one cannot help feeling that there is about him a streak of absurdity and charlatanism which makes it difficult to take him completely seriously, even while he is talking, and one gets the firm impression that his megalomania has far outrun his real power.[16]

As tensions – and the possibility of Indian military intervention – grew, the nizam's government realized it needed to bolster its armed forces. When asked by Monckton how long his forces could hold out against a full-blown Indian attack, General Syed Ahmed El Edroos, the commander of Hyderabad's army, replied. 'Not more than four days.' When asked the same question, the nizam responded: 'Not more than two.'[17] So, when a lanky blue-eyed Australian named Sidney Cotton offered to use his skills as a pilot to ferry in arms from Pakistan, he was welcomed with open arms and an open chequebook. The son of a Queensland cattle farmer, Cotton had a colourful background, ranging from seal-spotting and searching for lost explorers in Newfoundland to pioneering aerial photography in the run-up to World War Two. Posing as a businessman, he met Goering and other high-ranking Nazis and took them for joyrides while secretly filming German airfields, bridges and fortifications. Cotton had arrived in Hyderabad in early 1948 to investigate the possibility of exporting peanuts to the US. After seeing first-hand the effects Indian economic sanctions were having against a 'friendly and defenceless state', he was taken to meet Laik Ali. Cotton asked him 'if his government was prepared to spend £20 million to remain free'. Hyderabad's prime minister replied: 'You need not ask that question. The cost will not be counted.'[18] Cotton agreed to supply 500 tonnes of machine guns, grenades, mortars and anti-aircraft guns. He bought five second-hand Lancaster bombers that had been converted into civilian aircraft and hired eight three-man crews. The airlift of arms began in early June. In the end, most of what he transported would never be used.

On 25 May, with just weeks to go before he stepped down as governor-general and left India, Mountbatten summoned Menon to his office. The two talked well past midnight, workshopping ideas for what would be the Government of India's last attempt at a negotiated settlement of the Hyderabad problem. As he had done a year earlier in Simla, when tasked with drawing up the partition of India, Menon worked till dawn, chain-smoking to keep himself awake, to draft a solution. Named the Heads of Agreement, Menon's document contained eleven points that Hyderabad had to accept as a prerequisite for a settlement with India, including a plebiscite to determine the question of accession, the introduction of responsible government following the establishment of a Constituent Assembly elected on a 60 per cent non-Muslim basis and a cabinet with the same ratio. India would have the power to override legislation passed by the Assembly and Indian troops could be stationed within the state if India constitutionally declared a state of emergency. Osman Ali Khan would also agree to disband the Razakars.

Before the agreement could be presented to the nizam, it needed Monckton's approval and Patel's signature. Neither would be easy. Patel was recovering from a severe heart attack. He was also bitterly opposed to the concession on non-Muslim representation in a state that was 90 per cent non-Muslim, and, as he wrote to Nehru, 'sorely disappointed that after so much profitless discussion with so many Hyderabadi delegations, we are still thinking of producing formulas for their acceptance'.[19] Patel's anger was vindicated when Monckton refused to accept the Government of India's right to override legislation and a Constituent Assembly with a non-Muslim majority.

On 13 June, Mountbatten travelled to Dehra Dun where Patel was convalescing for a farewell luncheon. The Heads of Agreement he was carrying had been redrafted by Monckton to dilute the provision for overriding legislation and left out any reference to the composition of the Constituent Assembly. Patel refused to accept it. In H.V. Hodson's account of what happened next, Mountbatten was preparing to say goodbye for the last time when Patel asked: 'How can we prove to you our love and gratitude?' The governor-general replied: 'If you are sincere, sign this document.' 'Does agreement with Hyderabad mean so much to you?' Patel asked. 'Yes, because India's good name is at stake.' Patel then initialled the draft and embraced Mountbatten with tears in his eyes.[20] Menon was also travelling to Dehra Dun, but a delayed flight meant he got there after Mountbatten. As he later told the charge d'affaires at the US Embassy in Delhi, had he been the first to brief Patel he would have advised him not to approve the agreement. Mountbatten's obsession with 'obtaining another feather in his cap' by settling the Hyderabad problem had clouded his judgement.[21] Neither Menon nor Mountbatten nor Monckton realized that the Sardar was a step ahead of them: He had agreed to initial the Heads of Agreement knowing that the nizam would never accept it.

He was right. Khan demanded more concessions. Nothing could move him – not even a final appeal from Mountbatten reminding him that if he compromised he could go down in history 'as the peacemaker of South Asia and as the Saviour of your State, your dynasty and your people'.[22] On 17 June, at 1.15 p.m., after trying his best to change the nizam's stand, Monckton sent Mountbatten a telephone message with the single word: 'Lost'.[23] Boarding his plane at Delhi airport for the flight back to England, India's last viceroy and first governor-general turned to K.M. Munshi and said, 'I have had many jolts in my life, but never have I received such a shock as was given me by these people of Hyderabad.'[24]

~

If the Indian government needed a pretext for an invasion, it did not have far to look. Cotton's gun-running was one. The Australian claimed that he was merely conducting 'mercy flights' laden with medical supplies for hospitals hit hard by India's economic blockade. The Hyderabad government declared that it regarded his activities as 'an unsolicited gesture of sympathy'.[25] Meanwhile, armed clashes between Razakars and Indian troops in late July near Nanaj inside Hyderabadi territory led to the army capturing the village. Around the same time, P.V. Joshi, the commerce and industries minister in the Laik Ali government, resigned after claiming that Hyderabad police had joined the Razakars in looting, murder, arson and rape. In July, Patel ordered the confiscation of arms from all Muslim licensees in the province, even while weapons were being distributed to Hindus. With his backing, Congress party units from Hyderabad and the neighbouring states launched reprisal raids against the Razakars and their supporters. A pamphlet issued by the state Congress in Bombay in August 1948 claimed its militants had damaged railway lines at thirty-five different places, derailed two trains, set government buses on fire, blown up several bridges and railway stations and exploded five bombs near police stations in Hyderabad state. They also claimed to have killed 42 police officials, 205 constables, 361 Razakars, and 36 'Rohilas & Arabs' for the loss of just 17 'martyrs'.[26]

On 31 August 1948, India's new governor-general, C. Rajagopalachari, wrote to the nizam demanding that he ban the Razakars and allow the Government of India to station troops at Secunderabad to restore security in the state. Khan responded to say that allowing Indian troops into his territory was 'out of the question'. Meanwhile, rumours spread that millions of Indian Muslims would rise up and Pakistan would declare war if India invaded. The *Times* reported that Hyderabad's army had been strengthened to 40,000 soldiers and bolstered by supplies of arms, including anti-tank weapons. Laik Ali was quoted as saying: 'If the

Union government takes any action against Hyderabad, 100,000 men are ready to join our army. We also have 100,000 bombers in South Arabia ready to bomb Bombay.'[27]

Events now moved quickly. By the end of August, the Indian Army had almost surrounded Hyderabad. As the generals waited for their orders, Patel worked on the messaging. What would be a full-scale military operation would be known as 'Police Action'. It was not about Hyderabad's refusal to merge with the Union, but about solving the deteriorating and increasingly communal law-and-order situation. Addressing the Constituent Assembly in early September, Patel declared: 'The campaign of murder, arson and loot going on in Hyderabad rouses communal passion in India and jeopardizes the peace of the Dominion . . . We are therefore intimidating the Nizam accordingly.'[28]

Even at this late stage, Nehru was opposed to sending in the army, prompting an angry outburst at a meeting of the Defence Committee of the cabinet attended by Patel, Menon, Maulana Azad and Baldev Singh, the defence minister. According to two accounts of the meeting, one by Munshi and the other by the senior bureaucrat and Menon confidant M.K.K. Nayar, Nehru lashed out at Patel for his attitude towards Hyderabad. In Nayar's account, Nehru turned to Patel and said: 'You are a complete communalist and I'll never be a party to your suggestions and proposals.' Both writers recall Patel sitting in silence and then walking out of the room. The episode so shocked Patel that he had a heart palpitation and had to be put on oxygen. 'I thought, looking at him [Nehru], either he was mad, or I was a criminal . . . My blood was boiling,' Menon later recalled. He had had enough. He hurriedly drafted a letter of resignation and sent it to Nehru explaining that if that was the way he felt, there was no point in his being in the states ministry. Nehru apologized. Menon stayed on as the ministry's secretary.[29]

For India, the final straw would be Hyderabad's decision to refer the dispute to the UN. On 24 August, Zahir Ahmed, Hyderabad's external affairs representative, formally asked the Security Council to mediate. Ahmed's letter referred in detail to India's campaign of intimidation, threats of invasion and other breaches of the Standstill Agreement. The matter was included in the Security Council's agenda for 16 September.

At 4 a.m. on 13 September 1948, Indian troops poured into Hyderabad.[30] Although the three-pronged attack by forces under the command of Lieutenant General Maharaj Rajendrasinghji had been expected for weeks, Hyderabad's army appeared to be totally unprepared. Its maps were outdated and the bulk of the arms and ammunition Cotton had transported remained in the military godowns. Thousands of Razakars using crude guns, spears and stones were no match against Indian Army tanks. At 4.18 p.m. on 17 September, Laik Ali announced Osman Ali Khan's capitulation in a radio address: 'Early this morning the Cabinet felt that there was no point in sacrificing human blood against heavy odds.' He urged Hyderabad's 1.6 crore inhabitants to accept the surrender 'with courage and tolerance'.[31] Shortly afterwards, Laik Ali and members of his cabinet were arrested, along with Razvi, but Khan was allowed to remain free. Razvi would be sentenced to seven years' imprisonment. Laik Ali escaped from prison on 6 March 1949 and fled to Pakistan disguised as a woman. Hyderabad was now part of India.

The swiftness of the Indian victory is reflected in the official figures, which cited 1,273 Razakars and 807 soldiers of the Hyderabad state army as killed, as against just ten fatalities on the Indian side. There was no mention of civilian casualties, either directly as a result of the invasion or during the reprisals that followed. In his book *The Story of the Integration of the Indian States,* Menon gives a figure of 800, which is ludicrous. The first realistic tallies emerged in an article by the scholar Wilfred Cantrell Smith in *The Middle East Journal* published in 1950. Smith claimed it was 'widely held' that 50,000 Muslims died in Hyderabad and that 'other estimates by responsible observers run as high as 200,000'. 'The Muslim community fell before a massive and brutal blow, the devastation of which left those who did survive reeling in bewildered fear. Thousands upon thousands were slaughtered; many hundreds of thousands uprooted. The instrument of their disaster was, of course, vengeance.'[32] Later research by the scholar Lucien Benichou found there was a 'total upheaval in the fortunes of Muslims entailing not only a loss of livelihood and status, but often of life, honour and property'.[33]

Most of Smith's findings were based on the leaked contents of a confidential report by Pandit Sunderlal and Qazi Abdulghaffar commissioned by Nehru. On proclaiming victory in Hyderabad, Nehru had announced that 'not a single communal incident' had taken place. However, as news of atrocities began to emerge, he was pressured by the only Muslim Congressman in Delhi, Maulana Azad, the minister of education, to send an investigative team to the state. After visiting nine out of the sixteen districts of Hyderabad, Sunderlal and Abdulghaffar found there had been widespread anti-Muslim purges, primarily in the Marathwada and Telangana areas. 'At a very reasonable & modest estimate we think that the total number of deaths in the state may well have been somewhere between 30,000 & 40,000. There could in no way have been less than

25,000.'[34] They also found evidence that Indian soldiers had taken an active hand in the butchery. 'At a number of places members of the armed forces brought out Muslim adult males from villages and towns and massacred them in cold blood.'[35] Confidential notes attached to what became known as the Sunderlal Report detailed the gruesome nature of the Hindu revenge:

> We were shown wells still full of corpses that were rotting. In one such we counted 11 bodies, which included that of a woman with a small child sticking to her breast . . . We saw remnants of corpses lying in ditches. At several places the bodies had been burnt and we would see the charred bones and skulls still lying there . . . As for forcible conversions this too was a universal factor, almost everywhere we went. After the adult males of a locality had been killed, the women and children were generally 'persuaded' to adopt the Hindu faith.[36]

Nehru suppressed the report, and at Patel's urging cancelled the appointment of one of its authors as India's ambassador to the Middle East. Twenty years later, when news of the report finally surfaced, Indira Gandhi banned its publication, on the ground that it was injurious to 'national interests'. It was first published as an appendix to A.G. Noorani's *The Destruction of Hyderabad* in 2013. The killing of Muslims in Hyderabad remains the single largest massacre in the history of independent India.

11

'The Beauty of the Dawn'

In January 1948, V.P. Menon asked Louis Mountbatten to work his considerable charm on a gathering of eighteen prominent princes worried about the recent mergers of dozens of small states and their integration into Orissa and the Central Provinces. The mergers were a breach of the promises made by Patel in his first address as states minister on 5 July 1947 and then by Mountbatten in his speech to the Chamber of Princes three weeks later, that there would be no interference in the internal affairs of the states. Now Menon was being accused of threatening states that refused to merge with armed intervention. To the assembled potentates, these actions seemed a throwback to the despised Doctrine of Lapse propounded by Lord Dalhousie and one of the causes of the 1857 uprising.

Aside from the creation of West Pakistan and East Pakistan, the political map of India as it began its first full year of independence still resembled the tessellated pavement that Sir Bampfylde Fuller had described almost half a century earlier. The difference was that the stone tesserae represented the approximately 550 princely states that had given up their control of foreign affairs, defence and communications and had acceded, while the plain stone filling represented the eleven provinces that now made up the Indian Union. India was a single country, but it was fragmented geographically and politically. While several larger princely states were making strides towards representative government, the vast majority remained outposts of autocracy, too small to introduce efficient administrations, too conservative to contemplate democratic reform. Only by a process of integration could India hope to become a functional nation state. Menon and Patel would achieve this aim through a two-stage process – creating unions of states and merging smaller states with existing provinces such as Bombay or Orissa. Only the larger states, seventeen in number, among them Gwalior and Baroda, would remain as separate entities. However, even this promise, made by Menon when he met with their representatives on 8 December 1947 in New Delhi, would end up being broken.[1]

Luckily for Menon, Mountbatten not only wholeheartedly endorsed the need for the mergers of the small states, he also claimed the idea as his own, likening it to the annexation of the Grand Duchy of Hesse in Germany by Napoleon in 1806. Just as small states had no place in Europe 140 years ago, they had no place in India today, he told those present. He pointed out that the German princes gave up their powers but retained their palaces, private possessions and civil lists, leaving them better off than the larger states, which continued in power until they were annihilated by the revolution in Germany in 1918. He also was careful to exonerate Menon, despite knowing the extent to which he had been twisting arms to prevent the Balkanization of the subcontinent. According to Hodson, he told the gathering, 'Any suspicions which anyone might have had that he was putting excessive pressure on any Rulers to induce them to sign the various

Instruments would have been amply dissipated if they could have heard the unanimous praise which the Rulers showered on Mr. V.P. Menon.'[2] Nor, he said, was there any intention of applying the merger system to the larger and viable states. When it was Menon's turn to address the meeting, he promised that those states that had individual representation in the Constituent Assembly 'and which obviously had a future and possibilities of development' would continue to enjoy the same status as the provinces. After listening to the speeches, the Maharaja of Alwar curtly observed: 'If they wanted to live in Hell they should not be compelled to live in Paradise.'[3]

Perhaps moved by a sudden rush of empathy with the rulers, Mountbatten wanted to organize a larger gathering three days after his January meeting with the eighteen princes, to give an indication of the number of states that would be affected by integration. But Menon, ever the master tactician, stopped him, saying it was 'out of the question' for the governor-general to commit himself. He was instructed to confine himself to broad policy and to say only, without mentioning names or numbers, that while viable states would continue, non-viable states would be 'mediatised' – the jargon-laden term being used to describe the integration process. Among the princes seeking clarification of their position was the Raja of Jawhar. He would be one of the first to be 'gobbled up'.[4]

The Instruments of Accession signed just a few months earlier contained clear safeguards – or so the rulers believed. Article 5 stipulated that the Instrument's terms could not be varied without the ruler's acceptance conveyed by a supplementary instrument. Article 6 prohibited the new government from the compulsory acquisition of land within the state. The stoutest of bulwarks was Article 7, which read: 'Nothing in this Instrument shall be deemed to commit me in any way to acceptance of any future constitution of India or to fetter my discretion to enter into agreements with the Government of India under any such future constitution.'[5] The ink had been hardly allowed to dry on these Instruments before the States Department began to fill the vacuum left by the withdrawal of British paramountcy. Twelve months after Independence, all but a handful of the big states would either be merged into new unions or attached to existing provinces, sacrificing whatever identity they had on the altar of political unity. Patel made his stand clear after the first round of mergers in Orissa and Chhattisgarh had been completed in December 1947, asserting that 'Indian states could not long remain the citadels of autocracy'.[6]

In May 1948, Menon prepared a memorandum for the Indian cabinet, in which he argued that the three-subject accession was inadequate. New and larger unions were needed to bring the states in line with neighbouring provinces. On subjects such as industrial development, factory legislation, labour welfare, banking and insurance, the states had a lot of ground to make up. At this point in the document, Mountbatten wrote in red pen in the margin, 'Not in every case.' At the end of the document he noted, 'A preliminary flourish of the big stick.'[7]

In *The Story of the Integration of the Indian States*, Menon justifies his use of the big stick only when it could be proven to be in the interests of the county. 'The fact of the matter was that we did not realise that the weakness in the States' structure was the smaller States,' he later admitted.[8] Patel needed no validation. He simply could not tolerate the perpetuation of a feudal system which he believed was inherently incapable of survival. 'The ultimate test of fitness for the survival of any State was its capacity to secure the well-being of its subjects,' Patel told Menon as they debated how to approach the merger of the smaller states. 'By implementing their policy of merger, the Government of India would only be saving the rulers from the fury of their subjects newly awakened to a consciousness of their rights.'[9]

~

A fortnight before the transfer of power, twenty-six rulers in Orissa and fifteen in Chhattisgarh had formed the Eastern States Union, in the belief that united they stood a better chance of defending themselves against the Congress juggernaut. They were wrong. The union proved to be unviable. The states were scattered over a large area with no linguistic or ethnic bonds holding them together. By the beginning of 1948, barely a handful had allowed partial responsible government, setting the stage for ugly confrontations between the rulers and the local Praja Mandals. At Dhenkanal, only the presence of a tame leopard in the zenana prevented the takeover of the ruler's palace.

The trigger for the states ministry to act came when the establishment of an 'Azad Nilgiri Government' by the Praja Mandal in Nilgiri state, one of the members of the union, sparked a pro-raja uprising in November 1947 by adivasis armed with bows and arrows. When the state's ruler ordered armed tribals to attack Praja Mandal supporters and property, units of the Orissa Military Police Force took over the administration. Another concern for the states ministry was that Hyderabad might carve out a slice of the mineral-rich state of Bastar in Chhattisgarh for itself. Patel would later cite attempts by the nizam's agents to entrap its young ruler and convince him to merge with Hyderabad as shaping his views on partition. The prince's vulnerability to the machinations of the Political Department (which supported such a merger) led him to conclude 'that the best course was to drive out the foreigners even at the cost of the partition of the country. It was also then that I felt that there was only one way to make the country safe and strong and that was the unification of the rest of India.'[10]

As the situation in the Eastern States Union continued to deteriorate, Patel proposed that the states cede some of their powers to the neighbouring provincial governments of Orissa and Bihar. Aware of the potential backlash from the larger states in the union, he and Menon decided to target the smaller so-called B and C states first. Menon in particular knew that getting a deal would need a great deal of sweetening. 'Since they were surrendering their States for all time, it was but elementary justice that some form of quid pro quo should be conceded to them,' Menon later wrote.[11]

The draft merger agreement Patel and he carried to them would become a template for all future mergers over the next eighteen months. Under the agreement, the rulers would surrender all their governing powers in return for a guaranteed privy purse, amounting to approximately 10 per cent of the revenues of their states as they stood in 1947, subject to a maximum of Rs 10 lakh (this figure was sometimes exceeded). The privy purse would be tax-free, an important concession, given the high levels of taxation in India at the time. All rulers were allowed to retain their palaces and certain other property, their personal privileges and those of their immediate family and, most importantly, their titles. The agreement also provided that the rulers' authority, jurisdiction and power would be ceded in favour of the central and not provincial governments.[12] According to H.V. Hodson, Patel won approval for the policy at a cabinet meeting 'after one minute's explanation and no comment'.[13] The issue of privy purses and privileges would be a subject of controversy for decades to come.

On 13 December 1947, Menon and Patel travelled to Cuttack and invited the rulers of the Orissa states to a meeting. Though they sat on potentially rich deposits of minerals and coal, the states were mostly poor with incomes often too meagre to meet the requirements of administration. A 1939 enquiry had found that some of the more autocratic rulers were demanding that tenant farms pay around a quarter of their annual land rent just to meet the cost of royal marriages and religious ceremonies. In the case of Dhenkanal, the tenants were forced to hand over part of their income to fund a trip to Europe by the ruler's brother. 'This extra taxation prevails in almost all the Orissa States and it has been a source of considerable hardship to the people called upon to bear the heavy burden,' the enquiry report stated. 'No fundamental rights of citizenship are recognised. Civil liberty is crushed; and the people are daily oppressed with a feeling of potential danger to the security of life and property.'[14] Commenting on the negotiations in Cuttack, Menon wrote:

> They [the rulers] realised that their continued existence depended on the goodwill of their people and the support of the Government of India, both of which they lacked and that if, owing to agitation, the administration of their States were ultimately taken over by the Government of India, they might not even get the privy purses which were being guaranteed to them.[15]

By evening all the small states had agreed to a merger.

Convincing the larger states in the Eastern States Union proved more difficult. Pratap Singh Deo, the raja of Patna, wanted time to consider the offer. Patel was due to travel to Nagpur the following day and wanted the agreement before he departed. As Menon revealed to Hodson years later, he persuaded the Raja of Dhenkanal to tell Patna's ruler that if he and the others refused to sign 'he [Menon] was going to issue orders there and then that they must remain in Cuttack and that as soon as sufficient numbers of reserve police could be assembled, the States Ministry was going to occupy the states'.[16] When Singh Deo checked with Menon if there was any truth to the threat, he not only confirmed there was but also agreed to put in writing that if the ruler did not sign the agreement, 'the Government of India would be compelled to take over [his] administration'.[17] C.C. Desai, Menon's assistant, was even less tactful. When the prince of a small central Indian state pleaded for time to consider what he should do, Desai told him: 'Either you sign what we have got now or you do not sign at all, and you take the consequences of your action. Our Crown Reserve Police [*sic*] would walk into the State and you are free to take such steps as may be open to you.'[18]

The success of Menon's arm-twisting could be measured in the rapid-fire headlines it generated. 'Mr V.P. Menon visits state of Chhota Hazri', would be followed a day later by a brief note that 'HH the Maharajah of Chhota Hazri has arrived', culminating in the banner headline, 'CHHOTA HAZRI MERGED!'[19] The scoresheet at the end of the process was twenty states merging with Orissa, fifteen with the Central Provinces and two with Bihar.

Behind the triumphant headlines was a lingering sense of disquiet, with many princes smarting from having been compelled to act against their principles. Aside from having to cede power, they were furious that their status had changed overnight from princes to pensioners. In May 1948, the Intelligence Bureau reported that the rulers of Chhattisgarh 'felt humiliated and had accepted the mergers unwillingly'.[20] In the same month there were reports that a number of central Indian potentates had been meeting regularly with 'communal organisations' at Katra in Chhattisgarh's Raigarh district to formulate a plan 'to overthrow the Nehru Gov[ernmen]t'.[21] Menon's tactics also caused discomfort in Delhi, forcing him to defend himself before the prime minister and his cabinet. His defence was simple. Having already railroaded the

Orissa states into signing merger agreements, there was no question of reversing the process. A precedent had been set – one that would eventually embrace all the states. As Menon's biographer Narayani Basu writes: 'If he and Patel failed to merge Orissa and Chhattisgarh and if the model they had so painstakingly devised, backfired, it would reverberate across the remaining princely order and create precisely the kind of chaos India was looking to avoid.'[22]

~

Emboldened by his success in the Eastern States, Menon began working at a frantic pace, with one British official commenting after a meeting that he 'spoke more like a Fuehrer than ever before'.[23] Next in line was Kathiawar, where 222 states, described by Nehru as 'a crazy patchwork of territories . . . ridden by factions and jealousies', had defied earlier attempts at mergers and rationalization.[24] Larger states claimed suzerainty over their smaller neighbours; some states held isolated pockets of territory within the boundaries of others; and a multiplicity of customs duties and other barriers rendered communications and trade virtually impossible. On 17 January 1948, Menon addressed a conference of Kathiawar rulers at Rajkot, insisting that merger did not mean the Government of India was breaking its promises: 'They are only anxious that the question should be tackled in good time and that a fair and equitable solution should be arrived at as the result of a deliberate policy,' he observed. 'If this is not done, it is possible that events may get out of hand. This is the new problem before us.'[25]

The Kathiawar states tended to be more advanced than those in Orissa and Chhattisgarh. Their rulers were often well educated, popular with their subjects and enjoyed good relations with the Congress party. Many earned valuable incomes from customs duties at their ports. Menon's advice to them was to form a union of their own with an elected legislative assembly and a responsible government. He also promised to fix their privy purses at a higher level than had been done for the Eastern States. Menon's gentle art of persuasion worked. Once several of the larger states agreed to the merger, the smaller ones fell in line and the Union of Saurashtra was created. Once again, not all the rulers were happy with the merger. It was not the size of the privy purse that mattered, remarked the Maharaja of Bhavnagar. 'You cannot compensate me for parting with my land, my people and my rights, but whatever you think fit, you may give me. I am not going to say a word.' According to the Maharaja of Dhrangadhra, when he announced his decision to the people of his state 'there was stunned silence . . . Nobody had any comment to make and only one person, an elderly village head, said to me in Gujarati, "That is all very well Sir, I know what you have done, but who will now wipe away our tears?"'[26]

After Kathiawar it was the turn of the Deccan rulers, who met in February 1948 and agreed to a merger with the province of Bombay. In March, the Punjab 'hill states' were absorbed into a new centrally administered unit called Himachal Pradesh. The eight other Punjab states, including Patiala, Kapurthala and Faridkot, were merged in July 1948, with Yadavindra Singh becoming rajpramukh or governor. Menon's initial preference was for seven Rajput states – Kotah, Bundi, Tonk, Jhalawar, Banswara, Dungarpur and Pratapgarh – to merge with the Kathiawar Union. The rulers refused, insisting they would only unite with their fellow Rajputs. On 3 March, they formed the United States of Rajasthan. Having watched the arm-twisting first-hand, a secretary to the Maharaja of Bundi described Menon as a 'double-crosser of the first water'.[27] But Menon was not devoid of compassion. Visiting

Cochin in May 1949, he discovered that the royal house had a staggering 223 princes and 231 princesses, many now strapped for cash.

> I met some of these princes and princesses. As I talked with them I was reminded of an aviary in a certain State which possessed a rare collection of birds. When that State was integrated the popular [elected] ministry, apparently on the principle of ahimsa, let the birds loose! The poor creatures were very soon devoured by other birds and beasts of prey.[28]

Deciding that it would be inhuman to leave the Cochin royal family so vulnerable, he ordered that the Government of India continue giving allowances to its members.

Patel, meanwhile, was euphoric at the pace at which the map of India was changing. Addressing the rulers of Indore, Gwalior and Malwa at the inauguration of their union in June 1948, the usually gruff and no-nonsense states minister was positively elegiac:

> Let no bitterness or rancour spoil the beauty of the dawn which is now opening before you, let no unkindly thought besmirch the essential nobility of human nature; instead, let us all dwell on the pure vista of peace and progress which is now opening up and let us exploit to the full the many opportunities of service which are now being placed in the hands of us all.[29]

Patel's vistas 'of peace and progress' were not always accompanied by beautiful dawns. The merger of Punjab state had been preceded by extraordinary levels of communal violence and displacement of lakhs of Muslims, which Patel allegedly either turned a blind eye to or directly encouraged. Jathas or guerrilla groups targeting Muslims were provided with rifles, revolvers and ammunition by the Sikh rulers of Patiala and Nabha; Faridkot supplied jeeps and trucks; Kapurthala money; and Kalsia training facilities for RSS cadres. The commander-in-chief of the Indian Army, Claude Auchinleck, briefed the cabinet in late September 1948, saying: 'It is commonly believed that the rulers of the Sikh States of the Eastern Punjab are behind the campaign of extermination.'[30] The jathas would seek refuge in states where Boundary Force personnel were prohibited from entering. There they would rearm themselves, and with the support of state troops carry out more massacres of Muslims. In early September, the Maharaja of Faridkot told US embassy officials that 'Patel expressed satisfaction' after hearing that all Muslims had been evacuated from his state. The deputy prime minister also provided the maharaja with 800 rifles and 'remarked that before long [the maharaja] might have the task of defending territory other than that within the boundaries of his own State'. According to the embassy officials, Patel believed that

> . . . [given] the weakness of his own Government, . . . he [the Maharaja] has a better chance of controlling East Punjab through the medium of the Sikh Princes than through the pitiably inadequate provincial administration, and that he is currying favor with the rulers whom, until a year ago, he bitterly condemned as enemies of the people.[31]

The rift between Nehru, who was striving to make Muslims feel welcome in India, and his deputy, who was encouraging efforts to drive them out, would widen further over Patel's handling of the communal crises in Alwar and Bharatpur. Nehru suspected the rulers of organizing pogroms against Meo Muslim minorities in their states and had expressed his concern to Patel as early as on 30 September 1947. On 4 November, he again wrote to the Sardar citing alarming reports of atrocities and urged the states ministry to 'point out to them that what they are doing is objectionable and harmful. Further that we might stop all export of arms and petrol to these States.'[32] Patel ignored the request. 'The present atmosphere and condition in the country makes it necessary to handle the State questions with a degree of caution and tact,'[33] he argued. His reply infuriated Nehru, who sent his principal private secretary, H.V.R. Iyengar, to get a first-hand report on the communal situation. When Patel protested, Nehru defended his actions saying that his intention was not to go behind the Sardar's back but to get to the truth of what was happening in Alwar and Bharatpur. 'It seems our approaches are different, however much we may respect each other . . . If I am to continue as PM, I cannot have my freedom restricted and I must have a certain liberty of direction. Otherwise, it is better for me to retire.' Patel replied:

> I have no desire to restrain your liberty of direction in any manner. But when it is clear to us that on the fundamental question of our respective spheres of responsibility, authority and action, there is such a vital difference of opinions between us, it would not be in the interest of the cause which we both wish to serve to continue to pull on longer.[34]

Without consulting his prime minister, Patel directed the commissioner of Gurgaon to arrange for the evacuation of all the remaining Meos to Pakistan. When Nehru heard about the order, he immediately countermanded it and directed the Rajasthan government to return all the Meos from Alwar and Bharatpur to their original lands and rehabilitate them. But the order was never passed on to the officials. Patel was eventually forced to compromise and support a staggered programme of resettlement that was poorly implemented. One Meo refugee told the historian Shail Mayaram that he returned to Alwar because of Congress promises that he would retain his property. However, on arrival at his village, he discovered his house had been destroyed, his animals missing and he was returned only sixty of his original 600 bighas of land.[35] When Iyengar told Alwar's prime minister, N.B. Khare, that Nehru wanted him to accept the Alwar Meos back, his curt reply was: 'Once they enter the Alwar State they will be tried [*sic*] as rebels and shot.'[36]

On 7 February 1948, Patel finally bowed to pressure. He dismissed Khare and placed him under house arrest.[37] An investigation was held into his involvement in the massacres and the allegations that he had paid contractors to demolish mosques. Under interrogation, Khare estimated that as many 15,000 Muslims may have been killed. Bharatpur's ruler Brijendra Singh and his brother were also investigated for ordering armed robberies and looting in Meo areas. All three were cleared of wrongdoing. Interviewed by Robert Trumbull of the *New York Times*, Brijendra admitted to presiding over meetings of the RSS. 'He said that he had admired this organization which he thought was "something like the Boy Scouts".'[38]

Throughout the controversy, Menon stuck by Patel. In *The Story of the Integration of the Indian States,* he writes: 'Exaggerated accounts of his [Khare's] activities were being reported to us. It was alleged that the Meos were being hounded out of the State, their mosques were being demolished and that Muslim burial grounds were being desecrated. A section of the press played up these allegations.'[39]

Menon's dismissal of the reports not only clashed with Nehru's views but also with what Menon witnessed first-hand. In early 1948, he visited Alwar and confirmed what Edward Wakefield, joint secretary of the Political Department, and others were reporting and presented his findings to Patel. It was only years later, in a recorded interview with H.V. Hodson, that he admitted: 'I took Alwar and Bharatpur without their consent. There was a mad killing spree on there. The Diwan of Alwar [Khare] was encouraging mosques and graveyards to be demolished.'[40] In the end it was not Alwar's and Bharatpur's involvement in the massacres of Muslims, but their closeness to the Hindu Mahasabha and the RSS and possible links to the assassination of Mahatma Gandhi on 30 January 1948 that led to their administrations being suspended. Two months later the states were merged with Dholpur and Karauli to form the Matsya Union, with Dholpur's maharaja given the post of rajpramukh.

~

In 1948, Gaekwar Pratap Singh of Baroda presented Patel with an audacious list of conditions before he would merge with adjoining states. His demands included giving Baroda responsibility for all the western Indian states and to be crowned 'King of Gujarat'. Patel had little time for the ostentatious gaekwar who, when greeting prominent guests, fired salutes from a cannon made of solid gold. Prior to the transfer of power, Pratap had tried to extract a collateral letter from Patel, establishing that there would be no financial liabilities on acceding states and that Baroda's accession would be for 'legislation and policy only', and not for administration. Patel ignored him. The gaekwar had long epitomized the worst of princely excesses. Soon after breaking his father's laws against bigamy and taking Sita Devi as his second wife in 1943, Pratap Singh doubled his privy purse to the equivalent of $8 million. He then began advancing himself large sums from the treasury as undocumented and interest-free 'loans'. On one shopping spree in the US in 1940, the couple allegedly spent $10 million, mostly on luxury goods. As Independence loomed, they purchased a luxurious mansion in Monaco, and began plundering the royal treasury of cash and jewels. Among an estimated 300 pieces smuggled to their new home was a carpet embedded with 22 lakh Basra pearls, which sold for nearly $6 million at Sotheby's in 1992. Another item pillaged from the treasury was the seven-strand 'Baroda Pearls' necklace, one of the most extravagant pieces of jewellery ever created. Bedridden at the time, Patel deputed Menon to teach the gaekwar a lesson. The final showdown came in January 1949, when Pratap returned to Bombay after one of his long sojourns overseas. Told by Menon his state had no chance of surviving on its own, he broke down and signed the necessary documents. The Government of Bombay took over its administration in May 1949.

Border states were seen as particularly vulnerable. During 1948, intelligence officials in Delhi were receiving reports of Pakistani agents infiltrating Tripura and Cooch Behar to stir up communal tensions and merge them with East Pakistan. Tripura's regent, Prabhavati Mahadevi, was told that any assistance from India would come at the price of her state's merger with the Indian Union. The situation was more complicated in Cooch Behar, which sat astride the borders of West Bengal and Assam. Because of its special status, it was not merged with India until September 1949. On 1 January 1950, it lost its identity forever by becoming part of West Bengal. States that objected to merger arrangements included tiny Janjira south of Bombay and the much larger and more important state of Kolhapur. They were brought to heel through a mix of inducements ranging from threats of deposition to forcible annexation.

Rewa in central India proved another stumbling block, this time to the merger of thirty-five states in the Bundelkhand and Bhagelkhand regions. It was the largest of the states, and its young ruler Martand Singh was being egged on by his deposed father to resist the move despite promises of a liberal privy purse of Rs 10 lakh and of being made rajpramukh. Frustrated by his intransigence, Menon threatened to release his father, who had been jailed in 1945 for the murder of two members of his political staff, and to allow him to take over the state if he did not sign the merger agreement. In the end Gulab Singh was allowed to 'escape' from Delhi jail and spend a few days in Rewa. What transpired is not clear, but when his father was returned to jail, Martand signed the merger agreement and Rewa joined the Union of Vindhya Pradesh.

With the mergers came new expectations, and it soon became apparent that the powers still enjoyed by these newly created princely unions were hindering the government's development programmes. Summoned to a meeting in Delhi in May 1948, the rajpramukhs of Rajasthan, Madhya Bharat, Saurashtra, Vindhya Pradesh and Matsya were forced to sign new Instruments of Accession ceding to the Union the power to pass laws in respect of all matters falling within the federal and concurrent government lists. All through the process, the state rulers were reminded that they had two choices: to comply with the directives of the states ministry or to face the wrath of the Praja Mandals. Menon also dropped plenty of hints that the ministry had potentially incriminating files on the princes – which was probably not true as Conrad Corfield had succeeded in destroying or shipping out most of them. In an interview with G.M. Kelly of the Associated Press in 1948, Nehru said that India's longest stride down the freedom road had been the 'smashing of autocratic rule by the maharajahs of most of the subcontinent's . . .

princely states'. It was now up to their people to decide how long they would continue to pay gratuities to their former rulers.[41] As the American ambassador in New Delhi commented dryly: 'The Embassy feels that the proposals of the Government were placed before the princes in such manner that they had no alternative [but] to accept them.'[42]

~

The question that has vexed the few historians who have studied the fate of the Indian states after Independence is whether Menon and Patel intended from the outset to pursue a policy of integration that would come to embrace all the princely entities that existed after 1947. Initially their focus was only on the smaller states in Orissa and Chhattisgarh, which everyone, aside from their rulers, agreed were not viable. But within two years, what Patel proudly declared was a 'bloodless revolution' had embraced even the so-called viable states of Jaipur, Bikaner, Gwalior, Indore and Baroda, which Mountbatten and Menon had promised would be left alone. In their responses, both Menon and Patel have tended to emphasize the volatile situation that prevailed after Independence.

Menon claims that securing the accession of the rulers was always a 'stopgap' measure on the path to evolving a more permanent relationship between the states and the Government of India. But after the transfer of power, stopgap measures proved unviable as 'one crisis after another supervened to engross the attention of the Government of India', he elaborated.

> Firstly, we had to tackle the situation in Kathiawar. Then there was the two-way exodus of refugees, which threatened to engulf both Dominions in one big calamity. There followed the tribal invasion

> of Kashmir. Lastly, the situation in South India resulting from the non-accession of Hyderabad was causing us anxiety.[43]

For his part, Patel was particularly vexed by the Rajput states of western India, whose rulers he believed 'still dreamt of the power of their sword[s] and still thought of carving out a kingdom for themselves'.[44] He would compare the situation facing the government in early 1948 to 'a powder magazine, which a single spark may set ablaze'.[45] Compounding the crisis were warnings by defence strategists that Pakistan might attempt to compensate for its setbacks in Kashmir by launching a raid into Punjab. Intelligence reports from the Pakistani state of Bahawalpur stated that local regiments had been replaced by Pathans and Arabs and that troop levels had increased significantly. There were also reports of cross-border infiltration 'to do spying against the Indian Union'. On 28 January, Indian newspapers reported that 500 'Pathan raiders' had crossed the border of Jaisalmer state but were repelled by Indian forces. Pakistan denied the claim. The prospect of an agglomeration of weak, independent states as 'the front-line defence of the Indo-Gangetic Plains' in the event of an all-out war with Pakistan was concerning enough for Patel to reject as inadequate a proposal by Bikaner's prime minster, K.M. Panikkar, to create a 24-kilometre-wide buffer zone along the western border.[46] Size and viability would no longer matter, Patel decided, Punjab and Rajputana would be added to the list of states to be merged and integrated.

The lack of progress towards responsible government in most states was another reason for the two to act. Menon had initially indicated he was prepared to take a hands-off approach provided the states introduced full responsible government and could prove they had the capacity to deliver 'efficient administration and . . . provide adequate social and health services'.[47] States such as

Gwalior, Cochin, Bikaner and Kolhapur were quick off the mark in introducing constitutional reform in the weeks and months after Independence. But it soon became clear that in most states there was little if any progress towards adult franchise. The Instruments of Accession signed by the rulers contained no clauses committing them to democratize. They had been kept simple to make sure the princes signed them. Now, citadels of autocracy were the norm rather than the exception. Administrative standards were slipping, with food shortages being reported in Indore and the law-and-order situation deteriorating in states such as Udaipur. By December 1947, Menon told the American ambassador to India that he was considering a requirement that rulers of states that had acceded to India 'take practical steps towards the establishment of popular government'.[48]

As Patel pointed out in a statement to the Lok Sabha on 16 December 1947, the democratization of the states had long been the aim of the Congress. Yet, in their present condition most states were not suited for achieving this aim. Any delay in self-government could only lead to chaos and anarchy. 'Large-scale unrest' had already gripped the people of many states and there were 'rumblings of the storm' in others. Patel concluded his statement by pointing out that for the smaller states 'there was no alternative to integration and democratization'. No force would be employed against them. Whatever steps needed to be taken would take account 'of the circumstances and peculiar problems' of individual states.[49] Had he wanted to, Patel could also have cited section 3 of the sixth article of the Indian Independence Act, which allowed for the original terms of the Instruments of Accession to be altered by mutual agreement. The jury is still out on whether such an agreement was reached voluntarily or presented as a fait accompli.

12

The Wrath of Shiva

Having merged most of the smaller states into unions or into existing provinces, Patel and Menon now began to apply their tried-and-tested methods on the so-called 'viable states', which they had promised would remain autonomous because of their size and economic strength. Recalcitrant rulers were warned that popular movements were gaining strength, and if they waited too long they might be overthrown and lose everything. By coming on board they would win favour from their people and might be made the rajpramukhs of the merged units. Menon would conduct most of the face-to-face negotiations, leaving Patel to concentrate on his onerous tasks as home minister and deputy prime minister. Despite his increasing frailty, Patel, now aged seventy-three, remained a fearsome opponent. 'Whenever Sardar felt really incensed, his countenance assumed the visage of divine wrath,' his private secretary V. Shankar wrote. 'His eyes used to flash like lightning and sometimes one felt as if the opening of Shiva's third eye would follow. It was unnerving to anyone who would be a witness to that flash of anger.'[1]

When it came to defining what a viable state was, geography

and population were two important considerations, but not the only ones. Typically, these were also states that were well governed, economically advanced and had taken steps towards responsible government. Having signed Instruments of Accession, many were confident that their status as separate entities would be guaranteed. Indeed, Patel and Menon had repeatedly made such pledges. In early 1948, Patel told Sadul Singh of Bikaner that 'we do not ourselves initiate or encourage any merger proposal; nor do we accept any such proposal unless we are satisfied that it has the support and backing of both the ruler and the people concerned'.[2] Menon insisted there was no question that the status of any of the states that had joined the Constituent Assembly would be altered, a promise that was repeated in a speech to the Lok Sabha in March 1948 by N.V. Gadgil, who was deputizing for Patel. On 29 March 1948, Menon told a press conference: 'The bigger States like Cochin, Travancore, Mysore, Jodhpur, Jaipur, Bikaner, Bhopal etc., would stand as independent units.'[3] By the end of 1949, there were only three – namely, Mysore, Hyderabad and Kashmir.

In order to create what became known as Madhya Bharat, two major states, Gwalior and Indore, as well as nearly two dozen smaller ones would need to be merged. But it wasn't going to be easy. At one point, Patel and Menon found themselves delving into the intricacies of court intrigue and succession struggles, much like British residents had done in the past. Gwalior and Indore were age-old adversaries, having fought numerous wars, the bloodiest of which, Menon noted, had taken place when they were nominally at peace. They were also quite different from each other. While Indore's ruler Yeshwant Rao Holkar was a controversial figure who had twice married American women and appointed foreigners to key posts in his administration, Gwalior had moved towards responsible government; it enjoyed a well-endowed treasury and ran an efficient administration. Just days ahead of the transfer of power, Gwalior's ruler George Jiwajirao Scindia begged Mountbatten to give his state greater autonomy on account of its size and stature. Now, eight months later, he was pressing Menon for his state to not lose its identity by being absorbed into Madhya Bharat. As Jiwajirao's wife Vijayaraje Scindia would write scathingly in her memoir:

> For the princes to have so much as questioned the rationale, legality or usefulness of 'integration' – or to have even hinted that what they were being asked to do was hardly in conformity with the norms of democracy – would have instantly exposed them to the charge of being unpatriotic and anti-national reactionaries . . . [The Government of India] wanted to bring democracy in place of feudal rule, but that democracy did not extend to the people of the princely states, who were to be transferred to the new regime without being given an opportunity to decide their fate. They did not want arguments from the princes; they wanted capitulation.[4]

The two states were also important test cases, especially Gwalior, which would become the first twenty-one-gun state to lose its identity if it could be convinced to merge. Noted Menon: 'Sardar agreed that once Gwalior and Indore were integrated into one union, we should have to adopt the same policy in regard to all the States in the country.'[5] Patel's line of argument was that merger was to the advantage of the rulers. If the viable states were allowed to exist as separate units, the rights and privileges of the rulers would be at the mercy of the local legislatures and could not be guaranteed by the government in Delhi. While these principles made sense to Menon and Patel, they belied a host of complexities. In the haggling ahead, each ruler would compete for the position of rajpramukh, for the location of the state capital in his territory, for the maximum number of his own bureaucrats in the state apparatus as well as for his state's political representation in the new Madhya Bharat legislative assembly. And then there was the issue of personality.

Indore would prove to be the more difficult of the two princes to deal with. For all his faults, Yeshwant was a popular ruler. In 1948, Robert Trumbull of the *New York Times* accompanied the maharaja and his American wife Euphemia Crane – or 'Maharani Fay', as she was known – to the opening of a community development project in his state. The road was lined with loyal subjects and their car made frequent stops so that the couple could be garlanded with flowers. After the ceremony, Yeshwant and Trumbull drove unannounced into a small village. 'Every window and rooftop was crowded with men, women and children who showered the car with flowers, and the streets were made impassable by villagers of all ages who pushed and jostled just to touch the Maharaja's car. I never saw even Nehru given a reception like that.'[6] Yeshwant was also one of the few rulers that had read the political situation clearly. Shortly after Independence, at a meeting with Howard Donovan, the counsellor at the US Embassy in Delhi, he stated that Patel's plan for the princely states was to follow the Raj strategy of 'divide and rule' and thereby divest them 'of all the power they still possess'. He also told Donovan that Mountbatten had admitted to him that he had made a blunder regarding the states and urged them to take advantage of what he believed would be a period of chaos and organize themselves to fill any power vacuum that might develop. He claimed Mountbatten had told him: 'If you Indian princes within three years cannot organize yourselves and take the opportunity that lies ahead of you in all this chaos in British India, then you are not fit to be princes.'[7]

In May 1947, Yeshwant had appointed his chief of police, an Englishman named Ralph Horton, as his prime minister, despite protests from Patel. Horton was allegedly behind Indore's attempts to convince several rulers, including Jamnagar's and Baroda's, not to sign Instruments of Accession prior to Independence until they received better terms. He was also suspected, together with Colonel Harry Nedou, the head of the army, of stalling Yeshwant's signing of the Instrument of Accession until just hours before the Union Jack was lowered for the last time. Within a week of Independence, Patel was demanding that Horton be replaced by N.C. Mehta, a retired ICS officer, as a condition for formal acceptance of Indore's accession. On 21 August 1947, Yeshwant wrote to Patel saying he was prepared to interview Mehta, but that doing so must not impinge on his 'future sovereign right to approve my own Prime Minister'. Mehta's appointment was eventually accepted, but Yeshwant dismissed him a few months later, telling Patel he was disappointed with his performance. The maharaja's erratic behaviour prompted N.M. Buch, the secretary of the states ministry, to describe him as a 'stooge of Bhopal'.

> Albeit an extremely cultured and polished man, [Yeshwant] has almost no will of his own and is apt to come under the influence of personalities stronger than himself and liable to be easily misled by them. But once he makes up his mind to do a thing, he does it irrespective of the consequence: he is obstinate.[8]

That obstinacy was revealed when Yeshwant rebuffed Menon's demands that he merge his state into the Union of Madhya Bharat. On 16 April 1948, Jiwajirao and Yeshwant met Menon in Delhi to discuss the proposed merger. After two days of talks, both leaders were still adamant they wanted two unions, one centred on Gwalior and one on Indore. Menon told Jiwajirao that if he rejected the offer, he could only be the constitutional head of his state, whereas if he accepted the formation of one union, he would be the rajpramukh of all of central India. His privy purse and private properties would also be guaranteed by the Centre rather than being at the mercy of elected legislatures. A distraught Jiwajirao then turned to Menon and asked: 'Tell me honestly whether the integration of my State is in the interests of my people and myself. Tell me, as a friend, not as States Secretary.' Menon's response was: 'Considering all the circumstances and future possibilities, joining Madhya Bharat would be the best course of action.'[9]

As the discussions dragged on, Patel remained in the background, largely because of his failing health. But with no sign of compromise, Menon decided to include him in the negotiations. Shankar recalled:

> While the Rulers generally held Sardar in awe and esteem, these two [Indore and Gwalior] in particular stood [in] great fear of him. V.P. Menon as a rule successfully used the device of countering resistance or recalcitrance by the threat of taking them to Sardar. In the case of these two Rulers even that was not necessary; a mere hint that the point might have to be referred to Sardar was sufficient to bring them round.[10]

After lunch on 18 April, Shankar briefed his boss on the stalemate over the formation of the Madhya Bharat Union and of the frustration of the local leaders. 'I was not prepared for the explosion that followed,' he wrote later. He was asked to summon the prime ministers of Gwalior and Indore. 'As soon as they came, Sardar gave them a piece of his mind in a manner which I had seldom seen before. He told them plainly that he would see to it that one union was formed and that he would not tolerate any opposition to it.' Within a few hours Jiwajirao and Yeshwant had agreed to the merger of their states into one union. However, instead of welcoming the breakthrough, Menon was furious that Shankar had taken the prime ministers to see Patel without first informing him. Shankar was not present when Menon took his complaint to Patel, but it was clear that he was in no mood to listen and delivered his deputy a severe dressing down. 'The last I heard was V.P. Menon telling Sardar: "Very well, Sir, I shall now make the Rulers sign on the basis of one Union."'[11]

To facilitate the merger, Jiwajirao was made rajpramukh and Yeshwant uprajpramukh (deputy governor) of Madhya Bharat – posts they were promised would be for life. The final piece of haggling centred on their privy purses. Contrary to Patel's arguments, both state legislatures had been remarkably generous, setting Gwalior's at Rs 32 lakh per year and Indore's at Rs 18 lakh. However, Menon managed to bargain the sums down. Gwalior's privy purse was fixed at Rs 25 lakh and Indore's at Rs 15 lakh. Menon's final concession was to make Gwalior the winter capital of the new state and Indore the summer one.

~

Despite his appointment as uprajpramukh and his state's merger into Madhya Bharat, Yeshwant continued to tax the patience of Patel and Menon, who were demanding that he dismiss Harry Nedou from his staff, on suspicion of spying for Pakistan. Tall, well built and stoic, Nedou had served Yeshwant as military commander, senior adviser, ADC and part-time bodyguard for two decades. He was the son of Michael Adam Nedou, a Croatian architect who had emigrated along with his family from Dubrovnik to Lahore in the mid-1800s. Michael opened the first of what would be a small chain of elite hotels in Lahore in the late 1870s, followed by another property in Gulmarg in 1888 and then in Srinagar twelve years later. Nedou's was Srinagar's first luxury hotel and boasted the city's finest confectionery shop, famous for its jams and jellies. Its guests included the explorers Sven Hedin and Francis Younghusband as well as the Austrian mountaineer and one-time Nazi SS sergeant Heinrich Harrer. Following Partition, the hotel's bar was a favourite haunt of foreign correspondents seeking news from rum-soaked army officers about the latest developments in the Kashmir crisis. Nedou's continued to operate until sectarian violence led to its closure in the late 1980s.

Like his father, Harry Nedou spoke Urdu fluently, converted to Islam and married a Kashmiri woman. He began working for Yeshwant after the maharaja stayed in his Gulmarg property. According to Indian intelligence, he accompanied Yeshwant to the US following the death his first wife Sanyogita and encouraged him to marry Marguerite Lawler. When that marriage went sour, Nedou allegedly introduced him to Crane. The British found Yeshwant's behaviour appalling, comparing it to King Edward VIII's affair with Wallis Simpson. They refused to recognize Crane as maharani or their son Richard as the maharaja's legal successor. Following Independence, Yeshwant continued to lobby the states ministry to acknowledge Crane and his son. Patel's strategy was to ignore his numerous requests for meetings.

On 8 November 1949, the *Indian Express* ran a story headlined 'Holkar's ADC packs off following States Ministry Probe'. The article, no doubt the result of a selective leak by Patel, accused Nedou of spying for Pakistan and absconding with Rs 50 lakh of the maharaja's money. Nedou, the article also alleged, had been instrumental in trying to prevent Indore and other central Indian states from acceding to the Indian Union. As a Muslim holding a senior position in Holkar's retinue, he was suspected by Indian intelligence of being pro-Pakistan and of plotting with Bhopal's Hamidullah Khan to drive a 'dagger into the very heart of India' – a possibility that had so rattled Patel. After senior officials from the Central Intelligence Directive searched his home, Nedou packed his bags 'and suddenly left Indore for an unknown place' – most probably Pakistan, speculated the paper.[12]

Around the same time, Indian intelligence reported that Nedou and Crane were planning to smuggle Indore's crown jewels out of India to Pakistan using a private aircraft fitted out with long-range fuel tanks belonging to Indore state. The jewels were to be sold to New York's most famous jeweller, Harry Winston.[13] The States Department had evidence that Yeshwant had already peddled several valuable pieces to Winston, including the Dudley Necklace, comprising clusters of emeralds and diamonds, and the Inquisition Necklace, which had as its centrepiece a 45-carat emerald and was worn by Katherine Hepburn at the 1947 Oscars ceremony. Rather belatedly (and fruitlessly, as it would turn out) he was now asking to buy those items back.

Yeshwant's poor health was also causing concern, as it raised important questions of succession that Patel and Menon could not ignore. In Indore, as in other Maratha princely families, tradition dictated that only males could accede to the gaddi. The custom, enshrined in the covenant that Menon drew up on the merger of Indore state with Madhya Bharat, meant that Usha, his daughter with his first wife, could not be recognized as Yeshwant's heir. The impasse opened the possibility that Holkar's father Tukoji Rao, who had voluntarily abdicated in 1926 over the Bawla murder case and was also married to an American woman, would find himself back on the gaddi – a prospect that unnerved officials in the States

Department. Complicating an already knotty problem were Indian intelligence reports that Nedou and Crane were secretly trying to induce Yeshwant to disinherit Usha and 'to acknowledge Prince Richard Holkar as his successor'.[14] Nedou had to go, but removing him from Indore had potentially dangerous implications. Nedou's daughter Akbar Jehan was married to the Kashmiri leader Sheikh Abdullah. Any move against Nedou was likely to light the fuse of a political powder keg in India's most contested state.

In February 1950, Menon travelled to Indore to resolve the succession crisis and to convince the maharaja to sack Nedou. To his surprise, Yeshwant readily agreed to formalize Usha as his heir, but he stood by Nedou despite being presented with evidence of his 'criminal conduct'. When that approach failed, Menon told him that Patel's earlier assurances that he would look favourably at allowing him and his wife to transfer some of their assets abroad and travel overseas were dependent on his getting rid of Nedou. Patel was also demanding a promise from Yeshwant that he would stop selling his jewellery to Winston.

Patel's hard-line approach put him on a collision course with Abdullah, who was insisting on an enquiry that would exonerate his father-in-law. According to V. Shankar, Abdullah told Nehru he would resign if Nedou was removed. 'Nehru took up the matter with Sardar in view of the delicate position of the Kashmir problem and Sheikh's indispensability,' Patel's private secretary writes. 'But Sardar was adamant and refused to yield. He told Panditji that they could easily find a substitute for him.'[15] In the end, a face-saving formula was arrived at, where the allegations against Nedou were kept secret and he was allowed to leave Indore quietly without the opprobrium of charges being laid against him – charges which Yeshwant would refute if the matter went to court. Nedou moved back to Srinagar, where Abdullah made him the minister for tourism. However, in 1957, he squirmed his way back into the Holkar household, becoming the maharaja's senior adviser. When Yeshwant died from cancer in 1961, his seventy-one-year-old father Tukoji Rao made one final bid for the succession, writing to Home Affairs Minister Lal Bahadur Shastri that he was the seniormost member of the dynasty and that Usha had forfeited her right to the gaddi on account of marrying a Punjabi, thereby alienating herself from the people of Indore. His letter was ignored.

The greatest concentration of headstrong rulers was in Rajputana, where its mostly Rajput chiefs also tended to have strong followings among their subjects. The creation of a Rajasthan Union had been held up by disputes over who would become rajpramukh (a title claimed by Udaipur's ageing and invalid ruler, as he was the seniormost Rajput), which state would provide the union's capital, and the composition of an interim government representing all the states to prepare for elections. 'Negotiations with the rulers were difficult enough but those with popular leaders were even more so,' observed Shankar. 'I doubt if in any other part of India was there such inter-ruler jealousy as in Rajasthan.'[16]

It would take around half a dozen mini mergers before the Rajasthan that appears on today's maps came into existence, with Jaipur as its capital. After working tirelessly for more than a year on the creation of the new state, Patel nearly did not make it to the inauguration. On 29 March 1949, Shankar, together with Patel, his daughter Maniben and Hanwant Singh, the maharaja of Jodhpur, departed for Delhi in a twin-engine Dove aircraft for what should have been a routine ninety-minute flight to Jaipur. Shortly after passing Alwar, one of the aircraft's engines stopped functioning and the plane began to lose height. The pilot told Shankar he would try and belly-land the plane on a sandy riverbed to prevent it from catching fire. 'I was particularly hard on the poor Maharaja of Jodhpur whose corpulence was the butt-end of my jokes,' Shankar writes. 'Much to Sardar's amusement, I told him that he would have to be the last because if his figure got stuck in the exit, there would be no chance of anybody else getting through. Sardar was unruffled and unmoved.'[17]

After a bumpy but safe landing, the passengers and crew took shelter from the sun under a tree while the radio officer walked to the nearest village to seek help. Patel's heart condition made it impossible for him to trek the few kilometres to the nearest road. As night fell, a group of magicians turned up and entertained the party. Somehow, word of the plane's whereabouts reached the town of Sikar, and at around 9 p.m. three vehicles arrived at the crash site and took the party to Jaipur. It was not until two hours later that an anxious Nehru received confirmation that Patel and the others were safe.

At the ceremony for the inauguration of the union the next morning, Patel sat next to Jaipur's ruler Sawai Man Singh or Jai, as he was popularly known, who was shortly to be sworn in as rajpramukh. Aside from the rulers of the various princely states that were now to be part of Rajasthan, the ceremony was attended by about a thousand nobles and civil servants. Halfway through his inaugural address, Patel congratulated Jai for his elevation from being 'the first servant of Jaipur' to becoming 'the first servant of Rajasthan'. Not everyone was in such a celebratory mood. Embittered by the proceedings and the failure of Patel to remain in Jaipur to attend the opening of the new state legislature, Bikaner's Sadul Singh, once the leading proponent of accession by the states, retorted: 'Ties of blood extending over the last five centuries have been severed by a stroke.'[18]

Aside from giving up his hereditary right to rule, Jai had to give up cash, property and goods worth an estimated Rs 8 crore, as well as his Dakota, which his third wife Gayatri Devi used to fly to Delhi for her haircuts. The Government of India acquired Jaipur's railway infrastructure, including rolling stock, for a pittance. All official buildings were handed over, as well as many historical monuments such as Amber Fort and Jai Singh's astronomical observatories in Jaipur and Delhi. He also had to give up his army, which was merged with the Indian armed forces. To offset these losses, he was entitled to a slew of privileges, including a privy purse worth about Rs 18 lakh per annum, tax-free and for perpetuity, free medical care for himself and his family, provision of armed police guards and escorts, the right to fly his own flag on his residences, cars and planes, exemption from the Indian Arms Act of 1878, the right to register cars without payment and the use of red number plates, free electricity, exemption from customs duty, a state funeral with full military honours, qualified immunity from civil prosecution and, last but not least, a public holiday on his birthday. As far as the people of Jaipur were concerned, Jai was still their ruler. When he celebrated his thirty-eighth birthday just a couple of months after Jaipur's formal merger with Rajasthan, thousands lined the streets shouting 'Maharaja Man Singhji ki Jai' as he drove through what was now the state capital.

When the Indian government published its second *White Paper on Indian States* in March 1950, it adopted a self-congratulatory tone.

Glossing over the annexation of Hyderabad and the atrocities that followed, it described the process of integration as 'nothing short of a revolution'. A radical make-over from an autocratic set-up to a democratic order was never going to be easy. 'A modern system of Government has to be built in the States and in many of them a start had to be made from the very beginning. The task requires all the patience of the bricklayer; it also requires the vision of the planner and the skill of the engineer.'[19] The *White Paper* concluded by stating: 'The policy of integration and democratisation, which the Government of India have applied to the States, constituted the only solution of the problem of the States, and the only method of fitting in the states in the new setup of India. This was, therefore, no emotional approach, any expansionist policy, nor power politics.'[20]

There was no mention of the upheavals involved in this transformation. The judicial, administrative and bureaucratic functions of the states were now in the hands of the Union government, whose officials were rapidly filling posts once held by princely nominees. In one former Rajput state, the new administrator was a former deputy customs official with no experience in government administration. The retiring chief minister had no time to organize a proper handover, nor was a proper timetable received from Delhi. Instead of being allowed to take an active interest in the welfare of his former subjects, 'the ruler was forced to retire to the confines of his palace and the few surrounding acres of countryside which he had retained. The administration of the State was put back many years and the people suffered.'[21] Noted Kenneth Fitze, who served as the political agent in Indore and later as resident in Kashmir and Baroda: 'The Cabinets in some at least of the new conglomerations of States territory appear to have become a Tom Tiddler's ground for local agitators who were rewarded by high office for lean years of suppression and incarceration.' Because change had come 'too suddenly and like a cyclone', many states lacked strong service personnel with experience in local self-government and legislative work, 'the result being that the calibre, both intellectual and moral, of the Ministers in States Unions is terribly poor'.[22]

In places such as Orissa and Vindhya Pradesh, these shortcomings were compounded by factionalism and corruption. In Mayurbhanj, the largest of the Orissa states, the new regime had managed to turn its finances from a position of surplus to virtual bankruptcy in the space of a year. In Vindhya Pradesh, the industry minister was charged with taking kickbacks from a Lucknow dealer for the purchase of Chevrolet cars for official use. Even Menon was forced to admit that few of the officers sent by the States Department to take over the administration of the former states had the requisite experience in public affairs. Moreover

> . . . there was scant appreciation of the complexity of the problem of administrative integration, the process of integration had embraced every conceivable activity, and given rise in all directions to a basic urge towards uniformity and standardisation. But this urge often manifested itself in opposite and contradictory directions.[23]

Despite these drawbacks, Menon and Patel could justifiably pride themselves on achieving their goal of creating a politically cohesive India and of extending responsible, democratically elected government to the people of the states. No longer could the ruling princes run their states like fiefdoms; no longer could they remain unaccountable to the people. By the end of 1950, all of the princely unions, with the exception of Kashmir, had adopted the new Indian Constitution as their constitution.[24] Only Mysore, Hyderabad and

Kashmir remained as separate entities. Integration of the princely domains into the Indian Union yielded, in addition to territory and population, cash and investments amounting to almost Rs 100 crore, half of which had come from the bonds of just one state, Gwalior. In return, the Government of India had committed itself to paying privy purses costing around Rs 4.5 crore in the first year, an amount that would shrink with each succeeding year. Justifying the cost, Patel told the Lok Sabha in 1949 that the princes 'had done their bit and now it was time to do ours'. This was 'a small price to pay for the bloodless revolution' which had led to the 'great ideal of geographical, political and economic unification of India, an ideal which for centuries remained a distant dream and which appeared as remote and as difficult of attainment as ever even after the advent of Indian independence'. If the money received from the rulers of Madhya Bharat alone were invested, he added, the interest would cover the payment of all the privy purses.[25]

All that was now left for Patel was to enshrine the privy purses, privileges and dignities in the Constitution. He was absent from Delhi when the Congress party discussed the draft of Articles 291 and 362, which guaranteed those provisions. Opposition from some quarters in the Congress, including from Nehru himself, was vehement, prompting Patel to call a meeting of those party members who were critical of the draft clause. After the dissenters had had their say, Patel asked:

> Did you get Swaraj? Did you liquidate the States? Those of us who did it had pledged our word that constitutional guarantees would be given to the Rulers and the Civil Service. I don't know what the others who gave the pledge think. You can go to them if you like . . . We cannot start as a free country by breaking our promises.[26]

Articles 291 and 362 would be enshrined in the Constitution on 26 January 1950. But Patel would have little time to savour the victory. He died on 15 December 1950 in Bombay. He was aged seventy-five.

Patel's death was not unexpected. He had suffered a heart attack in March 1948, and in November 1950 had come down with a severe intestinal disorder followed by a stroke. But Menon felt the loss deeply. While there had been tension between the two men at times, Menon's pragmatism had complemented Patel's steadfastness. The same could not be said for Nehru, whose relationship with his deputy had been deteriorating since 1947. That there would be philosophical and political differences between such commanding and highly intellectual leaders of the left and right wings of the Congress party comes as no surprise. These differences worsened as the communal violence that accompanied Partition spun out of control, particularly in the Punjab, where the rulers of states such as Faridkot received a sympathetic hearing from Patel while Nehru desperately tried to prevent further killings of Muslims. The differences between the prime minister and his deputy were brought out sharply as India grappled with the crises in Junagadh, Kashmir and Hyderabad. Where Patel (and Menon) was urging the use of force to resolve the crisis, Nehru stuck to a more pacifist approach. Where Patel insisted that the princes be compensated for the sacrifices they had made, Nehru baulked at the expenditure of public money on their privy purses. But these were not unbridgeable differences. And, as Nehru acknowledged after Gandhi's assassination: 'The Sardar has been a tower of strength;

but for his affection and advice I would not have been able to run the State.'[27]

As for Nehru's relationship with Menon, it was coloured by his view that the suave Malayali was little more than Patel's puppet – an assertion that was far from the truth. M.K.K. Nayar, who joined the States Department in the late 1940s, recalls Nehru's fury at being told by his private secretary that Menon, a skilled mimic, would poke fun at the prime minister at the regular meetings with his senior secretaries. When Nehru confronted Menon with the information, he responded: 'As we have become independent, I didn't think it was necessary to bridle our sense of humour.'[28] Another illuminating story in Nayar's book, *Story of an Era Told Without Ill-Will*, concerns a complaint made to Patel by a Congressman regarding Menon's drinking habits. When Patel asked V. Shankar if his deputy had a habit of consuming liquor, he was told that he did, but only Scotch whiskey. Patel responded: 'Please advise all Secretaries to drink Scotch Whiskey.'[29]

In April 1951, the states ministry was wound up, despite protests from Menon that it was done with undue haste as it would have been very useful in building up the economies of the former states. His last achievement as secretary was to extract revenge on Baroda's gaekwar, Pratap Singh. A group of princes, including the gaekwar, had set up a Union of Rulers. Formally inaugurated in Bombay in February 1951, it comprised thirty-eight princes with Baroda as its president. Its declared purpose was 'to safeguard their common interest and well-being, as well as to promote social and cultural development of themselves and their families and to serve the Motherland in accordance with their best traditions in harmony with the progressive and stable elements in the country'.[30]

Menon was furious. He believed that Pratap Singh's real aim was to work up an agitation amongst the rulers as well as among the jagirdars and zamindars against the merger of the states. Reports reached the ministry that Baroda was also financing favourable press coverage of his plan. One maharaja told Menon that some rulers were waiting for war to break out between India and Pakistan in order to exploit the situation to get back their states.[31] As it happened, Pratap Singh was already under investigation for siphoning off funds from the state treasury overseas. On 14 April, a presidential order charged him with 'organising and financing various activities with a view to undoing the constitutional settlement arrived at with rulers of Indian States'. He was derecognized, and his title and privileges were conferred on his son. The action was seen as a warning to the princes to avoid extensive associational activity. Menon crowed that the move had the support of Parliament and both the local and international press. 'The government of India has struck back quickly. It is likely to have no more trouble from the princes,' he quoted the *Manchester Guardian* as reporting. 'I had the satisfaction at least of knowing that the edifice which we had built so laboriously would no longer be threatened, not from any princely quarter.'[32]

In May 1951, Nehru appointed Menon as the acting governor of Orissa. The posting to one of India's most backward states was seen as an act of revenge. When Patel had died six months earlier, Nehru had written two letters to Menon, one asking for the states minister's Cadillac to be returned to the prime minister's office, and the other saying the government would not pay the expenses of senior officials in Patel's department travelling to Bombay for his last rites. Menon responded by calling for a meeting of secretaries in the department and asking them to furnish him the names of those who wanted to attend. He then used his own money to charter a flight for himself and the other attendees. Menon remained in Orissa for just two months before a year-long stint in the Planning

Commission. After retiring from public life, he continued to tour India, giving lectures. Fulfilling a promise he made to Patel, he wrote two seminal books, *The Transfer of Power* and *The Story of the Integration of the Indian States.* In the late 1950s, he spent much of his time in the sprawling colonial-style bungalow he had built in Bangalore. He died of emphysema in 1964. A large part of the last year of his life was spent with his old friend H.V. Hodson.

13

Trouble on the Frontier

On 27 March 1948, a radio operator in Kalat near the rugged frontier separating Pakistan and Afghanistan tuned his shortwave receiver to the 9 p.m. bulletin from All India Radio, expecting to hear the usual denunciation of 'Pakistani aggression' in Kashmir. But that evening's bulletin was different. Quoting V.P. Menon, the official broadcaster stated that two months earlier Kalat had approached the Indian Union asking for accession to India but New Delhi had refused. The response from the Khan of Kalat, Ahmad Yar Khan, was swift. 'I am very much surprised to hear this mischievous news which I emphatically deny,' he wrote in a telegram to India's governor-general, Lord Mountbatten. 'Kalat Government has made no such request in any form whatsoever. I would request Your Excellency to contradict this announcement and release to press any correspondence that Indian Union may have received on behalf of Kalat Government.'[1] Three days later, Nehru stood up in India's parliament and announced that the AIR broadcast was unauthorized and untrue. Officials in Karachi were not convinced. India, they believed, was about to land troops by sea on the thinly populated coast of Makran and seize Kalat.

The case of Kalat, which prior to Partition was the third largest state in British India and for the previous six months had been independent, was no less contentious than that of Junagadh and Hyderabad. Its bid to maintain its sovereignty would lead to arguments over treaty obligations and accusations of cross-border meddling. As with Kashmir, Kalat's independence would end amid controversy, and the debate over whether its Khan signed the Instrument of Accession with Pakistan voluntarily or was forced to at gunpoint would continue. And, like Kashmir, the accession of Kalat fuelled an insurrection that lingers to this day.

Kalat was one of ten princely states that Pakistan inherited after Partition. Having to deal with a fraction of the number of states that Delhi did, the new government in Karachi faced fewer challenges than India in integrating these geographically and historically diverse entities. Bahawalpur and Khairpur, which shared borders with India, had been part of the Punjab States Agency. The North-West Frontier Province contained the states of Dir, Swat, Chitral and Amb. Of the so-called Baluchistan states, Kalat was the most important. The others were Las Bela, an enclave in Kalat, Kharan and Makran. All had originally been part of Kalat but were granted separate recognition by the British. Just before Independence, Pakistan's Constituent Assembly approved two forms of an Instrument of Accession, the longer of which was deemed proper for more developed states while the shorter applied only to the frontier tribal states. To both forms was appended a long list of subjects on which the dominion legislature could act in the states. By 14 August, the date of Pakistan's creation, no ruler had acceded to the dominion. Unlike India, where Mountbatten, Menon and Patel felt that India's very survival depended on getting as many states as possible to accede, Pakistan believed it had some breathing space by virtue of the fact that it had fewer states to deal with, and all of them had Muslim rulers presiding over Muslim-majority populations. Pakistan was also preoccupied with the crises in Kashmir and Junagadh, not to mention a refugee problem and reconstitution of its armed forces. But its assumption that all the states would neatly fall into its lap would prove premature.

~

Located on the other side of the Radcliffe Line from Bikaner and Jaisalmer, Bahawalpur was a seventeen-gun-salute state. It joined the ranks of the princely states under British paramountcy in 1833 after seeking the East India Company's protection against Ranjit Singh, the Sikh ruler of Punjab. Its sovereign in 1947 was Nawab Sadiq Muhammad Khan V, sixtieth in a line of descent that traced its origins to Al Abbas Ibn Abdul al Muttalib, an uncle of the Prophet Muhammad, through the Abbasid caliphs of Cairo and Baghdad. Bahawalpur was founded by Nawab Mohammad Bahawal Khan II in 1802 after the fall of the Durrani dynasty of Afghanistan that had occupied the region. Once stretching as far north as the Sutlej and Indus rivers, Bahawalpur had strategic importance and had been used as a base by the British for their campaigns in Baluchistan, Sind and Afghanistan.

Credit for turning a feudal backwater into a modern state with grand public buildings, canals, railways, and an efficient administration goes to Sadiq Muhammad Khan IV, who ascended the gaddi at the age of four and was invested with full powers at the age of eighteen in 1879. Unlike his traditionally dressed father, Sadiq Muhammad V belonged to the 'breeches and boots and flannels for cricket' school of ruler and prided himself on his European tastes, though he was also fanatical about his ancestry and wore a fez to emphasize his Abbasid roots. In 1882, the fabulously rich nawab with a penchant for white women (three of his wives were European), anonymously ordered from the Parisian firm La Maison Christofle a wooden bed decorated with 290 kilograms of sterling silver. At each corner of the bed was a life-size bronze figure of a naked woman with natural hair, movable eyes and arms, holding fans and horse tails. The four nudes represented the women of France, Spain, Italy and Greece. The bed's ingenious mechanics allowed him to set the figures in motion so that they fanned him while winking flirtatiously during a thirty-minute cycle of music from Gounod's *Faust* generated by a music box built into the bed.

Sadiq Muhammad Khan V ruled with a mix of piety and perversion. He was fanatical about his ancestry and, like Caliph Harun al-Rashid, he wandered the bazaars in disguise, sometimes as an ordinary camel driver, to gauge the mood of his subjects. The Sutlej Valley project, which turned thousands of acres of desert into productive farmland, made him fabulously rich. V.S. Naipaul, who visited the state while writing *Beyond Belief*, was told that the nawab built a separate building in the palace grounds for the English wives and their children so they would not know about his Indian wives. When the Pakistani army took over his palace after Partition, they found his collection of 600 dildos, some made of clay, some bought in England, some battery-operated. The army dug a pit and buried them, a local journalist told Naipaul.[2]

As independence approached, Bahawalpur's accession to Pakistan seemed a certainty because of its geographic location and demographic make-up. As its revenue minister, Penderel Moon, wrote, 'the state's people knew nothing of any other possibility'. Moon was therefore shocked when he learned that Sadiq Muhammad was considering either acceding to India or maintaining a quasi-independence in preference to swapping British paramountcy for Pakistan's.[3] In a rerun of the situation that rulers like Yeshwant Rao of Indore and Hanwant Singh of Jodhpur found themselves in, Muhammad had been swayed by advisers who believed that he might be able to extract more favourable concessions from the other side – in his case the Congress if he agreed to join India. He allegedly met with Nehru in London, and with Nehru's sister Vijaya Lakshmi Pandit at Bahawalpur's Sadiq Garh Palace in 1946, to discuss the terms of accession. However, Muhammad's ambivalence is revealed by his response to a British proposal to form a Rajputana States Confederation as a buffer between the two countries. When the nawab was offered the first presidency, he is reported to have responded: 'I believe we are all gentlemen here. My front door faces Pakistan, my servants' entrance faces India. I believe a gentleman usually enters his house through the front door.'[4] As the Pakistani historian Umbreen Javaid points out:

> Congress leaders were not interested in enticing Bahawalpur into the Indian Union. Moreover, since Bahawalpur was a Muslim State with a Muslim ruler and lay right astride the rail and road communications between Karachi and Lahore, its accession to India would be a deadly blow to Pakistan and must produce a violent Muslim reaction.[5]

Moon warned the state's prime minister, Mushtaq Ahmad Gurmani, that the nawab would be assassinated if he attempted such a course. Whether or not Gurmani notified him of the danger, all talk of acceding to India ended almost immediately.

On 15 August, the day after Pakistan's independence, the nawab adopted the title 'Jalalat ul Mulk 'ala Hadrat', or His Majesty the King of an independent Bahawalpur, a title which infuriated the new government in Karachi and was never recognized. Ten days later he issued a somewhat contradictory statement noting that the states had become 'fully independent and sovereign territories', while at the same time expressing the desire that his representatives 'participate in the labours and deliberations of the Pakistan Constituent Assembly . . . which will enable the two states to arrive at a satisfactory constitutional arrangement with regard to certain important matters of common concern'.[6] He then promptly departed to England for a holiday while some of the worst post-Partition violence engulfed his state. Eventually, however, and after an unspecified hitch, Bahawalpur's Instrument of Accession was signed and accepted by Jinnah on 5 October 1947.[7]

The accession of Khairpur, located in Sind and bordering the Indian state of Jaisalmer, occurred on the same day as Bahawalpur's. That things went relatively smoothly was largely thanks to the early death of Mir Ali Nawaz Khan, who had ruled the state from 1921 to 1935. The mir's death was blamed on his extreme obesity. The American journalist Webb Miller, best known for his graphic description of the violence inflicted on those who participated in Gandhi's Salt March, chanced upon him at the Cecil Hotel in Simla in 1930. 'His paunch was bespattered with soup spilled on its way from the plate to his distant mouth,' Miller observed, noting that the mir could not get his face closer than 60 centimetres to the table. The mir's opposition to Gandhi and the independence movement suggests his state would have gone further than Bahawalpur in wanting to maintain its autonomy. 'The interests of the Indian native rulers are identical with those of the British government,' the mir's minister told Miller. 'They believe if the present status is altered it will injure their interests.'[8] In 1931, the mir narrowly avoided being deposed after he was found guilty by the British of mismanaging the financial affairs of Khairpur and of indifference to his subjects' welfare as a result of his prolonged absences from his state. On his death in 1935 he was succeeded by his son Faiz Muhammad Khan.

Faiz Muhammad turned out to be an ineffective ruler of the state, which had a vast proportion of poor and illiterate subjects. Decades of mismanagement would see Khairpur's gun-salute status drop from nineteen to fifteen. '[Khairpur] carried a staggering burden of poverty, illiteracy, and ignorance,' the historian Wayne Wilcox writes. 'Each year after harvest the roads of Sind and Khairpur are filled with landless laborers, the haris, seeking a new field and a new master . . . Although the Indus and Sutlej slide together to nourish Khairpur's fields, the state is bleak and disquietingly isolated.'[9] Doubts over the mir's fitness to rule emerged soon after he began visiting England, where his guardian expressed dismay that the young prince displayed 'not a single boyish trait'. Over time his maladies included being 'vastly uxorious' – in other words, too in love with his wife – smiling for no reason and suffering from 'neurasthenia'.[10] His state of mind was thrown into doubt when he accidentally shot his nine-month-old son. The bullet penetrated the infant's stomach and right lung and exited through the back of his right shoulder. The infant survived and would go on to succeed his father.

In 1944, Faiz Muhammad was declared to be suffering from 'schizophrenic simples'; his powers were curbed and the resident of Punjab, J.P. Thompson, took over the state's administration. As the date for the transfer of power approached, Mountbatten recommended that Faiz Muhammad be formally deposed and a Regency Council be set up to rule on behalf of his son George Ali Murad, still a minor, to prevent a coup d'état by unscrupulous members of his family. On 20 July 1947, Faiz Muhammad was officially relieved of his rule and sent to Pune for rehabilitation.

Although Khairpur bordered Jaisalmer state, there was no pressure on Khairpur to accede to India and no urgency on the Pakistan side for its incorporation either. On 3 October 1947, the state's premier Ghulam Hussain Khan Talpur signed the Instrument of Accession while George was holidaying in Kashmir.

A similar lack of urgency applied to the so-called 'Frontier States' of Chitral, Dir, Swat and Amb, despite all four expressing their immediate desire to accede to Pakistan. Karachi's caution stemmed from the fact that Kashmir claimed Chitral and that Dir's accession might fuel tensions with Afghanistan. Swat and Amb were seen as islands of calm in an otherwise volatile region. The attitude of the Pakistani states ministry was to keep things that way.

Kashmir's abortive play for independence technically encompassed the eleven-gun-state of Chitral, which had recognized the suzerainty of the Kashmiri durbar since 1876. Following the lapse of paramountcy, Maharaja Hari Singh claimed that Chitral had no right to decide on its future without his permission. Chitral's ruler, however, told Jinnah as early as on 3 August 1947 that the state was 'exultantly' looking forward to joining Pakistan and 'redeeming its honour by shaking off the Kashmir suzerainty, of recovering the Gilgit districts ceded to Kashmir, and finally concluding a new honourable agreement with Pakistan in due course'.[11] Yet, when he telegraphed his willingness to sign an Instrument of Accession to Pakistan in early October 1947, it was ignored for fear of alienating Hari Singh. It was finally accepted on 18 February 1948, months after India had claimed Kashmir as its own territory. In May 1956, Nehru stated that India recognized no change in the status of Chitral and that he was unaware of any accession by it to Pakistan. The claim was probably made to shore up India's position in the event of any negotiated settlement with Kashmir.

Dir's location on the Afghan border and its obstinate ruler

posed a headache for Pakistan. Nawab Shah Jahan believed that the British would never really leave India, but if this 'miracle' were to happen, he wanted to be free to do what he liked. Using the threat of accession to Afghanistan, the nawab demanded a promise from Karachi that his relations with Pakistan would remain the same as they had been with Britain – namely, that he would retain control of the internal affairs of his state. Although he finally signed the Instrument of Accession on 8 November 1947, Shah Jahan refused to leave the state to confer with officials in Karachi until well into the 1950s. The state would remain a backwater for decades, with more kennels for the nawab's hounds than hospital beds. He refused to build schools, believing that too much education would see the end of his rule. When he finally ventured out of his state to meet with states ministry officials in Peshawar, he told reporters: 'There was no need for any constitutional reform, or rather any reforms in the State, because conditions are perfectly in order there and the peoples' entire satisfaction does not require any reform.'[12] Pakistan's patience finally ran out in September 1960, when border tensions led to armed clashes between Pakistani and Afghan soldiers. The nawab and his son were arrested for 'double dealing' with the Afghans and a minor son was installed in Shah Jahan's place.

The close relationship between the wali of Swat, Abdul Wadood, and Jinnah (the state's ruler had supported the referendum campaign for the North-West Frontier Province to become part of Pakistan) meant that his state's accession went without a hitch. In return for signing the Instrument of Accession on 3 November 1947, Swat was granted the lion's share of the disputed tribal area of Kalam, which was also claimed by Chitral and Dir. The leader of Amb, the smallest of Pakistan's states with an area of just 583 square kilometres, was also on close terms with the Quaid and wanted to accede immediately. But the state's insignificance meant that Jinnah ignored its entreaties for months. Amb's accession was finally recognized, almost as an afterthought, on 31 December 1947.

~

'The lofty peaks are our fortresses, the pathless gorges our friends,' runs a sixteenth-century Baluchi war ballad. Rugged, resource rich and occupying much of modern-day Baluchistan province, Kalat would prove to be the most vexatious of the states for Pakistan. Founded in 1638, it reached its zenith under Naseer Khan, who managed to unify the disparate Baluch tribes. By the end of the seventeenth century, Kalat embraced parts of Persia and Afghanistan and stretched southwards to the Makran coast on Pakistan's south-western flank. It first drew the attention of the British at the beginning of the 'Great Game' between Britain and Russia for control of Central Asia. Commanding several important passes into Afghanistan, including the Bolan, it was seen as a bulwark against any Russian advance into the subcontinent. After four decades spent fighting various Baluch clans, the British frontier official Sir Robert Sandeman signed a treaty with the Khan of Kalat in 1876. Under its terms, Britain was able to station troops in Kalat in return for generous subsidies and guarantees of tribal autonomy. To ensure that the frontiers of the Raj were contiguous with Afghanistan and to neutralize any threats to its military dominance, Britain divided Baluchistan with no regard for ethnic boundaries, giving part of it to Persia, part to Afghanistan and part to itself, which it called British Baluchistan. That left a truncated Kalat Confederacy and three smaller puppet principalities – Kharan, Makran and Las Bela. Uniquely among the Indian subcontinent's princely states, Kalat's ruler directly administered, through his wazir, only about one-third of his territory; the remaining portion was under the control of tribal chiefs known as sirdars, who owed him allegiance but resented interference in their affairs. Pakistan insisted that the 1876 treaty placed Kalat in the same category as other princely states of British India. However, Baluch nationalists read the document differently. They asserted that Kalat had direct treaty relations with Britain, which had recognized its independence and was therefore on the same footing as the British protectorate of Nepal.

Inspired by the anti-colonial struggle in India and the October Revolution in the Soviet Union, the first stirrings of Baluch nationalism appeared in the early twentieth century. The Kalat National Party (KNP), which demanded an 'independent, unified Baluchistan' and the restoration of those areas annexed by Britain, was formed in 1935 and was supported by Khan Ahmad Yar Khan. The British had little time for the khan, who was regarded by his one-time prime minister, Sir Edward Wakefield, as the heir to a 'tradition of craft and guile and endless intrigue . . . These, with poison and the sword, were the weapons with which he must maintain his position.' The khan's aim, Wakefield continued, was 'to convert his position of relative superiority into one of absolute supremacy'.[13] His aspirations were stymied by the fact that he controlled fewer than half of his state's eleven districts and had no official contact with the autonomous southern tribes.

In March 1946, Ahmad Yar Khan submitted a memorandum to the British Cabinet Mission visiting India affirming his intention that once the British withdrew, Kalat would return to the independent status it enjoyed prior to 1876. 'Kalat will become fully sovereign and independent in respect to both internal and external affairs, and will be free to conclude treaties with any other government or state . . . The Khan, his government, and his people can never agree to Kalat being included in any form of Indian union.' Kalat will, however, 'always be glad to enter into an alliance with any government which succeeds the British government in India on the basis of the strictest reciprocity', the memorandum stated. Khan also called for the principalities removed from Kalat under duress to return to its jurisdiction.[14]

The khan was initially on good terms with Jinnah, who allegedly asked him if the Muslim League could use the Makran coast for smuggling weapons should an armed insurrection be necessary to achieve his aim of a Muslim homeland. Relations began to sour when Khan demanded retrocession of the annexed areas, including the garrison town of Quetta and the strategically important Bolan Pass, to his state. Nehru, in his capacity as interim prime minister, opposed transfer of the territories on the grounds that Kalat was close to the border with Afghanistan. 'India cannot permit foreign forces and foreign footholds such as Kalat might afford near its own territories,' he said in July 1946.[15] While Pakistan was willing to issue a communique upholding Kalat's right to independence on the basis that it was a non-Indian princely state, it was not prepared to give up Quetta and other annexed areas.

From 19 July 1947 until a few days before Independence, Ahmad Yar Khan and his prime minister Muhamed Aslam held a series of talks in Delhi with Jinnah and Mountbatten at which Khan pressed his claims that the Khanate of Kalat should be treated as an independent and sovereign state. Mountbatten's initial reaction was non-committal, prompting a dressing down from Lord Listowel. London had come around to Nehru's viewpoint that an independent state close to the border of Afghanistan posed a geopolitical nightmare. Listowel argued that Kalat's claim to independence was contrary to the Government of India Act of 1935 and the Indian Independence Act.[16] Ignoring this advice, Khan and Jinnah issued a communique on 11 August 1947 acknowledging that Kalat was an independent sovereign state in treaty relations with the British government with a status different from that of other Indian states.[17] Three days later, Khan proclaimed his state's independence. Uniquely of all the subcontinent's princely states, Kalat was allowed to post an ambassador in Karachi and hoist the Baluchi national flag – a red Sword of Jihad on a green background. Elections were held, resulting in a landslide for the KNP, and Aslam was sworn in as the prime minister. Baluchi was made the official language.

Britain's high commissioner to Pakistan, Laurence Grafftey-Smith, described Karachi's acceptance of Kalat's independent status as being

> . . . of doubtful political wisdom and contrary to our interests elsewhere. This precedent may well encourage Hyderabad in maintaining its claim to independence in its negotiations with the Government of India . . . The admission of Kalat's claim means the emergence of a weak buffer state on the frontiers of Afghanistan, Iran and Pakistan.[18]

By now Jinnah also was beginning to have doubts about his decision. When Aslam travelled to Karachi in September with Douglas Fell, an ICS officer who had been appointed the state's foreign minister, they were told by Pakistan's foreign secretary Mohammad Ikramullah that the only topic on the table was Kalat's accession to Pakistan on the same terms as were being offered to other states. When Aslam and Fell returned to Kalat they presented the khan with five options: join the UK as a Crown colony, accede to India, accede to Iran, join Afghanistan or become part of Pakistan. The khan's preference was to apply to the UK for a protectorate status. Fell advised that Britain would not agree to making Kalat a protectorate as it still considered it an Indian state. The second option – acceding to India – was impractical, given the lack of any geographical link, and provocative. Fell was in favour of acceding to Iran, noting the country's strong ties with Baluchistan and the significant number of Baluchs who lived there, but he conceded there would be little appetite for the move in Tehran, which had enough problems on its hands. Joining Afghanistan was geopolitically risky, as Russia would have access to ports on the Indian Ocean if it ever took over the government in Kabul. The khan's strongly anti-communist sentiments also excluded this option. That left accession to Pakistan. The meeting ended without reaching an agreement.

Negotiations with the Government of Pakistan having stalled, Jinnah invited Ahmad Yar Khan to Karachi. The meeting did not go well. The khan hoped that Jinnah would accept a treaty of perpetual friendship, but the agreement that he presented was poorly drafted and not 'the kind of document which a political officer would have drawn up . . . The defects in the drafting alone would have antagonised a lawyer of the quality of Mr Jinnah,' noted Fell. The subsequent talks did not go well either, with the khan explaining his position in eloquent Urdu and Jinnah putting forward his views 'with equal elegance and eloquence in English'. As Fell would later recall:

> Unfortunately, though His Highness speaks English fluently, he does not find it easy to take in complicated ideas in that language, while Mr. Jinnah, being a Bombay Lawyer, is better at home in English than any other language and his Urdu is very poor indeed. Apparently, Mr Jinnah was as confident that he had persuaded the Khan as the Khan was confident that he had persuaded Mr Jinnah, and the only thing that the [Pakistani] Foreign Secretary agreed

upon was that neither of our principals had understood a word that the other had said.[19]

By now Baluchi nationalists were growing impatient. Addressing the Iwan-i-Am (lower house) of the Kalat state legislature on 14 December 1947, the KNP politician Ghaus Bakhsh Bizenjo, who had taken his inspiration for Baluch independence from Nehru and Gandhi, declared:

> . . . we have a distinct culture, and if the mere fact that we are Moslems requires us to amalgamate with Pakistan, then Afghanistan and Iran should also be amalgamated with Pakistan. They say we Baluch cannot defend ourselves in the atomic age . . . They say we must join Pakistan for economic reasons. Yet we have minerals, we have petroleum, and we have ports. The question is, what would Pakistan be without us? . . . We are ready for friendship with honour not in indignity. We are not ready to merge within the frontiers of Pakistan.[20]

On 25 February 1948, the KNP successfully sponsored a 'no-accession' bill in the Iwan-i-Am. The bill, however, stalled in the Iwan-i-Khas (upper house), where its members were unable to reach a final decision and proposed instead that the khan be given a three-month deadline to consider all aspects of the state's future. His patience exhausted, Jinnah entrusted Prime Minister Liaqat Ali Khan to travel to Kalat with some last-minute concessions. But the khan continued to equivocate, or as one military commander put it: 'He was trying to hunt with the hounds and run with the hare.'

Kalat's chances of remaining independent nosedived on 17 March 1948, when Pakistan recognized the feudatory states of

Las Bela and Kharan and accepted their demands for accession to Pakistan. The move, described by Ahmad Yar Khan as the 'political castration of the Baluch people', saw Kalat's territory halved and its access to the sea cut off. The khan threatened to protest to the International Court of Justice and the UN, prompting Pakistan to accuse him of plotting against its interests. Rumours began swirling that he was in secret talks with India for accession, that he was offering Afghanistan the use of its now-lost seaports and asking the British for protection.

It is at this point that the narratives diverge. In his memoir, Fell claims that he finally convinced the khan to sign an Instrument of Accession with Pakistan after warning him of the futility of armed resistance. Such a course of action 'could only have one ending and that quickly; the complete extinction of the State and the process would bring a lot of unnecessary suffering on the Khan's tribes' people'. Appealing to world opinion to support Kalat's case would be costly and ultimately futile. The only two countries likely to show any sympathy in Fell's view would be India and Afghanistan.[21] Despite opposition from Ahmad Yar Khan's brother Prince Agha Abdul Karim and hardliners in the KNP, Fell drafted a letter in which the khan apologized for the misunderstandings that had led to the impasse and stated that he was prepared to accede on whatever terms were demanded. After some redrafting by the khan, Fell left for Quetta on the evening of 27 March with the typed letter to present to A.S.B. Shah, secretary of the Ministry of States and Frontier Affairs. It was only the following morning that Fell was told about the AIR broadcast.

Shah believed the substance of the broadcast – namely, that the khan had been conducting secret talks about acceding to India. Fell was adamant that it was an attempt by Delhi to meddle in Kalat's affairs. Writing to Jinnah, he declared:

> Prima facie this is nothing but a piece of false propaganda carried on by an interested section in India with two motives behind; firstly to spoil the negotiations that are at present being conducted between Pakistan and Kalat; secondly to give false impression to the world that they are right in their policy in respect of Kashmir, Junagadh and Hyderabad Deccan.[22]

In Delhi, V.P. Menon was in damage-control mode, describing the claims made in the broadcast as 'utterly false'. 'Kalat approached us one or two months ago through one of the agents but we refused to have anything to do with Kalat, because we stand by our commitment that we will not touch a single state which rightly belonged to Pakistan,' he told a press conference. There would be no repeat, he said, by India of Pakistan's actions regarding Junagadh, nor was there any question of bribing Kalat, which was 'not worth the candle'.[23] He gave no explanation as to how the broadcast slipped past editorial controls. Addressing the Lok Sabha on 30 March, Nehru blamed 'an error in reporting'. He also said that a request by Kalat that India recognize it as an independent state and for permission to open a trade office had been ignored. Sections of the Indian press, however, claimed that Menon had committed a faux pas that had handed Kalat to Pakistan 'on a silver platter'.[24] The truth behind the AIR broadcast is unlikely to ever be told.

If Fell's narrative is correct, the AIR broadcast was irrelevant to the khan's decision to accede to Pakistan. Several Baluch historians, however, assert that the Instrument of Accession was illegal as it went against the February pro-independence vote in the lower house of the Kalat legislature. They also allege it was done under duress. On 22 March, Liaqat Ali Khan reportedly presided over a meeting of the three service chiefs to prepare invasion plans. Pakistani naval destroyers were deployed to Pasni and Jiwani on the Makran coast.

In his 'political autobiography', Ahmad Yar Khan claims he had no option but to sign the Instrument because 'things were moving fast towards a showdown'. Troops in Quetta were placed on high alert and the agent to the governor-general in Baluchistan was drawing up plans for a Hyderabad-style 'Police Action' against Kalat state.[25] In justifying his actions, the khan outlined a scenario where Pakistan's survival as a state would have been jeopardized by the igniting of a fratricidal war with the Baluchis, and a new menacing chapter of the 'Great Game' would have been unleashed.

> The army of Afghanistan could have easily entered into Baluchistan. India, too, could have sent her naval warships to the Makran coast, obviously to help the Baluchis, but in reality, this would have provided the best pretext for Russia to advance through Afghanistan and capture the ports on the Makran sea-coast.

Though unpopular, accession was necessary, he concluded. 'I abhorred the idea of mutual bloodshed of Muslims; and therefore acted the way I did.'[26]

Whatever the real story, the Baluchis would not go quietly. In April, the khan's brother Prince Karim left for Afghanistan to recruit a tribal army. But there would be no repeat of the surprise attack on Kashmir by tribal militias. Once Karachi found out about the planned invasion, troops transferred from the Punjab quickly overwhelmed Karim's militia. On 16 June 1948, Karim and twelve of his supporters were arrested. The rest of the militia dispersed, putting an end to the rebellion. But Baluchi resentment continued to simmer. In the early 1950s, Ahmad Yar Khan tried to mobilize tribal groups to reassert claims to Baluchistan's independence. After the commander-in-chief of Pakistan's army General Ayub Khan declared martial law in 1958, Ahmad Yar Khan was arrested and his palace bombed. In the following decades, attempts by successive Pakistani regimes to quell Baluchi nationalism would result in brutal repression and killings, as in Indian Kashmir. Pakistan continues to blame India for supporting what it describes as terrorist activities in the province.

14

Lost Among the Cobwebs

'The only thing that worries me about these trips is the crowd on the field when I land,' the twenty-eight-year-old maharaja of Jodhpur, Hanwant Singh, shouted over the roar of his single-engine Beechcraft to his guest, the British writer and photographer Jean Lyon, in early 1952. 'There are always mobs of people if they hear I'm coming. And these peasants don't know one end of a plane from the other. So far nothing has happened . . . knock on wood.'[1]

They were flying low over the dun-coloured desert of Bikaner state as its larger-than-life monarch prepared to address another election rally. Weighing in at 110 kilograms and a towering 192 centimetres tall, Hanwant was so self-conscious about his bulk he was always 'hunching his shoulders and ducking his head', Lyon observed. Fitting his massive frame into the cockpit of the tiny Beechcraft would have made for a comic scene as it prepared to take off from Jodhpur's aerodrome. Four years before, the headstrong Hanwant had whipped out a gun disguised as a pen and pointed it at V.P. Menon in protest at having to sign the Instrument of Accession. Less than three years had passed since he had been coerced into signing a merger agreement that saw his state absorbed into Rajasthan. Now he was getting his revenge by running against the Congress candidate in India's first election. His rather puzzling slogan was: 'A prince in free India should now rise to the level of the common man.'[2]

Lyon's description of her pre-election visit to Jodhpur is particularly poignant as Hanwant died after crashing the same aircraft a few weeks later just as votes were being counted. He would never know that weeks of campaigning with just four hours' sleep a night (helped by a daily dose of fifteen Dexedrine tablets) had resulted in a landslide election victory. With him on that fateful flight was his third wife Zubeida Begum, a professional singer whom he had met in the late 1940s when she was performing at his sister's wedding. She became his mistress and, despite protests from his first wife, the pair married and moved into Mehrangarh Fort while the rest of the family stayed at the newly constructed Umaid Bhawan Palace.

When Lyon was taken to Mehrangarh, she found the stables that once housed fifty elephants were empty. Of the more than a thousand servants employed by the royal family, only 200 remained . . . 'lost among the cobwebs'. Hanwant told Lyon that living off the government's privy purse of Rs 10 lakh was tough. 'I've had to cut the staff of all the palaces drastically. Last night when you first came in, you saw that there were no guards to guide you up to the palace, didn't you? Well, I can't afford them anymore.' When asked about how he financed his campaign, Hanwant laughed. 'Oh, I pull a button off a shirt now and again and sell it.'[3]

The majority of those yelling 'Bapji ki jai!' (Victory to our father!) and throwing coloured powders at his election rallies were peasants. 'They were people for whom royalty still glittered, and it was likely that the thought of turning against it had not yet occurred to them,' Lyon surmised. Addressing the adoring crowd, the maharaja proceeded to give the shortest electoral speech she had ever heard, consisting of just two brief sentences. 'We've had enough of this. Now let us go to the temple and think about God.'[4]

~

Of the 284 Indian princely families that were guaranteed privy purses and privileges at the time of the merger of their states into the Union of India, not all 'were pensioned off, and retired into their make-believe world of hunting and other pursuits', as some historians have claimed.[5] More than one-third would enter politics, either at the federal or state level before the end of 1971, the year in which the privy purses were finally abolished. Of the nine-to-twenty-one-gun states, half would field candidates – often but not always in opposition to the Congress. The Maharaja of Rewa never ran for office himself, but he sponsored twenty-three Congress candidates in the 1967 elections, the majority of whom were elected. Taking data from the general elections from 1962 to 1967, psephologist William Richter found that having a princely candidate run in a constituency raised the overall voter turnout and increased a party's chances of victory.[6] The greatest concentration of rulers-turned-politicians was among seventeen-gunners such as Jaipur, where Gayatri Devi, the wife of Maharaja Sawai Man Singh, would earn a place in the Guinness Book of Records for winning her seat with a 1,75,000-vote majority in her debut political performance for the centre-right Swatantra Party in 1962. By the late 1960s, the princes, thanks to their political clout, were in a better bargaining position than anyone could have predicted at the dawn of India's independence.

With a success rate of more than 80 per cent in the period from 1952 to 1971, princely candidates were eagerly sought after by political parties of almost every shade, including their greatest critic – the Congress. As the political economist Francine Frankel points out: 'Despite the loss of legal authority, the princes, as well as lesser members of the landed aristocracy, were able to exploit traditional vertical ties based on rank, caste, and economic dependence to perpetuate an aura of political legitimacy.'[7] Fear of losing their privy purses initially deterred many princes from running against the Congress. But as their confidence grew, so did their desire to seek revenge against a party they believed had broken its promises to them. As one ruler who spoke to the writer Taya Zinkin explained: 'The rulers are letting themselves be hanged with these financial strings. We ought to stand on our dignity like men and tell the Congress: "Take away your bribes. Let us fight you at the polling booth like Indians."'[8]

Among those who would change allegiances was Vijayaraje Scindia of Gwalior, who claimed she was drafted into politics against her will by Jawaharlal Nehru in 1957. Running as the Congress candidate, she outpolled her nearest rival V.G. Deshpande of the right-wing Mahasabha Party by two-to-one. Ten years later, she fell out with the Congress. Unable to decide which Opposition party to join, she ran simultaneously for the Swatantra Party in the state assembly and the Jana Sangh in the Lok Sabha. 'Our cavalcade merely had to pass near a village for that village to empty itself and form a procession behind us,' she recalls in her autobiography.[9] Her popularity swept her to victory in the seat of Guna for Jana Sangh with a margin of 2 lakh votes over her Congress rival, breaking Devi's record, and won her the state assembly seat of Karera. Her switch away from the Congress would doom the party to electoral oblivion in Madhya Pradesh for the next two decades. As the columnist Sunanda Datta Ray caustically observed: 'The old kingdom [of Gwalior] includes ten parliamentary constituencies where the maharani's word is law. No politician is ever elected there without her approval.'[10]

Princes also dominated the politics of Orissa, where more than half of the state's territory and one-third of its population belonged to the former princely states. Drawing heavily on candidates from royal families, the regional Ganatantra Parishad won thirty-one seats against the Congress's sixty-seven in the 1952 elections for the Vidhan Sabha. In 1957, the party increased its tally to fifty-one seats, forcing the Congress out of power. Princely candidates also challenged the Congress in Gujarat and Rajasthan. In the 1967 elections, nearly half of twenty-four royals who were elected to the Lok Sabha had run against the Congress, exacerbating the party's worst performance until then. In the state assemblies their success rate was even higher. It was only a matter of time before the Congress sought revenge. 'The Princes were asking for it,' remarked Rajendrasinh, the maharaja of Idar. 'Wherever we stood we just wiped them out. Now the feeling grew among Congressmen that this was a very dangerous group of people, so something had to be done to curb this particular group. It was as simple as that.'[11]

For Indira Gandhi, who had been in power for just over a year, there was only one way to avoid an electoral nightmare – institute a programme of populist measures that would put her opponents in their place. In the case of the princes that meant the abolition of their privileges and privy purses. But getting rid of them would not be easy. The dispensations enjoyed by the princes had been guaranteed under Articles 291 and 362 of the Constitution of India. Obtaining the two-thirds majority needed in the Lok Sabha to change the Constitution would require equal doses of cunning and coercion.

This would not be the first time that princely privileges had been drawn into the political debate. Indira's father Jawaharlal Nehru had been ambivalent about them from the beginning and had opposed moves to have them enshrined in the Constitution. Patel, however, insisted that the rights and privileges of the rulers must not be tampered with. Writing to Nehru from his sickbed in Bombay on 9 August 1949, he reminded the prime minister that the Rs 4.5 crore spent on the purses each year was 'comparatively an insignificant price to pay' for the unity of India. These commitments were consecrated in assurances by the head of state on behalf of all Indians, 'and it is our moral duty to ensure that these commitments are fully honoured both now and in future'. The Constitution should guarantee these undertakings. 'Any other alternative would not satisfy those who had accepted in good faith our pledges and our promises.' Having taken from the princes everything else that they valued, it would be wrong to 'show any nigggardly attitude in these matters . . . I consider it a matter of faith and honour, and I feel it would be moral cowardice on my part if I refrained from discharging this obligation,' he said, adding that he was ready to come to Delhi, despite his illness, 'merely for the sake of sponsoring these proposals'.[12] Nehru replied that the cabinet was 'a little surprised and taken aback by the fact that these privy purse payments, free of income tax were for perpetuity'. However, he conceded that because of the government's assurances, 'we have to abide by them, whatever the future might do'.[13]

Patel's death in December 1950 freed Nehru from the need to consult his deputy on contentious policy matters. But the prime minister moved cautiously. 'Many of us feel these privy purses are too bloated,' he wrote to a cabinet minister who had spoken out against the princes. 'Nevertheless, we have committed ourselves to them and we cannot easily walk through our commitments.'[14] Left with no alternative but to appeal to their patriotism, Nehru wrote a long letter in the autumn of 1953 to the hundred or so princes receiving more than Rs 1 lakh per year (the equivalent of approximately Rs 84 lakh in 2023), pointing out that payment of large sums of money to a functionless group could not be justified on any moral, political or social basis. In a democracy where the masses were growing in awareness and struggling hard to better their wretched lot, privy purses were an anachronism. 'Should we wait till the people put an end to this? Political wisdom consists in anticipating events and guiding them.' He ended his letter by appealing to the princes to come up with their own suggestions as to 'how best we can deal with this situation'.[15] After receiving no response, he wrote to the princes a second time, in June 1954, suggesting that those with purses of Rs 2 lakh to Rs 5 lakh should voluntarily contribute 15 per cent of their purse to developmental schemes in their states and invest 10 per cent in a national loan plan.

> A part of the privy purse might well be set aside for the development of their own people. Private properties, many of which are now a burden to the owner, might be used for purposes of social welfare and public advantage. But, apart from the monetary aspect, I should like the princes to line up with their people in other ways also and thus help in the great tasks which demand all our strength and energy.[16]

An unwillingness to break ranks publicly ensured that no constructive response was forthcoming, but privately princes from some of the larger states were acknowledging the reality that their glorified government pensions could not last forever. 'We ought to give the pensions back. The people will hold our tax-free money against us. This money is very little, but politically it is worth a lot to our enemies,' one prescient ruler told Taya Zinkin in 1957.[17]

There would be no changes made to princely privileges for more than a decade, aside from a policy introduced in 1961 that halved the amount when an heir succeeded to his father's title. An attempt to pass a resolution to abolish the privy purses raised at the Bhubaneswar session of the AICC by the right-wing politicians K. Kamaraj and Atulya Ghosh in 1963 was defeated because its opponents argued that it contravened the Constitution. By now Nehru had come to appreciate the soft-power potential of the erstwhile rulers, whatever his views on the privileges they enjoyed. Many were suave and cosmopolitan, making them perfect ambassadors for India.

Indira Gandhi developed her pathological dislike for the princes from an early age. She would inherit her father's strongly held views about malevolent maharajas and autocratic nawabs. And she would be exposed to their sense of entitlement first-hand. The year she spent at Rabindranath Tagore's Patha Bhavana school at Santiniketan in 1934 coincided with the presence of the princess of Cooch Behar, Gayatri Devi, who would later become maharani of Jaipur. Young, beautiful and liberated, Devi would spend her breaks surreptitiously smoking cigarettes behind the girls' toilet block while boasting of how she had bagged her first leopard at the age of twelve. As the writer Khushwant Singh wryly observed: 'Indira could not stomach a woman more good-looking than herself and insulted her in Parliament, calling her a bitch and a glass doll. Ayesha [Gayatri Devi] brought the worst out in Indira:

her petty, vindictive side.'[18] While campaigning in Jaipur against Devi's Swatantra Party in the 1967 election, Indira challenged the crowd to ask the maharajas

> . . . how many wells they dug for the people in their States when they ruled them, how many roads they constructed, what they did to fight the slavery of the British. If you look at the account of their achievements before Independence, it is a big zero there.[19]

Devi went on to win her seat, but eight years later Indira would get her revenge by locking her up in Tihar jail during the Emergency. Her crime: violating currency laws by not declaring £19 in sterling and a few Swiss francs found during a tax raid on one of her palaces.

When the results of the 1967 election came in, the Congress party had suffered its biggest setback since Independence – its majority reduced to just forty-five seats in the lower house, together with the loss of ten states. In May 1967, the AICC held a post-mortem meeting to analyse the party's poor performance. The Congress needed a makeover, the AICC concluded. With, 'the slow and tardy progress towards the goal of socialism' singled out as the main cause of the electoral setback, the privy purses were back in the firing line, not because of their cost to the exchequer but because of the political capital they might bring if their abolition became party policy. Congress treasurer Atulya Ghosh introduced a note calling the payments 'incongruous to the concept and practice of democracy'. Not all Congressmen shared Ghosh's view. No one, however, could ignore the fact that the Opposition Swatantra Party had won many of its forty-four seats thanks to princes running as candidates or lending their support. The AICC responded by proposing a radical ten-point programme, which included calls for the abolition of princely privileges such as exemption from import duties and civil prosecution, but not as yet the privy purses.

The AICC met again in July, this time amid rumblings from a faction known as the Young Turks. The grouping, which included Chandra Shekhar, who would briefly serve as prime minister from 1990 to 1991, and Mohan Dharia, the general secretary of the Maharashtra Pradesh Congress Committee and a member the Congress Forum for Socialist Action, was ostensibly supporting Indira against right-wingers in the party, including another future prime minister, Morarji Desai. Backed by Home Minister Yashwantrao Chavan, who coveted the deputy prime ministership, the Young Turks were angry that the ten-point programme excluded an earlier promise by Indira to nationalize banks and was too soft on the princes. Late at night, when the party leaders, including Indira, Desai and most of the delegates, had gone home, Dharia moved a resolution demanding abolition of the privy purses as well as the privileges of the former princely rulers. Dharia's amendment was approved by seventeen votes to four. Abolishing the last vestiges of India's princely order was now official Congress policy.

Reaction to the amendment reflected the disarray within Congress. S.K. Patil, an outspoken leader of the party's right wing, decried the move as 'stark madness'. Desai, who was the finance minister, termed it as a 'breach of faith'. Few others, however, protested. Congress president K. Kamaraj, who was Indira's implacable opponent, said nothing. Chavan remarked he had 'no problem' with the decision. The prime minister, enigmatic as always, merely expressed regret at the way the amendment had been introduced. It put her in a difficult position. If she went along with it, she would be breaking a promise her father had made to the states. If she tried to stop it, she would be seen as putting the interests of the princes above those of the poor. Her compromise was to make a rhetorical commitment to the resolution while promising to consult with the princes. Chavan was put in charge of the negotiations.

On 15 August 1967, the twentieth anniversary of Independence, a group of eleven princes – most of them MPs – inaugurated the 'Rulers of Indian States in Concord for India'. Although the declared purpose of the Concord included everything from protecting wildlife to preserving princely heritage, tradition and culture, its core activity was to fight abolition of the privy purses. Despite the grand-sounding title, it would fall prey to the same cracks and fissures that had stymied the effectiveness of the Chamber of Princes. Travancore and Kolhapur wanted the priority to be princely privileges rather than the privy purses, which put them at odds with the erstwhile rulers of the small states, who would face serious economic hardship if privy purses were abolished. The south Indian states were largely left out of the Concord, and Maharaja Mayurdwajsinhji Meghrajji of Dhrangadhra, its intendant general, was criticized for exercising 'dictatorial' powers. The traditional concerns of status and rank still bedevilled the princes. They lacked any real experience at lobbying politicians. Intermittent negotiations between the government and their representatives would drag on for more than three years, with both sides blaming each other for the lack of progress. As the journalist Dom Moraes eloquently observed, few princes could see beyond their immediate concerns and realize that 'if they wanted money, they would have to work for it'. Nor would they be able to use their titles 'like earned badges of honour'.[20]

The princes had a formidable foe in the politically ambitious Chavan. Before joining Nehru's cabinet in 1962, he had been the last minister of the bilingual Bombay province and the first chief minister of Marathi-speaking Maharashtra. In the 1967 general election, he was instrumental in getting a Parliament ticket from Kolhapur for Lieutenant General (retd) S.P.P. Thorat, a veteran of the Kashmir and Burma campaigns. Despite Chavan's canvassing of Thorat, the latter was defeated by the Rajmata of Kolhapur. During the campaign, Chavan had made disparaging remarks about the gaddi of the princes, 'comparing it with an old mattress, which should be discarded'.[21] In August 1967, he stood up before the Rajya Sabha and asked: 'Could a person who received Rs 150 a month, including dearness allowance, claim to have equal rights with those who received lakhs of rupees, tax free in perpetuity? Could a republic justify the existence of two classes of citizens?' In the debate that followed, many speakers referred to the government's commitments to the princes and the guarantees given them in the Constitution. But Chavan was unmoved. 'We are committed to providing the people . . . jobs, education, decent living conditions. What about commitments? The decision is clear. The course is set.'[22] Responding to Chavan's attack, Pratap Singh of Baroda, chairman of the Concord's steering committee, replied: 'Twenty-two years ago on this very floor, we were referred to as co-architects of independence. Today we are branded as reactionaries obstructing the path of an egalitarian society.'[23] Later, when asked how he felt about the prospect of losing his privileges, he told reporters: 'How will you feel if there is a demand to remove your clothes?'[24]

Chavan's forthrightness was enough to make the polo-loving Maharaja of Jaipur quit his cushy post as the Indian ambassador to Spain and return to India to fight alongside his fellow princes. In July 1967, Man Singh appealed directly to his old friend, Lord Mountbatten, to put international pressure on the Indian government, protesting that he would lose £180,000 if the purses were abolished and be forced to 'take up residence' in Britain. Mountbatten raised the matter with the Commonwealth Office, saying that he felt a 'deep sense of personal responsibility'. The proposed abolition was 'a breach of [his] solemn undertaking'.[25] As governor-general he had persuaded the rulers of the states to accept the arrangements for their privy purses and privileges and told them they could trust the Indian government. He had been mistaken. Now he was about to become the self-declared 'Ombudsman for the Indian Princes'.[26]

Instead of raising the matter publicly, Mountbatten drafted a personal letter to Indira Gandhi questioning the legality of the move to abolish the privy purses while at the same time sympathizing with the challenges she faced. John Freeman, British high commissioner in New Delhi, thought the intervention unwise. The privy purse was a subject of 'acute political sensitivity' on which Indira had 'a certain personal commitment'.[27] Despite being private and confidential, the letter's contents were leaked. On 2 September 1967, the Bombay weekly *March of the Nation,* which supported the Swatantra Party, ran a front-page story titled 'Mountbatten Suggests Caution'.[28] Indira chose to ignore the letter. Urged on by other princes, Mountbatten became bolder in his criticism of the Indian government in general and of Chavan in particular. 'It is absolutely monstrous that this man, Chavan (on whose head I had a price when I was Viceroy as he was a Goonda) should be breaking the pledges given by Nehru and Patel . . . What can we do about this?' he demanded of the Commonwealth Office.[29] Sir Morrice James, Freeman's successor as high commissioner, considered Chavan a potential prime minister and wanted Mountbatten restrained.

Chavan maintained the princes were simply not interested in

genuine negotiations or in making any compromises, an assessment that Indira gradually came around to share. 'As the prime minister, she had to weigh the pros and cons of the issue,' Chavan told the author T.V. Kunhi Krishnan.

> She had a wider view than I had. She had more information with her, more contacts, possibly better contacts. She was in a position to find out the truth about the whole situation and sift it from the untruth . . . But when she realised that the princes did not mean business, she did not hesitate a moment to go ahead with the bill, and I should say this to her credit that she took a correct position.[30]

By now the question of abolishing the privy purses had become entwined in the battle for supremacy in the Congress – a battle between the right-wingers in the Syndicate led by Kamaraj and Desai and Indira's own faction, known as Congress (R) – the initial variously standing for 'Reform' or 'Requisitionist'. In August, Indira won a decisive victory by getting V.V. Giri elected president of India over the Syndicate's preferred candidate Neelam Sanjiva Reddy, whom she suspected of conspiring to remove her from office and install Desai as prime minister. If she wanted to introduce bank nationalization or to dethrone the princes, she needed a compliant president. Giri would prove a loyal servant. His election, however, only served to exacerbate the Congress split. On 12 November 1969, the Syndicate-controlled Congress Working Committee expelled Indira from the Parliamentary Party, but several days later she was able to gather enough support from minor parties, including the communists, to confirm her leadership. Indira portrayed the fight for Congress not as a fight for power, but as 'a conflict between those who are for socialism . . . and those who are the status quo for conformism and for less than full discussion inside the Congress'.[31]

Matters came to a head in early 1970. Meeting with the Concord in January, Chavan reiterated that the government's intention was to implement the will of the people by abolishing purses and privileges. The princes responded by sending a 'memorial' to Giri, requesting that he seek an advisory opinion from the Supreme Court. The princes had no hope of a sympathetic hearing. According to the historian Granville Austin, Giri never sought the court's opinion. On 12 February, the Concord issued a 'Convention Statement' recalling their contribution to 'the creation of a new national unity' by having parted 'with their powers and jurisdictions'. The statement said the princes saw 'no great difficulty in the gradual utilisation of private wealth and income for public benefit'. They were in favour of using their purses for the public good by 'setting up funds or trusts for social service and public benefit'. But if the government persisted 'in proceeding arbitrarily, thereby jeopardising the honour and credit of our country', they would have to resist.[32] For Chavan, the statement only served to confirm his suspicions that the princes were only in it for the money. 'Even modern capitalists can perhaps give up their rights and privileges, but these people, entrenched so strongly in their own positions for centuries, would not like to lose them.'[33]

On 18 May 1970, Chavan moved for leave to introduce the Twenty-fourth Amendment Bill in the Lok Sabha to delete from the Constitution two articles and a portion of a third providing for the princes' purses and privileges. The bill was challenged by P.K. Deo, ex-ruler of Kalahandi and a member of the Swatantra Party, on the grounds that it was 'not open to the legal, legislative competence of the House to challenge the foundations of the Constitution'. Deo was supported by Balraj Madhok, a former RSS activist. Several royals, including Vijayaraje Scindia, the dowager maharani of Gwalior, joined parties allied with the Hindu nationalist cause. Many of their supporters remembered the assistance the princes had given to organizations such as the Hindu Mahasabha in the lead-up to Independence. The bill was introduced into the Lok Sabha on a voice vote but shelved until September. Chavan's biographer Krishnan speculates that Indira wanted to delay the introduction of the bill because she was negotiating secretly with the princes and a settlement that would see the princes forgo 50 per cent of their purses was imminent.[34]

When the bill to abolish the privy purse came up for discussion in the Lok Sabha in the last week of the monsoon session of Parliament in September 1970, Chavan was finance minister and Indira had taken charge of the home portfolio. The Congress was in power as a minority government, and she desperately needed to introduce some populist policies to buttress the party's position ahead of the next election, due in 1972. Bank nationalization was one of those measures. It had far-reaching implications for all sectors of the economy. In contrast, abolishing the privy purses, which cost the exchequer around 0.2 per cent of the annual budget, was not going to put more food on the table of peasants in Bihar. As the Maharana of Udaipur remarked, the amount was so pitiful 'it wouldn't buy every Indian a picture postcard'.[35] But it was a politically sensitive issue, one that could be used in an ideological battle, as Indira framed it, between the forces of progress and those of reaction.

Introducing the bill to abolish princely privileges in the Lok Sabha, she pitched it 'as an important step in the further democratisation of our society . . . [representing] the momentum of social change in our country'. She appealed to the princes to cooperate with the government 'in doing away with certain institutions which are not in harmony with a society striving for equality and social justice'. History, she said, was replete with instances where 'what was sacrosanct in one age was considered inhuman in another'. Finally, she warned that 'either we bring about change peacefully and with consent, or the change will come in a manner which I am sure this Parliament and this country would not like'.[36] Countering her argument, Desai responded by slamming the bill as 'fraudulent and deceitful and . . . not consistent with the spirit of the Constitution'. Failure to honour commitments made to the princes would be a breach of faith. Speaking on behalf of the Concord, the Maharaja of Dhrangadhra said there was no greater hardship than the dishonour the government was inflicting on the rulers. The glorious chapter written by the founding fathers was now being 'brought to an inglorious end'.[37] On hearing Indira's threats, Vijayaraje Scindia opined: 'I could not help being reminded of how Lord Dalhousie had justified his annexation of Oudh, because not to have done so would have been wrong in the eyes of God.'[38]

With the support of socialist and communist parties, a bill was introduced to abolish the privy purse and princely privileges. It was passed by 336 to 155 votes in the lower house. But when it reached the Rajya Sabha, it failed to get the required two-thirds majority. When the votes were tallied, 149 members had voted for the bill and seventy-five against. It had failed by just one third of one vote. The reasons offered for the narrow margin included bad weather, which prevented two MPs from boarding their flight in Calcutta, a member of the Dravida Munnetra Kazhagam (DMK) party absenting himself, and a Congressman leaving for the toilet when the vote bell rang. The bill's passage was also stymied by Charan Singh, the powerful chief minister of Uttar Pradesh and leader of the agrarian-based Bharatiya Kranti Dal (BKD). Singh opposed the privy purses bill on the grounds that it would constitute a breach of a solemn agreement made by, and on behalf of, the country's leaders at the time, and also because it represented a step towards abolition of private property, which he insisted was fundamental to democracy. Singh also believed that Indira's attempt to abolish the privy purse was little more than a 'political stunt', given that the payments were minuscule compared with the amount of tax payments that were evaded outright by 'big Capitalists and industrialists', which, he said, was 'equivalent to 180 times the amount of the privy purse'.[39] Knowing that the BKD had three members in the Rajya Sabha, Indira sent word that in return for voting for the bill Singh could stay on as chief minister until 1974. Singh said no. Indira was furious. After the vote failed, the Maharaja of Bikaner said to her: 'You have saved us.' She responded: 'We will execute you.'[40]

Soon after the defeat of the bill, the cabinet held an emergency meeting, and after a seventy-five-minute discussion issued what became known as the 'Midnight Order'. Having recognized the princes, the president could derecognize them. A note was prepared for the cabinet, which was cleared by the law ministry and then signed by the home secretary. Cabinet then met and, without dissent, approved derecognition. The decision was conveyed to Giri in Hyderabad in a communication sent by an Air Force plane. At around 11.30 p.m., he was roused from his bed and handed the cabinet note. A few minutes later he formally issued an order under Article 366 (22) of the Constitution, derecognizing the princes with immediate effect. The same plane carried the signed order back to Delhi, landing at 1.34 a.m. Indira's principal secretary, P.N. Haksar, 'justified' the 'decisive' turn in a letter to the prime minister on 5 September 1970: 'The President has the unquestioned power to derecognize . . . There is widespread support in the country for putting an end to an antiquated system.'[41]

Giri's actions caused an uproar. Indira's opponents in the Congress (O), one of the party's splinter groups, compared her to

Stalin and Hitler. Meanwhile, eight former rulers brought a suit before the Supreme Court of India challenging the presidential order. Anticipating the possibility of a court battle, the Concord had set aside funds and had engaged top lawyers to plead their case. Their petitions were based on three main arguments: the president had no power to withdraw the recognition of a ruler once he had been recognized; the order violated the constitutional mandates in Articles 291 and 362; and derecognition of the princes en masse was an arbitrary exercise of power for a collateral purpose. The government responded to say the petitions were not maintainable because the right to receive a privy purse was 'a political agreement' and was 'in the nature of a political pension' and not a property right. Since the government had inherited the concept of paramountcy from the Crown, recognition of 'rulership' was a 'gift of the Presidency' and an act of the state. Therefore, the government argued, the courts were excluded from enforcing agreements with the princes.[42]

As they awaited the court's decision, a mood of pessimism pervaded the now defunct royal houses, with one prince mournfully remarking to Dom Moraes: 'With Indira in control of everything, we expect a biased decision.'[43] He was mistaken. On 15 December 1970, after a four-day huddle, the Supreme Court rewarded the princes with a nine-to-two ruling that the president's order was 'ultra vires', illegal, and on that account inoperative. The president's powers did not extend to 'withdrawing recognition of all the rulers by a midnight order'. Justice Shah, who delivered the majority judgment, held: 'Neither the paramountcy of the Grand Moghul who could give subedarships to his generals as he pleased, nor the paramountcy of the British Crown has descended to the President.'[44]

Their extinction had been stayed. The princes could still enjoy their privileges and privy purses. Summing up the verdict of the

Supreme Court, the *Times of India* wrote: 'The President proposes, the Supreme Court disposes. This is how the drama centring on the privy purses of the princes has ended for the moment.'[45] Mountbatten felt vindicated, gloating to Charles Curran, director general of the BBC, that Indira had received 'a very bloody nose' in consequence of ignoring his warnings.[46]

Once again, hubris had got the better of him. It would be a punch-drunk Indira who would deliver bloody noses to those who dared to defy her. Twelve days after the verdict, she addressed the nation on All India Radio to announce an early election. Bank nationalization and abolition of the privy purse 'were welcomed by large masses of people throughout the country . . . [but] reactionary forces have not hesitated to obstruct . . . these urgent and vitally necessary measures'.[47] The impatience of the people was 'being exploited by political elements'. Time was a luxury India could not afford, she insisted. 'The millions who wait for food, shelter, and jobs are pressing for action. Power in a democracy resides with the people. That is why we have decided to go to our people and seek a fresh mandate from them.'[48]

Although the trigger for the election had been the judicial setback on the privy purse matter, Indira campaigned hard on the powerful slogan of 'Garibi Hatao' (abolish poverty), and when the results were announced in March 1971, she had won a thumping victory. She now had the magical two-thirds majority she needed to amend the Constitution. With her triumph, any chance of survival of the princely order vanished. As Ann Morrow writes, the princes 'were as vulnerable as the deer they had tied up between two lighted posts to be pounced on by a tiger at viceregal shoots'.[49]

Indira would leave her prey panting in the heat for nearly a year before coming in for the final kill. Faced with a civil war in East Pakistan and a flood of refugees entering West Bengal, India intervened in December 1971, inflicting a humiliating defeat on Pakistan and aiding the creation of the new state of Bangladesh. Realizing that this time they needed all the help they could get, the princes again turned to Mountbatten, who once more appealed to Indira 'to be generous', adding that her father 'would have approved of [it]'.[50] His appeal fell on deaf ears, and in the closing days of the winter session of Parliament the Constitutional Amendment Bill was reintroduced. On 2 December, the Lok Sabha debated and passed the Twenty-sixth Amendment in a single day. Introducing the bill, Indira blamed its earlier failure to pass on 'a technical failure . . . the will of the people was not in doubt'. [51] The bill to derecognize the princes and abolish their privy purse and privileges became law on 28 December 1971. A year later, Zulfikar Ali Bhutto would follow her lead and issue his own presidential order abolishing the privy purse and privileges of the rulers of the states that had acceded to Pakistan.

The rights and rituals of a cobwebbed past were now relegated to the status of historical footnotes, just like the Raj had been a quarter of a century earlier. For some, like the jurist Nani Palkhivala, the real losers were not so much the princes as the common man.

> The basic issues involved in the case were not concerned with privileges and privy purses – with the booming of salute guns or the counting of our devalued currency; the basic issues centred round the sanctity of the Constitution and public morality . . . If privy purses could be stopped by executive action, the most unsafe investment in the world would be the securities of the Indian Government.[52]

One of the most vocal critics of Indira's constitutional coup was Patel's private secretary, V. Shankar, who wrote that abolishing the privy purses without compensation was 'an unprecedent act in the annals of India's constitutional history . . . The utter impropriety, immorality, unconstitutionality, lack of chivalry . . . and ingratitude of the transaction begs description.'[53] Ironically, the legislation was born, debated and passed in a Parliament built on land that Maharaja Madho Rao of Jaipur had ceded to the British for their new capital in exchange for a handful of villages in the Punjab.

Epilogue: 'No More Boodle'

'Sometimes one thinks of the past. One thinks of the entertaining, of playing a role,' Jayachamarajendra Wadiyar confessed to Bernard Weinraub of the *New York Times* in late 1973. Weinraub was interviewing the ailing head of the Mysore royal family in a dimly lit room of the Amba Vilas Palace piled high with books, magazines and records. A few years earlier, up to 30,000 people had jammed the palace courtyard for the annual ten-day long Hindu festival of Dussehra. Magicians and clowns entertained the masses and a royal elephant knelt before Srikantadatta, believed by his followers to be the reincarnation of Lord Vishnu. 'It was quite pleasant, of course, but there's no sense lingering on the past, is there? You have to make the best of what's available now.'[1]

Bhawani Singh of Jaipur, technically India's last maharaja as he was placed on the gaddi just a couple of months before the privy purse and titles were abolished, was equally sanguine about the new dispensation. 'The government recognizes you as "Mr" now. But some people still use the titles. And around Jaipur things haven't changed that much. People still look to the old rulers for solutions to problems like getting electricity and roads,' he told the freelance writer Susan Yerkes in 1984. Instead of looking to the durbars for provision of welfare services such as education and public healthcare, the inhabitants of the erstwhile states had to deal with much more remote and bureaucratic authorities in the state capitals or in far-off Delhi. 'Unfortunately, no matter how we may play down our image, the people of India will always look up to a king figure. We're not used to democracy, nor will we be,' Singh said.

> The people will always expect a ruler. The Hindu religion has been based on that concept of the undivided family, the village chief, somebody sitting in a chair to sort out their problems, from village to state level. We still get regular requests. We have trust funds to help our people.[2]

While 'Bubbles', as he was known, enjoyed an income stream from palaces leased to the Taj Hotel group and could look back on a decorated career as a lieutenant-colonel in the 10th Parachute Regiment, the ex-ruler of neighbouring Bikaner was very down at the heel when Ann Morrow interviewed him and his wife in the mid-1980s. 'We have nothing left, no more boodle: it has been nothing but grief and heartache. My mind is adjusted now to the plastic cup; that is all that matters,' Karni Singh complained.[3] The days of throwing banquets in his rose-red marble palace with an eight-piece orchestra, filet de pomfrets and 'American Rognons Swann, plats de Bikaner, Havana cigars and monogrammed cigarettes for the ladies' were a distant memory. The couple were reduced to living in one room of their tumbledown palace, eating at an old card table and patching up the walls with distemper.[4] Further west in Gujarat, the Maharao of Kutch pleaded with Mountbatten for help, claiming that he could no longer live in India as his 'reduction to the status of a private citizen will expose [him] to harassment'. Given his state's continuous loyalty to the Crown, he enquired if he could acquire British citizenship or permission to reside permanently in Britain. Mountbatten forwarded his letter to the Commonwealth Secretariat, adding: 'Madan Singh's letter is really rather pathetic . . . I need hardly say that I will go surety for him.'[5]

Among those shedding no tears for the end of the princely order was Karan Singh, the ex-maharaja of Kashmir, who told Morrow that while some of his compatriots had endured hardship or faced psychological problems, 'theirs is not a sob story. It does not evoke a well of sympathy.' Continued Singh: 'Does it matter what you had in your palace? "Oh, my Lalique," the Princes say, but there are starving millions in India; you must get things in perspective.'[6] Singh's views, though widely shared, need to be put in context. He was a rising star in the Congress, and at the time of making those remarks had become India's youngest cabinet minister at the age of thirty-six, filling the tourism portfolio in Indira Gandhi's cabinet.

~

In 1992, Chintamanrao Patwardhan, the eighty-eight-year-old raja of the tiny no-gun-salute ex-Maratha state of Kurundwad (senior) surprised his princely peers by filing a suit in the Supreme Court of India claiming that Indira had violated constitutional guarantees to the princes when she abolished the privy purse. 'These rulers never would have gone along with Lord Mountbatten and joined India if they hadn't been given a guarantee that their rights would be respected,' a lawyer familiar with the case said at the time.[7]

The suit failed, but it showed how the question of whether Mountbatten led his princely flock to safety or down the garden path remained an agonizing one for the former royals, even decades after

Independence. Did the viceroy know that the promises he made to the princes could not be kept? Did V.P. Menon and Vallabhbhai Patel violate the guarantees contained in the Instruments of Accession by compelling the states to sign merger agreements? Was the abolition of the privy purse unconstitutional? In the case of the small states, there is a general consensus (rarely shared by their rulers) that they could never be economically viable or function as modern and efficient administrative units. However, some of the larger states, such as Gwalior, Cochin, Bikaner and Bhavnagar, had introduced a measure of responsible government. The questions around them are more contentious: Why could the future of these larger states not have been decided by their people – something the Congress had been demanding since the 1930s? Menon's justification for speeding up the process of integration was to avert an escalation of the chaos that had engulfed the subcontinent after the transfer of power. Simultaneous crises in Junagadh, Kashmir and Hyderabad, the refugee catastrophe triggered by Partition, coupled with his belief that popular uprisings would depose autocratic rulers, left no 'breathing time', he said, for evolving 'a scheme of permanent relationship between the States and the Government of India'.[8] However, the historian Barbara Ramusack argues otherwise. Had the Congress not been confronting these multiple emergencies, they would probably have taken a harder line against the states. 'It was in the best interests of the Congress to entice as many princes as possible with sweet gifts and to take a hard line with the few who refused their offers,' she asserts. 'Most princes acceded for a variety of reasons including patriotism, the advice of their ministers, the pressure of popular political leaders in their states, and a sense of abandonment.'[9]

The accession-versus-chaos theory also ignores the very high probability that any form of independence would have been short-lived. The states that flirted with dreams of sovereignty, including Hyderabad, Junagadh, Bhopal, Indore and Travancore, would almost certainly have understood the economic and security benefits of merging with the Indian Union – and done so peacefully. Jinnah's influence is overstated. While he certainly had a vested interest in keeping both Hindu and Muslim dynasties out of the Indian Union and took an active role in supporting Hyderabad's bid for independence, he had only minimal impact on the course of integration. As the history of post-Independence India shows, the greatest threats to national unity would come from tribal insurgencies in the northeast, the Tamil-language movement of the 1960s, demands for a Sikh homeland, Kashmiri separatism, the Naxalite movement in West Bengal and the ongoing Maoist rebellions in central India. So acute was the fear of India splitting apart at the periphery that in 1958 the Lok Sabha passed the Armed Forces (Special Powers) Act, which is still used with ruthless abandon today.

Menon's biographer Narayani Basu rejects the charge of betrayal by V.P. Menon and Patel outright:

> It is perfectly true that V.P. and Patel were not above – when neither their powers of persuasion or offers of empty honours worked – engaging in a judicious mix of arm-twisting and veiled threats. But they did not set out to betray the princes. Nor is there the slightest evidence to prove these charges.[10]

The Instrument of Accession was always going to be a stopgap measure to ensure that an orderly transition took place. 'Given the bloodcurdling events that were to follow independence and Partition, it is hardly likely that either Patel or V.P. hatched a long-term plot to hoodwink the princes.'[11] But this ignores the fact that states like Baroda or Bikaner, which were transitioning to modern administrations and were repeatedly promised by Menon that they would stay as separate entities, ended up being absorbed into larger units in much the same way as tiny Katodia (population in 1901 of 347, privy purse in 1948 of Rs 192) was absorbed into Saurashtra. It was a one-size-fits-all strategy that steamrolled its way across India, from Manipur in the east to Jaisalmer in the west.

Narratives of victimhood rang as hollow in 1947 as they do now. As the curtain began to come down on the Indian empire of the British, the princes were their own worst enemies. They never presented a common front or a coherent agenda. Nor did they face up to the inevitability that their patrons and protectors in the Government of India would abandon them once India was granted independence. Most were too fearful of change to institute real reforms and too divided to form a common front against the nationalists. Adding to their ossification was their fear of being overthrown by popular unrest and the constant messaging from Congress leaders that their days were numbered. Old habits died hard. Their attempt to enlist the support of Mountbatten when their privy purses were under threat smacked of a throwback to colonial times when they would go running to the Raj to quell protests by their subjects. Today Indira Gandhi is viewed by many as their Durga, the lay goddess who brought about the princes' destruction.

Menon and Patel were not plagued by self-doubt. Their priority, their long-cherished dream, was the creation of a democratic nation state stripped of all traces of autocracy, inequality and imperial leftovers. Unifying India, as they did in just two years, was by any consideration an astonishing feat. Arrayed against them were hundreds of princes unwilling to give up their palaces, their treasuries and their ancestral lands. Some claimed their descent from the sun, some were the illegitimate offspring of Baluchi warlords, a few were obdurate individuals barely out of their teens who spent their summers gambling in the casinos of Cannes and Deauville. Regardless of how much blood they had spilled coming to the gaddi, their rule was guaranteed by their British protectors. Each durbar had its own legal code, its own protocols and its own etiquette based on religion, caste and language. And every single ruler – no matter whether his fiefdom was the size of Italy or no larger than a mela ground – had the legal right to declare independence on the transfer of power or to form a federation with other lotah-sized realms and choose between Nehru's India or Jinnah's Pakistan. Menon and Patel were acutely aware that leaving decisions regarding accession and integration to the people of the states, as many rulers demanded, would have unleashed chaos, which their nascent country could not afford. While they warned those rulers who dragged their feet on accession that they would face the wrath of their subjects – or in extreme cases armed intervention – they never encouraged popular uprisings. Their appeal to the rulers and to their subjects alike was to work in the cause of national unity and stability. In the vast majority of cases, it worked.

~

Since 1947, the princes have had to reinvent themselves, firstly as rulers with limited sovereignty, then as figureheads and finally, after 1971, as mere citizens. In a world where privilege and entitlement carry negative connotations, it is easy to write off monarchies – and dynasties – in general. Some royals have reassembled the relics of their glorified past and tolerated the ignominy of tourists taking selfies in what were once their private durbar halls. Others have invested in the preservation of their princely heritage or have made the most of the resources at their disposal. Instead of organizing tiger hunts and grouse shoots for visiting viceroys, some have become champions of wildlife conservation. Those that have entered politics know that they can no longer rely on their princely past to gain re-election. Far from being transformed into a 'fantasy for post-modern consumption',[12] they remain a part of the social, political, economic and cultural fabric of India.

As private citizens, many find it hard to escape the traditions of palace life. The term 'erstwhile' is hardly ever used in today's India. 'Maharajas' sporting diamond-buttoned achkans and 'maharanis' wearing strings of Basra pearls still make for great copy in the gossip and fashion magazines, even though their titles have carried no legal weight since 1971. Nor has their brand value diminished. Air India still invites its premium passengers to enjoy its 'Maharajah Lounges' in airports around the country. The smiling, mischievous potentate with his upturned moustache, instantly recognizable internationally as a symbol of both luxury and hospitality, became the airline's mascot in 1946. Since then, he has appeared in dozens of iconic travel posters, including being shown rescuing a mermaid on a beach in Sydney wearing nothing but a turban and swimsuit and skiing down icy mountains in Europe on a snowboard that had morphed into a bed of nails – his doings sparking 'many a discussion in teashops, coffee houses, bus stops', notes historian Jim Masselos.[13]

While nostalgia for the gilded past might tempt tourists to take the 'Maharajah's' flying carpet from New York to Delhi and then check into a refurbished hunting lodge in Rajasthan populated with taxidermized tigers, it has limited value in the India of today and only reinforces unfortunate cliches. More than just cheerleaders for the Raj, the princes were important patrons of the arts, found roles as eminent statesmen on the world stage, employed many of pre-Independence India's most able administrators, produced some of its most stunning architecture and laid the foundations for several of its most important and dynamic urban centres such as Mysore, Baroda and Hyderabad. If they can prove their calibre again, this time in devising new ways of taking India forward, there are many roles for them to play.

Notes

List of abbreviations

IOR: India Office Records, British Library

JP: *Jinnah Papers*, edited by Z.H. Zaidi

MP: Mountbatten Papers, University of Southampton

NA (UK): National Archives, London

NA (US): National Archives, Washington

NAI: National Archives of India, New Delhi

NMML: Nehru Memorial Museum and Library, New Delhi

SPC: *Sardar Patel's Correspondence*, edited by Durga Das

SWJN: *Selected Works of Jawaharlal Nehru*, edited by Sarvepalli Gopal, et al.

TOP: *The Transfer of Power, 1942–47*, edited by Nicholas Mansergh et al.

Prologue: The Last Durbar

1. The figure of 562 is drawn from the Butler Committee of 1927, which was appointed to clarify the relationship between the states and the aramount Power, that is, Britain. The number was adopted in the first *White Paper on Indian States* published in 1948 and is the number referred to by V.P. Menon in his seminal *The Story of the Integration of the Indian States*.

2. Francis Wylie, 'Federal Negotiations in India, 1935–39', in C.H. Philips and Mary Doreen Wainwright (eds), *The Partition of India: Policies and Perspectives, 1935–1947*, 519.
3. Philip Mason, *A Shaft of Sunlight: Memories of a Varied Life*, 200.
4. Leonard Mosley, *The Last Days of the British Raj*, 195.
5. V. Shankar, *My Reminiscences of Sardar Patel*, vol. 2, 175.
6. D.V. Tahmankar, *Sardar Patel*, 19.
7. *The Scotsman*, 18 January 1948.
8. B. Krishna, *Sardar Vallabhbhai Patel: India's Iron Man*, 434.
9. Menon in conversation with the author. Leonard Mosley, *The Last Days of the British Raj*, 170.
10. V.P. Menon, *The Story of the Integration of the Indian States*, 113.
11. Leonard Mosley, *The Last Days of the British Raj*, 64.
12. V.P. Menon, *The Story of the Integration of the Indian States*, 104.
13. Press communique, 25 July 1947, *TOP*, vol. 12, 347–53.
14. G.H. Philips (ed.), *The Evolution of India, 1858 to 1947: Select Documents*, 438.
15. Philip Ziegler, *Mountbatten: The Official Biography*, 410.
16. Leonard Mosley, *The Last Days of the British Raj*, 194.
17. Alan Campbell-Johnson, *Mission with Mountbatten*, 141.
18. Ibid., 165.
19. Nisid Hajari, *Midnight's Furies: The Deadly Legacy of India's Partition*, 117.
20. Reginald Coupland, *Report on the Constitutional Problem in India*, 152.
21. Presidential Address at the All India States Peoples' Conference, Ludhiana, 15 February 1939, *SWJN*, vol. 9, 420.
22. Manu Bhagavan, 'Princely States and the Hindu Imaginary: Exploring the Cartography of Hindu Nationalism in Colonial India', *The Journal of Asian Studies*, vol. 67, no. 3, August 2008, 888.

1. The 'Iron Man' and the Civil Servant

1. Larry Collins and Dominique Lapierre, *Mountbatten and the Partition of India, August 16, 1947–June 18, 1948*, 36.

2. Alan Campbell-Johnson, *Mission with Mountbatten*, 41.
3. Larry Collins and Dominique Lapierre, *Freedom at Midnight*, 86–87.
4. 'Statement by Prime Minister Attlee on the Transfer of Power in India', 20 February 1947, *Middle East Journal,* vol. 1, no. 2, April 1947, 211.
5. Penderel Moon (ed.), *Wavell: The Viceroy's Journal*, 494–96.
6. Alan Campbell-Johnson, *Mission with Mountbatten*, 174.
7. Leonard Mosley, *The Last Days of the British Raj*, 86.
8. Viceroy's Interview, no. 7, 25 March 1947, *TOP*, vol. 10, 17.
9. Alex von Tunzelmann, *Indian Summer: The Secret History of the End of an Empire*, 218.
10. Balraj Krishna, *Sardar Vallabhbhai Patel: India's Iron Man*, 47.
11. Ibid., 58.
12. Jawaharlal Nehru, *An Autobiography*, 27.
13. Patrick French, *Liberty or Death: India's Journey to Independence and Division*, 51.
14. Balraj Krishna, *Sardar Vallabhbhai Patel: India's Iron Man*, 296–97.
15. Sikata Panda, 'The Strategy of Integration: Bismarck Vis-à-Vis Vallabhbhai', *International Journal of Research in Humanities, Arts and Literature,* vol. 6, no. 7, July 2018, 52.
16. P.N. Chopra, *The Collected Works of Sardar Vallabhbhai Patel*, vol. 7, 164.
17. Ibid., 116.
18. *The Times of India*, 10 May 1939, 9.
19. Penderel Moon, *Wavell: A Viceroy's Journal*, 384.
20. Abel to Mountbatten, 27 March 1947, *TOP*, vol. 10, 27.
21. Narayani Basu, *V.P. Menon: The Unsung Architect of Modern India*, 235.
22. Ibid., 15.
23. Ibid., 26.
24. Ibid., 80.
25. Ibid., 152.
26. Robert Trumbull, *India as I See It,* 77.
27. Narayani Basu, *V.P. Menon: The Unsung Architect of Modern India*, 176.
28. Linlithgow to Amery, 21 September 1942, *TOP*, vol. 2, 1000.

29. V.P. Menon, *The Transfer of Power in India*, 358.
30. Ibid., 363.
31. K.M. Panikkar, *Indian States and the Government of India*, xvi–xvii.
32. Romesh Dutt, *The Economic History of India in the Victorian Age*, 32.
33. Annie Besant, *Essays and Addresses*, vol. IV, 228.
34. Urmila Phadnis, 'Gandhi and Indian States: A Probe in Strategy', in S.C. Biswas (ed.), *Gandhi: Theory and Practice, Social Impact and Contemporary Relevance*, 363.
35. Anand Hingorani (ed.), *Mahatma Gandhi: To the Princes and Their People*, fn. 1, 329.
36. Ibid., 362.
37. Pran Nath Chopra, *The Collected Works of Sardar Vallabhbhai Patel: 1 January 1935–31 December 1935*, 81.
38. Sarvepalli Gopal, *Jawaharlal Nehru, 1889–1947*, 359.
39. Jawaharlal Nehru, *Toward Freedom: The Autobiography of Jawaharlal Nehru*, 99.
40. Ibid., 101.
41. *The Collected Works of Mahatma Gandhi*, vol. XXVII, May–July 1925, 208–209.
42. Popaptal Chudgar, *Indian Princes under British Protection: A Study of Their Personal Rule, Their Constitutional Position and Their Future*, 7.
43. More salacious stories were to come from the pen of Jarmani Dass, who served as a minister in Bhupinder Singh's administration. Dass describes how in the so-called love chamber inside the Leela Bhavan or Palace of Gaiety, expert surgeons would alter the breasts of the ruler's mistresses to be shaped like peaches or Alfonso mangoes. Another team of doctors was employed to help the ruler retain his sexual vigour, which, as he approached his fifties, was flagging. For a somewhat sensationalized account, see Jarmani Dass, *Maharaja: Lives and Loves and Intrigues of Indian Princes*.
44. *Indictment of Patiala: Being a Report of the Patiala Enquiry Committee Appointed by the Indian States' People's Conference*, 36.

45. 'Resolution on Indian States', Haripura session, February 1938, *Congress Handbook*, 258.
46. Ian Copland, *State, Community and Neighbourhood in Princely North India, c. 1900–1950*, 94.
47. Narendra Singh Sarila, *Once a Prince of Sarila: Of Palaces and Tiger Hunts, of Nehrus and Mountbattens*, 143.
48. Ian Copland, *State, Community and Neighbourhood in Princely North India, c. 1900–1950*, 95.

2. The Bonfire of Vices

1. Stephen Ashton, *British Policy Towards the Indian States*, 83.
2. See, for instance, Leonard Mosley, *The Last Day of the British Raj*, 185–86.
3. K.M. Panikkar, *An Introduction to the Study of the Relations of Indian States with the Government of India*, n.p.
4. Francis Wylie, 'Federal Negotiations in India, 1935–39', in C.H. Philips and Mary Doreen Wainwright (eds), *The Partition of India: Policies and Perspectives, 1935–1947*, 520–21.
5. Stephen Ashton, *British Policy Towards the Indian States*, 256.
6. Penderel Moon, *Wavell: A Viceroy's Journal*, 143.
7. Wylie to Mountbatten, 12 August 1947, *TOP*, vol. 12, 682.
8. Madeleine Moëd, *The Political Department and the Retraction of Paramountcy in India, 1935–47*, 172.
9. Charles Tupper, *Our Indian Protectorate*, 108.
10. *Proclamation by the Queen in Council, to the Princes, Chiefs, and People of India*.
11. Barbara N. Ramusack, *The Indian Princes and Their States*, 82.
12. Bampfylde Fuller, *The Empire of India*, 235.
13. *Report of the Indian Statutory Commission*, vol. 1, 83.
14. Herbert Matthews, 'Princely States Pose Another India Problem', *The New York Times*, 22 June 1947.
15. Mary Minto, *India, Minto and Morley, 1905–1910*, 345.

16. Gurmukh Nihal Singh, *Indian States & British India: Their Future Relations*, 6.
17. Edwin Montagu, *An Indian Diary*, 21.
18. Sir Herbert Thompson, *Icarus Went East*, 125.
19. Margaret Bourke-White, *Halfway to Freedom: A Report on the New India*, 166.
20. K.M. Panikkar, *His Highness the Maharaja of Bikaner: A Biography*, 55.
21. Walter Lawrence, *The India We Served*, 185.
22. Humphrey Trevelyan, *The India We Left*, 217.
23. Henry Cotton, *New India; or, India in Transition*, 25.
24. Gordon Casserly, *Life in an Indian Outpost*, 161.
25. *Notes of Instructions to Assistants and Officers of the Political Department of the Government of India*, xii–xiv.
26. Ian Copland, *The Princes of India in the Endgame of Empire, 1917–1947*, 46.
27. Popatlal L. Chudgar, *Indian Princes Under British Protection: A Study of Their Personal Rule, Their Constitutional Position and Their Future*, 101.
28. Madeleine Moëd, *The Political Department and the Retraction of Paramountcy in India, 1935–47*, 75.
29. Narayani Basu, *V.P. Menon: The Unsung Architect of Modern India*, 285.

3. Allies and Agitators

1. Trevor Burridge, *Clement Attlee: A Political Biography*, 285.
2. Philip Ziegler, *Mountbatten: The Official Biography*, 116.
3. Sarah Bradford, *The Reluctant King: The Life & Reign of George VI, 1895–1952*, 395.
4. H.V. Hodson, *The Great Divide: Britain, India, Pakistan*, 357.
5. Edmund Wakefield, *Past Imperative: My Life in India, 1927–47*, 210.
6. V.P. Menon, *The Story of the Integration of the Indian States*, 59.
7. House of Lords Debates, 'India: Statement by Cabinet Mission', 16 May 1946, vol. 141, 271–87.

8. Conrad Corfield, *The Princely India I Knew: From Reading to Mountbatten*, 146.
9. Penderel Moon, *Wavell: The Viceroy's Journal*, 34.
10. K.M. Panikkar, *An Autobiography*, 147–48.
11. G.M. Nandurkar (ed), *Sardar's Letters Mostly Unknown–I*, vol. IV, 258.
12. V.P. Menon, *The Story of the Integration of the Indian States*, 55.
13. Philip Ziegler (ed.), *Personal Diary of Admiral the Lord Louis Mountbatten: Supreme Allied Commander, South-East Asia, 1943–1946*, 201.
14. Interview no. 2, 24 March 1947, *TOP*, vol. 10, 11.
15. Rajmohan Gandhi, *Patel: A Life*, 407.
16. Leonard Mosley, *The Last Days of the British Raj*, 197.
17. Corfield to Abell, 27 March 1947, *TOP*, vol. 10, 31.
18. Leonard Mosley, *The Last Days of the British Raj*, 163.
19. 'Mr Jinnah's Statement on Partition', 1 May 1947, *TOP*, vol. 10, 543.
20. 'Address to the All India States Peoples' Conference, Gwalior', 18 April 1947, *SWJN*, vol. 2, 268–70.
21. Record of interview between Mountbatten and Nehru, 22 April 1947, *TOP*, vol. 11, 361–62.
22. Sarvepalli Gopal, *Jawaharlal Nehru: 1889–1947*, 359.
23. Ian Copland. *The Princes of India in the Endgame of Empire, 1917–1947*, 245.
24. Viceroy's Personal Report, no. 7, 15 May 1947, *TOP*, vol. 10, 836.
25. 'Nehru to Mountbatten', 11 May 1947, *TOP*, vol. 5, 756–57.
26. Narayani Basu, *V.P. Menon: The Unsung Architect of Modern India*, 253.
27. Ibid., 254.
28. Minutes of Viceroy's Eleventh Miscellaneous Meeting, 10 May 1947, *TOP*, vol. 5, 732.
29. H.V. Hodson, *The Great Divide: Britain, India, Pakistan*, 309.
30. R.J. Moore, *India in 1947: The Limits of Unity*, 56.
31. Minutes of the Meeting of the Viceroy with the Indian Leaders, 2 June 1947, *TOP*, vol. 11, 39.
32. Viceroy's Personal Report, no. 8, 5 June 1947, *TOP*, vol. 12, 159.

33. V.P. Menon, *The Story of the Integration of the Indian States*, 82.
34. Alan Campbell-Johnson, *Mission with Mountbatten*, 125.
35. M.N. Das, *Partition and Independence of India: Inside Story of the Mountbatten Days*, 233.
36. Leonard Mosley, *The Last Days of the British Raj*, 180.
37. Firman, 11 June 1947, *JP*, vol. 2, 191.
38. Lord Birdwood, *India and Pakistan: A Continent Decides*, 44.
39. 'Disposal of Crown Representative's Records, Papers Circulated for Leaders' Conference 13 June 1947', NAI, Sadar Patel Papers.
40. Minutes of Viceroy's Eighteenth Miscellaneous Meeting, 13 June 1947, *TOP*, vol. 11, 320–29. Corfield failed to mention that the 'weeding out and destruction, under capable supervision, of such records as (a) possess historical interest, and (b) are patently valueless for purposes of future reference' had been approved towards the end of Wavell's viceroyalty. Wakefield to Corfield, 7 November 1946, *TOP*, vol. 11, 249.
41. 'Fifty-five days to go', *The Economist*, 26 June 1947.

4. A Basket-full of States

1. Viceroy's Personal Report, no. 10, 27 June 1947, *TOP*, vol. 11, 687.
2. Prem Nath Chopra (ed.), *The Collected Works of Sardar Vallabhbhai Patel, 1 January 1947–31 December 1947*, 139.
3. V.P. Menon, *The Story of the Integration of the Indian States*, 89.
4. Balraj Krishna, *Sardar Vallabhbhai Patel: India's Iron Man*, 347.
5. V.P. Menon, *The Story of the Integration of the Indian States*, 88.
6. Menon to Patrick, 8 July 1947, *TOP*, vol. 12, 1.
7. Leonard Mosley, *The Last Days of the British Raj*, 169.
8. V.P. Menon, *The Story of the Integration of the Indian States*, 94.
9. Ibid.
10. H.V. Hodson, *The Great Divide: Britain, India, Pakistan*, 358.
11. V.P. Menon, *The Transfer of Power in India*, 549.
12. Leonard Mosley, *The Last Days of the British Raj*, 193–194.
13. Rajmohan Gandhi, *Patel: A Life*, 308.

14. H.V. Hodson, *The Great Divide: Britain, India, Pakistan*, 367–68.
15. Viceroy's Personal Report, no. 14, 23 July 1947, *TOP*, vol. 12, 338.
16. *White Paper on Indian States* (1948), 47–48.
17. V.P. Menon, *The Story of the Integration of the Indian States*, 103.
18. Ibid.
19. 'Nehru to Gaekwar of Baroda', 23 May 1947, *SWJN*, vol. 2, 257–59.
20. R.J. Moore, *Escape from Empire*, 318.
21. Narayani Basu, *V.P. Menon: The Unsung Architect of Modern India*, 287.
22. W.H. Morris, 'Thirty-six Years Later: The Mixed Legacies of Mountbatten's Transfer of Power', *International Affairs*, vol. 59, no. 4, September 1983, 624.
23. V.P. Menon, *The Story of the Integration of the Indian States*, 104.
24. K.M. Panikkar, *An Autobiography*, 160–61.
25. Conrad Corfield, 'Some Thoughts on British Policy and the Indian States, 1935–47', in C.H. Philips and Mary Doreen Wainwright (eds), *The Partition of India: Policies and Perspectives, 1935–1947*, 531.
26. Conrad Corfield, *The Princely India I Knew, From Reading to Mountbatten*, 159.
27. Leonard Mosley, *The Last Days of the British Raj*, 197.
28. V.P. Menon, *The Story of the Integration of the Indian States*, 113.
29. Alan Campbell-Johnson, *Mission with Mountbatten*, 137.
30. Press communique, 25 July 1947, *TOP*, vol. 12, 347–53.
31. R.J. Moore, *Escape from Empire*, 313.
32. Larry Collins and Dominique Lapierre, *Mountbatten and Independent India, August 16, 1947–June 18*, 1948, 44–46.
33. Nisid Hajari, *Midnight's Furies: The Deadly Legacy of India's Partition*, 117.
34. V.P. Menon, *The Story of the Integration of the Indian States*, 109.
35. Ann Morrow, *Highness: The Maharajahs of India*, 11.
36. Narendra Singh Sarila, *Once a Prince of Sarila*, 207–08.
37. Ibid., 209.
38. Mountbatten to Listowel, 4 August 1947, *TOP*, vol. 12, 529–30.

5. Dangerous Liaisons

1. Travancore, Memorandum by Secretary of State for India, 14 July 1947, *TOP*, vol. 12, 152–53.
2. Ramachandra Guha, *India After Gandhi: A History of the World's Largest Democracy*, 45.
3. Travancore, Memorandum by the Secretary of State for India, 14 July 1947, *TOP*, vol. 12, 154.
4. Balraj Krishna, *Sardar Vallabhbhai Patel: India's Iron Man*, 327.
5. Thomas J. Nossiter, *Communism in Kerala: A Study in Political Adaptation*, fn. 40, 99.
6. A.S. Memon, *Triumph and Tragedy in Travancore*, 23.
7. Penderel Moon, *Wavell: The Viceroy's Journal*, 112–13.
8. Itty Abraham, 'Rare Earths: The Cold War in the Annals of Travancore', in Gabrielle Hecht (ed.), *Entangled Geographies: Empire and Technopolitics in the Global Cold War*, fn. 18, 119.
9. Ibid., fn. 61, 113.
10. Ibid., 106.
11. Ramachandra Guha, *India After Gandhi: The History of the World's Largest Democracy*, 42.
12. A.S. Memon, *Triumph and Tragedy in Travancore*, 382.
13. Itty Abraham, 'Rare Earths: The Cold War in the Annals of Travancore', in Gabrielle Hecht (ed.), *Entangled Geographies: Empire and Technopolitics in the Global Cold War*, 117.
14. Thomas J. Nossiter, *Communism in Kerala: A Study in Political Adaptation*, 92.
15. Viceroy's Personal Report, no. 14, 25 July 1947, *TOP*, vol. 12, 336.
16. Ibid.
17. Viceroy's Personal Report, no. 15, 1 August 1947, *TOP*, vol. 12, 453.
18. Speech at Junagadh, 13 November 1947, in Sardar Patel, *On Indian Problems*, 10.
19. Reginald Coupland, *Indian Politics*, 1936–1942, 201.
20. Ian Copland, *The Princes of India in the Endgame of Empire, 1917–1947*, 250–51.
21. R.J. Moore, *Escape from Empire: The Attlee Government and the Indian Problem*, 311–12.

22. 'Notes of a Meeting between Monckton, Mountbatten, the Nawab of Chhatari and Menon', 3 August 1947, *TOP*, vol. 12, 497.
23. Sumantra Bose, *Roots of Conflict, Path to Peace*, 7.
24. Ibid., 16.
25. Larry Collins and Dominique Lapierre, *Freedom at Midnight*, 444.
26. A Note on Kashmir, 17 June 1947, *TOP*, vol. 11, 448.
27. Kwasi Kwarteng, *Ghosts of Empire: Britain's Legacies in the Modern World*, 120.
28. Ibid., 110–11.
29. Victoria Schofield, *Kashmir in Conflict: India, Pakistan and the Unending War*, 29.
30. Alan Campbell-Johnson, *Mission with Mountbatten*, 140.
31. Kwasi Kwarteng, *Ghosts of Empire: Britain's Legacies in the Modern World*, 123.
32. Alan Campbell-Johnson, *Mission with Mountbatten*, 120.
33. Larry Collins and Dominique Lapierre, *Mountbatten and Independent India, August 16, 1947–June 18, 1948*, 39.
34. Harbans Singh, *Maharaja Hari Singh*, 297–98.
35. Patel to Hari Singh, 3 July 1947, *SPC*, vol. 1, 32–33.
36. Hastings Lionel Ismay, *Memoirs*, 433.
37. Robert G. Wirsing, *India, Pakistan, and the Kashmir Dispute*, 22–31.
38. Philip Ziegler, *Mountbatten: The Official Biography*, 420.
39. Conrad Corfield, 'Some Thoughts on British Policy and the Indian States, 1935–47', in C.H. Philips and Mary Doreen Wainwright (eds), *The Partition of India: Policies and Perspectives, 1935–1947*, 531.

6. 'A Dagger into the Very Heart of India'

1. 'Secret Report to Jinnah', 20 August 1943, IOR, R/1/1/3913.
2. Ian Copland, 'The Princely States, the Muslim League, and the Partition of India in 1947', *The International History Review*, vol. 13, no. 1, February 1991, 51.
3. Larry Collins and Dominique Lapierre, *Mountbatten and Independent India, 16 August 1947–18 June 1948*, 43.

4. Ian Copland 'The Princely States, the Muslim League and the Partition of India in 1947', *The International History Review*, vol. 13, no. 1, February 1991, 59.
5. Statement by M.A. Jinnah, 15 June 1947, *JP*, vol. 8, 31.
6. Choudhary Rahmat Ali, *Pakistan (the Fatherland of the Pak Nation)*, 145–48.
7. Ian Copland, 'The Princely States, the Muslim League and the Partition of India in 1947', *The International History Review*, vol. 13, no. 1, February 1991, 43.
8. Sadula Khan to Yousaf A. Haroon, 7 July 1947, *JP*, vol. 3, 153–54.
9. N.B. Khare, *My Political Memoirs or Autobiography*, 298.
10. Lothian to Fitze, 25 January 1943, *TOP*, vol. 3, 538.
11. Note by Sir W. Croft and Mr Turnbull, 25 April 1946, *TOP*, vol. 12, 338.
12. Sarvepalli Gopal, *Jawaharlal Nehru: A Biography*, 338.
13. Kirpal Singh (ed.), *Select Documents on Partition of Punjab–1947: India and Pakistan*, 86.
14. Ibid., 87.
15. Nisid Hajari, *Midnight's Furies: The Deadly Legacy of India's Partition*, 88.
16. Jack Bazalgette, *The Captains and the Kings Depart: Life in India, 1928–46*, 131.
17. Nisid Hajari, *Midnight's Furies: The Deadly Legacy of India's Partition*, 84.
18. K.M. Panikkar, *An Autobiography*, 164.
19. Viceroy's Personal Report, no. 16, 8 August 1947, *TOP*, vol. 12, 604.
20. Enclosure, 18 August 1947, *SPC*, vol. 5, 342–43.
21. Alastair Lamb, *Birth of a Tragedy: Kashmir 1947*, 8.
22. Bhopal to Mountbatten, 22 July 1947, *TOP*, vol. 12, 292–95.
23. Balraj Krishna, *Sardar Vallabhbhai Patel: India's Iron Man*, 336.
24. Ibid., 335.
25. Ibid., 339.
26. Narayani Basu, *V.P. Menon: The Unsung Architect of Modern India*, 320.
27. Ibid., 340.

28. V.P. Menon, *The Story of the Integration of the Indian States*, 113.
29. Onkar Singh Babra, *Ek Maharaja ki Antarkatha*, 92.
30. K.M. Munshi, *The End of an Era, Hyderabad Memories*, 47.
31. K.M. Panikkar, *An Autobiography*, 138.
32. Balraj Krishna, *Sardar Vallabhbhai Patel: India's Iron Man*, 348.
33. Conrad Corfield, 'Some Thoughts on British Policy and the Indian States, 1935–47', in C.H. Philips and Mary Doreen Wainwright (eds), *The Partition of India: Policies and Perspectives, 1935–1947*, 532–33.
34. Nawab of Bhopal to M.A. Jinnah, 2 August 1947, *JP*, vol. 4, 146–48.
35. Nawab of Bhopal to Mountbatten, 14 August 1947, *TOP*, vol. 12, 729–31.
36. Balraj Krishna, *Sardar Vallabhbhai Patel: India's Iron Man*, 347.
37. H.V. Hodson, *The Great Divide: Britain, India, Pakistan*, 427.
38. Bhopal to Sardar Patel, 26 August 1947, *SPC*, vol. 5, 361.
39. Philip Ziegler, *Mountbatten: The Official Biography*, 413.
40. Indore to Mountbatten, 31 July 1947, *TOP*, vol. 12, 435.
41. Indore to Nehru, 6 August 1947, NA (US), Decimal File 845.01, Internal Affairs of States, India, Government. Mandates, Recognition, 9 August 1947–7 December 1949.
42. Viceroy's Personal Report, no. 15, 1 August 1947, *TOP*, vol. 12, 454.
43. Ibid.
44. Viceroy's Interview, no. 177, 4 August 1947, *TOP*, vol. 12, 508.
45. Viceroy's Personal Report, no. 17, 16 August 1947, *TOP*, vol. 12, 768.
46. Grady to Marshall, 7 August 1947, *JP*, vol. 4, 308.
47. Maharaja of Indore to M.A. Jinnah, 9 August 1947, in ibid., 307.
48. Maharaja of Indore to Pandit Nehru, 6 August 1947, *TOP*, vol. 12, 556.
49. Narayani Basu, *V.P. Menon: The Unsung Architect of Modern India*, 321.

7. Endgames of Empire

1. Charles Allen and Sharada Dwivedi, *Lives of the Indian Princes*, 82.
2. Nicholas Mansergh and E.W.R. Lumby, *Constitutional Relations Between Britain and India*, 351.

3. Mountbatten to the Maharaj Rana of Dholpur, 29 July 1947, *TOP*, vol. 12, 393.
4. Minutes of the Meeting of the Viceroy with the States Negotiating Committee, 3 June 1947, *TOP*, vol. 11, 84.
5. Edward Wakefield, *Past Imperative: My Life in India, 1927–47*, 167.
6. Note on Discussion between Cabinet Mission, Maharawal of Dungapur and Raja of Bilaspur, 4 April 1946, *TOP*, vol. 12, 129.
7. Vijayaraje Scindia, *Princess: The Autobiography of the Dowager Maharani of Gwalior*, 160.
8. Ibid., 161.
9. Viceroy's Personal Report, no. 16, 8 August 1947, *TOP*, vol. 12, 591.
10. Rear Admiral Viscount Mountbatten of Burma to the Earl of Listowel, 8 August 1947, in ibid., 585.
11. 'New Delhi to Secretary of State', 7 August 1947, NA (US), Decimal File 845.00, Internal Affairs of States, India, Political Affairs, 20 May 1947–23 August 1947.
12. Ian Copland, *The Further Shores of Partition: Ethnic Cleansing in Rajasthan, 1947*, 203–39.
13. Note by J. Thompson, 14 April 1942, IOR R/1/1/3770.
14. Note by F.V. Wylie (for the viceroy), Simla, 21 May 1941, IOR R/1/1/3764.
15. Note by Lord Ismay on talk with Jawaharlal Nehru, Simla, 3 October 1947, Mountbatten Collection, British Library, 90.
16. 'Conversations with the Maharaja of Indore', 20 August 1947, NA (US), Decimal File 845.01, Internal Affairs of States, India, Government. Mandates, Recognition, 9 August 1947–7 December 1949.
17. Ian Copland, *State, Community and Neighbourhood in Princely North India, c. 1900–1950*, 282.
18. Narayan Bhakar Khare, *My Political Memoirs; or Autobiography*, 321.
19. Shail Mayaram, *Resisting Regimes: Myth, Memory and the Shaping of a Muslim Identity*, 179.
20. Patel to Khare, 7 August 1947, *SPC*, vol. 5, 387.
21. Edward Wakefield, *Past Imperative: My Life in India, 1927–47*, 218.

22. Francis Tuker, *While Memory Serves*, 390.
23. Ibid., 335.
24. Viceroy's Personal Report, no. 17, 16 August 1947, *TOP*, vol. 12, 768.
25. Accession of Radhanpur State to the Dominion of India, NAI, Progs, Nos. 8(30)-PR, 1947, Ministry of States.
26. Larry Collins and Dominique Lapierre, *Freedom at Midnight*, 260.
27. Narendra Singh Sarila, *Once a Prince of Sarila*, 213–14.
28. Philip Mason, *A Shaft of Sunlight: Memories of a Varied Life*, 214.
29. Kenneth Fitze, *Twilight of the Maharajas*, 87.
30. Narayani Basu, *V.P. Menon: The Unsung Architect of Modern India*, 316–17.
31. V.P. Menon, *The Story of the Integration of the Indian States*, 116–17.
32. *White Paper on Indian States* (1950), 176.
33. John R. Wood, 'Dividing the Jewel: Mountbatten and the Transfer of Power to India and Pakistan', *Pacific Affairs*, vol. 58, no. 4, Winter 1985–86, 661.

8. A Pawn in a Chess Game

1. Michael Edwardes, *The Last Years of British India*, 208.
2. Keki N. Daruwalla, *Ancestral Affairs*, 5.
3. Ibid., 27.
4. Michael Edwardes, *The Last Years of British India*, 208.
5. Bhutto to Jinnah, 4 September 1947, *JP*, vol. 8, 266.
6. Leonard Mosley, *The Last Days of the British Raj*, 185.
7. Rakesh Ankit, 'The Accession of Junagadh, 1947–48: Colonial Sovereignty, State Violence and Post-Independence India', *The Indian Economic and Social History Review*, vol. 53, no. 3, 2016, 375.
8. Ibid., 375.
9. Annexure to Enclosure to PS-161, 5 September 1947, *JP*, vol. 8, 268.
10. Bhutto to Liaqat Ali Khan, 16 September 1947, in ibid., 270–73.
11. Michael Edwardes, *The Last Years of British India*, 195.
12. Jinnah to Mountbatten, 18 September 1947, in ibid., 274.
13. Mountbatten to Jinnah, 22 September 1947, in ibid., 279.

14. Srinath Raghavan, *War and Peace in Modern India*, 36.
15. H.V. Hodson, *The Great Divide: Britain, India, Pakistan*, 430.
16. Alan Campbell-Johnson, *Mission with Mountbatten*, 278.
17. Ismay to Mountbatten, 17 September 1947, *JP*, vol. 8, 273.
18. Srinath Raghavan, *War and Peace in Modern India*, 41.
19. Regional Commissioner, Rajkot, to Ministry of States, 21 September 1947, *JP*, vol. 8, 278.
20. Nisid Hajari, *Midnight's Furies: The Deadly Legacy of India's Partition*, 170.
21. Ibid., 171.
22. Shah to Yusuf, 24 February 1948, *JP*, vol. 8, 440–41.
23. H.V. Hodson, *The Great Divide: Britain, India, Pakistan*, 436.
24. V.P. Menon, *The Story of the Integration of the Indian States*, 134.
25. Ronald Stead, 'India Untangles Tragic Web of Politics, Partition, and Religious Unrest', *The Christian Science Monitor*, 16 October 1947, 13.
26. Menon to Desai, 19–20 October 1947, MP, MB1/D203.
27. Note by Shattock, in Lionel Carter (ed.), *Partition Observed*, Document 171, 454.
28. Ibid.
29. The ruler of Manavadar was not so lucky. After the sentry on duty at Manavadar's palace was killed by Indian soldiers, they arrested the sheikh who was kept in custody under very harsh conditions for several months. See Terence Creagh Coen, *The Indian Political Service: A Study in Indirect Rule,* 138.
30. Rajendra Lal Handa, *History of Freedom Struggle in Princely States*, 333.
31. Srinath Raghavan, *War and Peace in Modern India*, 62.
32. Rajmohan Gandhi, *Patel: A Life*, 437.
33. Bhutto to Mountbatten, 9 November 1947, MP, MB1/D204.
34. V.P. Menon, *The Story of the Integration of the Indian States*, 317.
35. Rakesh Ankit, 'The Accession of Junagadh, 1947–48: Colonial Sovereignty, State Violence and Post-Independence India', *The Indian Economic and Social History Review*, vol. 53, no. 3, 2016, 394.
36. *The Times,* 11 November 1947, 4.

37. Balraj Krishna, *Sardar Vallabhbhai Patel: India's Iron Man*, 364.
38. Alan Campbell-Johnson, *Mission with Mountbatten*, 278–79.
39. Faiz Muhammad Khan and others to Louis Mountbatten, 28 November 1947, *JP*, vol. 8, 390.
40. Ibid.
41. Buch to New Delhi (C/21-1), 2 January 1948, NAI, 85 (3)-PR (47), Ministry of States.
42. Buch to Shiveshwarkar, 2 January 1948, NAI, MoS, 85 (3)-PR (47), Ministry of States.
43. New York to New Delhi, 18–19 February 1948, MP, MB1/D204.
44. A.B.S. Shah to M. Yusuf, 26 February 1948, *JP*, vol. 8, 399–402.
45. Rakesh Ankit, 'The Accession of Junagadh, 1947–48: Colonial Sovereignty, State Violence and Post-Independence India', *The Indian Economic and Social History Review*, vol. 53, no. 3, 2016, 397.
46. *Dundee Courier*, 4 May 1948.

9. The Vale of Tears

1. Narayani Basu, *V.P. Menon: The Unsung Architect of Modern India*, 370–71.
2. Ibid., 371–72.
3. Prem Shankar Jha, *Kashmir 1947: Rival Versions of History*, 135.
4. 'Kashmir', 24–31 July 1949, *SWJN*, vol. 11, 416.
5. Lord Birdwood, *Two Nations and Kashmir*, 25.
6. Nehru to Patel, 10 May 1947, *SPC*, vol. 4, 113.
7. G.M. Nandurkar (ed.), *Sardar Patel, in Tune with the Millions*, vol. 2, 156.
8. 'Concord on Kashmir', 5 August 1952, *SWJN*, vol. 19, fn. 8, 266.
9. Nicholas Mansergh, *Survey of British Commonwealth Affairs: Problems of Wartime Cooperation and Post-War Change, 1939–1952*, 237.
10. Karan Singh, *Heir Apparent: An Autobiography*, 41.
11. Victoria Schofield, *Kashmir in Conflict: India, Pakistan and the Unending War*, 41.
12. Hasan Zaheer, *The Rawalpindi Conspiracy, 1951: The Times and Trial of the First Coup Attempt in Pakistan*, 63.

13. Joseph Korbel, *Danger in Kashmir*, 68.
14. *The Statesman*, 4 February 1948.
15. Victoria Schofield, *Kashmir in Conflict: India, Pakistan and the Unending War*, 43.
16. Lord Birdwood, 'The Problem of Kashmir,' *Journal of the Royal United Services Institution*, vol. 99, no. 594, 211.
17. Victoria Schofield, *Kashmir in Conflict: India, Pakistan and the Unending War*, 43.
18. Nisid Hajari, *Midnight's Furies: The Deadly Legacy of India's Partition*, 183.
19. Rajmohan Gandhi, *Patel: A Life*, 435.
20. Pran Nath Chopra (ed.), *The Collected Works of Sardar Vallabhbhai Patel: 1st January 1947–31st December 1947*, 204.
21. Joseph Korbel, *Danger in Kashmir*, 71.
22. Patel to Baldev Singh, 7 October 1947, *SPC*, vol.1, 37.
23. Alastair Lamb, *Kashmir: A Disputed Legacy*, 126.
24. Mehr Chand Mahajan, *Looking Back*, 269.
25. Karan Singh, *Heir Apparent: An Autobiography*, 57.
26. Robert Trumbull, 'Kashmir City Left in Ruins by Rebels', *The New York Times*, 11 November 1947, 1.
27. Margaret Bourke-White, *Halfway to Freedom: A Report on the New India*, 206–07.
28. Ibid., 161.
29. Alan Campbell-Johnson, *Mission with Mountbatten*, 224.
30. V.P. Menon, *The Story of the Integration of the Indian States*, 378–80.
31. 'Despatch no. 405, 21 April 1948, American Embassy, New Delhi', NA(US), Decimal File 845.00, Internal Affairs of States, India, Political Affairs, 14 April 1948–13 May 1948.
32. Victoria Schofield, *Kashmir in the Crossfire*, 145.
33. Ian Stephens, *Horned Moon: An Account of a Journey Through Pakistan, Kashmir, and Afghanistan*, 109–110.
34. C. Bilqees Taseer, *The Kashmir of Sheikh Muhammad Abdullah*, 146.
35. Phillips Talbot, *An American Witness to India's Partition*, 353.
36. Srinath Raghavan, *War and Peace in Modern India*, 107.

37. US Embassy, Delhi to Secretary of State, Kashmir Dispute, 14 November 1947, NA(US), Decimal File 745.45F, Political Relations of States, Relations; Bi-Lateral Treaties, India and Pakistan, 30 January 1948–4 February 1948.
38. Prem Shankar Jha, *Kashmir, 1947: Rival Versions of History*, 64.
39. Victoria Schofield, *Kashmir in the Crossfire*, 149.
40. The view that the Instrument of Accession was signed on 27 October is also supported by the account contained in 'Despatch no. 405, 21 April 1948, American Embassy, New Delhi', NA(US), Decimal File 845.00, Internal Affairs of States, India, Political Affairs, 13 April, 1948–13 May 1948.
41. Alastair Lamb, *Kashmir: A Disputed Legacy*, 136.
42. Prem Shankar Jha, *Kashmir, 1947: Rival Versions of History*, 62.
43. Philip Ziegler, *Mountbatten: The Official Biography*, 446.
44. Larry Collins and Dominique Lapierre, *Mountbatten and Independent India, 16 August 1947–18 June 1948*, 39.
45. Nisid Hajari, *Midnight's Furies: The Deadly Legacy of India's Partition*, 195.
46. Saroja Sundararajan, *Kashmir Crisis: Unholy Anglo-Pak Nexus*, 119.
47. Robert Trumbull, 'Ex-GI, Kashmir Leaders, Reveals He Quit After Murder Attempts', *The New York Times*, 29 January 1948.
48. Karan Singh, *Heir Apparent: An Autobiography*, 85.
49. Nehru to Patel, 3 June 1948, *SPC*, vol. 1, 200.
50. Sarvepalli Gopal and Uma Iyengar (eds), *The Essential Writings of Jawaharlal Nehru*, vol. 2, 329.
51. HC India to Commonwealth Relations Office, IOR, L/P&S/13/1845B.
52. Saxena to Patel, 27 July 1949, *SPC*, vol. 1, 45.
53. Patel to Nehru, 3 July 1950, in ibid., 317.
54. Robert Trumbull, *As I See India*, 100.
55. *The Hindu*, 4 October 1948.
56. H.V. Kamath, 'Sardar Vallabhbhai Patel: Some Memories', *Bhavan's Journal*, 16 January 1982, 63.
57. Balraj Krishna, *Sardar Vallabhbhai Patel: India's Iron Man*, 397.

58. Jayaprakash Narayan, 'Sardar Patel: A Reappraisal', *Bhavan's Journal*, 22 December 1974, 37.
59. A.G. Noorani, 'Roots of the Kashmir Dispute', *Frontline*, 27 May 2016.
60. Ramachandra Guha, 'Opening a Window in Kashmir', *World Policy Journal*, vol. 21, no. 3, 2004, 81.
61. Donovan to the Secretary of State, July 23, 1948, NA(US), Decimal File 845.00, Internal Affairs of States, India, Political Affairs, 18 May 1948–30 September 1948.

10. The Killing Fields

1. V.P. Menon, *The Story of the Integration of the Princely States*, 335.
2. Lucien D. Benichou, *From Autocracy to Integration: Political Developments in Hyderabad State, 1938–1948*, 208.
3. Record of interview between Mountbatten and Jinnah, 12 July 1947, *TOP*, vol. 12, 121.
4. Narayani Basu, *V.P. Menon: The Unsung Architect of Modern India*, 340.
5. Philip Ziegler, *Mountbatten: The Official Biography*, 452.
6. K.M. Munshi, *The End of an Era, Hyderabad Memories*, 77.
7. Manu Bhagavan, 'Princely States and the Hindu Imaginary: Exploring the Cartography of Hindu Nationalism in Colonial India', *The Journal of Asian Studies*, vol. 67, no. 3, August 2008, 910.
8. H.V. Hodson, *The Great Divide: Britain, India, Pakistan*, 488.
9. Ibid., 490.
10. Ibid., 492.
11. Narayani Basu, *V.P. Menon: The Unsung Architect of Modern India*, 349.
12. Lucien D. Benichou, *From Autocracy to Integration: Political Developments in Hyderabad State, 1938–1948*, 204.
13. Mir Laik Ali, *Tragedy of Hyderabad*, 183.
14. Ibid., 185.
15. Philip Ziegler, *Mountbatten: The Official Biography*, 454.
16. Alan Campbell-Johnson, *Mission with Mountbatten*, 380–81.

17. Vasant Kumar Bawa, *The Last Nizam: The Life and Times of Mir Osman Ali Khan*, 229.
18. Sidney Cotton, *Aviator Extraordinary: The Sidney Cotton Story*, 229.
19. Patel to Nehru, June 1948, *SPC*, vol. 7, 212.
20. H.V. Hodson, *The Great Divide: Britain, India, Pakistan*, 486.
21. Donovan to the Secretary of State, 23 July 1948, NA(US), Decimal File 845.00, Internal Affairs of States, India, Political Affairs, 18 May 1948–30 September 1948.
22. K.M. Munshi, *The End of an Era*, 176.
23. D.V. Tahmankar, *Sardar Patel*, 230.
24. K.M. Munshi, *The End of an Era*, 176.
25. Lucien D. Benichou, *From Autocracy to Integration: Political Developments in Hyderabad State, 1938–1948*, 226.
26. Sunil Puroshotham, 'Internal Violence: The Police Action in Hyderabad', *Comparative Studies in Society and History*, vol. 57, no. 2, 2015, fn. 35, 444.
27. K.M. Munshi, *The End of an Era*, 180.
28. Sardar Patel Statement on Hyderabad in the Constituent Assembly, *SPC*, vol. 7, 236–37.
29. M.K.K. Nayar, *Story of an Era Told Without Ill-Will*, 138.
30. The British Commander-in-Chief General Bucher urged the intervention be delayed in case India's enemies linked the operation with the death the day before of Muhammad Ali Jinnah. He was overruled by Patel.
31. *The New York Times*, 18 September 1948.
32. Wilfred Cantwell Smith, 'Hyderabad: Muslim Tragedy', *The Middle East Journal*, vol. 4, 1950, 46.
33. Lucien D. Benichou, *From Autocracy to Integration: Political Developments in Hyderabad State, 1938–1948*, 236.
34. 'Confidential notes attached to the Sunderlal Committee Report', in A.G. Noorani, *The Destruction of Hyderabad*, 368–69.
35. Ibid., 375.
36. Ibid., 372–74.

11. 'The Beauty of the Dawn'

1. The seventeen were Mysore, Gwalior, Baroda, Jaipur, Jodhpur, Udaipur, Kotah, Bikaner, Cochin, Rewa, Kolhapur, Patiala, Mayurbhanj, Travancore, Indore and Alwar. Hyderabad was named as the seventeenth state on the assumption that it would eventually accede.
2. H.V. Hodson, *The Great Divide: Britain, India, Pakistan*, 495.
3. Stephen Ashton, 'Mountbatten, the Royal Family, and British Influence in Post-Independence India and Burma', *The Journal of Imperial and Commonwealth History*, vol. 33, no. 1, 2005, 77.
4. Ibid.
5. *White Paper on Indian States* (1948), 52–53.
6. Balraj Krishna, *Sardar Vallabhbhai Patel: India's Iron Man*, 442.
7. Stephen Ashton, 'Mountbatten, the Royal Family, and British Influence in Post-Independence India and Burma', *The Journal of Imperial and Commonwealth History,* vol. 33, no. 1, January 2005, 76.
8. V.P. Menon, *The Story of the Integration of the Indian States*, 152.
9. Ibid.
10. Inauguration of the Provincial States Advisory Board, November 1948, in Harekrushna Mahtab, *The Beginning of the End*, 9.
11. V.P. Menon, *The Story of the Integration of the Indian States*, 152.
12. D.R. Mankekar, *Accession to Extinction: The Story of the Indian Princes*, 121.
13. H.V. Hodson, *The Great Divide: Britain, India, Pakistan*, 494–95.
14. *Report of the Enquiry Committee Orissa States*, 17.
15. V.P. Menon, *The Story of the Integration of the Indian States*, 106.
16. D.R. Mankekar, *Accession to Extinction: The Story of the Indian Princes*, 119.
17. V.P. Menon, *The Story of the Integration of the Indian States*, 159.
18. Terence Creagh Coen, *The Indian Political Service: A Study in Indirect Rule*, 132.
19. Robert Trumbull, *As I See India*, 76.
20. Note on anti-merger activities, 12 May 1948, NAI, 8 (31)- P/48, Intelligence Bureau, Ministry of Home Affairs,

21. Confidential report from DI, G.R.P. Bina, dated 20 December 1948, NAI, C 9-Q/48, CI Agency.
22. Narayani Basu, *V.P. Menon: The Unsung Architect of Modern India*, 388.
23. Stephen Ashton, 'Mountbatten, the Royal Family, and British Influence in Post-Independence India and Burma', *The Journal of Imperial and Commonwealth History*, vol. 33, no. 1, 2005, 76.
24. Nehru to Menon, 20 February 1948, NMML, Nehru Papers.
25. V.P. Menon, *The Story of the Integration of the Indian States*, 175.
26. Charles Allen and Sharada Dwivedi, *Lives of the Indian Princes*, 329–30.
27. 'Formation of the United State of Rajasthan', 1 April 1948, Central File, Decimal File 845.00, Internal Affairs of States, India, Political Affairs, 13 April 1948–13 May 1948.
28. V.P. Menon, *The Story of the Integration of the Indian States*, 275.
29. Patel on the Inauguration of the Gwalior–Indore–Malwa Union, *SPC*, vol. 7, 581.
30. Shahid Hamid, *Disastrous Twilight*, 261.
31. Confidential Despatch no. 213, 23 September 1947, American Embassy, New Delhi, NA(US), Decimal File 845.00, Internal Affairs of States, India, Political Affairs, 12 October 1947–5 February 1948.
32. Nehru to Patel, 4 November 1947, *SPC*, vol. 5, 380.
33. Patel to Nehru, 5 November 1947, in ibid., 380–81.
34. Patel to Nehru, 24 December 1947, V. Shankar (ed.), *Sardar Patel, Select Correspondence*, vol. 2, 147.
35. Shail Mayaram, *Resisting Regimes: Myth, Memory and the Shaping of a Muslim Identity*, 205–06.
36. N.B. Khare, *My Political Memoirs; or Autobiography*, 305.
37. Dep. PM to Dep. High Commissioner for Pakistan, 26 February 1948, NAI, Prasad Papers, 5-R/48.
38. Robert Trumbull, 'Princely State of Bharatpur Placed Under Dominion's Authority While Check on Violent Group Is Made', *The New York Times*, 11 February 1948, 16.
39. V.P. Menon, *The Story of the Integration of the Indian States*, 240.
40. Narayani Basu, *V.P. Menon: The Unsung Hero of Modern India*, 409.

41. G.M. Kelly, 'Independent India Learns Freedom Lessons Slowly, but Leaders See Progress', Associated Press, 10 April 1948.
42. Ian Copland, 'The Integration of the Princely States: A "Bloodless Revolution"?', *South Asia*, vol. 18, no. 1, 141.
43. V.P. Menon, *The Story of the Integration of the Indian States*, 144.
44. Speech by Patel at Alwar, 25 February 1948, IOR, L/P&S/13/1387.
45. Patel to Rajendra Prasad, 24 June 1948, *SPC*, vol. 6, 384.
46. Ian Copland, *State, Community and Neighbourhood in Princely North India, c. 1900–1950*, 182.
47. Ambassador, New Delhi, to Sec. State, Washington, 31 December 1947, NA (US), Decimal File 845.00, Internal Affairs of States, India, Political Affairs, 12 October 1947–5 February 1948.
48. Ian Copland, 'The Integration of the Princely States: A "Bloodless Revolution"?', *South Asia*, vol. XVIII, 1995) 137.
49. *White Paper on Indian States*, 1948, 47–48.

12. The Wrath of Shiva

1. V. Shankar, *My Reminiscences of Sardar Patel*, vol. 1, 185.
2. Karni Singh, *The Relations of the House of Bikaner with the Central Powers, 1465–1949*, 343.
3. Ibid.
4. Vijayaraje Scindia, *Princess: The Autobiography of the Dowager Maharani of Gwalior*, 160.
5. V.P. Menon, *The Story of the Integration of the Indian States*, 220–21.
6. Robert Trumbull, *As I See India*, 80.
7. 'Indore, Donovan', 20 August 1947, NA(US), Decimal File 845.01, Internal Affairs of States, India, Government. Mandates, Recognition, 9 August 1947–7 December 1949.
8. Buch to Shankar, NAI, File no. 83-Q, 1952, Central India Agency.
9. V.P. Menon, *The Story of the Integration of the Indian States*, 222.
10. V. Shankar, *My Reminiscences of Sardar Patel*, vol. 1, 185.
11. Ibid., 186.
12. *Indian Express*, 8 November 1949.

13. Undated telegram, Foreign, New Delhi to Regional Commissioner, Madhya Bharat, *SPC*, vol. 8, 513.
14. Harry Nedou: Question of Sale of Certain Jewellery of H.H. of Indore in America, NAI, 9.1 (20), PB-51.
15. V. Shankar, *My Reminiscences of Sardar Patel*, vol. 2, 112.
16. Ibid., 4.
17. Ibid., 7.
18. Ian Copland, *The Princes of India in the Endgame of Empire, 1917–1947*, 266.
19. *White Paper on Indian States* (1950), 1–2.
20. Ibid., 145.
21. Lord Birdwood, *A Continent Decides*, 45–46.
22. Kenneth Fitze, *Twilight of the Maharajas*, 159–60.
23. V.P. Menon, *The Story of the Integration of the Indian States*, 423–24.
24. Article 370 of the Indian Constitution conferred on Kashmir the power to have a separate constitution, a state flag, and autonomy of internal administration. The article was abolished in 2019.
25. *White Paper on Indian States* (1950), 123–24.
26. K.M. Munshi, *Indian Constitutional Documents: Pilgrimage to Freedom, 1902–1950*, 174.
27. Bipan Chandra (ed.), *India After Independence*, 190.
28. M.K.K. Nayar, *Story of an Era Told Without Ill-Will*, 144.
29. Ibid., 149.
30. William L. Richter and Barbara Ramusack, 'The Chamber and the Consultation: Changing Forms of Princely Association in India', *The Journal of Asian Studies*, vol. 34, no. 3, May 1975, fn. 20, 759.
31. V.P. Menon, *The Story of the Integration of the Indian States*, 410.
32. Ibid., 413–14.

13. Trouble on the Frontier

1. Ruler of Kalat to Louis Mountbatten, 27 March 1948, *JP*, vol. 8, 189.
2. V.S. Naipaul, *Among Believers: An Islamic Journey*, 355–56.
3. Anabel Lloyd, *Bahawalpur: The Kingdom that Vanished*, 120.

4. Ibid., 120–21.
5. 'Bahawalpur State: Effective Indirect Participation in Pakistan Movement', *Journal of the Research Society of Pakistan*, vol. 46, no. 2, December 2009, 197.
6. *Dawn*, 25 August 1947.
7. There was speculation that the hitch that delayed the signing of the accession agreement related to some last-minute behind-the-scenes manoeuvring. Moon maintains that the nawab's preference was for independence: 'If we went cap in hand to Pakistan, we should put ourselves at their mercy and enable them to assert the Paramountcy of the old British Indian Government. The Nawab and Gurmani were anxious to avoid this and considered it both possible and desirable that Bahawalpur should maintain a quasi-independent existence.' See Penderel Moon, *Divide and Quit*, vol. 1, 157.
8. Webb Miller, *I Found No Peace*, 204–05.
9. Wayne Wilcox, *Pakistan: The Consolidation of a Nation*, 118.
10. Shruti Kapila, 'Masculinity and Madness: Princely Personhood and Colonial Sciences of the Mind in Western India, 1871–1940', *Past and Present*, no. 187, May 2005, 144–46.
11. 'Ruler of Chitral to M.A. Jinnah', 3 August 1947, *JP*, vol. 8, 97.
12. *Khyber Mail*, 21 December 1954.
13. Edward Wakefield, *Past Imperative: My Life in India, 1927–47*, 136.
14. Selig Harrison, *In Afghanistan's Shadow: Baluch Nationalism and Soviet Temptations*, 23.
15. Nehru to Khan Abdus Kamad Khan, 10 July 1946, *SWJN*, vol. 15, 444.
16. Listowel to Mountbatten, 2 August 1947, *JP*, vol. 8, 142.
17. 'Draft Communique', 14 August 1947, in ibid., 144.
18. The high commissioner of UK in Pakistan, Draft Letter, 22 September 1947, IOR, L/P&S/13/1846.33.
19. Douglas Fell, *Memoir of Douglas Fell: The Last Prime Minister of Kalat State*, 42–43.
20. Selig Harrison, 'After the Afghan Coup: Nightmare in Balochistan', *Foreign Policy*, no. 72, Fall 1978, 143–44.

21. Douglas Fell, *Memoir of Douglas Fell: The Last Prime Minister of Kalat State*, 42–43.
22. 'D.Y. Fell to Jinnah', 30 March 1948, *JP*, vol. 8, 191.
23. T.C.A. Raghavan, *The People Next Door: The Curious History of India's Relations with Pakistan*, 13.
24. Alleged Negotiations Between Kalat and the Government of India, 2 April 1948, NA(US), Decimal File 845.00, Internal Affairs of States, India, Political Affairs, 13 April 1948–13 May 1948.
25. *Inside Balochistan: Autobiography of Mir Ahmed Yar Khan*, 161.
26. Ibid., 162–63.

14. Lost Among the Cobwebs

1. Joan Lyon, *Just Half a World Away: In Search of the New India*, 146.
2. Ibid., 134.
3. Ibid., 147.
4. Ibid.
5. Hugh Tinker, *India and Pakistan: A Political Analysis*, 40.
6. See William Richter, 'Electoral Patterns in Post-Princely India', in Jagdish N. Bhagwati et al. (eds), *Electoral Politics in the Indian States: Three Disadvantaged Sectors*, 1–77.
7. Francine Frankel, *India's Political Economy, 1947–1977: The Gradual Revolution*, 74.
8. Taya Zinkin, *India Changes*, 210.
9. Vijayaraje Scindia, *Princess: The Autobiography of the Dowager Maharani of Gwalior*, 196.
10. *The Canberra Times*, 24 December 1979.
11. Charles Allen and Sharada Dwivedi, *Lives of the Indian Princes*, 275.
12. Patel to Nehru, 9 August 1949, *SPC*, vol. 8, 598–600.
13. Nehru to Patel, 11 August 1949, in ibid., 601.
14. Nehru to H.K. Mahtab, 20 December 1951, NMML, Hare Krishna Mahtab Papers, File 29.
15. Sarvepalli Gopal, *Jawaharlal Nehru: A Biography*, vol. 2, 79.
16. 'A Letter to the Princes of the Indian States', 10 September 1953, *SWJN*, vol. 23, 219–20.

17. Taya Zinkin, *India Changes*, 210.
18. Khushwant Singh, *Why I Supported the Emergency: Essays and Profiles*, 21.
19. Quentin Crewe, *The Last Maharaja*, 225.
20. Dom Moraes, *Mrs Gandhi*, 153.
21. T.V. Kunhi Krishnan, *Chavan and the Troubled Decade*,166.
22. Ibid.
23. D.R. Mankekar, *Accession to Extinction*, 243.
24. T.V. Kunhi Krishnan, *Chavan and the Troubled Decade*, 167.
25. Minute by Garner of a Meeting with Mountbatten, 26 July 1967, NA(UK), FCO 37/44, no. 4.
26. Stephen Ashton, 'Mountbatten, the Royal Family, and British Influence in Post-Independence India and Burma', *The Journal of Imperial and Commonwealth History*, vol. 33, no. 1, 78.
27. Rakesh Ankit, 'Mountbatten and India, 1964–79: After Nehru', *Contemporary British History*, vol. 35, June 2021, 576.
28. Ibid., 578.
29. Mountbatten to Sir P. Gore-Booth, 27 November 1968, NA(UK), FCO 37/364, no. 1.
30. T.V. Kunhi Krishnan, *Chavan and the Troubled Decade*, 172.
31. Granville Austin, *Working a Democratic Constitution: The Indian Experience*, 180
32. *Indian Express*, 13 February 1970.
33. T.V. Kunhi Krishnan, *Chavan and the Troubled Decade*, 267.
34. Ibid.
35. Ann Morrow, *Highness: The Maharajas of India*, 356.
36. Lok Sabha Debates, Fourth Series, vol. 44, no. 26, col. 261.
37. Ibid., col. 296.
38. Vijayaraje Scindia, *Princess: The Autobiography of the Dowager Maharani of Gwalior*, 205.
39. Paul Brass, *An Indian Political Life: Charan Singh and Congress Politics, 1937 to 1961*, n.p.
40. A senior member of Gandhi's staff interviewed by Granville Austin, *Working a Democratic Constitution: The Indian Experience*, fn. 59, 228.

41. Jairam Ramesh, *Intertwined Lives, P.N. Haksar and Indira Gandhi*, 185–86.
42. Granville Austin, *Working a Democratic Constitution: The Indian Experience*, 230–31.
43. *The New York Times*, 14 February 1971.
44. D.R. Mankekar, *Accession to Extinction*, 230.
45. T. V. Kunhi Krishnan, *Chavan and the Troubled Decade*, 272.
46. Stephen Ashton, 'Mountbatten, the Royal Family, and British Influence in Post-Independence India and Burma', *The Journal of Imperial and Commonwealth History*, vol. 33, no. 1, 2005, 79.
47. Granville Austin, *Working a Democratic Constitution: The Indian Experience*, 232.
48. Ananth V. Krishna, *India Since Independence: Making Sense of Indian Politics*, 100.
49. Ann Morrow, *Highness: The Maharajas of India*, 236.
50. Stephen Ashton, 'Mountbatten, the Royal Family, and British Influence in Post-Independence India and Burma', *The Journal of Imperial and Commonwealth History*, vol. 33, no. 1, 2005) 77.
51. Lok Sabha Debates, Fifth Series, vol. 16, no. 54, col. 139.
52. Nani Ardeshir Palkhivala, *The Constitution and the Common Man*, 14.
53. V. Shankar, *My Reminiscences of Sardar Patel*, vol. 2, 212.

Epilogue: 'No More Boodle'

1. Bernard Weinraub, 'A Maharaja Bows to the Present', *The New York Times*, 22 November 1973, 2.
2. Susan Yerkes, 'A Modern Maharaja', *The Illustrated London News*, vol. 272, 55.
3. Ann Morrow, *Highness, The Maharajas of India,* 240.
4. Ibid., 363.
5. Rakesh Ankit, 'Mountbatten and India, 1964–7', *Contemporary British History*, vol. 35, no. 4, 2021, 581.
6. Ann Morrow, *Highness: The Maharajahs of India*, 192.
7. *The Vancouver Sun*, 24 December 1992.

8. V.P. Menon, *The Story of the Integration of the Princely States*, 144.
9. Barbara Ramusack, *The Indian Princes and Their States*, 274.
10. Narayani Basu, *V.P. Menon: The Unsung Architect of Modern India*, 299.
11. Ibid.
12. Barbara Ramusack, *The Indian Princes and Their States*, 279.
13. Jim Masselos, 'Decolonised Rulers: Rajas, Maharajas and Others in Post-Colonial India', in Robert Aldrich and Cindy McCreery (eds), *Monarchies and Decolonisation in Asia*, 56.

Select Bibliography

Abraham, Itty, 'Rare Earths: Travancore in the Annals of the Cold War', in G. Hecht (ed.), *Entangled Geographies: Empire and Technopolitics in the Global Cold War*, MIT Press, Cambridge, Mass., 2011.

Allen, Charles, and Sharada Dwivedi, *Lives of the Indian Princes*, Arena, London, 1986.

Ankit, Rakesh, 'The Accession of Junagadh, 1947–48: Colonial Sovereignty, State Violence and Post-Independence India', *The Indian Economic and Social History Review*, vol. 53, no. 3, 2016, 371–404.

——— 'Mountbatten and India, 1964–79', *Contemporary British History*, vol. 35, no. 4, 2021, 569–96.

Ashton, Stephen, *British Policy Towards the Indian States: 1905–1939*, Curzon Press, London, 1982.

——— 'Mountbatten, the Royal Family, and British Influence in Post-Independence India and Burma', *The Journal of Imperial and Commonwealth History*, vol. 33, no. 1, January 2005, 73–92.

Austin, Granville, *Working a Democratic Constitution: The Indian Experience*, Oxford University Press, New Delhi, 1999.

Bangash, Yaqoob Khan, *A Princely Affair: The Accession and Integration of the Princely States of Pakistan*, Oxford University Press, Corby, 2015.

——— 'Betrayal of Trust: Princely States of India and the Transfer of Power', *South Asia Research*, no. 26, 2006, 181–99.

Basu, Narayani, *V.P. Menon: The Unsung Architect of Modern India*, Simon & Schuster India, New Delhi, 2020.

Benichou, Lucien D., *From Autocracy to Integration: Political Developments in Hyderabad State, 1938–1948*, Orient Longman, Chennai, 2000.

Bhagavan, Manu, 'Princely States and the Hindu Imaginary: Exploring the Cartography of Hindu Nationalism in Colonial India', *The Journal of Asian Studies*, August 2008, vol. 67, no. 3, August 2008, 881–915.

Lord Birdwood, 'The Problem of Kashmir', *Journal of the Royal United Service Institution*, vol. 99, February 1954, 206–18.

——— *Two Nations and Kashmir*, Hale, London, 1956.

Bourke-White, Margaret, *Halfway to Freedom: A Report on the New India*, Simon & Schuster, New York, 1949.

Campbell-Johnson, Alan, *Mission with Mountbatten*, Robert Hale Limited, London, 1951.

Cantwell Smith, Wilfred, 'Hyderabad: Muslim Tragedy', *Middle East Journal*, vol. 4, no. 1, January 1950, 27–51.

Chaudhuri, Muhammad Ali, *The Emergence of Pakistan*, Columbia University Press, New York, 1967.

Chopra, Pran Nath (ed.), *The Collected Works of Sardar Vallabhbhai Patel: 1st January 1947–31st December 1947*, Konark Publishers, Delhi, 1990.

Creagh Coen, Terence, *The Indian Political Service: A Study in Indirect Rule*, Chatto & Windus, London, 1971.

Collins, Larry, and Dominique Lapierre, *Freedom at Midnight*, Collins, London, 1975.

——— *Mountbatten and Independent India, August 16, 1947–June 18, 1948*, Vikas, New Delhi, 1984.

Copland, Ian, 'The Further Shores of Partition: Ethnic Cleansing in Rajasthan, 1947, Past and Present', no. 160, August 1998, 203–39.

——— 'The Integration of the Princely States: A "Bloodless Revolution"?', *South Asia*, vol. 18, 1995, 131–51.

——— *The Princes of India in the Endgame of Empire, 1917–1947*, Cambridge University Press, Cambridge, 1997.

——— 'The Princely States, the Muslim League and the Partition of India in 1947', *The International History Review*, vol. 13, no. 1, February 1991, 38–69.

Corfield, Conrad, 'Some Thoughts on British Policy and the Indian States, 1935–47', in C.H. Philips and Mary Doreen Wainwright (eds),

The Partition of India: Policies and Perspectives 1935–1947, George Allen & Unwin, London, 1970.

——— *The Princely India I Knew, from Reading to Mountbatten*, Indo British Historical Society, Madras, 1975.

Coupland, Reginald, *Indian Politics 1936–942: Report on the Constitutional Problem in India, Part Two*, Oxford University Press, Oxford, 1943.

Daruwalla, Keki N., *Ancestral Affairs*, Fourth Estate, Noida, 2015.

Fell, Douglas, *Memoir of Douglas Fell: The Last Prime Minister of Kalat State*, Sayad Hashmi Reference Library, Karachi, 2010.

Fitze, Kenneth, *Twilight of the Maharajas*, John Murray, London, 1956.

Frankel, Francine, *India's Political Economy, 1947–1977: The Gradual Revolution*, Princeton University Press, Princeton, 1979.

French, Patrick, *Liberty or Death: India's Journey to Independence and Division*, Flamingo, London, 1998.

Fuller, Bampfylde, *The Empire of India*, Pitman, London, 1913.

Gandhi, Rajmohan, *Patel: A Life*, Navajivan Publishing House, Ahmedabad, 1991.

Gauba, Khalid Latif, *His Highness: Or, the Pathology of Princess*, Times Publishing Company, Delhi, 1930.

Gopal, Sarvepalli and Uma Iyengar (eds), *The Essential Writings of Jawaharlal Nehru*, vol. 2, Oxford University Press, New Delhi, 2003.

Groenhout, Fiona Elizabeth, 'Debauchery, Disloyalty and other Deficiencies: The Impact of Ideas of Princely Character upon Indirect Rule in Central India, c. 1886–1946', PhD Thesis, University of Western Australia, 2007.

Guha, Ramachandra. *India After Gandhi: The History of the World's Largest Democracy*, Pan Macmillan, New Delhi, 2017,

——— 'Opening a Window in Kashmir,' *World Policy Journal*, vol. 21, issue 3, 2004, 79–94.

Hajari, Nisid, *Midnight's Furies: The Deadly Legacy of India's Partition*, Amberley, Stroud, Gloucestershire, 2017.

Harrison, Selig, *In Afghanistan's Shadow: Baluch Nationalism and Soviet Temptations*, Carnegie Endowment for International Peace, New York, 1981.

Hodson, H.V., *The Great Divide: Britain, India, Pakistan*, Atheneum, New York, 1971.

Indictment of Patiala: Being a Report of the Patiala Enquiry Committee Appointed by the Indian States Peoples' Conference, Bombay, 1930.

Jeffrey, Robin (ed.), *People, Princes and Paramount Power: Society and Politics in the Indian Princely States*, Oxford University Press, Delhi, 1978.

Jha, Prem Shankar, *Kashmir, 1947: Rival Versions of History*, Oxford University Press, Bombay, 1996.

Khare, N.B., *My Political Memoirs; or Autobiography*, J.R. Josh, Nagpur, 1959.

Korbel, Joseph, *Danger in Kashmir*, Princeton University Press, Princeton, 1954.

Krishna, Balraj, *Sardar Vallabhbhai Patel: India's Iron Man*, Indus, New Delhi, 1995.

Kunhi Krishnan, T.V., *Chavan and the Troubled Decade*, Somaiya Publications, Bombay, 1971.

Laik Ali, Mir, *Tragedy of Hyderabad*, Pakistan Co-operative Book Society, Karachi, 1962.

Lamb, Alastair, *Kashmir: A Disputed Legacy: 1846–1990*, Oxford University Press, Karachi, 2003.

Lloyd, Anabel, *Bahawalpur: The Kingdom that Vanished*, Vintage, Gurgaon, 2020.

Lyon, Joan, *Just Half a World Away: In Search of the New India*, Hutchinson, London, 1955.

Mahajan, Mehr Chand, *Looking Back: The Autobiography of Mehr Chand Mahajan*, Asia Publishing House, New York, 1963.

Mankekar, D.R., *Accession to Extinction, The Story of the Indian States*, Vikas, Delhi, 1974.

Manor, James, 'The Demise of the Princely Order: A Reassessment', in Robin Jeffrey (ed), *People, Princes and Paramount Power: Society and Politics in the Indian Princely States*, Oxford University Press, Delhi, 1978.

Mason, Philip, *A Shaft of Sunlight: Memories of a Varied Life*, Deutsch, London, 1978.

Mayaram, Shail, *Resisting Regimes: Myth, Memory and the Shaping of a Muslim Identity*, Oxford University Press, Delhi, 1997.

Memon, A.S., *Triümph and Tragedy in Travancore*, Current Books, Thrissur, 2001.

Menon, V.P., *The Story of the Integration of the Indian States*, Orient Longman, Bombay, 1956.

——— *The Transfer of Power in India*, Princeton University Press, Princeton, 1957.

Minto, Mary, *India, Minto and Morley, 1905–1910*, Macmillan, London, 1934.

Moëd, Madeleine, 'The Political Department and the Retraction of Paramountcy in India, 1935–47', Unpublished master's thesis, Rhodes University, 1988.

Moon, Penderel (ed.), *Wavell: The Viceroy's Journal*, Oxford University Press, London, 1973.

Moore, R.J., *Escape from Empire: The Attlee Government and the Indian Problem*, Oxford, Clarendon Press, 1983.

Morris-Jones, W.H., 'The Transfer of Power, 1947: A View from the Sidelines', *Modern Asian Studies,* vol. 16, no. 1, 1982, 1–32.

——— 'Thirty-Six Years Later: The Mixed Legacies of Mountbatten's Transfer of Power', Royal Institute of International Affairs, vol. 59, no. 4, Autumn 1983, 621–28.

Morrow, Ann, *Highness: The Maharajas of India*, Grafton Books, London, 1986.

Mosley, Leonard, *The Last Days of the British Raj*, Weidenfeld and Nicolson, London, 1961.

Munshi, K.M., *The End of an Era, Hyderabad Memories*, Bharatiya Vidya Bhavan, Bombay, 1957.

——— *Indian Constitutional Documents: Pilgrimage to Freedom, 1902–1950*, Bharatiya Vidya Bhavan, Bombay, 1967.

Nanda, B.R., 'Nehru and the British', *Modern Asian Studies*, vol. 30, no. 2, May 1996, 469–79.

Nandurkar, G.M. (ed.), *Sardar's Letters Mostly Unknown-I*, vol. IV, Sardar Vallabhbhai Patel Smarak Bhavan, Ahmedabad, 1977.

——— *Sardar Patel: In Tune with the Millions*, Smarak Bhavan, Ahmedabad, 1975–76.

Nayar, M.K.K., *Story of an Era Told Without Ill-Will*, DC Books, Kottayam, 2014.

Noorani, A.G., *The Destruction of Hyderabad*, Tulika Books, New Delhi, 2013.

Nossiter, Thomas Johnson, *Communism in Kerala: A Study in Political Adaptation*, University of California Press, Berkeley, 1982.

Panikkar, K.M., *An Autobiography*, Oxford University Press, Madras, 1977.

——— An *Introduction to the Study of the Relations of Indian States with the Government of India*, M. Hopkinson, London, 1927.

——— *His Highness the Maharaja of Bikaner: A Biography*, Oxford University Press, London, 1937.

——— *Indian States and the Government of India*, Kaushal Prakashan, Delhi, 1985.

Patel, Vallabhbhai, *For a United India: Speeches of Sardar Patel, 1947–1950*, Publications Division, Ministry of Information and Broadcasting, New Delhi, 1967.

Phadnis, Urmila, 'Gandhi and Indian States: A Probe in Strategy', in S.C. Biswas (ed.), *Gandhi: Theory and Practice, Social Impact and Contemporary Relevance*, Indian Institute of Advanced Study, Simla, 1969.

——— *Toward the Integration of Indian States*, Asia Publishing House, Bombay, 1968.

Philips, C.H., and Mary Doreen Wainwright (eds), *The Partition of India: Policies and Perspectives, 1935–947*, Allen & Unwin, London, 1970.

Puroshotham, Sunil, 'Internal Violence: The Police Action in Hyderabad', *Comparative Studies in Society and History*, vol. 57, no. 2, 2015, 435–66.

Raghavan, Srinath, *War and Peace in Modern India*, Palgrave Macmillan, Basingstoke, 2010.

Ramesh, Jairam, *Intertwined Lives, P.N. Haksar and Indira Gandhi*, Simon & Schuster, New York, 2018.

Ramusack, Barbara, *The Indian Princes and Their States*, Cambridge University Press, Cambridge, 2004.

——— *The Princes of India in the Twilight of Empire: Dissolution of a Patron-Client System, 1914–1939*, Ohio State University Press, Columbus, 1978.

Report of the Enquiry Committee Orissa States 1939, Orissa Mission Press, Cuttack, 1939.

Richter, William, 'Electoral Patterns in Post-Princely India', in Jagdish N. Bhagwati et al. (eds), *Electoral Politics in the Indian States: Three Disadvantaged Sectors*, Manohar Book Service, Delhi, 1975.

Richter, William L., and Barbara Ramusack, 'The Chamber and the Consultation: Changing Forms of Princely Association in India', *The Journal of Asian Studies*, vol. 34, no. 3, May 1975, 755–76.

Saiyid, Dushka H., 'The Accession of Kalat: Myth and Reality', *Strategic Studies*, vol. 26, no. 3, Autumn 2006, 26–45.

Sarila, Narendra Singh, *Once a Prince of Sarila: Of Palaces and Tiger Hunts, of Nehrus and Mountbattens* , I.B. Tauris, London, 2008.

Sarvepalli, Gopal, *Jawaharlal Nehru: A Biography*, vol. 2, Jonathan Cape, London, 1984.

Schofield, Victoria, *Kashmir in Conflict: India, Pakistan and the Unending War*, I.B. Tauris, London, 2021.

Scindia, Vijayaraje, *Princess: The Autobiography of the Dowager Maharani of Gwalior*, Century, London, 1985.

Shankar, V., *My Reminiscences of Sardar Patel*, vols 1 & 2, Macmillan, Delhi, 1974–75.

Singh, Karan *Heir Apparent: An Autobiography*, Oxford, Delhi, 1982.

Singh, Karni, *The Relations of the House of Bikaner with the Central Powers: 1465–1949*, Munshiram Manoharlal Publishers, New Delhi, 1974.

Symons, Richard, *The Making of Pakistan*, Faber and Faber, London, 1950.

Tahmankar, D.V., *Sardar Patel*, Allen & Unwin, London, 1970.

Talbot, Phillips, *An American Witness to India's Partition*, Sage, Los Angeles, 2007.

Tinker, Hugh, *India and Pakistan: A Political Analysis*, F.A. Praeger, New York, 1967.

Trevelyan, Humphrey, *The India We Left*, Macmillan, London, 1972.

Trumbull, Robert, *As I See India*, William Sloane, New York, 1956.

von Tunzelmann, Alex, *Indian Summer: The Secret History of the End of an Empire*, Henry Holt, New York, 2007.

Wakefield, Edward, *Past Imperative: My Life in India, 1927–47*, Chatto & Windus, London, 1966.

White Paper on Indian States (1948), Government of India Press, New Delhi, 1948.

White Paper on the Indian States (1950), Government of India Press, New Delhi, 1950.

Wilcox, Wayne, *Pakistan: The Consolidation of a Nation*, Columbia University Press, New York, 1963.

Wirsing, Robert G., *India, Pakistan, and the Kashmir Dispute: On Regional Conflict and Its Resolution*, St. Martin's Press, New York, 1998.

Wolpert, Stanley, *Shameful Flight: The Last Years of the British Empire in India*, Oxford University Press, Oxford, 2006.

Wood, John R., 'Dividing the Jewel: Mountbatten and the Transfer of Power to India and Pakistan', *Pacific Affairs*, vol. 58, no. 4, Winter, 1985–86, 653–62.

Wylie, Francis, 'Federal Negotiations in India, 1935-39', in C.H. Philips and Mary Doreen Wainwright (eds), *The Partition of India: Policies and Perspectives, 1935–1947*, George Allen & Unwin, London, 1970.

Zinkin, Taya, *India Changes*, Chatto & Windus, London, 1958.

Acknowledgements

When my editor at Juggernaut books, Parth Mehrotra, asked if I would like to write about the role of V.P. Menon and Vallabhbhai Patel in the integration of India's princely states, it felt like an impossible task. Some sources put the number of states at over 700 and even the figure of 562 that was officially accepted was daunting. How could I do these states – large and small, great and degenerate – justice while fitting them into the wider narrative of India's march to independence and its aftermath? To attempt the story of how Menon, Patel and Mountbatten avoided sabotaging decades of nationalist struggle by cajoling hundreds of rulers to join India in the space of just a few weeks, could not have been done without the support of the talented team at Juggernaut books. With me at the beginning of my journey was Nandini Mehta, who sadly retired before the final manuscript was delivered. Her place was ably taken by Anjali Puri, who in true Menon–Patel style arm-twisted and cajoled me into keeping focused on the core of this narrative whenever I became too bedazzled by the inner world of the princes. My gratitude also goes to my publisher Chiki Sarkar for providing inspiration and encouragement for what is our third book together. A special thanks must go to Robin Jeffrey and Ian

Copland, whose work on the princes I've long admired, for giving their time to reading over earlier versions of this manuscript and making insightful suggestions. My appreciation also goes to the staff at the collections I utilized, especially the National Archives of India in New Delhi, and the India Office Records at the British Library in London. Finally I would like to acknowledge my partner April for standing by and supporting me through the long journey that this book represents. Without her belief in me this book would not have seen the light of day.

Index